FAST ESCAPE

Bonnie W. Vause, Ed. D.

Published by Edenton Branch Books, LLC

Printed in the United States of America

DEDICATION

I would like to dedicate my first novel *Fast Escape*, to my husband, who has always remained beside me during many adventurous paths: undergraduate school, graduate school, and completion of my doctorate in education in 2012. Eric has worked hard to assist me in the publishing of *Fast Escape* and made many sacrifices. He is the most patient man on the face of the earth.

Our oldest daughter, Erika, has been very helpful and supportive. Our youngest daughter, Amanda, read the manuscript and provided many helpful changes. Thank you both for believing in me.

To our three granddaughters: Anna-Brooke, Gracyn-Harper, and Meredith Thomas. Each of you brings such happiness to my life. My prayer and wish for you is to always be determined in life and know you can do anything. I have tried to model "Perseverance" throughout my entire life. I love each of you with all my heart.

TABLE OF CONTENTS

ACKNOWLEDGMENTS

PROLOGUE

Chapter I - SECRETS OF THE HEART   1

Chapter II - THE CHILD WITHIN   14

Chapter III - SHADOW VILLAGE ELEMENTARY   33

Chapter IV - BEHIND THE COTTON MILL   46

Chapter V - THE GUNTERS   55

Chapter VI - GOING HOME   71

Chapter VII – FACING REALITY   86

Chapter VIII - DEMONS IN THE NIGHT   98

Chapter IX - OLD FRIENDS   114

Chapter X - REUNITED   125

Chapter XI - BRADFORD EXCHANGE   139

Chapter XII - HIGHEST BIDDER   150

Chapter XIII - THE LIES BENEATH   160

Chapter XIV - TRUTH IN THE LIES   172

ABOUT THE AUTHOR   189

ACKNOWLEDGMENTS

Throughout the process of writing *Fast Escape*, many individuals have taken time to assist me. I would like to give acknowledgement to my husband who has provided me with positive reinforcement and encouragement. I would also like to give a special thanks to my two daughters for their ongoing support of reading the manuscript and their feedback. A special thanks to Jo Ann Bushong for her reassurance and Dr. Bob Bushong for always providing inspiration to me as a teacher leader. Prior to his death, I promised to pursue my dreams. Thank you to my community as a whole for actively sharing in feedback and your contributions. I am blessed to have awesome neighbors in South Meade.

I would like to offer an extra special thanks to the following individuals. Without their assistance and insight portions of my book could have not be completed. You are valued contributors to my success of writing *Fast Escape*.

First, I would like to thank my husband Eric for standing beside me throughout my career as an educator and as an author. You are my motivation. Thank you for believing in me and never doubting my dreams. My adult daughters: Erika and Amanda, thank you for your inspiration. My three granddaughters: Anna-Brooke, Gracyn-Harper, and Meredith Thomas, I hope that one day you will understand why we moved "Nan's" office into the den! Just maybe one day when you read Fast Escape you will find a connection and likewise preserver with your dreams.

My colleagues, especially my Paraprofessional, Latanja Dunkins, Johnston County School central office administration/Board of Education, thank you for cheering me on during the process of writing *Fast Escape*. Dr. June Atkinson, your book, *T-Shirt Named Zee* was an inspiration for me to write. Thank you for being an awesome friend and mentor. You have shared words of wisdom to empower the teachers under your leadership as the Superintendent of North Carolina Public Schools.

PROLOGUE

Dr. Elizabeth Davenport wrestled frantically with unwelcome strangers that disturbed her sleep. She often compared them to disgruntled relatives who show up at a family gathering without a proper invitation. Her visitors showed worn appearances reserved strictly for her nightmares, and taunted her with agitating precision, always knowing exactly which nerve to strike.

Elizabeth described her encounters as abstract lines aimlessly searching for answers to her past. Snatches of phrases and disembodied voices would invade her senses as she tried desperately to make sense of it all. She would welcome the visits if they would present gifts of gratitude to their host, but there was nothing in return except darkness and confusion. The encounters were dreadful, forcing her to face bits and pieces of her past through the eyes of evil.

Peace was nowhere to be found in the blackness of her room. Her body was once again stuck in slow motion as the nightmare clawed at her mind. She was in a familiar hall that housed an old wooden twin bed. The wood felt splintered and worn in her hands and all too familiar. Falling to the floor were curled stark white paint chippings that had been tampered with by the hands of Lizzy, the frail young child underneath the thin sheets, curling the bed covers underneath her chin. A man's voice roared and echoed in the darkness but the words were unclear.

A discarded crate appeared, such a seemingly mundane thing, yet it caused panic to crawl into her throat, threatening to spill over into a blood-curdling scream. The words, poisoned with the sickly sweet scent of plums, escaped her as she tried desperately to cling to a single image of a clothesline swinging softly in the breeze.

The onset of the nightmare became unbearable as Elizabeth's body jerked and arched in hopes of waking to the beauty of her lavishly adorned bedroom. Her vision remained blurred as she begged for release from the horrifying grip of the darkness. She did not want to be locked inside the frail child's body whose life was stained with unspeakable secrets she wanted to avoid at all costs.

Please, not another restless night, she thought. She tried to surface, reaching for anything familiar to pull herself back into consciousness. Each time she would come close, rounding the edges of wakefulness, the frightening images would pull her back under and upon herself. Like the crashing of waves, she was helpless to the tide.

With a final, desperate throe, Elizabeth jerked her body upwards and managed to awaken her mind. Sitting bolt upright in her bed, she realized the attempt to hold her hostage had not been successful. She also knew the fight to remain in the present would resume.

As she sat at her desk exhausted, Elizabeth reminded herself that nightmares are not unusual, most people experience them. The vividness and power of the nightmares could only be attributed to her past and an over-active imagination. No matter how much she tried to reassure herself, however, the dreams lingered in her mind as something more than just a nightmare.

It was time to read. Her personal office contained a wealth of researched-based literature that facilitated healing for the mentally wounded. She hoped to find solace as she reached for the thick book on the bottom shelf of the bookcase.

To justify the turmoil within her life, Elizabeth often reminded her husband that she carried the weight of her patients' shattered lives within her heart. It made her mind and spirit more susceptible to bouts of insomnia. She was quick to add that lately she had been more aggressively overwhelmed due to long days of patients suffering from intense emotional pain.

Elizabeth knew her explanation was sufficient, and she need not worry about providing further details of her personal struggles.

As the day continued, Elizabeth listened with compassion as her patients exposed their deepest secrets in hopes of finding answers. She was a renowned researcher who provided strategies her colleagues considered helpful in treating their patients, but she felt nothing less than a personal failure when she could not silence the demons that relentlessly haunted her own mind.

CHAPTER I

SECRETS OF THE HEART

During a conference, Dr. Elizabeth Davenport shared clinical observations about a child she called Little Lizzy, explaining how the turmoil in this child's life would certainly manifest as she matured into adulthood. Her intention was to reinforce to the attendees that research in psychological disorders is vital to treat patients like Little Lizzy. She added that empathy was also crucial if a positive outcome in a patient's mental wellness was expected.

Dr. Davenport often compared the patient's nightmares to those of a car traveling without a map. The audience was in awe of her metaphor of nightmares, concluding they had the ability to blindfold one's mind. It could cause severe impairment of a patient's senses, making it impossible to recognize speed signs, location markers, and most importantly, stop signs. Once the sense of sight is impaired, the patient's road trip leads to the possibility of a fatal wreck.

The patient's identity was confidential. Her colleagues understood the oath she had taken, and did not expect it to be exposed at the symposium. The renowned Dr. Elizabeth Jones Davenport was subtly seeking knowledge and possible consultation from members of the audience to assist the child who cried for help within her own soul. The patient's identity stood helplessly waiting in need of disclosure.

Often at the tip of Dr. Davenport's tongue the name, "Eliz" was replaced by "Lizzy" as she stood in front of her colleagues, exemplifying poise and dignity.

Dr. Davenport's previous conference came close to disaster as the name Lizzy gushed from the mouth of the well renowned doctor, yet in an all too familiar voice...the voice of the child she faced in her nightmares. She stood speechless -- the facial structure of a fragile child mirrored on the top

1

of the podium was none other than the face of Lizzy. Had a mere slip of the tongue opened the floor for suspicion to blossom among her colleagues? Would they demand more details?

Much to her relief, quietness lingered over the conference room as she quickly gained her composure. Standing with profound assurance, she spoke, "My fellow colleagues...we all have to be willing to expose our personal life experiences, our deepest, darkest feelings, and provide insight from within to reach and educate our colleagues. We must give meaning through exposure of one's hidden secrets. I have opened my life to this audience, giving you the actual name of a beloved relative that has been deceased some forty years, a precious relative I proudly call an asset to my research in the field of psychology. It is with grace and pride that I share her name. With understanding of her conflicts, I find it an honor to share a kindred spirit. Yes, I am a descendent of Lizzy Jones, a frail child who suffered with severe anxiety, mental distress, and a life filled with emotional pain. She was a strong, vivacious woman, and her soul is resting in peace in the arms of our faithful Heavenly Father."

With distinct poise, Dr. Davenport added, "I anticipate that by sharing my own life experiences, you, my colleagues, have learned it is crucial to peel back the layers of our personal wounds and conflicts in order to share and allow each other to gain knowledge that could promote healing for our patients."

As she left the podium, her colleagues gave her a standing ovation to show their approval. Several uttered words of praise and admiration.

Thankful to be heading home, Elizabeth waited patiently for her flight so she could be in the arms of Harrison Davenport, her husband whom she missed tremendously, to feel his unconditional love and the safety of his arms. The mere mention of his name made her beam like a light on a dark night guiding the lost boats to shore. Harrison had rescued her soul from the haunting memories on numerous occasions.

Elizabeth reflected upon the conference. She felt that her slip of the tongue nearly revealed her secrets and that her hidden childhood nearly exposed to her colleagues. She felt her quick thinking brought a spark of inspiration to those listening and would allow her colleagues to reflect upon the outstanding professional she strived diligently to become. With a peaceful heart, she laid her head back to enjoy the flight to North Carolina, her home.

As the plane landed, calmness entered her soul. She felt Harrison's presence before she ever laid eyes on him. It was their secret, the one secret she never minded possessing; they were close by without ever being able to see each other. Sure enough, when she stepped off the plane, Harrison, her soul mate, was waiting to embrace her. Silence was golden...the tightness of their arms spoke fluently of their love.

Upon entering the driveway of their home, Elizabeth's eyes sparkled with enthusiasm. She was glad to be back in her comfort zone. She was home.

"Let's get you inside and settled. While you're showering, I'll bring your luggage inside," Harrison said, placing the key inside the locked door. That was music to Elizabeth's ears. She glanced at the clock in the kitchen. "I'm glad you're home," he said.

"Oh no…goodness, it is about time for our favorite *LifeTime* movie. It's supposed to be a thriller tonight." Elizabeth fell asleep halfway through the movie. Harrison shook his head. It was apparent Elizabeth was struggling. Suddenly, she woke up at the touch of Harrison's hand combing through her hair.

"Sorry, I fell asleep. This trip was harder than usual. Something isn't right Harrison. I can feel it in my entire being. It is like a cloud of horror in my spirit."

Elizabeth stood and announced she was ready to call it a day. Managing to force a smile, she slipped under the soft cotton sheets.

The beam of light flickering through the wooden décor shutters inside the Davenport's bedroom signaled a beautiful day on the horizon. The couple had moved to a gated, secluded subdivision near Brevard, NC on December 24th, 2000. No doubt, Christmas was a glorious season Elizabeth looked forward to each year. Beautifully decorated streets brought calmness to her hectic schedule. She enjoyed gazing at the dancing stars in the misty blue sky; breathing the refreshing scent of cinnamon Christmas candles. Soon the magical spell of Christmas filtering in the air would engulf their lovely home.

The hint of hope also gave peace of mind for her rigorously organized life with her soul mate, Harrison Davenport, a handsome man with thick black hair sprinkled with a slight suggestion of salt and pepper. Elizabeth's description of her husband was indeed that of a trustworthy man who had tirelessly provided a safe and secure home for his wife.

Elizabeth, in her mid-fifties, was an accomplished child psychologist. Her days were busy and enjoyable as she nurtured the children who shared their feelings of hopelessness, clutching to her as their savior. She identified with their hidden pain and easily won their trust.

Harrison was seven years older than his wife was. Elizabeth was his best friend, and the only woman he had ever truly loved. With nearly thirty-five years in nuclear energy research, Harrison was looking forward to retirement. Spending more time with his beautiful wife was high on his agenda. A new beginning awaited the Davenports, and they were both anxious to move into a new phase of their lives. Elizabeth was immensely appreciative to have the opportunity to live a life of luxury with Harrison. Their dream home was an added bonus.

After many years of hard work and sacrifices, Harrison approached retirement with a desire to celebrate their thirty years of marriage with a well-deserved gift...a beautiful and elaborate dream home. Harrison shared the blueprints with his wife as he quickly reminded her that she would assist with the interior design. Elizabeth was ecstatic as she wiped tears from her eyes, nodding to show her approval. Life with Harrison had been so rewarding. She loved him profoundly for his devotion to their marriage and his precise plans for their future. Their life together had evolved into a storybook adventure that got better with each new chapter.

Harrison married his bride with no denial that she had a kind of ambition he had never seen in another human being. He was also well aware that Elizabeth had an unusual need for security and followed a well-planned daily agenda that allowed for limited deviation. He displayed unconditional love for his wife, attributing her somewhat overbearing demands to a dysfunctional childhood. He often backed down when their discussions became too uncomfortable for his wife. Her disapproving body language spoke loudly if pushed beyond her self-determined boundaries.

Despite his need to probe, Harrison understood and respected the quietness within his wife's soul. He knew there was a deep well of frustration within Elizabeth and he worried that one day it might explode outward. Harrison could not fathom the details locked securely inside. He had grown to respect her personality quirks, obsessive-compulsive disorder, and other issues ruling her life. He realized that these problems were what gave her the understanding to provide help and freedom to her patients, even if she could not give it to herself.

Harrison was astonished at the resources she was able to access to render aid to her patients. In his eyes, Elizabeth was close to being perfect, minus a few quirky traits. He yearned for the gratifying day when he would rescue Elizabeth from the demons that had tried to overtake her mind for decades. He wanted to be the man who captured the demons who refused to relinquish their grip on his wife.

Publicly, Elizabeth was a perfect image of success. She portrayed self-confidence, a wholesome personality, vibrant beauty, and dark black hair that mirrored long strands of silk. Her deep brown eyes brought pure sunshine on the darkest day. Yet, Harrison also acknowledged his wife was vulnerable.

He often felt that she was the gatekeeper of her dysfunctional childhood, cursed as it were. The locked doors of her heart kept Elizabeth from much deserved freedom. However, it was apparent the key was made of hard steel, hidden securely by its master, and provided protection against all intruders, even her beloved husband.

The Davenport's weekly agenda was carefully prepared, reviewed, typed, and placed on the bar for easy access on the last day of each week. Order

4

provided a calming effect on Elizabeth's mind; any deviation had the potential to cause panic. Elizabeth was a woman on a mission to abolish a childhood that brought her sorrow and pain. She depended on Harrison to be strong, trustworthy, and socially dominant. They were proud of the life they had built together. Each enjoyed spending time reading, talking, and watching their favorite movies, their love safeguarded by respect and privacy.

Harrison had a pot of coffee on the warmer waiting for his wife while brewing a second pot at the same time. Elizabeth walked into the kitchen with a dazzling smile on her face, absorbing the satisfying aroma from the freshly brewed coffee as it floated in the air.

"Good morning, Harrison. I love opening the bedroom door to the smell of coffee, such a pleasant way to start my morning."

"I am always amazed at how much you appreciate such small things, like a simple cup of coffee," Harrison responded with a gentle smile.

"But Harrison, you're forgetting…it isn't just a simple cup of coffee. It's the way you say 'I love you' to me each day with a special blend of gourmet coffee beans," she said, playfully.

Harrison marveled that a fresh pot of gourmet coffee could produce such brightness in her sleepy eyes. "Elizabeth, as soon as your feet hit the hardwood floors each morning you have no problem finding something to be thankful for; what a pleasure it is to see you smile so early." Her ability to find pleasure in simple things was one of the things he admired most about her. She could be so uncomplicated at times, but she could also become an unsolvable puzzle without warning. Life with Elizabeth was never dull.

It was apparent that when it came to specifics in her life, she left no stone unturned. Harrison thought of her love for the sweet aroma of freshly ground gourmet coffee beans. Using the coffee grinder, she meticulously extracted their fragrance.

She believed that the aroma of fresh ground coffee beans contained spiritual properties and that it contained the power to shield their home from negative energy.

Their home, filled with warmth, was inviting to others. Elizabeth had carefully designed a safe haven from her dysfunctional life lurking beyond the railroad tracks in Shadow Village. The result was much like a serene Norman Rockwell painting. It had the power to overcast negative energy…including a painful childhood. Harrison was proud of his wife's eagerness to extend hospitality to their social circle within the neighborhood while also including her patients.

It was apparent that Elizabeth had placed padlocks on the doors of her heart in hopes of keeping outsiders from snooping. Harrison wanted to lend a hand to his wife, help her escape from her torment. He searched endlessly to find where she hid the padlock keys. If he could only unlock the doors, the ghosts would be free. She refused to grant the right to anyone to pry into her childhood. Doors to her personal affairs remained securely fastened to prevent the ghosts of Shadow Village from exposing her silent pain, and they were surely not a welcomed guest in their home.

Harrison, a reserved man of great stature, was trustworthy. He had worked hard to provide a life of comfort and security in hopes of replacing the dysfunctional childhood his wife suffered in silence. Yet if he tried to force Elizabeth to open the door to her secrets, she would abruptly remind him of her need for privacy.

Elizabeth referred to her childhood by coining the term "adventurous childhood" with deep pockets of secrets. Secrets that were buried deep within her soul, far from civilization in a tiny closet of her heart and soul; each secret housed amongst soiled rags hanging tightly meshed with pain, sadness, and a sprinkle of hope. She held tightly to the hope.

She had become a master at controlling her environment and keeping herself floating above the drowning waves of day-to-day tasks. Harrison was aware of his wife's strategies to avoid situations that caused her to dwell on uncomfortable topics. It seemed when life's circumstances bombarded his wife's mind, she silently repeated her motto, "In the midst of chaos, a rigid schedule keeps a person grounded." Since this worked for her, Harrison felt he had no justification to question her ability to cope with stress.

Periodically, Harrison would compassionately pry open the doors of Elizabeth's heart. The word "hope" met him at the entrance. Hope seemed to be consistent as an entrance to her hiding place. When he noticed a slight crack offered by hope, the doors would open temporarily for discussion. As soon as Harrison moved to take advantage of the opening, his lovely wife would quickly slam the doors. Once the silence was broken, Elizabeth always reminded her husband of the rules of her heart, saying, "Hope remains the key to my freedom from the doom of the village. I will unlock the doors slowly… as I see fit. Please don't rush me."

With this said, Elizabeth would boldly state, "End of discussion. Let's move forward." Through the years, Harrison had not been successful in walking through the doors of his wife's heart for more than a moment, but he remained hopeful.

The day began as usual for the Davenports – breakfast consisting of wheat toast topped with honey and several cups of freshly ground gourmet coffee. The morning news slowly penetrated their ears as they continued dodging between morning conversations and the normal distractions of preparing breakfast.

They did not know that the early morning news reports would be so important or that they might bring life- altering information into their peaceful sanctuary.

Elizabeth faintly heard the reporter's promise of upcoming breaking news. After breakfast, she began to clear the dishes, carefully rinsing cups thoroughly with warm water, placing each at the back of the dishwasher, forks erected in a straight line in the basket, and plates perfectly aligned in the proper order on the bottom rack.

The couple retreated to the clear glass table to review their daily agenda. With her head bent over their papers, Elizabeth reminded him that she had five patients on her schedule and several meetings afterward but planned to be home by 5:45 p.m. When she raised her head, she saw that Harrison was no longer at the table. Growing anxious at this breach in their routine, Elizabeth raised her voice to show her disapproval of his disappearance.

"Harrison, are you listening to me?" Elizabeth asked as she tried to summon her husband's undivided attention. "Hello...I'm speaking to you. I think you've abandoned ship."

Harrison answered in a firm tone. "Elizabeth, please. I am listening to this special report. This is the third time I've heard breaking news, so surely it is important." Elizabeth knew by the firmness in his voice that Harrison was serious, so she ceased her chatter, came closer to the den, and stood behind the sofa.

She had no doubt her husband's interest in the breaking news report was nothing more than a bad storm rising.

Elizabeth muttered, "By all means, the weather report requires your undivided attention."

Harrison's fascination with the weather had always been appealing to Elizabeth as it brought back fond memories of her deceased grandfather whom she loved dearly. Nonetheless, with her husband's refusal to respond, Elizabeth granted full attention to his demand as she playfully locked her lips, throwing the key over her shoulder.

Harrison's eyes were fixated on the flat screen television with a look of deep seeded concentration as the breaking news scrolled across the bottom once again. He took his final sip of coffee with a gulping swallow and said, "Elizabeth, you need to see this. It's important."

Because of her husband's obsession with storm chasing, Elizabeth was not concerned about his demand. She walked closer merely to be respectful.

Elizabeth sensed her husband's concern and made her way to his side. By focusing on the colors in the den rather than the news, she was able to quell the rising sense of fear in her heart. It was a coping skill that she had developed that she considered to be a retreat to her safe haven. She was in awe of the house—no, the home—they had built together, and in love with the man who was able to see past her flaws and remain faithfully in love with her.

Harrison stood in the den with utmost authority. It was apparent that the news report had his attention. Elizabeth thought of the many hours Harrison had spent sketching the details of their safe haven, revising each draft once she noted some minor detail omitted. The final project was the epitome of beauty. Suddenly Harrison bellowed, "Elizabeth, my goodness woman, stop daydreaming, and listen to the news report. Sweetheart…this is serious."

Harrison was deeply concerned about the effect the current news report would have on his wife. He envisioned her retreating to the sofa to avoid significant details of the apparent devastation blasting on the morning news. Harrison could feel the shadows from the dark truth lingering at the top of the ceiling calling Elizabeth's name, screaming to take her mind hostage.

"OK, Harrison, I'm listening. But, what's the urgency?" Elizabeth wanted to know as she playfully crossed her legs with perfect poise. He now had her full attention. She uttered an apology for the earlier sarcasm; the rambling of the mind and mouth was what she called it.

Harrison was more concerned with his wife's ability to deal with the upcoming news. He remembered all too well the nights she spent plagued with nightmares that sought to unravel her childhood, afflicting her with insomnia and anxiety. Harrison had finally gained his wife's full attention, but she still did not understand why his face was white as a ghost. That is, until she heard the two words that struck fear in her heart and continuously haunted her nights: 'Shadow Village'.

Silence rang in her ears. Shadow Village, her hometown, was located 150 miles south of Brevard, N.C.

The television screen displayed pictures of blazing flames that were on the way to destroying the entire mill village.

The streets where she walked barefooted with her brothers and friends…the hometown she left behind for a better life. Never once had she wished for the residents of Shadow Village to be engulfed in blazing flames.

The small mill village was located across the tracks in the town of Shadow Village, S.C. The news continued to show red, yellow, orange, and blue flames consuming the village with a roaring sound that seemed to extend stridently into their den. The blazing fire was so vivid it seemed to have a mind of its own.

She looked at Harrison and asked in a desperate and frantic tone, "What happened?"

Harrison had little to say as he listened intensely, trying to soak up every detail. "Be quiet so I can hear Elizabeth. I can't tell you anything until I hear the full report."

His anxious wife was now pacing from room to room searching for comfort from her coffee mug. She was in damage control mode and could feel the panic rising in her soul. She needed to escape the shadows of the glaring flames as they consumed the village of her tragic childhood.

Elizabeth felt her throat tightening as she tried to call out Harrison's name. She wanted—no needed—reassurance that all would be well as soon as the fire was contained. Yet, she knew in her heart that not all was well.

Truth was beaming through the darkness, searching for light.

Quietness fell on Elizabeth's shoulders, the same quietness she knew all too well as a child escaping under the tethered sheets on her discolored wooden bed, located in the hall of the family mill home.

The memories were returning, and Elizabeth felt lightheaded and sickened to her stomach. She retreated to the sofa in the den, ready to check out of reality as Harrison continued to listen to the news. The flames seemed amused by her unsettledness, mocking her through the television screen, calling her to come and entertain the dominance they had inflicted upon the mill village.

Barely escaping the doom of poverty as a young teenager seemed to be enough punishment, yet Elizabeth felt she was under personal attack as cotton fibers burned and manipulated the weak minds living in her hometown. Watching the events unfold before her eyes seemed as painful and overwhelming as being a resident of Shadow Village.

Feeling fearful and helpless, she curled up on the leather sofa in the fetal position, pulling a white feather comforter across her lap. Holding tightly to the end of the blanket, she searched for a safe haven to rescue her weary thoughts. She found her agenda and reviewed her schedule repeatedly until she had memorized the details of each time slot.

If only her mind would slow down to a normal pace, it was racing in circles, reminding her of the black snake that once slithered and coiled across the porch of her old mill home. She knew if Harrison unlocked the steel doors of her heart, the ghosts would gush out with the roaring flames and consume their beautiful life.

Elizabeth felt strongly that once a person's spirit was clear, followed by good character and conduct, then the haunting of their past would find peace. She could only hope and pray that her spirit was clear of the past, and she was not sure if withholding information from her husband would deem her unfit and justify the tormenting devastation taking place before her eyes.

The wicked flames that continued to blaze out of control screamed for Elizabeth. The ghosts were calling her name. She was not sure why she was summoned. She did not have the courage to be the ringmaster of the torment, to reveal the unimaginable events that had taken place in the mist of Shadow Village. With little assurance, she prayed she would not have to heed the call. She remained in the fetal position on the sofa, one ear toward the television.

Freedom awaited her if only she could find the means to cross the cold tracks behind the cotton mill. Fleeing such an offensive life would enable her to experience a pleasant environment filled with love and respect. She felt more at peace when she obtained the master keys to her childhood.

She stored all the hurt and pain in a safe place many decades ago, her heart and mind held her secrets. She was not about to disclose them to anyone. Her worries were behind the dilapidated cotton mill as she crossed the railroad tracks at the tender age of nearly twenty. She had been in search of a better life with the hope of experiencing peace for her heart and mind. Elizabeth felt refreshed when her new life became reality a few months after moving into a rented room on Maple Leaf Avenue. Her life had been supposed to remain calm.

The news continued to echo in Elizabeth's ears as she laid her blanket at the foot of the sofa, walked over to stand beside her husband in the den, and felt the fear bloating her veins. The unsettledness that surrounded the den was becoming foggy, and she needed answers. Not even Harrison could control her anxiety level or rescue her from the demons.

Harrison seemed to understand. He took her hand and led her back to the sofa, assuring her that he would provide updates, telling her she really needed to just rest, review her agenda, and settle down. He promised to sort everything out.

Grateful that Harrison had taken charge; Elizabeth sat at the end of the sofa and laid her head on the armrest. She began reminiscing about her freedom from a shameful life and the pride she felt when she thought she was free of the haunting ghosts. It was a hot July afternoon. There he stood in the upscale furniture gallery with a serious look upon his face. With a quick swipe across his forehead, the customer was no doubt in need for assistance.

The man introduced himself to the newly hired Elizabeth as Harrison Davenport. "How might I assist you, Mr. Davenport?" Elizabeth had asked, eyes taking note of his indecisive mannerism.

"Well, I'm browsing for the perfect ottoman," he replied as his eyes scanned the store. He handed Elizabeth a sales paper with his right hand while pointing to a cluster of high-end ottomans.

"I see you're eyeing a new selection we just placed on the floor. They are from a popular New York designer. Each designed with the finest woven fabric and embellished with triple layer silk fringe that extends to the floor." It was the most expensive ottoman in the gallery show room, a show room known for its famous designers, and the styles and flair that held the human eye captive. Elizabeth watched to see her customer's facial expressions, hoping he would be interested in making a purchase.

"Well, it looks like I see the perfect ottoman for me." Her customer walked toward the middle of the showroom. He pointed to a beige ottoman with elaborate details. The square shaped ottoman had inverted pleats on each corner. In the center, an oversized button adorned with black silk fabric perfectly matched the long stands of double-layered black fringe. The fringe covering the perimeter of the masterpiece was eye appealing to Harrison.

"I'll have to warn you that your selection comes with risk," Elizabeth said as she followed her customer. This was a cunning way to investigate the man in front of her, towering over most men in the store.

"It comes with a warning? Never imagined an ottoman coming with a warning disclosure," Harrison chuckled as he approached the piece of furniture, placing his hands on the fine silk.

"Well, the warning would be appropriate if you are the owner of a pet. The fabrics are too delicate. You may need a more durable fabric for paws, claws, and pet hair."

With a quick reality check, Elizabeth added the importance of owning the one of a kind designer ottoman. She needed to make a sale so she could pay her rent. The commission would be substantial and ease her mind. She crossed her fingers, hoping she had not been too forward, praying he would purchase the ottoman. Offering her his contact information for a possible future causal lunch would be an added bonus.

Harrison assured Elizabeth that he liked the design and was not the owner of a pet. He indeed would be purchasing the ottoman for his apartment. Elizabeth completed the sale, noticing his polite facial expressions and the kindness in his voice. When their eyes met, Elizabeth felt her cheeks blushing red. Harrison's sleek black hair and his olive skin were impressive. She took a deep breath trying to slow the fast beating of her heart.

Never had she met a man that made her feel lightheaded.

Their short and intensely romantic courtship led to a commitment of marriage. Taking the hand of Harrison Davenport, reciting their wedding vows at the altar of a quaint chapel in South Carolina as Victoria Holiday stood beside her as the maid of honor. Victoria clung to Elizabeth and told her how much she would miss her but noted that it was time for her to make a new life far from Shadow Village.

Living on Maple Leaf Avenue had been dreams come true for Elizabeth, but she must move on in her role as the wife of Harrison. Victoria helped the new couple with the purchase of a small home in Columbia, South Carolina and blessed them as they began planning for a bright and productive future together. Each vowed to stay in contact.

Elizabeth had gained respect for Victoria when she had been her landlord. Victoria had exhibited all the characteristics of a well-educated woman with a hint of appealing sophistication. She had provided excellent care and guidance to her young tenant. The thought of leaving Victoria was hard, but Elizabeth was more at ease because she knew they would be a phone call away and hopefully visiting throughout the year for special occasions.

Elizabeth would be a generous host and wait on Victoria. It was a known fact that Victoria lavished all her tenants with tender love and care. Surely, nothing would ever blemish their love for each other.

"Victoria, I'll repay your kindness by being a generous hostess if you'll visit Harrison and me." Elizabeth tightly hugged her friend goodbye for the hundredth time.

"Well, that would be lovely," Victoria said with a chuckle, embracing Elizabeth while vowing to write and call often.

Elizabeth would need to ease her mind from the separation anxiety she was experiencing. She knew the key would be relinquishing her old life and replacing it with gratitude as the new bride of Harrison.

She was grateful for the opportunity to be distant from the cotton mill village she had once called home. She would not miss the faintness of the midnight train blowing its whistle as it rambled closer to the mill dock. She had always wondered if the echoes would stop once she crossed the cold tracks. If possible, there was no doubt it would take many years to fade completely.

From that day, she planned to make her new life rich with positive energy. She and Harrison would build a grand life together far from Shadow Village.

The current news report blasting from the television brought Elizabeth out of her deep thoughts as she faintly heard her husband repeating the words of the current conditions in Shadow Village. She was tuning him out, reconnecting to her old life and visualizing how she and Harrison made their last drive from Shadow Village, vowing to never cross the cold tracks again with the exception of darkening the doors of Victoria Holiday on Maple Leaf Avenue.

Elizabeth had worked hard to replace the painful childhood of living in a cotton mill village. She searched for peace of mind with the assurance of a promising future. She had found a glimmer of hope as the wife of Harrison.

It had not been easy for her to accomplish such a difficult task as cremating the ghosts of Shadow Village. Upon marriage, she was too young to have the skills to tame the demons that haunted her mind, but rather than surrender to the ghosts, she took them hostage. She hid them, their terror, and torment deep inside her heart where they could not escape. Elizabeth felt she could protect her new life with Harrison and bear the pain in silence with a soundproof heart.

Yet Elizabeth was no fool, and she knew one day the ghosts would escape and forcefully call her name.

Distressed, she decided to let Harrison keep her updated. That would be much better for her sanity. Harrison was quiet as he watched with tension visible on his face. Elizabeth knew he was in protection mode and would make all the bad disappear. If there were a way, Harrison would surely bring peace.

Through the years as the wife of Harrison, her inner struggles, nightmares, and daily insecurities had never completely ceased. It had been over thirty years, but as she sat on their sofa, the same ghosts were pounding on the steel walls of her heart wanting their freedom. She longed to master her demons and shield her old life from others. She wondered if the day had come when she would encounter the ghosts, and be forced to explain their identities to the man she called her husband.

Only time would tell if Harrison would continue to support his wife. She felt the ghosts of Shadow Village coming alive within her soul.

She remembered how unmerciful they had been for weeks as she struggled to rest each night. The ghosts wanted out. They were visible and she felt defenseless against their clutching hands on her shoulders.

Elizabeth pondered the possibility of Harrison accepting damaged goods as his partner of thirty years. It was shameful enough that he knew she was from the other side of the tracks. Being forced to relinquish the details of hurtful disturbances in her life was more than Elizabeth could bear. There was silence in the room. Harrison had turned the television off and stood staring at his wife. He walked over, bent down, and kissed her forehead, then turned and walked away.

CHAPTER II

THE CHILD WITHIN

It was a cool, misty morning in Shadow Village, a small town located near the border of South Carolina. Lizzy was approaching the tender age of ten. She had excellent survival skills and was wise beyond her years. She wore clean but faded second-hand clothes, clothes Lizzy considered new even though her brothers reminded her that the previous owner's name was stitched into the collar of each garment.

Lizzy was thin with long, lanky legs and arms. Her dark sand-colored hair was thick but short. She often daydreamed of growing long hair so she could be beautiful like her friends at school. It was important to have long hair because, according to Lizzy, it increased a girl's self-esteem, and she made it known that she dreamed of one day being among the elite who sported long locks of silky hair. Lizzy was excited about anything that might add to her appearance, and the monthly haircut was not on her list.

"Albert Joe, don't you think I would be beautiful if I looked more like Pippi Longstockings?" Lizzy asked her elder brother one afternoon while on the tire swing tied to an old oak tree in their backyard.

"Well Lizzy, maybe so…minus that orange-red hair Pippi Longstockings sports," Albert Joe replied as he pushed his sister with extra force.

"Anything that will add to my looks would be a bonus. Hey, Albert Joe, you think you can find a secret hiding place for the Pyrex bowl Mama uses to cut my hair?"

"Not sure Lizzy 'cause Mama would get a long switch after my legs if you rat me out."

"Albert Joe, shame on you. I would never rat you out."

"Besides Albert Joe, if that darn bowl was missing, it would surely end the jagged haircuts that make me look like a freak. Mama's precious Pyrex bowl has been used for generations, and she is determined to use it on my head."

"Albert Joe, how come I'm the only one sitting in the backyard with a glass dome on my head for monthly haircuts? It makes me angry when those scissors clatter against the glass, rounding the bowl to the finish line."

"Alright Lizzy, I'll see what I can do. Gosh, golly, gee! Stop chattering and I'll swing you across the ditch."

"Thanks Albert Joe, you're the best brother a girl could have."

Teachers considered Lizzy well-mannered and well above average; yet, they were often concerned about the young girl who showed compassion for others but simultaneously seemed withdrawn. While Lizzy was helping others, her teachers felt that she yearned for a helping hand for herself. Even as they raved about Lizzy being an asset to the classroom, they noticed that she was a people pleaser. She was a curious girl with big dreams for her future.

Lizzy had hopes for a better life beyond the railroad tracks, and one day her dreams would become reality. Unlike most of her friends in the village, Lizzy could envision a real neighborhood with beautiful homes, manicured yards, and colorful flowers aligned against freshly painted white fences. If she did not stay focused, she might become a permanent resident. Even worse, the idea of joining many of her ancestors in the local insane asylum was not a choice she would dare entertain.

She was aware that her family and the residents of the cotton mill village frowned on her dreams. It was not acceptable to dart across the tracks even in one's private dreams. As Lizzy's grandmother would say: "They would forever be tarnished cotton." Any successful village escapee became an outcast, but Lizzy was willing to take the risk. It was well worth the effort to find happiness and peace of mind.

Lizzy felt trapped in a society within a society offering only a life sentence of poverty. Lizzy dreamed of the day she would break away from her heritage.

She did not plan to become a cotton mill worker. Having abandoned that thought years ago, Lizzy planned to get a formal education beyond high school. She dreamed of becoming a doctor of psychology, but Lizzy was also a realist. She was a frail girl who lived in poverty in a cotton mill village, but she was determined to hold on to hope. She did not mind working hard, and she was always looking for a break, a chance to learn more, for an opening that led from the cotton mill village.

Her hope was comparable to the kites she and her father flew on the ditch bank in late afternoons. It allowed her to soar high above the clouds of poverty. She surely did not foresee spending her adulthood turning the handle of a dilapidated tub washer; wringing water from wet clothes on laundry day. Nor did Lizzy want to chase the chickens for food, fetching the plumpest animal and placing the helpless creature on the chopping block.

"Albert Joe. Run. Come hide with me under the kitchen table while they butcher the chickens. You don't want to see the eyes of our captured pets because it is just too heart wrenching."

"I'm coming, Lizzy," Albert Joe shouted as he ran under the fig tree making his way into the kitchen to come to his sister's side. "Lizzy, you're not having one of those panic attacks are you? Close your eyes and soon it will be over Lizzy. I'll stay right here with you. Heck, I knew you were going to start up that crying. Hush up Lizzy. Please don't cry."

"Well, Albert Joe, I can't stand to see the animals butchered and all that blood on the tree stump is frightening. I'll have horrible nightmares. Please wash it off when Daddy finishes the killings. Please Albert Joe, do it for me."

"Now, hush up, Lizzy. You're getting all worked up for no reason. I'll wash the tree stump if it will make you feel better. But you must stop worrying."

"Albert Joe, my goodness. I think Daddy killed "Miss Wheeler." She was my favorite chicken. I can't sit at the kitchen table and eat Miss Wheeler. That would be just awful; she was a good chicken."

"Lizzy, I told you not to go naming the chickens and taking up with them. I saw you trying to wrap that chicken in a blanket the other day while you were in your playhouse. Mama will get the switch after you if she catches you playing house with the yard animals."

"Is it over Albert Joe? Is there a lot of blood on the tree stump?" Lizzy asked her brother as she uncovered her eyes.

"Yes, it's over and Daddy is coming in the house. I told you I would wash the darn tree stump, stop worrying. Come on Lizzy, get up and run to the sofa or you'll see the chickens in the bucket and you'll probably faint. My goodness, at least we have something to eat and don't have stand in line and wait for a box of food."

"Albert Joe, I told you that was a special chicken. That was Miss Wheeler and Mama knew I loved that chicken. Shame on her for telling Daddy to kill my pet chicken I'll never eat chicken again. I would much rather go hungry than eat my friend."

"Lizzy, hush up you're such a drama queen."

"Goodness, Albert Joe. Give a girl a break. My best friend just got the axe and you're rushing me. I should be mourning the loss of Miss Wheeler."

Silence was a rare commodity in the Jones' one bedroom dwelling that housed her parents and two brothers. It was welcome, especially after a weekend filled with noise, partying, and uncertainty for the future. Occupying the hall of the house as her bedroom did not dismay Lizzy at all. She actually felt fortunate to occupy the small space because it gave her a safe place to escape during family conflicts. The small bed and table encompassed her spirit and provided strength for Lizzy to survive in a home filled with constant turmoil.

Adults provided little encouragement for Lizzy to rise above the misty dew on the trees of this small cotton village. Poverty owned the hard-working people of Shadow Village, and Lizzy never let go of her dream of crossing the cold tracks that separated the village from the land of opportunity. Lizzy's plan was alive in her soul, and she was determined to work hard until her dark brown eyes gripped the land of opportunity.

Peeping through the holes in the worn out sheet, Lizzy glanced at her music box and the graceful plastic ballerina portraying perfect poise. She carefully placed her feet on the cold linoleum floor and kissed the ballerina's golden silky hair, acknowledging how fond she had grown of her music box through the years. The classical tune soothed her weary mind during restless nights.

Lizzy also dreamed that her hair would one day be as picturesque as the hair of her beautiful ballerina. She was elated the glass Pyrex bowl was not a miniature size since her mama was obsessed with bowl haircuts.

Continuing her morning ritual, Lizzy tiptoed to the unheated bathroom that adjoined the back porch of her house. Young, but wise, the young girl was well aware timing was a major factor if she would be the first to occupy the bathroom. Sharing a bathroom with a family of five was nothing to look forward to. If she dared be late, she would have to clean up behind Albert Joe and Samuel before she could use the bathroom.

Being Katie Mae and Buck's only daughter required Lizzy to be proactive in every aspect of her young life. It was important to be the first to greet the cold floors, the unheated bathroom, and most importantly, the first to savor the warmth of her mom's homemade, buttered grits. Lizzy had learned to operate her life in survival mode, to be a step ahead of adversity. Lizzy knew that adversity had no boundaries and no warning. She had to be on guard for chaos to sweep through her home at any given moment.

Monday, the first day of the school week, brought the warmth in the small classroom from the clanking steam pipe furnace and a hot lunch in the basement of the quaint elementary school. A feeling of pride overwhelmed Lizzy as she thought about entering the halls of her school in Shadow Village. She enjoyed her teachers' encouragement to excel as she embraced each day and absorbed new skills from the words in her books.

She beamed with anticipation of new knowledge, forming a strong bond with characters and believing they added meaning to her life.

Lizzy loved the smell of a new book and cherished the opportunity to devour the pages, often pretending she was the main character's best friend. Reading not only provided encouragement and sometimes escapes, but it also opened windows of opportunity where Lizzy could view a gleam of hope. In her eyes, the future surely had to be splendid and simply fantastic.

The most important task for Lizzy was to learn from her teachers as she excelled in her studies. She would continue to work hard and be successful. Her dreams were safe within her mind for the time being as were all her secrets. Anyway, she did not mind waiting.

Lizzy loved her teachers and cherished the opportunity to learn in a safe environment. Maybe one day, she would even be a teacher.

The old brick school not only provided warmth and a hot meal, but it also extended safety so different from her home life. It would be a good week for Lizzy. The long walk to the bus stop did not seem bothersome because it gave her time to prepare for the school day and form answers to possible questions in the correct manner when her teacher called upon her.

Lizzy supposed her anxiety was due to living in a dysfunctional home, a home where many uncertainties faced her as she entered the front door. Lizzy was sure her teachers could see through the sadness in her eyes. Yet, she tried hard to cover the pain by helping others even less fortunate than her.

As she entered the bus, an aroma trickled into her nostrils. Could it be the smell of new crayons, freshly sharpened pencils, crisp paper, or the luxurious bagged lunches of the students across the tracks? Personally, Lizzy had no clue how a pre-made bagged school lunch actually tasted or how to prepare such. She only knew the smell was different and pleasant as the doors of the bus opened and the aroma engulfed her nostrils. Bagged lunches were non-existent to the children of the mill village; only the students across the tracks got their hands on them.

The bus doors closed tightly sweeping the distinct aroma of homemade bread to the back of the bus. This alerted Lizzy that her friends were aboard the bus. Lizzy walked slowly to her seat while daydreaming of the day she would be the rightful owner of a character tin lunchbox with a hand held handle to carry her home made lunch. She would then be similar to her wealthy friend, Tori Belk.

"Hi Lizzy," Tori whispered in a mysterious voice as Lizzy continued to walk at a slow pace to her seat.

"Good morning, Tori. I love your new lunch box. It is simply beautiful."

Tori held her new tin lunch box at eye level so Lizzy could view the colorful picture painted on the front resembling a Norman Rockwell painting.

"It's a Victorian house surrounded with beautiful flowers and colorful pigeons perched perfectly on the branch of a huge oak tree." Tori said with pride. "Mama declares it looks like our home Lizzy, you know, all beautiful and perfect."

"That's good Tori," Lizzy replied as she disregarded the only daughter of the wealthy Mr. and Mrs. Belk who had adopted Tori; providing her with the best of everything.

"Maybe I can one day have such a nice lunch box, Tori. If not, my second wish would be to have a new crisp brown bag like Piper Thomas and Rexi Lane."

"Well, everyone knows Piper Thomas and Rexi Lane can't afford anything but a brown bag to carry their lunch," Tori said with malice in her eyes.

"Tori, that isn't a nice thing to say about Piper and Rexi. You should be nicer to your friends."

"Whatever, Lizzy," Tori shouted making a hissing sound as Lizzy walked past her. Tori slouched down, rolling her eyes at two girls sitting across from her and continued to make a hissing snake noise.

"What you looking at?" Tori said with a bully tone causing the girls to bite their nails.

"Nothing Tori, we like your lunch box," The girls replied.

With lunch on her mind, Lizzy did not have time to worry about Tori, knowing her mood would most likely swing into another direction as soon as they arrived at school. Lizzy had to concentrate on escaping from Tori when they went through the lunch line. Having Tori in her business would be devastating.

Lizzy was appreciative of free lunch at school but her cheeks blushed red as an eligible recipient. She would peer over her shoulder to see if anyone noticed her non-payment. It could be her lucky day if she could hurry and scoot by the cafeteria cashier without hesitation. However, she knew there were many more school lunch lines to shuffle through with her head bent down to hide her blushed cheeks as onlookers smirked.

It should not be so degrading to receive a hot meal at school. There was no such thing as a "free" lunch, for the required payment was in the form of labor. Soon after the privileged students completed their lunch, the lunchroom was crowded with underprivileged students with a list of chores posted on the cafeteria wall including picking up trash, cleaning the tables, and placing chairs on top of tables. Lizzy felt there was a high price to pay for being poor at the cost of humiliation.

She would hurriedly clean the tables and run outside to join her friends, hoping no one had noticed she was not on the playground, desperately trying to blend in with her peers.

Lizzy felt lonely, sad, and empty hearted the day Tori spotted her cleaning the tables in the cafeteria. Lizzy's face turned all shades of red. She hung her head downward hoping Tori would not speak to her. Suddenly, Lizzy turned to see who was tapping her on her shoulder.

"Lizzy, have you seen your brother Albert Joe? You think he has finished his chores in the cafeteria?" Tori asked with compassion in her voice and a sympathetic look in her eyes.

"No, sure haven't seen him anywhere, Tori. He is probably running laps on the playground. Might be in the boy's bathroom. Just look around, and you'll find Albert Joe. He's so tall you can't miss him, he towers over everyone," Lizzy cheerfully replied in hopes of defraying Tori from taunting her.

"Sure. I'll look for him and thanks, Lizzy. You're a nice friend, and I like you a lot. You want to run some laps with me when you finish your chores? Maybe we can look for Albert Joe," Tori asked with a friendly smile.

"I would like to run some laps with you, Tori, sounds like a good thing to do. I'm sure Albert Joe will catch up with us soon." Lizzy replied with a sigh of relief at having dodged Tori's questioning which would most likely turn into a bullying game.

"Wait for me outside the cafeteria door, I'll be there soon."

"Sure, Lizzy. I'll wait for you and don't worry! I promise not to tease you," replied Tori as she ran out the door with a mischievous smile on her face. Lizzy worked fast to finish her chores and met up with Tori as planned crossing her fingers that her odd friend would not break her promise and bully her.

"So, why do you want to see, Albert Joe?" Lizzy asked with a warm smile as she walked beside Tori.

"Actually, I'm fascinated with Albert Joes' love of pigeons, and I have a new lunch box that my mom bought me other day at the hardware store. It has a beautiful painting of pigeons that I think Albert Joe will just love."

"Tori, you showed me your new lunch box this morning on the school bus. It is really pretty and I'm sure Albert Joe will be excited to see the pigeons since that is his favorite bird," Lizzy said, recalling how nice Tori was currently acting and wondering if she would snap and distort her face at any moment. Tori remained cordial and friendly for the time being.

"Come on Lizzy, there's Piper and Rexi. We can all run laps together before Ms. Allen calls us to get in line. Maybe they can help us find Albert Joe," Tori shouted.

"Sure Tori, we can also glance around the playground and see if we can find arrowheads while we run," Lizzy said as they caught up with their friends.

Lizzy gained her composure, hoping Tori would not rat her out to Piper and Rexi, revealing Lizzy and Albert Joe had to clean the cafeteria because they were poor. Tori was nice to her; but Lizzy had also seen an evil spark in Tori's eyes when she got angry, and she was known for playing mean pranks on anyone who ticked her off. It was Lizzy's goal to keep on Tori's good list of friends.

"Albert Joe, don't you think all students should be treated equally and everyone gets free lunch?" Lizzy asked her elder brother as they hurriedly cleaned the cafeteria tables one day.

"Heck Lizzy. Where do you come up with all that stuff? I ain't thought 'bout no free lunches. I just eat 'em up and also snatch up a few bites of leftovers on the trays them rich kids leave when I'm cleaning," Albert Joe replied with pride beaming in his eyes. "Lizzy, I ain't got the time to think about who gets what. Anyway Ms. Walker saves the scraps for my birds; packs them in a paper bag for me twice a week," Albert Joe reported. "So, way I see this Lizzy, I ain't eating free; I am getting my fair share for my pigeons with the left over scraps. Heck, I should be paying Ms. Walker because she is the best cafeteria manager we ever had at our school and she ain't even going to charge me for the scraps."

"Well, you don't see eye to eye with me on this because I strongly feel all students should be treated equally, and no one should be punished because they are poor. All students should eat free." Lizzy placed her washcloth in the bucket, making sure her hand did not touch the murky water.

"Lizzy don't worry what others think of us."

"You're so busy defending your right to the leftovers for your pigeons; you didn't even notice I beat you washing tables. Pay closer attention, Albert Joe," Lizzy shouted as she ran out the cafeteria door looking over her shoulder to get a glimpse of her brother trailing behind.

Albert Joe yelled as he sprinted out the cafeteria door, "Lizzy, just leave it alone. You go running your mouth and my pigeons will not get free food. Don't go writing a letter to someone protesting again."

"What's your problem Lizzy?" Ms. Allen quickly asked. "I overheard Albert Joe, and what type of protest is on your mind this time, young lady?"

"Well, it isn't a secret Ms. Allen…the poor students have to clean in order to receive a hot meal at school, all because our parents can't afford to pay for our lunch. I just feel this justifies unfair treatment, Ms. Allen." Lizzy explained. "I want to help change the rules so everyone eats free, and we are all treated equally. Albert Joe is afraid I'll mess up his arrangement with Ms. Walker…she saves scraps for his pigeons."

"Wise beyond your years, you sound like a politician my dear," Ms. Allen added as Lizzy continued to rally for her approval.

"Don't you agree with me Ms. Allen? No student should ever feel embarrassed because they are poor and this policy stinks."

Her teacher nodded again to show she was indeed very proud of the stand Lizzy had taken to bring equality to their school.

"Lizzy, you run along and get some fresh air and try not to worry, my dear," Ms. Allen raised her arms, scooting Lizzy toward the playground to run her laps prior to the end of recess.

Lizzy chattered as she briskly walked toward the large playground hanging her lightweight sweater around the back of her head, pretending she had long hair like the other girls in her classroom. Suddenly she felt a sharp tug on her head as something flew to the ground. It was her white sweater and it was now no longer white. It was filthy.

"Tori, why did you yank my sweater off my head? Just look at my sweater. It is all dirty because of you."

"Lizzy, you look odd with that white sweater flopping around your back like a cape and everyone knows your hair is short. That sweater you sport is so cheap, not even real cotton. I know it is made of polyester," Tori replied with a flicker of disgust on her face.

"Tori, sometimes you are weird, you act nice to me, and then you are just plain mean," Lizzy snapped as she continued to brush off the dirt from her sweater.

"Tori, I just don't know about you. I think you have something wrong with you," Lizzy shouted at her unreliable friend who was now gazing in the trees, mesmerized by the birds perched on the branches.

Lizzy caught up with Piper Thomas and Rexi Lane who were good friends. Both were from poor families and could identify with her. Besides, their fathers also worked at the cotton mill.

"Lizzy, is Tori acting strange again?" Piper Thomas asked as Rexi Lane listened with empathy for Lizzy.

"Yep but she can't help it. I think she is a bad seed, has a faraway look in her eyes when she says mean things. Sometimes Tori can be nice though," Lizzy explained to Piper and Rexi, hoping they would understand Tori was not always mean.

"You got that right, Lizzy. Tori is a weird person and I think she is disturbed, you know like someone with two people living inside them," Piper Thomas said as they ran laps.

"She's an only child and just spoiled," Lizzy wanted to excuse her friend's behavior. "Anyway, she and Albert Joe are good friends, so I'm hoping he'll be a good role model."

"If I were Albert Joe, I would be very careful," Piper had a frown on her face as she twirled her hair. "Tori might hurt one of his pigeons. She sure does stare at Albert Joe's pigeons in a weird way. Just the other day, I saw Tori teasing one of his pigeons with breadcrumbs. Once the baby pigeon swooped down to fetch a bite, Tori stomped on the bread with her foot and laughed."

"Goodness. Maybe Tori is a bad seed," Rexi said with concern.

"Piper, I'm glad you and Rexi are nice and I think you both are so pretty. Thank you for being the same every day."

"Thanks Lizzy, and you are really a nice friend and don't worry about Tori's mean words. Just ignore her because everyone knows she is moody,"

Piper Thomas said, as Rexi shook her head in agreement. "Lizzy, you are pretty, too. We like you because you are nice to everyone."

Lizzy rose the following morning with a renewed spirit, looking forward to a brighter day at school…that is, in the lunchroom. At school, Lizzy pondered the lunch menu behind Ms. Allen's desk. Soup was truly on the menu for lunch. Yuck!

Lizzy hated soup; it reminded her of the Jones' potluck meals served every Sunday. She found the menu rather repulsive.

In fact, Lizzy disliked all soups in huge pots and compared them to the white thin slop jars filled to the rim with community leftovers, which was food fed to their hogs.

Rounding up the slop jars and washing them was a chore Lizzy despised, but it was necessary so her dad could retrieve food from the village neighbors to feed their livestock.

Yep, to Lizzy all soups had that same look and smell…multiple food groups mixed in one enormous pot. Lizzy decided her lunch would consist of milk and fruit. She would skip the community soup pot, even though she had to clean the tables regardless of what she ate.

She gulped her milk down while finishing the last bite of her apple. The soup on her tray remained untouched.

Lizzy grabbed the wet towel and washed each table before running outside as fast as her legs would carry her. Just maybe her friends did not see her entering the playground late again as on the previous days.

She spotted Tori and Albert Joe looking at the pigeons on Tori's new lunch box. Lizzy could only hope Tori was having a good day and would be nice to Albert Joe. At least she did not have a faraway look in her eyes.

"Lizzy told me you were looking for me yesterday, Tori. I sure do like your lunch box," Albert Joe held the tin box close to his eyes, taking in every inch of the scenery. "Gosh, wish I had a prime lunch box. Tori, you have one fine masterpiece.

"I'm amazed that a girl would have a lunch box with pigeons painted on it, Tori. So, your mom bought this at the local hardware store? Bet it cost a lot of money."

Albert Joe slowly returned the lunchbox back to its rightful owner.

"You can have my lunch box, Albert Joe. You want it? If you'll promise to be my best friend, you can have it. So, go ahead and tell me you'll be my best friend for always."

"Nope, I can't take your lunch box. I do appreciate the offer, Tori, and that was mighty nice of you to offer but it belongs to you."
Albert Joe had a big smile upon his face. "How would you like for me to bring a real pigeon to school so you could hold it, Tori? I'll see if I can bring my favorite pigeon one day just for you."

"Sure, Albert Joe I would love to hold a real live pigeon. Never seen one up close just flying in the sky and at the courthouse where they perch on the top of the building. Sometimes they come down when we throw breadcrumbs on the ground, but I've never held one. Thanks, Albert Joe. You're my best friend."

"I'll let you know soon, Tori. Thanks for sharing your lunchbox with me. It's really nice, and I like it a lot. I have to run my laps on the playground, so I'll see you later, Tori." Albert Joe was more interested in joining his friends that had already started their laps. "Darn, I'll be last all because of Tori."

Tori was excited that Albert Joe liked her lunchbox. She ran over to Lizzy with the news. "Albert Joe is bringing a pigeon to the school for me to see and possibly hold."

"Good, Tori. I'm glad you and Albert Joe are friends." Lizzy pulled a hangnail from her pinky finger while looking deep into Tori's mysterious and blank eyes. Tori saw the blood oozing from Lizzy's tiny finger. She smiled while handing Lizzy a black napkin she pulled from her pants pocket.

Lizzy could not believe Tori liked pigeons; no other girl she knew liked any type of bird. Lizzy thought it was odd that Albert Joe and Tori had so much in common, but she was also fond of the idea of a rich girl like Tori taking her time to befriend kids that were from a poverty stricken cotton mill village.

The following morning Albert Joe caged a beautiful pigeon with snow white feathers tipped with a touch of bluish color that sparkled when the rays of the sun shined upon them. Once the bus came to a stop Tori's eyes saw the pigeon in the cage and lit up like a Christmas tree in Central Park. Albert Joe and Lizzy boarded the school bus.

"Now Albert Joe, son...you know the rules. Keep that bird in the cage, or I'll have to ask you to get off and walk the rest of the way to school." The bus driver echoed as Albert Joe went toward the back of the bus.

"Ah! That is the most beautiful pigeon I've ever seen Albert Joe. Can I hold him?"

"Well, not until we get to school 'cause Mr. George reminded me, I must leave the pigeon in the cage," Albert Joe stated.

"Last time I took my bird out its cage, it frightened some of the little kids, and Mr. George nearly plunged into the ditch with all the screaming that was going on. Besides, I gave him my word I wouldn't let my pigeons out of their cage if Mr. George let me take them on the bus with me."

"I understand. Soon as we get off the bus can I hold it?" Tori asked with her eyes still wide open, filled with anticipation of touching the bird Albert Joe had caged and securely sitting on his lap.

"Sure, Tori I'll take my pigeon out and you can rub the feathers. They are so soft. You'll fall in love with 'Lady Blue'." Albert Joe was grinning from ear to ear.

"Lady Blue? How did you come up with such a name Albert Joe?"

"Well, I figured with snow white feathers with a bluish tip the only name that would give justice was 'Lady Blue'. Besides, Lady Blue is a special pigeon." Albert Joe proclaimed.

"How's that Albert Joe?" Tori asked with suspicion echoing in her voice.

'Cause, Lady Blue can soar higher than any other pigeon I've ever had. She resembles a beautiful dove in the sky; blends in with the fluffy clouds," Albert Joe explained as his friend with the beautiful lunch box continued poking her fingers in the cage for Lady Blue to nibble.

All of a sudden, Albert Joe was screaming at the top of his lungs. Mr. George slammed on the brakes and book sacks flew to the front of the bus, lunch boxes bounced off the seats while thermos bottles rolled in the bus aisle.

"What's going on back there?" Mr. George asked, looking up to see Lady Blue flapping her wings around the bus frightening the younger children.

"Albert Joe! You gave me your word, son!" Mr. George shouted as he pulled the yellow bus on the side of the dirt road. He got out of his seat and made his way toward the back of the bus where the action seemed to be taking place. He stopped once he saw the empty birdcage near Albert Joe's seat.

"But Mr. George, I didn't do it, Tori…" Albert Joe tried to say as he felt Tori's elbow punching his ribs.

"Hush up, Albert Joe. You'll get me in trouble. I just wanted to touch Lady Blue's feathers, feel their smooth edges with my fingers," Tori sported a sparkle in her eyes that Albert Joe could not resist.

"Albert Joe, what happened, son?" Mr. George asked as he stood looking at Albert Joe and Tori.

"Well sir, the cage door jarred open when you turned the corner and Lady Blue flew out. It was an accident Mr. George." Albert Joe declared.

"Alright, but you can't bring your birds on the bus again. You hear me, Albert Joe?" Mr. George said with a firm tone in his voice as Albert Joe plucked Lady Blue off a piece of freshly baked bread that had landed on the floor.

"Get your pigeon, Albert Joe, and lock the cage tightly so we can safely get to school." Mr. George shouted shaking his head in the negative as he sat down in the driver's seat and continued on the route.

"OK Albert Joe. I can't wait until we arrive at school. I'll meet you under the huge oak tree. See you there." Tori marveled at the bird that sat perfectly still in the cage as if it had been super glued to the perching post.

As the bus arrived at school, Lizzy waited patiently in her seat while everyone unloaded. Being at the back of the bus provided her with the opportunity to be the last person to seize the beautiful landscape on Maple Leaf Avenue.

Lizzy's mind was cluttered with the episode of Albert Joe's pigeon flying around like a mad bird on an Alford Hitchcock movie as she spotted her brother at the front of the bus. "Albert Joe. What the heck happened? How did Lady Blue get out of her cage?" Lizzy asked with accusing eyes searching for Tori on the school grounds.

"I'm not sure Lizzy. I securely closed the cage door with a bread tie this morning. Tori and I was talking and next thing I knew; Lady Blue was out of the cage." Albert Joe explained.

"Did Tori let Lady Blue out?"

"Well, yes, but Tori swears it was an accident," Albert Joe said while shaking his head in disbelieve of Tori disobeying Mr. George's rule.

"Lizzy, Tori had a weird look in her eyes when Lady Blue was flapping around the top of the bus. She was spellbound, and I declare at one point she looked evil. Don't think she meant no harm," Albert Joe got off the bus holding Lady Blue's cage tightly with both his hands. The bird resembled a stone statue in a museum.

"Tori is a good friend, but I think she is also odd. You need to be careful so you don't get in trouble," Lizzy warned her brother as they walked toward the school.

"Lizzy, don't be mad at Tori. Sometimes people can be nice and also awkward at the same time." Albert Joe felt compelled to defend Tori.

"Well Albert Joe, you're right. She is a nice girl but she is also very odd and downright mischievous."

"I don't know what those big words are Lizzy…like 'miscivuss' hope it doesn't mean Tori is terrible 'cause I really have taken a liking to her." Albert Joe looks at his sister for clarification.

"Albert Joe, that's not how you pronounce "mischievous. What I meant was for you to be careful because Tori could be a bad seed. You have to watch your back all the time with bad seeds," Lizzy warned her elder brother.

As Albert Joe walked ahead of his sister he shouted, "Lizzy, you are such a worry wart but I love you."

They each walked toward the big brick school building that had a canopy of beautiful oak trees providing much needed shade on all four sides. Lizzy's mind was in space as she thought how nice it would be if the mill village had nicely landscaped yards and streets. Suddenly she hears someone shouting her name. She spotted her friends Karen and Sharon Moore who were talking to someone.

As Lizzy walked closer, she saw Albert Joe whose hands remained glued to Lady Blue's cage while Tori carried his book bag. He was chatting to

Karen and Sharon Moore who were spellbound at her elder brother and Lady Blue. Tori was pulling at Albert Joe's arm; signaling she wanted to move on. Albert Joe obliged his dominant friend and faded into the crowd leaving Karen and Sharon looking puzzled at his disappearance.

Lizzy let out a snicker at the sight of Karen and Sharon Moore who were wearing matching floral maxi dresses accented with tie-dye canvas shoes. Lizzy could not help but admire their spunk to be different, though she would never wear such an ensemble in public. Lizzy stopped and chatted and then she politely excused herself.

As Lizzy got closer to the front of the school building she saw Albert Joe and Tori under an oak tree admiring Lady Blue who was still perched perfectly still in her locked cage.

Lizzy decided to join the group and watch Albert Joe coach Lady Blue as she performed for the crowd of excited spectators, knowing the finale would bring a loud cheer.

The bell rang and everyone moved toward the entrance doors of the school leaving the schoolyard empty. It was time for class to start on this bright warm day. Albert Joe was feeling pride for bringing Lady Blue to school until he heard the echo of Mr. Parrish's words in his ears.

Later on Albert Joe passed Lizzy at the water fountain. Lizzy whispered to her brother, "I'm having a great morning Albert Joe, are you?"

"Sure Lizzy. Everyone loved Lady Blue as she faded into the fluffy clouds soaring in the sky. That was a sight to behold. Think I won some new friends with Lady Blue's help." Albert Joe turned to go back to class. "See you later Lizzy."

Lizzy joined her friends, realizing they only had a few more minutes and it would be time to go back to class. She was sure the rumor mill had made its round to her friends that did not get to see Lady Blue prior to the morning bell ringing. Lizzy knew she would have to arrange for Albert Joe to bring his prize pigeon to school for show-and-tell but he would have to walk because there was no way Mr. George would allow Albert Joe's birds back on the bus after the incident. Tori had ruined the possibility of Lady Blue or any other bird riding the yellow school bus in the near future.

Soon a group of girls found Lizzy. They asked about Albert Joe's beautiful pigeon he had released in the sky, if Lady Blue would surely fly to their home and be perched in the pigeon hotel, as Albert Joe had claimed. Everyone was eager for Lizzy's answer.

"Yes, Lady Blue and all of Albert Joe's pigeons are very intelligent and they always come home." Lizzy assured the girls who wanted more information about Albert Joe's pigeon hotel. Lizzy felt compelled to release pertinent facts to the inquisitive spectators and answered as many questions as possible prior to entering the classroom.

"Well, you see, Albert Joe built it all by himself," Lizzy said with pride adding her brother was a master at raising his prize pigeons and well skilled in constructing their home.

"Albert Joe loves his pigeons and takes good care of them," Lizzy assured her friends who were huddled together listening to Lizzy's speech of perfection. Suddenly, all attention went toward Ms. Allen as the well-respected teacher raised her hand to signal that it was time to get back to class and resume their work assignments.

Everyone ran towards Ms. Allen pleading for Lizzy to finish her story during afternoon recess. Everyone was fascinated at the thought of a young boy raising birds in a cotton mill village.

For now, she had to get back to class and concentrate on learning. Lizzy entered her classroom and reviewed her daily agenda so she would be ready. As she read over the agenda for the third time, trying to memorize transitions, she noticed her class would be visiting the school's library. A smile immediately appeared upon her face.

The thought of visiting the school's library made Lizzy's day much brighter.

It was her favorite place to visit at school as it offered wonderful adventures. Lizzy found acceptance and peace of mind by bonding with the characters as she read under her sheet each night. She had to decide upon a book as Ms. Allen reminded everyone it was nearly time to leave. It was such a hard decision for a girl with such a profound love of books to make. Lizzy just could not bear the thought of having to make a choice between the books. She wanted both books in her procession.

She checked out her favorite landscaping book that was full of beautiful homes and colorful flowers which adorned huge gardens. The librarian was in the process of stamping Lizzy's book when she noticed the young girl eyeing a book that had been left on the nearby book cart. Lizzy's long slender fingers reached for the book and she began to fixate on the pictures as she slowly turned each page; then placed it back on the cart.

"*Charlotte's Web*," said the slender woman standing behind the counter. "That was a favorite of mine when I was a young girl, Lizzy. Did you want to check out a second book today?" Ms. Jefferson asked with an accepting smile and eyes that showed approval of Lizzy's love of books.

"Yes. Thanks Ms. Jefferson for allowing me to check out two books. I'll take good care of them. I promise." Lizzy turned and walked away from the counter smiling and clutching her books with both hands. She turned her head and whispered, "You're the best librarian in the world."

Tori were next in line at the librarian's desk. Noticing the books Lizzy was holding securely underneath her arm she whispered, "That's my favorite book you're holding prisoner Lizzy. I was going to check it out." She had a piercing look in her eyes as she reached out to claim Lizzy's books.

"I was looking for *Charlotte's Web* Lizzy 'cause it is my favorite book, give it to me now."

"It is my favorite book also. I'm glad you like it," Lizzy replied, hoping Tori would stop her spiteful gazing that Lizzy coined as 'silent eye bullying'. Tori followed Lizzy who was sitting at a table looking at her books. Tori purposely bumped Lizzy's head with the dull end of her hardback book and immediately apologized as she scanned for an empty chair at Lizzy's table.

"Lizzy, you look like you are holding your books hostage," Tori chuckled with a smirk on her face; finding a seat across from Lizzy. "What's wrong, do I make you nervous?" Tori whispered across the table with her slightly oversized lips that were perched and ready to sling intimidating language at any given moment. "I have a special power, Lizzy. I can cast spells on people. I talk to dead people…spirits. I want to make you nervous enough to crap a clinker."

"Nope, I'm not nervous and you have a foul mouth that needs be washed out with lye soap. Besides, I love the library and being around all the wonderful books. They help me to escape reality. I sorta get lost in the characters." Lizzy lifted her chin to portray confidence to the moody Tori who was for sure escorting multiple personalities on this day. Lizzy refused to be intimidated.

"We're a lot alike, Lizzy. I love books, reading, and writing same as you. Sometimes my mom even calls me a bookworm. Anyway, I find it is easier for me to learn by reading," Tori preached as she slowly held out her hand to retrieve Lizzy's book.

Lizzy ignored the odd behavior and held her books tightly with both hands as she slowly lower them toward her lap. An unexpected jerk from a hand abruptly came from across the table. Tori had Lizzy's book in her possession.

Refusing to be intimidated by the evil hawk eye Tori was now glaring, Lizzy pretended to be undisturbed by Tori's actions. Lizzy answered questions from the ill spirited girl sitting across from her. It was apparent to Lizzy that evil was silently speaking through Tori's dilated pupils.

"Learning has always been easy for me, Tori. Books offer a world away from any distractions. It's hard sometimes when you're the only girl in the family. I have two brothers, and they both like to tease me. I just retreat to reading when I feel I've had enough of them and I've had well enough of you Tori…you stop your bullying." Lizzy leaned across the table and snatched her book from Tori's greedy hands.

Tori was shocked and sat in awe that Lizzy was up for a challenge. She would appease the frail, poor, but seemly intelligent Lizzy…for the moment.

"Well, I surely don't know what it is like to have siblings because I'm an only child. Sometimes I wish I had a brother. I think it would be nice to have a big brother like Albert Joe," Tori smiled to show her approval of Lizzy's elder brother.

"I would torture the poor soul if I had to actually share my things," Tori added with a weird laugh as she stood beside Lizzy's chair with her eyes fixated on the prized books in Lizzy's lap.

A cold chill entered Lizzy's body as Tori touched her shoulder. Lizzy squirmed in her seat in hopes the strange sensation would leave as Tori's hand moved. Refusing to look at Tori's eyes, Lizzy continued their conversation, ignoring her weird friend's demeanor as she quietly stood and pushed her chair under the table.

"Albert Joe is a good brother but he can get on your nerves sometimes. His entire world is his pigeons. He stays in his tree house when he has free time."

"I like Albert Joe a lot and I also like Lady Blue. She is a beautiful pigeon. I'm glad Albert Joe let me take her out of the cage on the bus," Tori added. "Even thou he broke Mr. George's rules."

"Oh no he didn't, Tori. Albert Joe would never do that. You took Lady Blue out of her cage and Albert Joe got in trouble with Mr. George," Lizzy proclaimed while throwing a darting glare.

"Well, guess we better get in line, looks like Ms. Allen is ready for us to get back to class," Tori replied without defending herself from the allegations. They both walked toward their teacher, knowing it would soon be time for school to dismiss.

Once she heard the bell ring Lizzy hung her head in dismay. As she boarded the school bus, the quietness in the schoolyard echoed another day that had come and gone.

The bus doors slowly closed and Lizzy moved toward the back, sitting down to rest and enjoy the ride home. She felt something under her foot. Reaching down Lizzy found the bread tie that Albert Joe had used to secure Lady Blue's cage in a tight wad. She also found the remains of crushed snacks that had apparently fallen out of lunch boxes during the pigeon outrage that occurred on the morning route to school. She placed the trash from the bus floor in her crinkle brown paper bag and stuffed it back inside her book sack.

Once the bus went over the railroad tracks, she heard the screeching sound of the bus doors opening as it came to a stop.

"See you tomorrow Lizzy," Mr. George said waving as he closed the bus door.

"Thanks for the ride Mr. George. See you tomorrow," Lizzy shouted as she jumped off the last step of the bus.

The long walk home was always interesting because the neighborhood dogs would run with excitement to meet the kids. Some of the boys would stop and play a game of marbles, and several of the girls would scramble in their homemade book sacks to find a piece of chalk to draw squares on the rocky payment for a quick game of hopscotch.

A flying object caught Lizzy's attention. It had to be her weird and simple-minded neighbor up to his mean pranks. Lester Gunter was known for terrorizing the children in the neighborhood. Lizzy tilted her head up toward the cotton mill water tower. Sure enough, she spotted crazy Lester Gunter grasping the metal ladder with one hand and reaching into the front bib pocket of his nasty overalls with his other hand searching for figs to throw at the children walking on the street. "Lester Gunter, you better get down from that water tower before Mr. Johnson calls the law on you," Lizzy shouted.

Lester Gunter continued to throw rotten figs as he climbed higher on the ladder. Once he reached the top, he commenced to jumping around like a monkey in a cage. The children ran for safety as the figs fell like hail, splashing on the tar pavement. Lester Gunter continued to jump and laugh as he threw his rotten figs. "Lester, you're acting like a maniac. Get down off that water tower," Lizzy demanded to no avail as everyone scattered.

As the day ended, Lizzy was very tired as she prepared for bedtime. She had looked forward to ending her day by reading. She could hardly wait to slide under the faded, thin sheets and clutch her book. Walking toward her hall bedroom, she placed her library book under her pillow and settled into bed. Her mind was tired, and she needed a good night's sleep.

Lizzy held tightly to her book for protection, waiting for the inevitable to occur but hoping it would not cause her as much disturbance as the previous nights. Praying for a peaceful night's rest had become a nightly ritual for Lizzy.

She nodded off into a light sleep with the book clutched tightly in her hands. Lizzy knew that unwanted nightmares could approach the foot of her bed at any time, seeking an opportunity to enter her and take her mind captive.

Lizzy's last task prior to surrendering to the nightmares was to close the lid to her beautiful music box and place her flashlight on the tiny wood table beside her bed.

As the ballerina folded into the box, Lizzy crawled back into her bed, gently placing her book under the pillow. Quickly pulling the thin sheet over her head, Lizzy put her hand under her pillow and held onto her book. She felt that, if she held tightly, the book would protect her from the intrusion of the monsters that harbored the hall bedroom.

She gave in to the demands of the darkness once the familiar coldness surged within her body, paralyzing her limbs, calling her name. Lizzy knew there was little she could do to stop the nightmares. It was ready to overtake her body.

The monstrous nightmares were realistic, and they had haunted this frail young girl for years. Lizzy could always recall vivid details...the cries of babies, the echoes of someone running up and down steps, blankets, lots of blankets and total blackness...blackness that made her feel anxious. She would often wake up shaking in fear and unable to fall back asleep.

Lizzy knew one day she would be free of the nightmares and she would at last experience inviting pleasant dreams with vivid pictures of beautiful homes, flowers, and children playing on the sidewalks as the birds chirped in the trees.

CHAPTER III

SHADOW VILLAGE ELEMENTRY

The halls of Shadow Village Elementary School filled with a cracking sound from the pine wood boards that lined the floors of the old three-story school building. The steam heat made the floors feel warm and cozy.

Lizzy glanced at the schedule written on the clean chalkboard. She admired the white chalk placed neatly on the wood board ledge that was clearly without a dust of the white chalk. Order and structure were appealing to Lizzy, and her school days were structured by the mind and hand of her devoted teacher. Lizzy's smile gave complete approval of her environment. She felt secure in her classroom, far from the nightmares behind the cotton mill.

Lizzy took out her book and prepared for class. It was easy to find her place in the reading book; she always placed a four-leaf clover between the last pages read on the previous day. On that day, a necklace made of clovers fell to the floor when Lizzy opened her book.

Everyone scrambled into their appointed small groups located in various places within the classroom. The students knew Ms. Allen's daily rhyming drill "Scramble, scramble, with me... to the count of one, two, and three, find your places as you walk, being careful not to talk."

The students beamed with excitement as they scrambled to one of four corners in the classroom. Ms. Allen reminded the students to get in the correct corner by pointing to posters listing students' names.

Everyone knew corner number one was the home of students who read fluently above grade level; corner number two housed students who read on grade level with the potential of moving up to corner number one by mid school year.

Ms. Allen reminded her students daily that it took hard work and dedication to move from corner two to corner one.

Then there was corner number three for emergent readers who needed to learn basic sight words. With a classroom of twenty-eight students, corner number three resembled Ms. Tart's local candy store where students hung out after school. Students in that corner had potential, but they lacked the support of engaging family members to embrace the importance of learning. At least that is what Lizzy had overheard Ms. Allen say to the principal while tending to adult business.

It was a known fact that in order to make an exit from corner number three, students had to be self-motivated and work hard to excel in reading. Ms. Allen reminded everyone it required dedication and perseverance to learn. She often reminded her students that determination would allow them to be lifelong learners and productive individuals. The names on the posters in each corner changed as students mastered skills. Their peers clapped as they graduated to a higher level.

Ms. Allen patiently reminded her students to stay on task. She encouraged them to work together and help each other with the reading unit. With everything in order, Ms. Allen took a seat behind her worn oak desk. It was time for class to begin.

Her desk was unique as it was shared with two students, their desks attached to each side. Everyone enjoyed viewing the threesome arrangement as it added to the cozy surroundings within the classroom.

The fourth corner contained a small basket of books on a large colorful woven rug donated by Mr. Jack Bradford, the supervisor of Shadow Village Cotton Mill. The students were proud of it and took special care of it, but Lizzy had some bottled up suspicion about the generous gift from the prominent mill supervisor.

Lizzy was wise for her age and often too suspicious. She knew the gazing eyes of Mr. Jack Bradford expected something in return for his so-called "generosity."

At least that is what the "porch women gossipers" had revealed just the other day. Katie Mae would not approve of her daughter being in the company of these women in the mill village, but Lizzy enjoyed tending to adult business.

Lizzy naturally sought out the less fortunate. On many occasions she would tap the twin boys on the shoulder and ask for their books. Smiling, the boys knew this meant Lizzy would check out the books for them. When the school librarian completed the transaction, Lizzy would nod at Roy and Troy, twins, who knew their books were safe with Lizzy.

After school, the books always magically appeared in their ragged book sacks. Lizzy was practicing her vow to treat others the way she wanted to be treated, but it was also her way of rebelling against the school's policy not to allow students of color to check out books.

Equality was not a term Lizzy understood, but she was interested in learning more. Checking out books in the library for Roy and Troy made her feel helpful, so Lizzy searched for books she felt would intrigue the twins.

Roy and Troy Smith were Lizzy's friends, but they got little respect from their peers. The Smith brothers did not seem concerned that their boisterous and rambunctious younger sister was a notch above them in all academics.

Emma Jean Smith participated in the third corner that housed emergent readers. She was bullied and called an "overgrown moth" by her classmates.

"You stop that name calling John Ross. That's just mean." Lizzy walked closer toward Emma Jean who had a handful of rocks, aimed at John Ross's head.

"He's been bullying me all day," Emma Jean Smith told Lizzy as she handed over the collection of rocks, minus one she had stashed in her pants pockets.

"John Ross, you should leave now, or I'll tell Ms. Allen you're being a bully to Emma Jean Smith."

John Ross turned and stuck up his middle finger at Lizzy then fell hard on the ground. He did not move but sobs were audible, as Lizzy got closer to his body.

"That'll teach you to call me names John Ross Johnson. Bet you'll have a goose egg on your forehead for weeks," Emma Jean shouted as she ran toward the playground in a gallop that could out beat any sprint runner.

Lizzy helped John Ross off the ground; he was holding his forehead with both hands as he screamed profanity at Emma Jean Smith who was galloping towards the school building. She was merely a speck in sight of the injured bully.

"I'm going to get that girl. Ms. Allen will send her to the office for throwing a rock at me. That Emma Jean is nothing but a zebra, a no good idiot."

"John Ross, if I were you I would tell Ms. Allen you need to see the school nurse and forget the tattling," Lizzy instructed the injured boy.

"Shut up Lizzy, you misfit. I'm going get that galloping zebra. That Emma Jean Smith is nothing but a son of a biscuit eater, a half breed—that's what she is," John Ross screamed as he waved his hands in the air for Ms. Allen's assistance.

"Are you coming John Ross?" Ms. Allen shouted while shaking her head wondering what the boy had gotten into.

"John Ross. You better not tattle on Emma Jean. You started this fight. Besides, John Ross, do you really want everyone to know you got beat up by Emma Jean Smith? You'll be known as a boy sissy for sure."

"Already told you once Lizzy shut your trap or I'll shut it for you."

"Your words don't scare me. Also, I gotta warn you I have Emma Jean

Smith's rock collection in my pocket. That is, minus the one she just used." Lizzy cocked her head toward the fallen boy and stuck her tongue out at him.

"From the looks of things you're not in any condition to do much anyway John Ross. Think you might require some medical assistance. Your forehead has a red goose egg. It may crack at any minute and spill black blood on the ground. Ha! Ha! Emma Jean whipped your butt some kinda bad."

Lizzy knew Emma Jean was no saint. She often bellowed profanity and enjoyed slinging her stashed rocks at the bullies. To make matters worse her twin brothers did not understand why her skin was much lighter brown than their other family or why she was often left out of their family portraits.

They also enjoyed bullying her and assisted others in the same practice.

Between her foul language and stashed rocks, Emma Jean always had the upper hand on her offenders. She was a strong-willed, street-smart, seasoned fighter. She could throw rocks farther than any bully. They declared Emma Jean Smith was born with rubber bands inside her arms and hands.

Emma Jean Smith was a survivor, and Lizzy admired her friend's strong traits.

Lizzy did her share of speaking up for justice. She refused to believe the gossiping porch ladies even though she enjoyed knowing the up-to-date news. While eavesdropping one day after school, Lizzy spoke up in defense of her friend.

"You have no right to say Emma Jean is a misfit in the Smith family. Besides, the color of Emma Jean's skin is flawless, beautiful and surely doesn't have wrinkles!"

As she abandoned her friends, she bellowed over her thin shoulder she was tired of drawing hopscotch outlines. Running home, she wiped tears welting in her eyes. She loved her one true friend, Emma Jean.

It was true there were many things Lizzy did not understand when it came to the Smith family. With guilt, she kept a close ear to the gossiping porch ladies, especially when they spoke in reference to Mr. Jack Bradford's eye for Emma Jean's mother, Jasmine. Lizzy was way too young to comprehend such gossip. It made her feel awkward.

Mr. Horace Smith, the father of the Smith children, worked at the cotton mill as the only tow motor mechanic of color. His nickname was "Black Jack" Smith, a name coined by the cotton mill supervisors. He had no idea his paycheck reflected lower wages than other mill hands. Besides, salaries were confidential. Mr. Horace Smith had no idea the mill supervisors visited his house while he was working late shift.

Horace Smith was a hard worker who reported on time and often stayed later after he had clocked out, at the end of his shift. For his hard work and devotion to the mill, his supervisor allowed the Smith family to live amongst the mill residents in the village. Black Jack Smith was willing to use his skills around the clock to feed his family and the mill supervisors were willing to work him around the clock, if they needed him.

To prevent harassment toward the Smith family a huge cotton field separated their house from the other residents in the village. Also, there were boundary lines set for the Smith children within the village. This was very disturbing to Lizzy since she shared a kindred spirit with Emma Jean Smith.

When the bullies called Lizzy names, Emma Jean would come to her rescue, reaching for the rocks in her pants pockets. Lizzy thought Emma Jean Smith had potential to learn but Lizzy had doubt Emma Jean would be successful in school if her friend could not learn to control her hot temper.

One day Lizzy got wind that the twins wanted to join the bully club and had been instructed to taunt Emma Jean with crow sounds and pecking noises in order to be initiated into the club. The twins were also told to pull Emma Jean's long frizzy hair so the club members could feed it to the overgrown black hawks that gathered on the school grounds, pecking for fresh food.

If the twins were successful, they would have a front seat at the bullies' secret clubhouse that was a small dwelling, resembling a cage made out of dilapidated boards and haphazardly nailed to the branches of a crooked oak tree. "Bully Headquarters - Keep Out" had been sprayed on the front of the dwelling to frighten off non-members.

At the expense of their sister's well-being, the twins climbed the weathered plank stairs nailed to the crooked tree trunk to join their bully friends. Using a small razor blade, each boy sliced his middle finger to draw fresh blood to smear on the walls of the tethered door to signify loyalty. After the meeting, the bullies threw their right hands in midair and in unison smashing a high five.

For days, Emma Jean was their prime target, and she was spared no mercy as they taunted her at school and any other opportunity given within the rising and setting of the sun.

The scene was not pretty as the twins waited for their sister on the playground, the club members standing against the fence waiting for the hair pulling to take place as planned. Lizzy had tipped her to the twin's deviate plan, and Emma Jean was well prepared for her brothers and the club members.

The twins called Emma Jean to the fence, claiming to have some candy for her. Emma Jean saw the big black hawks on the fence as the club members continued to throw breadcrumbs toward the ground. Emma Jean approached her brothers with an innocent demeanor. As she got three feet from them, she reached in her back pocket and pulled out a water gun filled with her secret recipe of pepper and water and a pinch of salt. She commenced to hose the twins in the face causing them to stumble and one by one fall to the ground, covering their eyes with their dirty hands.

Emma Jean ran toward the bullies who were standing against the fence. The bullies ran as fast as they could…frightened to death of the frizzy yellow-skinned girl reaching in her pockets slinging rocks faster than Babe Ruth could throw a ball. Emma Jean's aim was directly on target as each boy fell to the ground begging for mercy from Emma Jean Smith.

Emma Jean showed no mercy as she reached into a small marble bag and pulled out blackberries, smashing the berries all over the face of each boy, making sure that John Ross got more than his share. Each boy got up crying like a baby out of milk. They ran as fast as they could, trying to dodge the rocks Emma Jean continued to sling, aiming at their heels. Lizzy watched from a distance and figured the bullies deserved what they were getting. She quickly dismissed a slight tinge of guilt.

When Lizzy entered the principal's office, Emma Jean was sitting on one side of the principal's desk in a large chair. Her long legs were dangling as her bellbottom jeans swayed to the tune of a freedom.

Emma Jean had won, and she had the look of victory on her face. She winked at Lizzy to assure her all the rocks were safely scattered on the playground, and the only true evidence upon her body were the blackberry stains that covered her light brown hands.

Lizzy glanced around the office and on the opposite side of the room sat several boys. Emma Jean's twin brothers tried to cover the blackberry stains on their faces with their hands. Lizzy looked at John Ross whose heels had large red marks that were now bleeding.

The nurse entered the office gazing around to find the injured students so she could cleanse and bandage the wounds. The boys shouted for a washcloth to remove the blackberry stains prior to others witnessing their apparent loss to Emma Jean Smith.

Lizzy's eyes scanned John Ross once again and she chuckled, calling him a bloody monster.

"Shut up Lizzy, you're a zebra lover!" John Ross shouted. "We hate you. You ain't nothing but a frizzy headed piss ant."

"You . . . well, you're a nosey brat. Think we'll call you brat ratter. Maybe Lizzy Pissy would fit you better."

"Alright boys, better lower your voices," the nurse instructed as she continued to care for their needs. Lizzy walked by the boys toward the principal's office with a smirk upon her face, grinning from ear to ear. Revenge was sweet to Lizzy. She detested a bully.

"Lizzy, I understand you were on the playground when the fight took place between Emma Jean Smith and these boys. Can you tell me what

Emma Jean did to these boys? The boys have rock marks on their hands, legs, and heels, not to mention the blackberries smashed all over their faces. They are simply a mess, and it seems Emma Jean Smith is the culprit."

"No sir. I can't tell you in good faith what Emma Jean did to the boys, but I can tell you Emma Jean was outnumbered by the bullies. They planned the attack on her. This was an outright premeditated attack on a girl, Mr. Parrish."

The principal agreed that the boys were wrong to plan such an attack. Emma Jean had caused bodily harm to the boys, and the episode would cost her two days of suspension from school.

Lizzy stood up and went to Mr. Parrish's desk: "How can you in good conscience give Emma Jean Smith two days at home and not give the bullies any time? That is very unfair, Mr. Parrish. With all due respect to you as my principal, this calls for a protest."

"A protest? What do you mean Lizzy? You need to explain yourself, young lady."

"Well, it seems to me you're being too harsh on Emma Jean Smith; and you're letting the bullies get off light. They started this fight, Mr. Parrish...think I might have to get Ms. Allen help me with a letter to the superintendent...let him know we have a group of bullies at our school."

"Now, wait a minute, Lizzy. I think you're being too outspoken for a young girl."

"Well, Mr. Parrish, I do apologize if I sounded disrespectful, but I answered your question to the best of my knowledge. You just didn't take my word as the truth," Lizzy argued.

"OK, Lizzy, you win. I understand Emma Jean is a girl, and she was the target of bullies. I'll give them all three days at home to think about their actions. Is that fair Lizzy?"

"Well, Mr. Parrish. I'll have to say 'No.'...once again, Emma Jean didn't start the fight. She was outnumbered, and they targeted her because of the color of her skin. It is true that Emma Jean beat the boys up but only because she was prepared. If she had not been prepared, these bullies could have hurt her. So, I say give her two days in school suspension and the bullies three days at home."

"Prepared? Well, let me think about this, Lizzy, because I have concerns about students coming to school with rocks in their pocket; prepared to fight. Thank you for answering my questions truthfully. Now, you are excused to go back to class. Don't discuss this with anyone," Mr. Parrish warned Lizzy as he stood and shook her hand.

"Sure Mr. Parrish. I'll never say a word about the beating the boys got from Emma Jean Smith, but I'm sure everyone already knows. If not, they'll know when they see the blackberry stains on their faces," Lizzy chuckled as she left the principal's office, winking at Emma Jean Smith as she passed.

As Lizzy entered the hallway, the school librarian faced her. "You look like you're on a mission, Lizzy. Are you protesting, being a politician?"

"Well, both I guess, Ms. Jefferson. You see, some boys were being bullies, and I was a witness so I had to tell the truth to help Emma Jean."

Ms. Jefferson patted Lizzy on the shoulder and winked, giving Lizzy's approval for standing up to bullies.

"See you later, Ms. Jefferson. I need a book from the library and can't wait to stop."

Lizzy walked back to her classroom with assurance that justice had been served. She refused to say a word to anyone about the events that took place in the principal's office, but she could not wait for the rumors to fly around like a windstorm. It would not be long before everyone would know the bullies had blackberry smashed on their faces.

After school, Lizzy looked for Emma Jean Smith. She spotted her standing under the big old oak tree in the front of the school. "Emma, come here. Need talk to you." Emma Jean approached Lizzy with a smile.

"Lizzy, what you want with me? You shouldn't be seen talking to me. You might get in trouble with Mr. Parrish."

"Emma Jean, I'll not get in any trouble because I've done nothing wrong. It is a free country, and I can talk to you if I well please."

"Now, listen to me, Lizzy. You gotta stay clear of the bullies. They know you helped me. You hear me, Lizzy? They might hurt you."

"I'm not afraid of those boys. Besides, Albert Joe will defend me if I need him. Don't worry, Emma Jean. All will be well. I'm just glad they didn't hurt you."

"Thanks for being my friend, Lizzy. I ain't too pretty and will never be smart like you, but I have always liked you Lizzy, cause you stand up for people, you're a good friend, Lizzy."

"Thanks, Emma Jean. I'll help you with your reading once you're out of detention. Now, you be really good when you come to school tomorrow. Go directly to the school suspension room. Take your punishment, and don't talk to anyone, like Mr. Parrish instructed."

"OK, Lizzy. Thanks again for helping me."

"Sure Emma Jean. You are an exciting human being. You have good attendance in school, and that says a lot about your character," Lizzy added.

"Lizzy, do you think I'm a rotten crow's egg like the bullies chant?" Emma Jean asked tearfully.

"No, Emma Jean. You're just a little mouthy, but that's not a bad thing. Emma Jean, if I can teach you to read, you'll excel in school and that will make you feel better. You'll see, Emma Jean. I'll teach you to read, and the bullies will leave you alone for good."

Lizzy continued to encourage her friend. "Emma Jean, if I can teach you to read, you can make it over the tracks with me once we graduate from high school."

"Lizzy, I've never wanted to remain in the village. Everyone knows if you stay here there is nothing to look forward to but a lifetime of working long hours at low wages in that stinking cotton mill."

"You got that right. But, you'll never get out of the village unless you learn to read, Emma Jean. Well, we better get on the bus or we'll get left," Lizzy said as they walked together to board the bus.

"OK, Lizzy. You teach me to read and we'll make a get-a-way once we graduate from high school...just like you told me." On the bus, Emma Jean sat directly behind Mr. George in her assigned seat.

Lizzy went toward the back, found a seat that was empty and sat next to the window where she could look at the houses and dream about living on Maple Leaf Avenue.

"Is everyone on the bus?" Mr. George asked as he looked in the big mirror to make sure all his riders were properly seated. "Off we go. Now, everyone must stay seated."

The last wheel crossed the tracks with a loud sound, followed by a bump that made the students laugh as they intentionally bounced out of their seats. The bus had just crossed over the railroad tracks into the cotton mill village. Mr. George blew his horn as he turned around and came to a complete stop so the kids could get off.

"See you in the morning. Have a good evening," Mr. George shouted as everyone got off the bus, waving as he closed the bus door.

Lizzy walked home with her head down; she wondered if the children on the other side of the railroad tracks had tormenting nightmares, if the darkness that haunted her at night caused anxiety in their bedrooms.

Lizzy's mood changed as she thought of the blackberries Emma Jean Smith had smeared on the bullies. Lizzy could not help but laugh at the beating the boys got at the hands of Emma Jean Smith.

Running toward her house, Lizzy took a deep breath. She wished she did not have so much to do once she got home. She would purposely find a quiet place and hide out with her favorite book. Read until she heard her mom screaming her name. Concentrating on reality, the young girl skipped home.

After finishing her chores, Lizzy remembered her promise to Emma Jean. With her teacher's assistance, Lizzy was confident she could tutor Emma Jean in one of the corners of the classroom.

If Lizzy was successful in teaching Emma Jean to read, just maybe they could be neighbors on Maple Leaf Avenue. That sounded like a grand idea to Lizzy.

The next day in school, Lizzy was startled by a loudly ringing bell. She was working feverishly to complete her homework before going home. On the bus, Lizzy thought of the chores that awaited her, and she knew that completing her homework at home was sometimes impossible.

The sound of the bus going over the tracks snapped Lizzy out of her thoughts.

She noticed the textile mill workers sitting on the side porch, munching peanuts and drinking soda as they took puffs from a shared cigarette. Several of the workers had poured peanuts in their soda bottle. Lizzy thought that was as gross as sharing one cigarette.

Mr. George yelled, "Last stop."

The children knew the drill: everyone had to get off once the bus pulled into the dirt street beside the tracks to turn around. The door opened slowly, and the mill village children nodded to the driver as they got off. As everyone unloaded, Lizzy thought they looked like crickets as each jumped off the last step and headed home.

Several boys, holding jars with holes in the lids, chased the girls trying to throw bullfrogs on them. Emma Jean was not their target as she walked alone toward her house. Another group of boys ran toward the nearby park for a game of baseball.

Lizzy noticed Albert Joe staring at the boys running toward the park and knew he wanted to catch up with his friends. "Albert Joe, you going to play ball with the boys? Mama said we needed to go straight home once we got off the school bus, so you better come on with me or you'll be in trouble. Mama will have that long, thin switch waiting for you if you're late," Lizzy reminded her older brother. "Might just tell Mama where you are, unless you buy me some penny candy from Mr. Thompson's candy truck."

"Lizzy, you know I want to play ball with the boys. Heck, I'll buy you some penny candy if you'll keep your trap shut. What do you want...B-B Bats or some chewy Mary Janes?" Albert Joe asked as he dug deep in his front pants pocket making his loose coins jingle.

"Come on, Lizzy. Walk with me to the ballpark and think about Mr. Thompson's candy truck coming around the corner. That is a nice tradeoff for not telling on me. Besides, you can get some cold water from the new water fountain at the ballpark. It sure is good and cold. Lizzy, you'll like it."

"Well, guess I could walk with you and check out the water fountain, but I'll only look at it. I don't drink out of the community water fountains at the ballpark. I know you boys put your mouth on the waterspout. That's just gross. I'll head home after I see the fountain and start on my chores. I don't want to be late and get the switch."

The two siblings walked side-by-side, talking about their day at school and how they enjoyed riding the school bus. Lizzy did most of the talking, and Albert Joe allowed his younger sister to chatter on because he thought she was interesting and somewhat wise. Besides, he wanted to catch up on the gossip in the neighborhood.

"Lizzy, tell me all about Mr. Roscoe Johnson and the cotton mill. I know you gotta have some bustin gossip that needs to depart from them lips of yours. You're always full of gossip."

"Well…I'll catch you up on the latest if you'll let me have the first scoop of grits and all the extra butter in the middle of the pot. You know Albert Joe, the little dip that forms and all the butter pours into it…just waiting for the spoon to enter and scoop it away," Lizzy gushed with her eyes wide open as if she had won million dollars.

"Goodness, Lizzy, is that all you want for the gossip update? Sure. You can have the first scoop of grits and all the butter that comes with it if you'll chatter away with the latest gossip. Besides, I always let you have first dibs on Mama's buttery grits. I kept my word the other day, Lizzy. You forget already?"

"OK, let me see." Lizzy closed her eyes, trying to recall all she knew on the latest gossip. "Well…there is so much gossip I don't know where to start. But, let me think…yep, this will be good to know. I was next door playing in the yard, you know…trying to catch a doodle bug worm in a big hole that went deep into the earth."

"Lizzy, what does your worm catching have to do with latest gossip? Besides, you're going to get bitten one day by those fuzzy creepy worms you pull out of the ground. You better be careful."

"I have some good juicy gossip for you, but you're bothering my thought waves. Stop calling my worms creepy. They are not creepy worms. They're beautiful, and I always put them back in their rightful home so your smelly frogs don't eat them."

"Well, are you going to tell me, Lizzy, or make me wonder all day?"

"Goodness sake, indeed, Albert Joe. Give me a minute to get all this straight in my head before I tell you. Can't you give a girl time to organize her thoughts? I'll start with how Mr. Roscoe Johnson owns everything in the cotton mill village. Heard he owns the ballpark you can't wait to get to and play ball. Bet you didn't know that. Also, the word is out that Mr. Roscoe Johnson owns the timber mill, and even the mill homes that he rents to the residents.

In fact, according to rumors, Mr. Roscoe Johnson donated the tract of land where the village church was built. He owns the preacher too. Yep. He tells the preacher which sermons to preach on Sundays to keep order in the village."

"Lizzy, don't be ridiculous. Do you really believe all the gossip? Are you kiddin' me? How could one man be so wealthy? Besides, Mr. Roscoe Johnson is a good man far as I know. I think you've gotten hold some wrong gossip, Lizzy."

"Shame on you, I have not floundered upon idle gossip. It is the truth. Besides, I don't gossip…I only repeat the honest to goodness truth. So you need to apologize to me or I have a good mind to tell Mama you are playing ball with the boys after school."

"OK Lizzy. I'm sorry. There, I said it so you better not go home telling Mama I got off the bus and went straight to the ballpark. I will put a frog under your pillow if you do. It will pee on you, and you'll have warts all over your face. You'll have to go to the wart doctor, and let her spit on your warts. That'll be the talk of the neighborhood, Lizzy."

"Enough of your frog talk, Albert Joe. I'll tell you some more good truth if you'll close your trap."

"Well, let's see…have you been made aware that the church Mr. Roscoe Johnson donated is from extra bricks that were left after the cotton mill was built? Let me set the record straight. It is a replica of the textile mill except the house of worship has a huge steeple with a cross. According to my sources, on the base of the steeple, the rightful owner's name is engraved to show proper ownership. Bet you didn't know that." Lizzy looked at her brother to show she did indeed know the facts about Mr. Roscoe Johnson and their neighborhood.

"Lizzy, I'm sure you're probably right about the extra bricks from Mr. Roscoe Johnson's cotton mill, you gotta remember…this is adult business and you're still a child." Albert Joe warned his younger sister who he felt was wise beyond her years. Yes, he knew Lizzy worried way too much about the goings on in the cotton mill village.

"Well, bet you didn't know this piece of information."

"What's that little sis?"

"Seems Mr. Roscoe Johnson took donations from the local merchants to pay for the ballpark he already owned. In other words, Mr. Johnson told the village residents he donated the ballpark when he was actually paid by the local merchants. Bet you didn't know that." Lizzy skipped beside her older brother, waiting for him to reply.

Albert Joe stopped in the middle of the road and turned to his sister, "Lizzy, how in the world do you come up with all this stuff?"

"I have already told you, I heard it from the porch ladies. I don't give out names of my resources. And, it isn't gossip, because they know everything going on in the neighborhood. It's just plain updates of the truth. Without these ladies, everyone would be in the dark about our neighborhood."

"Lizzy, go on over to the water fountain and get you some cold water to soothe that over-heated, blabbering mouth of yours. I'll be home before dark, and don't you rat on me." Albert Joe shouted as he ran onto the ball field, laughing at his sister's quirky ways, knowing she would not go near the water fountain.

"OK, but you better not be too late or Mama'll get you. See ya."

Lizzy skipped toward her house. She had a lot on her mind and knew her evening would be busy with chores. She could not help but think that her parents thought Mr. Roscoe Johnson was such a generous man to give so much of his wealth to the village community, but Lizzy had her own opinion of Mr. Roscoe Johnson.

She knew he appeared to be a very generous man, but she believed the porch women and their updates of the truth.

Lizzy knew there was something that did not seem right about Mr. Roscoe Johnson's demeanor. She often sensed trouble as large as an avalanche brewing when she saw the astute businessman. It was no secret to the village residents that Mr. Roscoe Johnson operated the cotton mill village in a dictatorial manner. It was also no secret he sought the assistance of his main cotton mill supervisor, Mr. Jack Bradford. The street-smart young girl suspected something underhanded at the expense of the mill residents, just as the porch women had declared.

Lizzy heard someone calling her name as she approached the railroad tracks that led toward her home. Turning, she saw Albert Joe running to catch up with her.

Lizzy could not help but think that Albert Joe had thought long and hard about his tardiness and the long thin switch that awaited him if he was late arriving home. Disobeying Katie Mae was not something to take lightly. Lizzy was a witness to her mom entertaining the pleasure of watching Albert Joe walked slowly with his head bent downward in shame. As he approached the tall hedge bush that aligned the side of their mill home he quickly snatched the perfect stem. Lizzy was glad her elder brother had made a good choice.

CHAPTER IV

BEHIND THE COTTON MILL

"Albert Joe, what happened? Why you comin' home? Why didn't you play ball with the boys? Afraid of that switch getting your legs?" Lizzy had a mischievous grin on her face as she stared at her tall brother.

"Lizzy, I ain't afraid of no switch. Mr. Roscoe Johnson came to the ballpark recruiting some of the boys to come to the mill so they could see the new machinery. I thought it might be a good time to head home 'cause Mama told me I was too young to be thinking about working at the mill. The other boys went with Mr. Johnson. Since I can't play ball by myself I decided to head home. Anyway, I knew you would tell on me, and I didn't want you to get a big switching when you found that big frog under your pillow tonight," Albert Joe had a serious look on his face.

"You better stop it or I'll surely tell on you," Lizzy yelled.

"Oh Lizzy, I was just kidding. Can't you take a joke? Besides, I wouldn't let you squash my frog. I'll just tell Mama you been listening to the porch ladies gossip, and she'll get your butt for sure."

"Well, you're nothing but a tattle tale. See if I tell you anything else in our life time," Lizzy shouted as she walked ahead of her brother.

"Lizzy, I promise I won't tell on you. I was just kidding because I like it when you get all mad and turn fifty shades of red. You're such a silly girl. You do need to stop listening to gossip all the time. That ain't a good thing for a young mind to take in. Those women need to stop their gossip too," Albert Joe added.

"Why are you asking me for updates if you think I don't need to listen to the gossiping porch ladies? Some of my sharing is firsthand information. Just the other day I witnessed a harsh fight among several employees and Mr. Roscoe Johnson. Heard and saw it myself."

As they approached the Chaney ball tree, Lizzy stopped and turned to her brother. "You're really bothering me. I'm mad because you think I just like to hear gossip and spread it to everyone. But, I've never told anyone but you. Now, I wish I hadn't even told you what I heard from the porch ladies. Now, let me set the record straight; I've witnessed some of the truth with my own eyes and ears."

"How's that Lizzy? What did you hear?" he asked.

"Well, since you're so concerned, I'll tell you," Lizzy paused. "You better not repeat it or I'll call you a gossiping porch boy. You hear me?" Lizzy said to her older brother as she broke her code of silence.

"It is obvious Mr. Roscoe Johnson has always been seen as a saint for his goodness to the community, but Mr. Roscoe Johnson is robbing the workers. He has paid lower wages than the amount they agreed on with a firm handshake. So, you see…he is not a nice man. Besides, my gut tells me the mill workers are justified in accusing Mr. Roscoe Johnson of subjecting the people of the village to captivity through genetic poverty. Don't you think it is strange how generations repeatedly become instant members of the textile mill workforce?" Lizzy continues while Albert Joe stood under the chaneyball tree with his ears perched to hear his sister pour out her heart.

"Lizzy, I've never heard a young girl speak such big words and be so full of information. Not to mention you using the term "gut" to justify your claims. You need to focus more on working hard in school and not worry about all the mess going on in the neighborhood. What makes you so interested in all this stuff?" Albert Joe asked.

"Well, funny to me you want me to stop listening but you always want the most updated news. Now, to me that is a double standard. Also, I already work very hard in school. I'm a very intelligent girl." She replied defensively. "You need to decide what you want; the updated truth or me acting like a regular girl, you know…all prissy and naïve. Besides, I'm much wiser than anyone gives me credit. One day you'll see 'cause I'm going to be a doctor. I refuse to stay here and be a porch lady or a mill hand worker."

"Lizzy, you will be fine. Just hold up, and take it one day at a time. We'll all be fine, but this is our life now, and we have to be happy as it is. Besides, you can't leave your potbelly pig behind. What would Sugar do without you?" Albert Joe asked jokingly as Lizzy bent to get her book bag off the ground.

"Goodness. Those stinky Chaney balls have stained my book bag. Yuck. That is an awful smell. It'll never come out in the wash no matter how many times it's scrubbed with Mama's lye soap.

"I'm sure Mama can get the stains out in the wash. Now, before we go inside, let me make it clear. The gossip stays between us. You hear me?" Albert Joe reminds Lizzy.

"I told you it isn't gossip. It is the truth. So, why can't you believe me?"

Albert Joe touched Lizzy's hand as they walked through the door. "I hope one day you make it out of here 'cause you deserve much better. I'm not too smart in school and most likely be right here rest of my life, fighting for my fair and overdue raise from old man Roscoe Johnson."

"Albert Joe, have you ever really thought about the low wages Mr. Roscoe Johnson pays the workers? There is no way out of this mill village; so there must be some truth to what the porch ladies are talking about, don't you think?"

Concerned for her brother's future, Lizzy pointed to the swing and said, "You want to swing on the porch with me before we head in and start on our chores?"

"Sure, I'll swing with you. But we have to hurry before Mama knows out we're here and hollers for us to come in and get to work." They laid their belongings down and sat on the weathered swing. It was time to pick her for some juicy neighborhood gossip as they swung and basked in the sun. He was searching for information on Emma Jean Smith's mother...and it seemed Lizzy had little information on that gossip so he may have to pick his younger sister for any good gossip at the tip of her tongue.

Albert Joe began quizzing his sister as they inhaled the fresh smell of honeysuckles on the front porch. "Lizzy, I been thinking about what you told me...what else do you know about his bank account, Old Mr. Roscoe?" Albert Joe asked.

"Well, seems Mr. Roscoe Johnson was arguing that his goodness extended to all mill workers and their families...said he had never lied to his mill workers about his bank account. But, according to the mill workers, there is an investigation to see if his bank account has hidden secrets," Lizzy declared with a big grin.

As they continued to swing, Lizzy added, "Only time will reveal the truth, and everyone knows an investigation could take years. But, I bet you those chattering lips of the porch ladies will continue to say that Mr. Roscoe Johnson is a millionaire at the expense of his overworked and underpaid employees."

Thinking for a moment, she added, "Bet the investigation will prove Mr. Roscoe Johnson is not a righteous man. Those same chattering lips will spread the word that he shared a small percentage of his fortune with Mr. Jack Bradford."

"Come on, Lizzy. We gotta get going and do our chores." He said as he got off the swing. Albert Joe told his sister, "Lizzy, your mind is on overload for a young girl." He had a stern but sympathetic smile. "Come on, we have things to do before we both get the switch."

"I know, but I just can't help myself. Seems my mind is made up when it comes to Mr. Roscoe Johnson. Might be due to the voices I always hear from the gossiping porch ladies. I surely feel what they say about Mr.

Roscoe Johnson must be true. He always has a deceitful look in his eyes. Besides, how could he ride around in his black Lincoln if he wasn't a big fat greedy pig like Sugar?"

Albert Joe laughed at his sister's comparison of Mr. Roscoe Johnson and her pet pig, Sugar. "Now Lizzy, your mind is really wandering. Come on. Let's get started on the chores."

Lizzy could not resist finishing their talk as they worked on their chores. She chattered on as they worked together. Lizzy stopped and turned to Albert Joe with a suspicious eye as he emptied the trashcan, and she took the final piece of clothing off the line. "You better keep this information to yourself. You looking like you might run and blab on me."

"Well, the accusations could be true, Lizzy. Maybe Mr. Roscoe Johnson refused to share the earned wages with the workers."

"You should know that Mr. Roscoe Johnson has always seemed to be very dishonest. His eyes are squinted with greed just like Sugar's." Convinced that he was indeed the greediest man she had ever seen, Lizzy felt it was her job to convince Albert Joe and others of the same.

"The fact is Mr. Roscoe Johnson can be described as a fat, pot belly pig that bullies the mill village residents and stops them from departing in the darkness of the night."

"Lizzy, maybe escaping the cotton mill village was something Mr. Roscoe Johnson made sure didn't happen. Besides, you need stop and think about who would do the manual labor at the cotton mill if all the workers crossed the tracks." Albert Joe said with a loud laugh that startled her.

"We gotta get inside and finish up our chores." They both went toward their house quickly. Albert Joe opened the door for his sister, and they parted ways.

Albert Joe thought long and hard about his conversation with Lizzy. He had to admit that maybe his intelligent sister, a third grader, had unraveled the yarn of Mr. Roscoe Johnson's web and understood the traditional cycle the wealthy man had spinning in his textile mill with Mr. Jack Bradford's assistance.

Besides, even Albert Joe knew many of the boys started working in the mill in the fourth grade. He knew that prior to stepping on the bus that waited impatiently each morning most of the boys had worked several hours in the cotton mill. He also had heard from the mill boys that Mr. Roscoe Johnson requested that the bus stop behind the cotton mill for safety of the children loading.

Lizzy pointed out numerous times the real reason was to hide the young boys working in his mill. It was a well-known fact that working the under aged boys was hidden from main society. Had Lizzy unraveled all the secrets, the goings on of the neighborhood by listening to the porch women?

The next day at school Lizzy heard some devastating news. Rumor had it that Albert Joe was going to be a full time employee at the cotton mill. He would not even have the opportunity to complete school. It seemed that Mr. Roscoe Johnson had handpicked him for a full time position, and this made Lizzy sick to her stomach. She searched for her older brother at recess.

"Albert Joe, come over here now. Did you realize Mr. Roscoe Johnson has a full time position for you once you complete the school year?" Lizzy asked with tears in her eyes.

"Yes Lizzy, I heard it today. I'm not too excited, but guess I need to help Mama and Daddy out by drawing a check at the cotton mill," Albert Joe said in his defense. "It's not so bad Lizzy. I'll have the extra benefit of free soda, peanuts, and plenty of beef jerky. Don't cry Lizzy, I'll be just fine. Your teacher is looking for you, run on now. Get back in line and go to class before you get in trouble." Albert Joe went the opposite way from his sister.

Lizzy got in line with her friends but she could not help thinking about Albert Joe's future and Mr. Roscoe Johnson's bribery in exchange of her brother's education. Albert Joe saw it as an opportunity to help their parents.

After lunch, Lizzy did her usual cleaning of the cafeteria tables and headed out the door to find Albert Joe. She had just a few minutes to speak with her brother so she had to be swift with her plan. As she looked toward the huge oak tree, she spotted him standing with his friends. "Albert Joe, come over here. It's very important."

"Lizzy, what can't wait until we get home?" he asked. "This better be important, or I'm going be really mad at you."

"Well, first thing, you need to think long and hard before quitting school. You need to finish school so you can cross those cold tracks and have a better life. If you go to the cotton mill and work, you'll never make a decent living."

"Please Lizzy, just stop it. You're such a worrywart. Why can't you be a regular girl and play games with your friends instead of worrying about grown up business? I'll see you on the bus after school." Albert Joe hugged Lizzy's neck as he turned toward his friends, shaking his head at his younger sister.

When the school bell rang for dismissal, Lizzy ran to the bus. Standing on the top step, she peered over the seats looking for Albert Joe. She saw him at the back of the bus and walked toward him. "May I sit with you?"

"Sure, Lizzy, sit down." Albert Joe snatched his sister's book bag and placed it on the floor of the bus.

"Give me my book bag, Albert Joe. It'll get all dirty on the floor and have stains all over it. I can't carry a dirty book bag." Lizzy reached for her book bag brushing the gritty dirt off as she scolded her elder brother. "You should know by now that I don't like for my things to get filthy."

When the bus stopped, all the cotton mill kids got off. Most of the boys headed toward the ballpark; the girls headed home. Albert Joe and Lizzy walked side-by-side. He listened to Lizzy's chattering long enough and then decided to change the conversation to soothe his tired ears.

"Come on, just think if we can get the chores finished before supper maybe we can run behind the skitter truck when old man Thompson blasts the smoke and makes his getaway. Don't say a word about my new job at the cotton mill." Albert Joe warned his sister as they raced home. "Let me do the explaining to Mama and Daddy 'cause they may get upset."

"Listen. I hear a bell ringing, Albert Joe. That's the sound of the candy truck, and you promised to buy me a piece of candy. Remember?"

Lizzy ran toward the ringing bell with her mouth watering at the thought of sweet candy upon her lips. "I'm not sure why Mr. Thompson is so early but you need to make good on your promise, or I'll spill the beans on you," Lizzy reminded her brother as the old truck rounded the corner.

"Yep sure do remember my promise? Once Mr. Thompson's candy truck comes to a stop, you can run over and ask to see the special treats he has to offer today. Remember, only one piece of penny candy and that's all," Albert Joe firmly said.

The candy truck was in sight and Lizzy was jumping up and down as if it were Christmas morning. Eustice Thompson, the youngest son of Mr. Thompson, was sitting in the passenger seat of the candy van. He was a creepy teen who enjoyed staring at the children as they lined up to purchase candy from his father. In fear, the children always stood a good distance from the truck when Eustice Thompson was assisting his dad on the route.

Lizzy waved her arms in the air for Mr. Thompson to stop. At the expense of Albert Joe's pocket change, she asked Mr. Thompson if he had a candy necklace.

Mr. Thompson had three in his candy box. "Eustice, give Lizzy her candy necklace," Mr. Thompson shouted to his dysfunctional son. Suddenly a hand appeared underneath Mr. Thompson's arm. It was the hand of Eustice Thompson. His hand was not hard to recognize with his long nasty fingernails. Lizzy stepped back as Eustice teased her with the candy necklace swinging it in midair.

"Eustice, stop your mess. Get back in the cab, you're frightening the children," Mr. Thompson instructed his son as he took the candy necklace from Eustace's clinched fingers and handed it to Lizzy.

Her eyes lit up at the sight of the candy that was in a colorful pattern, threaded on a thin piece of elastic. She was overjoyed.

"Mr. Thompson, do you have any B-B Bats or Mary Janes? 'Cause I want one of each. Albert Joe is paying," Lizzy informed Mr. Thompson, letting out a loud chuckle.

A loud grunting voice hollered from the cab of the truck, "I ate the last one Lizzy; ain't got no more." Eustice continued to scream out with gruesome laughs that frightened Lizzy. Seeing his patron was nervous, Mr. Thompson popped his son on the head with a broom handle with hopes of detaining his inappropriate behavior.

"Hush up Eustice. You promised to be nice to the children if I allowed you to come with me on the route. Now sit quietly in the cab or I'll take you home," Mr. Thompson shouted to his son.

Peering at the front of the candy truck, Lizzy saw Eustice Thompson looking like he was still in his Frankenstein Halloween costume. He stuck his fingers in his nose and pretended to eat his catch as he laughed aloud.

"Pay my son no mind Lizzy. Eustice is a little strange. It's a jacked up mess. I think the boy is mixed up in the head. Been acting crazy since the day he fell off our cow Bessie when he was a young lad," Mr. Thompson reported as he placed Lizzy's candy inside a tiny brown bag. "That'll be five cents, young lady."

Albert Joe stepped up to the side window of the candy truck and reached deep into his pant pocket to pay Mr. Thompson for Lizzy's candy. "Here you go, Mr. Thompson. Thanks for the candy; I'm sure Lizzy will enjoy her loot." Albert Joe turned to find his sister standing under a tree counting the candy pieces on her necklace and sticking her tongue out at Eustice Thompson.

"Hey, Mr. Thompson, what time you be by our house with your skitter truck?" Albert Joe asked, knowing Mr. Thompson had to go home and most likely eat some supper before starting his second job. "I'd say just before night fall, be watching for me 'cause Mr. Roscoe Johnson just paid to have my tanks filled with some pricey skitter spray. Salesman claims it'll blast thick blue smoke fumes a mile high in the sky. You children will have a good ole time tonight chasing my truck."

Mr. Thompson added as he cranked his old candy truck with his deranged son hanging out the passenger's window. Eustice Thompson seemed to be enjoying scaring the little children with his distorted facial expressions and puckering his chapped lips as he spit out the truck window.

Waving at Albert Joe and Lizzy, Mr. Thompson shouted out his window, "See y'all later this evening on my skitter truck. Be ready to run after the smoke."

Albert Joe looked at Lizzy with disappointment. He muttered, "Now Lizzy, I told you to get one piece of penny candy. You got a necklace that cost me three cents, and then you added B-B Bats and a Mary Jane. I just paid five cents, you little rat," Albert Joe scolded.

"Well, you told me it was 'penny candy' and the sign on Mr. Thompson's truck advertised the same. So I figured you only owed three cents for my candy. I know you said one piece but, I thought it was worth three cents to keep such important details from Mama and Daddy," Lizzy pointed out while nodding her head.

"You'll surely make a good lawyer one day. You have an answer for everything," Albert Joe chuckled as he patted his sister on the head.

Once supper was done, Albert Joe reminded Lizzy that it was about time for Mr. Thompson to turn the corner on their street and blast blue smoke from his new skeeter tank. "Lizzy, the skeeter truck will be here in few minutes. You want to come with me outside and wait for Mr. Thompson under the Chaneyball tree?" Albert Joe was trying to get Lizzy out of the house, away from their parents because he knew Lizzy would open her trap and spill her guts to them; he could not take a chance on that happening.

"OK. I'll come with you but it isn't called a skeeter truck. It is a 'mosquito' truck." Lizzy corrected as they both headed out the front door.

Albert Joe praised his sister, "Lizzy...thanks for keeping your trap shut. I'm proud of you for keeping your word. Look. Here comes the skeeter truck. I mean... the mosquito truck."

They both stood near the street waiting for Mr. Thompson to blow his horn that signaled it was clear for the kids to chase after his truck. Once they heard the horn, everyone standing along the side of the street ran into the thick blue smoke, screaming to top of their lungs as they chased the skeeter truck, laughing up a spell.

Lizzy was standing too close to Mr. Thompson's truck as it came to a complete stop. Something grabbed her hand. "Eustice Thompson you better let go of my arm before I bite you." Lizzy screamed as Eustice released his grip and yanked her hair. Eustice quickly raised the window to escape her verbal attack. The truck continued blasting fumes into the air. The children screamed as they waded into the smoke.

Katie Mae was standing on the front porch when they returned from their nightly chase of the blue smoke. "OK, you two, it's time to come in for the night," she reminded her two older children as she closed the front door.

Albert Joe came in first and sat on the sofa looking at his parents "I need to tell you both about a job offer from Mr. Roscoe Johnson," he whispered, noticing Lizzy in the room with her ears perked-up.

Lizzy was hoping her parents would disapprove but the look on their faces told her it was a done deal between Albert Joe and Mr. Roscoe Johnson. With sadness, Lizzy abandoned the idea of Albert Joe escaping the cotton mill.

Albert Joe seemed excited to be among the mill workers as Buck gave his blessing and reminded Albert Joe about the perks of being a mill hand worker.

"Albert Joe, you'll get bottle of soda and pack of peanuts during your break at the mill. That's nice to look forward to when you're tired," Buck chuckled.

"Wow, the generosity of the owner of the textile mill, Mr. Roscoe Johnson. Cost about ten cents, at the most," Lizzy added with sarcasm in her voice.

Lizzy's decision-making skills had proven to be greater than those of her parents. Was she adopted? That thought was increasingly appealing to Lizzy as she sat listening to their approval for their oldest son to quit school and become a mill hand worker. Lizzy could not wait to get out of their presence. She was sickened at the thought of Albert Joe being a prisoner in the cotton mill village. He deserved to escape to a better life, but it seemed Albert Joe was destined to carry on the legacy of the family.

"Get in yonder and head to bed. Both gotta rise early Saturday morning and get started on your chores. Y'all have long day's work. Scoot on to bed," Katie Mae said to Albert Joe and Lizzy.

Lizzy stood and held her head down as she left the room. She only wished she could have a good night's rest but nighttime was not always considered pleasant.

With her flashlight, library book, and a sheet over her head, Lizzy prepared to greet the darkness of the night with fear.

CHAPTER V

THE GUNTERS

The early morning sun was peeping through the windows as Lizzy prepared to start her day. She walked slowly to the bathroom on the screened-in back porch; taking her time washing and preparing for breakfast. Lizzy did not want to hear the nonsense about Albert Joe quitting school to work full time in the cotton mill. Saturdays should be a fun day, not stressful.

"Lizzy, I saved the first scoop of grits for you with lots of butter," Albert Joe said as she walked into the kitchen.

"Thanks, but think I'll pass on the grits this morning. Not too hungry," She raised her head and asked to be excused so that she could begin her chores.

Lizzy walked out the back door as she reviewed her chore list. She could not help thinking about the events that had taken place the night before. She felt Albert Joe was about to make the biggest mistake of his life, and there was nothing she could do to stop him.

Walking toward the shed, Lizzy almost stumbled over an old wood crate. Bending down she picked it up and placed it against the shed. She noticed the faded letter "H" scribbled on top of the lid. "Wonder what that stands for?" Lizzy said aloud as she went inside the shed and picked up the hoe.

She was lost in thought. Suddenly she heard loud gurgling sounds. It had to be Old Lady Gunter or her socially awkward grandson who was probably poised and ready to jump out at her. In fear for her life, Lizzy walked faster toward the garden.

Glancing over at the Gunter's house, she thought how frightful the place looked with overgrown trees covering most of the front porch and the overflowing thorn bushes that had long branches waiting to prick human skin. The Gunter's lived on the same street as the Jones family, and Lizzy had a clear view of the house from her backyard, especially from the garden. It was rumored that the Gunter's house was haunted. That frightened Lizzy even more.

Lizzy thought the rumor had to be true; Old Lady Gunter smelled like a pot of stale witches' brew. Anyone would run for their life at the sight of the bulging oversized warts on her face. Lizzy was convinced the warts validated her wicked persona.

As Lizzy started pulling up grass, she glanced at the haunted house and couldn't help but wonder why Old Lady Gunter didn't visit Mabel Jean, the village witch doctor. Mabel Jean could use her secret mumbo jumbo language to speak to the warts while spitting her slimy saliva all over them. Everyone knew Mable Jean could rub any size wart and make them disappear with her witch magic. Besides, Mabel Jean had removed several small warts on Lizzy's fingers that had been caused by Albert Joe's frogs.

Lizzy remembered how she closed her eyes while being led behind a mysterious curtain into a dark room that smelled of herbs, blood, and rotten figs. Lizzy's eyes always remained closed during the ceremony to prevent the witch's evil spirit from entering her soul; it was necessary to keep your eyes closed, according to Albert Joe.

Lizzy did not like the thought of a witch doctor; it frightened her but Katie Mae explained the witch doctor was a perk for the residents in the cotton mill village because visiting a medical doctor was too expensive and Mabel Jean used the barter system.

Buck Jones was the head of his family. A proud man that always presented Mabel Jean with a freshly killed chicken, cut into small pieces including the eyes and beak. Albert Joe taunted Lizzy by declaring Mabel Jean used the dead chicken's eyes and beaks to make her witch's brew. Lizzy always refused to carry the bucket that held the remains of the dead chickens when she was taken to Mabel Jean's house of horror.

It was getting rather hot in the garden, so Lizzy went inside. She got a clean glass and poured water from the jug she had hidden in the refrigerator. Returning to the garden, she saw Old Lady Gunter rummaging in the large tin trash bin in her back yard. Then she heard a door slam. Lizzy was startled.

Lizzy turned to find Albert Joe standing over her with a distorted facial expression.

"What the heck you doing? You scared me to death, sneaking up on me like that," Lizzy squawked as she yanked more weeds from the ground. "What's up with you making a frightful look upon your face? You want to give me a heart attack?"

Albert Joe grinned as he handed the hoe to his sister. Lizzy why don't you try using the garden hoe to pluck out the weeds? Lizzy, you're supposed to be an intelligent girl and you should at least give the Gunter's the opportunity to be neighborly. You can be very rude sometimes, little sister."

"Thanks Albert Joe, but I can pull weeds much faster with my bare hands and also bypass the splinters from that dilapidated wood handle. And, don't tell me to give Old Lady Gunter and her grandson a chance to prove they are neighborly or normal. I know both of them are crazy and mean. Please go on about your business and stop making such a frightful face at me." Lizzy shook her head at her elder brother as she threw her hands up in the air.

"Lizzy, hate tell you this, but I found your water hidden in the refrigerator and drank me some of it. I also slobbered in your water jug." Albert Joe laughed as he ran from Lizzy who was now standing with the raised hoe in her hand.

"You better be kidding me. You stay away from my water jug. That is not for your nasty mouth to be drinking from like a goat. You hear me?" Lizzy screamed. "I've a good mind to tell Mama about your afternoon ball games."

"I was just kidding you. Take it easy. Looks like you might have some company soon. Old Lady Gunter and Lester are both at the fence staring at you. Better be careful, or she'll cast a spell on you that not even Mabel Jean can undo." Albert Joe was now laughing uncontrollably as he fell on the ground, rolling around like tumbleweed in an open field.

Lizzy thought about the day she walked under the Gunter's fig tree with its lanky limbs poised to grab her entire body and hang it on the branches. She imagined meeting her death as rotten figs poured over her head. *What a dreadful sight to behold* she thought as she raked the now dried weeds into the crate she had found against the shed, praying she did not get a splinter in her hands.

She closed the weathered crate's lid so the weeds would stay put until she made it to the dumpster at the back of the lot. That is when she noticed Old Lady Gunter and Lester were still standing at the fence, just waiting for her to pass them on her way to the dumpster.

What could she do? She had to run to the dumpster with the crate and then back to the shed. Putting the crate back where she got it would save her from having to explain why she disobeyed her dad's instructions not to use it for packing weeds.

She knew it would not be long before numerous rotten figs flew through the air. Yet, she had to finish her gardening and move on to the next item on her list or she would be in trouble with her mama. She surely did not want to set her off since she could already be in major trouble with her dad for using his old crate.

Lizzy ran as fast as she could with the weeds packed securely in the crate. The dumpster seemed five miles away. After she dumped the weeds, she turned to see where the weird neighbors were and could not find them anywhere. With a sigh, Lizzy ran back to the shed.

Once she made it back she placed the old crate in its rightful place, but she felt something was brewing with the neighbors. As she headed home, she noticed the ditch a few feet in front on her. If she could just get across the ditch then she could run fast and soon be safely inside her house.

Lizzy knew the neighbors had to be hiding somewhere. Suddenly she remembered…the fig tree. That is where they must be waiting. It was Lester Gunter's favorite hiding place; he could fill his pockets with rotten figs as he waited for his prey.

Lester Gunter was described by the village residents as simple- minded. However, his accuracy in throwing figs was legendary. No one could throw figs as far as Lester Gunter. Not even Emma Jean Smith.

As Lizzy left the shed, she felt something hit her knee once, twice, and on the third time, she knew it was Lester throwing rotten figs at her. Aiming for the knees was his trademark. Lizzy ran as fast as her frail legs could carry her. It was still a long way to the back door of her home.

The only thing separating Lester and Lizzy was a few feet of her yard and the old rusty chain link fence that Lester was leaning against. Lizzy tried to get up but fell down in the ditch several times.

Lucky for her, the ground was dry as a bone except for several pods of juice that were from the rotten figs thrown in the crevice.

Lizzy partially stood, knowing she had to run for her life. As she got her balance and stood straight, Lester threw a handful of rotten figs at her, hitting her dress. She brushed the figs off her clothes and walked toward the fence to face the fig-throwing maniac.

Lester Gunter was shirtless beneath his blue, ragged overalls stained with the rotten figs that he had stashed in his front bib pocket. His bare feet were stained and filthy. Lester Gunter was jumping in mid air and making gurgling sounds that offended Lizzy's sensitive ears. She was not afraid; she was tired of the Gunter's mess.

Lizzy's closeness to Lester confirmed that he was surely in need of a hot tub of water and a bar of lye soap to cleanse his body and greasy hair. He reeked of filth, and his hands and feet were black as tar. He was a jacked up mess. Sight for sore eyes.

The brave Lizzy knew the words would flow from her mouth if she could only get Lester Gunter to stop jumping so he could hear. Once she spoke her message, she would determine if she should stay or run. Most likely, run for shelter.

Lizzy stood with a firm look in her eyes, glaring at the jumping man as fig juice sprayed everywhere. She screamed Lester Gunter's name, demanding that he stop throwing figs. Lester jumped even higher and started to laugh with a high screeching tone that was almost unbearable.

Lizzy picked up a fig off the ground and held it above her head, aiming at Lester's face. Lester saw Lizzy's arm swing around and ran like a jackrabbit, taking refuge behind the nearest bush. Lizzy stood quietly, not sure what she should do. Suddenly she jumped when she felt something touch her left shoulder. She turned and was eyeball to eyeball with Albert Joe.

"Goodness. You frightened me almost to death again. But, I'm sure glad you're here!" Lizzy screamed. She told her older brother about simple-minded Lester Gunter and his fig throwing fit. Albert Joe laughed, and the two of them walked backwards until they reached their home. Lizzy scrubbed her hands with lye soap.

As they drank water on the screened-in back porch, Lizzy asked Albert Joe, "Where you think Lester Gunter is hiding? I wish we knew the whereabouts of that maniac; then we could be prepared for him next time he decides to attack me with those rotten figs."

"Lizzy, I wouldn't worry about the whereabouts of Lester Gunter." Lizzy planned to keep a watchful eye at all times.

Lizzy was sure Lester Gunter would be making his rounds in front of her house on his rusty red bike as he scattered rotten figs in their yard. She wondered why the neighbors had not already sent him to Dix Hill where some of her relatives were residents. Besides, everyone knew Lester Gunter was downright mean to the children in the village. Lizzy was concerned he was going to hit some child in the eye during one of his rotten figs rampages. She felt Lester should be sent away, for good.

Lizzy and Albert Joe finished drinking their water and headed outside to complete the rest of their chores. They heard a siren coming from the front of their house and quickly ran toward the road to see what was going on. As they approached the corner, they saw a sheriff's car driving into their driveway.

Lizzy stood erect in front of the house, easing closer to the tree trunk. With a solemn look upon her face and lips pursed to speak at any moment as if she were in charge of the family business, she kept her eyes upon the situation brewing in the driveway, on standby if needed and then her stomach seemed as if it had knots tightening within. She had no idea why a sheriff would be at her house and was afraid she may find out some bad news soon.

"Oh my goodness, Albert Joe something just fell from the sky," Lizzy shouted when she felt a plop on her head. Looking upward, she saw her younger brother throwing Chaney balls from the lowest tree branch where he was perched. Sam was full of laughter at the sight of Lizzy's frightened expression. Lizzy cocked her head giving Sam a stern look, demanding he come down from the tree. It was apparent that he was not going to make a move toward the ground.

"Sam, what the heck you doing up there in that tree? Get down right now or I'm going tell Mama, and you'll get the switch."

"No switch for me. Mama said no switch for her baby boy," Sam shouted as his chubby legs dangled in midair and his lips muttered words mixed with uncontrollable laughter.

"Samuel Jones, you get down before you fall and break your arm!" Lizzy demanded, pointing her index finger as means of scolding her rambunctious younger brother.

"No Lizzy. I not come down," Sam laughed while nodding his round head toward the pigs running around the house like a whirlwind. The sight of the pigs made him continue to gush out bouts of giggles as he slowly made his way down from the tree and ran toward the plank front porch. His sandy blonde hair was in his eyes causing him to stumble and nearly fall.

"Albert Joe, what's going on? Can you please help me out, inform me?" Lizzy asked her brother in a panicked tone, picking at her nails.

"I'm not sure, but we might as well stand here and find out. Be brave Lizzy, don't be nervous." Albert Joe immediately reached for his sister's sweaty hand to comfort her. Lizzy held tightly as she gazed around to find the whereabouts of little Samuel. She heard his voice and turned to see her baby brother near the front door.

Lizzy knew it was common to see a sheriff's car in the driveway, especially when her dad had been drinking, but lately things had been calm. She was puzzled to see the sheriff making a house call.

Albert Joe and Lizzy made their way toward Sam who was standing in front of the screen door still bellowing out laughter to the top of his lungs. "Let's stand here for a minute and see if we can hear anything," Lizzy whispered. "Hush up Sam."

Buck and Katie Mae continued to speak with the sheriff when suddenly Sam started to laugh uncontrollably causing Katie Mae to glance toward the front porch. "You children get on in there and stay out of trouble. Samuel darling, Mama will be right there, be a good little boy."

"Mama looks really mad. You better start cleaning up any mess you've made," Lizzy instructed her siblings as they all went inside the house.

Lizzy saw deep concern in her mother's eyes while speaking with the sheriff. Katie Mae nodded her head, apparently agreeing to do as instructed by the sheriff. Lizzy was standing inside the screen door when her mama looked up and saw her tending to adult business. Lizzy knew it was not acceptable to be nosey and quickly scooted away from the door to check on her brothers.

Albert Joe and Sam were on the sofa looking out the window, still engaged with the scene outside. Lizzy walked slowly toward the kitchen to help with supper. She could smell the vapors from the kettle pot filled with the homemade dumplings her mother had already started.

Lizzy stirred the pot with a wooden spoon and turned the flame down on the gas burner so the dumplings would not burn.

Albert Joe and Sam ran into the kitchen with a sack of penny candy from Mr. Thompson's candy truck. They were sitting at the kitchen table savoring the taste of forbidden sugar before supper.

"Albert Joe! You of all people should know Mama will skin you alive for eating candy before supper. Have you lost your mind? Why would you allow Sam to follow your example? You will surely get the switch for letting him eat candy!" Lizzy warned in a motherly tone.

"Yep, guess I'll be in hot water, Sam. I'm breaking house rules so give me the candy loot. We'll eat it later," Albert Joe quickly held out his hand for Sam's candy.

Sam's tiny hands refused to give up his penny candy inside the wrinkled brown bag. Albert Joe jerked the candy from Sam who was flapping his hands in the air to escape his brother's robbery attempt.

Sam let out a loud scream that pierced their ears. "You are a mean brother, Albert Joe; I'm telling on you." He shouted as he continued to yell out bolting screams and tiny tears slowly fell down his tender cheeks.

"Now, you should be ashamed of yourself. You being the oldest should never have given Sam a candy bag. That is against the rules. Now, look what you've done. Sam is crying, and I'm telling you, you better do something to stop him or we'll both be in hot water," Lizzy warned with a disgusted look on her face as she briskly walked toward her youngest brother. She wiped his chubby cheeks with a clean fluffy cloth.

Lizzy kissed Samuel on the cheek as she stroked his silky hair. "Hush up Sam, all is fine." Suddenly, a loud banging on the door frightened the children. Lizzy jumped sky high as both of the boys fell out of their seats letting out a screeching scream. Loud gurgling screams continued to follow the banging on the back door.

Albert Joe and Lizzy ran to the door, instructing Sam to remain in the kitchen. They found Old Lady Gunter standing half bent over with an old cracked ball bat in her wrinkled hand banging as hard as she could swing on their back door.

"You better fetch your stinking pigs from eating my good figs or I'm going to use my pellet gun on them. Ain't going to have any figs for jelly cause of those beasts! Old Lady Gunter screamed as she continued to swing the bat and banged their back door. "You come and fetch your darn pigs from my yard...you brats."

"What's a pellet gun? Will it hurt the pigs?" Sam asked Lizzy with tears welting in his big sky blue eyes.

"Don't worry Sam. This is grown up stuff. Mama and Daddy will take care of it," Lizzy bent down, picked up her younger brother, and tried to settle his worries.

Old Lady Gunter turned and grunted as she slowly limped toward the front of the house, making her way under the tree where everyone had moved. The sheriff screamed for peace and quietness when Old Lady Gunter swung the bat at his knees. She missed him and hit the Chaneyball tree causing the smelly, round, rock-like fruit to fall on their heads.

"Alright that's enough of this Ms. Gunter. Put that bat on the ground, or I'll have to handcuff you," he warned.

Watching from the window with her brothers, Lizzy wondered how the Sheriff would restrain such a filthy old woman. Albert Joe and Samuel asked for details. "Hush," Lizzy commanded sternly. "I can't hear anything because you're talking too loud."

Lizzy watched the sheriff escort Old Lady Gunter to her haunted house and return leading two pigs with swollen bellies. Lizzy's father took the rope and led the pigs to the back of their house. He called for Albert Joe to come and assist him.

Albert Joe went running out the back door the minute he heard his name. "Now, Albert Joe, I need you to take these pigs to their pens. Use the water hose to rinse away the rotten fig juice stench. Now, do a good job. You hear me, son?" Mr. Jones said to Albert Joe who was anxious to appease his father's directives.

"Yes sir, I'll wash the pigs down real good, Daddy. Come on you stinking fig pigs," Albert Joe shouted to the animals as he led them toward the water hose. He washed the pigs and put them in their pen. Then he came in, announced that all was taken care while eyeing the dinner table. He was ready to eat supper.

"Alright children, time to wash up for supper. I've fixed some dumplings for the family. I think it's time to settle down from all the drama. You all eat and get ready for bed." The children knew that Katie Mae's patience was thin, and they dared not disobey.

Her mother's dumplings were no longer as inviting due to the odor floating in the air. Lizzy was praying the fig pudding warming on the stove would be overcooked and inedible. Mama's buttered biscuits would be just fine without the fig pudding oozing out the middle.

Not a word was uttered except from Buck who arrived from outside just in time for supper. He made way to the stove and asked for a spoon. "Why you need a spoon, Buck? You need to sit down so we can say the blessing and eat a meal together." Katie Mae had a puzzled look on her face as she darted a glare at her husband.

"Well, I was going to stir the fig pudding on the stove before it sticks to the pot like cement. But, I'll just let it stick if it is too much trouble to get a spoon from you."

Buck shouted as he sat down at the head of the table. "Might fresh the air a little. There's a bad odor in the house, Katie Mae."

"Buck, I hate to be bearer of bad news, but there's a reason for the bad odor. It is from the crud and filth in our backyard. The aftermath of the pig drama that just took place."

"Remember, Buck? You told Albert Joe to hose the pigs down and put them in their pen. The boy did what you said and the pig hosing left a pool of water in our backyard. That's what you smell. It's coming in through the windows and will stink for days," Katie Mae explained.

Buck stuck his head out the screen door. "Oh drat. What a mess he made and the smell is unbearable. You're right, Katie Mae. That smell is coming in the house, and it'll settle in the walls, the curtains, and even our clothes." Buck had a slight dismay in his voice as he eyed Albert Joe.

"Well, Buck...what should I do?" Katie Mae asked. "Do you want me to close the house up tight? If so, we'll surely melt in here."

"Whatever suits you Katie Mae I'm telling you, that's an awful smell. I'm going have borrow some gas masks for us to save our lungs." Buck playfully chuckled. "Why don't you let me close the windows half way? Maybe that'll help. Next time, maybe Albert Joe can use some common sense and carry the pigs out back."

"May I be excused from the table?" Lizzy asked. "I'm really tired and need to check over my assignment before I go to sleep."

Lizzy was ready for the day to end and was puzzled why her dad was blaming Albert Joe for the awful smell. With permission from her mom, she left the table and went to her tiny hall bedroom to read one of her favorite books in hopes of settling her anxiety.

It was time to think about the new day approaching as the sun slowly disappeared behind the trees. At last, the house was quiet and peaceful.

The next morning Albert Joe was dressed by the time the sun rose, and ran outside to nourish the pigs with sour slops and water in hopes of winning his dad's favor. The pigs were sound asleep until the slops meant for their trough splattered everywhere. When the cool slops hit their bellies, the pigs started to squeal. They rolled in the mushy mud as if they enjoyed being prisoner in the barbed wire fence. Perhaps it was sacred ground compared to Old Lady Gunter's fig pasture.

"I told those pigs that if they didn't want to smell rotten figs, then they'd better stay inside their fence," Albert Joe announced when he returned. "They might end up in the slaughter house and on to Old Lady Gunter's Thanksgiving table," Albert Joe added with a loud chuckle that made Sam bellow out a playful laugh.

"What if the pigs were splattered with some warm fig jam? Now that would be a smelly belly," Sam shouted as he fell on the floor laughing, rolling around like a ball.

"Well, the thought of those pigs being splattered with fig jam should be enough to keep them behaving today, little Sam. Let Albert Joe and your sister get dressed and head out for the school bus." Katie Mae continued clearing the breakfast table, bending down and tenderly stroking her youngest son's hair. "Sam, you're such a handsome baby boy with your big sky blue eyes."

Katie Mae turned and saw the innocent look on his face and softly summoned him to her side. "Sammy baby, come to Mama, you're just too cute, now get off that floor before you get all fifty from that mucky mess Albert Joe and Lizzy most likely trampled onto Mama's clean floors."

"OK. I'll get up," Sam squealed as he looked up at his mother who was hovering over his tiny body with her arms reaching for him.

"You're Mama's baby boy, come...you shouldn't be wallowing on the floor." Katie Mae reached down, retrieved her youngest son from the linoleum floor, and held him tightly in her arms as she showered him with attention.

Katie Mae needed to finish cleaning the kitchen before settling into the chair with Sam. She softly said, "Sam, Mama has your favorite cartoon playing. Take this warm chocolate milk, and sit in Daddy's favorite chair, Sweetie. Tom and Jerry will be on shortly. I'll be in there to rock you after I get Albert Joe and Lizzy out the door and finish cleaning the kitchen."

Sam took his milk and resigned himself to the cozy rocking chair to wait for his mama to join him while Katie Mae shouted, "Lizzy, you better rush your brother and get out the door or the bus will leave you both."

"Yes Mama. We'll be ready and out of the way shortly," Lizzy replied.

Albert Joe fussed as he dressed. He claimed he did all the morning chores.

"Albert Joe, you sound like a whiny baby. I have just as much to do before getting ready for school as you do, so hush your trap," Lizzy stood with her hand on her hip, staring at her elder brother. "Can't you please change those high water pants?"

Albert Joe wanted to argue with his sister, but he knew there was not a chance he would win either battle, so he rolled his eyes and continued to complete his chores before the bus arrived. Lizzy nodded her head in satisfaction, thinking she had won the argument, except for the high water pants Albert Joe was still wearing.

Lizzy spotted Lester's dilapidated red bike against the edge of the broken gate as she approached the Gunter's house. The thought of Lester Gunter being up early and ready to pounce on her was almost unbearable. She slowly walked toward the Gunter's house, looking around uneasily for crazy Lester.

"Albert Joe, slow down. May need your help 'cause I can smell Lester Gunter for sure," Lizzy shouted, but Albert Joe kept running to the bus stop.

"Hurry Lizzy, we can't be late for the bus."

"I'm doing my best. Slow down and wait for me."

As soon as Lizzy thought she was safe, she heard a gurgling noise behind her and the sound of flapping baseball cards on the spokes of a bike. Could it be Lester so early in the morning?

"Goodness, Old Lady Gunter, what you doing on Lester's handle bars? You're going fall off and kill yourself. You're too old to be acting so foolish," Lizzy shouted.

Old Lady Gunter was perched like a black hawk on Lester's handlebars with her apron, full of rotten figs, flapping in the wind. Lester began to peddle the bike so fast that the chain broke and the bike jerked. Old Lady Gunter fell off the handlebars.

Her eyes looked like saucer cups full of rotten fig pudding as she rolled into the grassy ditch. Lester lost control of the bike as he tumbled into the ditch landing beside his grandmother. Both were face down. Lester's bike bounced against the textile mill fence and splattered into a million pieces as figs flew through the air; several landing on Lizzy's forehead and her clean clothes.

"Lester Gunter! You had better hope you have a major injury 'cause if you don't I'm going to give you one. You are a freaking nut. What in the world are you two doing riding a bike that way? You're going to get yourself killed!" Lizzy exclaimed as she leaned over the ditch to see if the weird neighbors were breathing. Lester made a loud gurgling noise, causing Lizzy to jump as she screamed for Albert Joe's assistance.

"The dew is still fresh on the grass, Lester Gunter. You're an absolute idiot for frightening a young girl who already has enough anxiety without your mean pranks. Now I'll have a horrible day at school," Lizzy hollered once she made sure Lester and his grandmother was not hurt badly.

"Lester, I know you can hear me! Now, you get yourself out of the ditch and help your crazy grandmother. I'm going to be late getting to the school bus. You hear me, Lester Gunter?"

Lizzy was in tears as she looked up and saw Albert Joe running toward her. Albert Joe would know how to handle the situation, even though she was not sure how he could rescue the two knuckleheads who were lying face down in the ditch.

"Lizzy, what's going on?" Albert Joe yelled as he ran over to the chaotic scene of smelly figs and the tangled up Günter's. Albert Joe paused. "My goodness what is that lying in the ditch making that gurgling noise?"

"Why that's crazy Lester Gunter and his grandmother. They nearly frightened me to death, and I'm a wreck myself. That crazy Lester should be locked behind bars in the asylum."

About that time, Lester Gunter stood up and jumped as high as he could. He shook his body, slinging grass and fig fragments.

"What the heck are you and your grandmother trying to do to my sister? Don't you know it isn't nice to frighten children? Help your grandmother to your house and you both stop bothering Lizzy," Albert Joe instructed.

"OK, Albert Joe," Lester Gunter grunted as he looked around for his red bike. He pulled on his grandmother's arm. "Granny, get up so I can find my bike." Continuing to grunt, Lester Gunter added a jumping motion that frightened Lizzy even more as his filthy feet sprang upward.

Suddenly, Lester Gunter pulled his grandmother out of the ditch, bent over, threw her over his shoulder, jumped up, and muttered as he ran toward their haunted house. Figs splattered all over the pavement, the ditch, and Lizzy's clothes.

"Oh no. What am I going to do?" Lizzy cried, pointing to her rotten fig-soiled dress and shoes. "I'll miss the bus, and then I'll be in big trouble."

"Lizzy, you'll be fine. You have ten minutes to run home and get cleaned up before the bus arrives. Mr. George would never intentionally leave you, Lizzy. Now run on and get cleaned up."

Lizzy ran home and changed clothes. She wiped her face with a wet dishtowel and grabbed a fresh cloth to take with her to school. She would have the opportunity to spot clean if needed once she got to school. Now she had a bus to catch.

Lizzy was out of breath when she arrived at the bus stop just in time. Lizzy reached for the cloth in her backpack and repeatedly wiped her arms. She wanted to make sure she did not have the rotten fig stench on her body. She pulled out a small bottle of Jergen's lotion to rub on her skin.

All day Lizzy wondered what in the world Lester and Old Lady Gunter were trying to do so early in the morning. She decided it must have been revenge because her family's pigs had feasted on the Gunter's rotten figs. Anyway, she was sure Lester and his grandmother had plenty more pranks coming Lizzy's way.

That afternoon, Albert Joe met Lizzy on the bus. "Hey, Lizzy, how did your day go at school?" Albert Joe asked as they got off the bus. He looked around to see if the Gunter's were nearby.

"I had a good day. Glad to see Emma Jean back in class. Still feel it was unfair she spent two days in the suspension room. Not justice at all."

"Walk beside me Lizzy. I'm thinking Lester Gunter will be somewhere waiting to start his pranks. I'll protect you." Albert Joe proudly said.

"Thanks for helping me this morning when crazy Lester and his grandmother tried to frighten me to death. That Lester seems to be getting really crazy lately. Don't you think? I'm glad I have a big brother like you to walk me home."

"Don't be afraid of him or Old Lady Gunter. I'm sure they're harmless...just a little nutty," Albert Joe was trying to reassure his sister that they weren't trying to 'cause her bodily harm." Lizzy had little faith in his words as she clutched her book bag.

"Well, if we make it to the house without a fig fight with Lester Gunter, do you want to play a round of penny porch poker with me, Albert Joe?"

"Sure Lizzy. I love to play penny porch poker, but I don't have any pennies on me."

"Hey, I know where we can get some," Lizzy whispered.

"Where Lizzy? You going to steal them from Mr. Thompson's candy truck?" Albert Joe chuckled.

"No, Albert Joe, I don't steal. Besides, I saw Mama carry a bag of pennies into her bedroom the other day. I hid behind the door and watched her pull out a big blue piggy bank with the word 'Baby' on its side. Sam watched Mama drop the pennies in the slot. The clanging noise made him giggle," Lizzy reported.

Albert Joe went inside and returned with a hand full of pennies. "Lizzy, we can play several rounds. Look. I got all Sam's pennies." Albert Joe was amused at his robbing of their baby brother's piggy bank.

"Albert Joe, we only need a few. Remember: we have to return them. If not, Mama will get the switch to us. Don't you let any fall between the cracks," Lizzy warned.

"Lizzy, I didn't see Sam or Mama in the house. Think they might be in the garden? Maybe we can play penny porch poker a little longer."

"Bet I win," Lizzy announced as she threw the first penny and watched for it land on the crack of the porch plank.

"Lizzy, I hate to be the bearer of bad news, but I saw the bowl on the table. Remember, that orange bowl? So, you better start on your chore list and hide out in the garden."

"Thanks for the warning. My hair surely doesn't need to be cut again. I wish I could crack that bowl with a bat. Maybe Old Lady
Gunter would let me use her bat. I just hate the clattering sound of the scissors, Albert Joe."

You're not concentrating because I just won again.

They heard their mama yelling, "Albert Joe? Lizzy! Where are y'all?"

Lizzy hissed, "Oh, no. Albert Joe, you better gather up Sam's pennies and hide them or we're going be in hot water. I'm going to jump in the swing."

"We're coming Mama. Taking a little time to swing before we do our chores," Lizzy shouted, hoping their mama didn't find out they had used Sam's pennies.

"Run, Albert Joe. She's coming around the house."

Albert Joe got up off the porch and ran like a thief who had just robbed a bank. Lizzy was praying her elder brother would hurriedly put all the pennies back in Sam's piggy bank without being caught.

"Lizzy, where's your brother?" Katie Mae asked sternly.

"He's inside, Mama. Albert Joe is getting ready for his chores, and I'm heading inside to do the same."

Lizzy got out of the swing and ran inside before her mama's foot hit the first doorstep. She was aware of her mama's next sentence, and Lizzy did not want to hear such nonsense. She would make a quick get away before Katie Mae had the opportunity to place the Pyrex bowl on her head. It was hair-cutting day.

Katie Mae, the wife of Buck, was the mother of three young children: Albert Joe, Lizzy, and Samuel. She was a beautiful woman with long wavy brown hair and a shapely body that was admired by most men in the mill village and throughout the small town of Shadow Village. Katie Mae spent her days making the Jones house as much of a home as she could with the little resources that were made available to her. Buck was not able to provide Katie Mae with the many things she desired. Katie Mae wanted more but had to settle for reality.

Continuous bickering and hostility marked the early years of their marriage, but with time, Katie Mae and Buck seemingly worked out their differences. They attempted to insert a new page in the family album that showed a happier family, but there was a time that Shadow Village's police knew the family's home address by heart. They often responded with haste when neighbors called for assistance because Buck had hit the bottle too many times. No one was sure if Buck drank because of the arguments, or if the arguments were because of Buck's drinking.

Either way, the result was usually at the expense of Katie Mae or one of the children.

When Officer Joe arrived at the home, Buck and Katie Mae would be over their spell of differences and sitting in the swing as if all was fine. The sadness and distressed look on Lizzy's round face as she stood behind the living room curtain hid a different tale that would be untold.

"Now Buck, you and Katie Mae need to settle your differences like man and woman. No need to cause this entire ruckus and worry the children," Officer Joe said. Before getting into his car, he nodded to Lizzy who remained in the shadow of the window curtain.

During those early days, Buck seldom took orders seriously. He was a man who ruled his home, wife, and children. Katie Mae belonged to him, and jealousy, fogged with alcoholic rage, was often at the root of the arguments that ended with Katie Mae wearing sunshades, even inside and on cloudy days, for weeks to hide his "love" for her.

Albert Joe and Lizzy watched from the living room window as their parents fought like wrestlers in the front yard. They tried to protect Sam, the baby, from the ruckus, but that became impossible when the show moved into the house. The children learned to hide and protect themselves by running for safety—anywhere to be safely out of harm's way as objects flew around the room. Albert Joe referred to these times as 'Bucky and Katie's throwing attacks,' which could last for hours.

After years of fighting, Buck and Katie Mae sat their two older children down and explained that things were going to be much better. Katie Mae sat quietly on the worn sofa. Buck said, "Kids, the fighting has ended. There will be no more front yard brawls. Your mama and I are sorry for our behavior, and our home will be a much happier place." Katie Mae nodded her head in agreement, as a small tear of bitterness crept down her flawless skin. She was silent, depressed.

Lizzy wanted desperately to believe her father's words, but this young girl had doubt. She had heard these words one too many times. They are lies, words that meant nothing to Lizzy.

Lizzy wanted to believe that their mother was indeed the attentive, loving mother she claimed to be, but Lizzy had witnessed the truth—the volatile life of being a child in the Jones household—too many times. She knew the rules of the game, and she stayed focused on her inevitable escape from the torment inflicted upon her by the hands of those who should have loved and protected her—not hating and hurting her.

Throughout the following months, things did settle down somewhat at the Jones' home. Lizzy concluded it was because their mama had turned all her attention toward their younger brother, Samuel. Lizzy also considered the fact her dad was in a drunken stupor, passed out on the sofa, from the time he left the cotton mill on Friday afternoons until the sun rose early on Monday mornings.

One morning while walking to the bus stop, Albert Joe reported with hopes of his wise sister to agree, "Lizzy, things are getting better for us—guess Mama is concentrating on bein' a better mother. Don't you think, Lizzy?"

"Mama is consumed with Sam, not us. All we hear are lies, Albert Joe, lies, and empty promises."

"Well Lizzy, best I understand Sam is going to college. Maybe Mama is busy making sure his piggy bank stays full of pennies. I know she makes monthly deposits at Banker's Savings & Loan downtown."

"Albert Joe, Sam is a little boy, he isn't going to college. Where did you hear such talk?"

"I heard Mama telling Sam they had to walk downtown to the bank and make their monthly deposit in his college account yesterday. Mama didn't know I could hear her, so please don't say anything," Albert Joe pleaded. "I'll get a switching for sure."

"I'm sure Mama has an account set up for all three of us, so don't fret Albert Joe." Lizzy knew her words were false as soon as they left her mouth, but she wanted to help ease her brother's mind. He worked hard to help her and her parents—it was the least she could do to ease his worries. And she knew that, even though it hurt her that she couldn't be the one to make her mama happy like she so desperately wanted to do, at least her mama found joy and peace in her baby boy, her porcelain baby doll...Samuel.

Lizzy did find it odd that her mother bonded only with her baby brother but had little motherly instinct for her other two children. It reminded her of Girl, their family dog who gave birth to three puppies, but she had only nursed one of them. The others were left to fend for themselves. Lizzy prayed that Girl would come around and accept all her newborn puppies.

"Mama, I don't understand all this. I guess the puppies she rejected need me to care for them. Do you have any tiny bottles, so I can feed them if Girl continues to refuse to be a good mother?" Lizzy asked Katie Mae one sunny afternoon as she sat close to the puppies and their mother, Girl.

"I'll see, Lizzy, but be patient with Girl. Give the mother dog some time. Maybe she'll nurture her newborns. Let's wait a few days before we buy some milk and see what happens," Katie Mae said as Lizzy continued rocking the tiny puppies in her arms.

Two days later, Lizzy woke up to the sound of the shovel hitting the dirt in the backyard. Lizzy had so many questions. "Mama, what's wrong with Girl? How could she leave her puppies to die?"

"Lizzy, I'll try to explain this so you'll understand, my dear. You see, sometimes animals bond with their offspring and sometimes they reject them. The newborns that are rejected don't always survive, Lizzy, but that's a part of life, my dear. Besides, some newborns are easier to nurture than others."

Lizzy still didn't understand Girl's unnatural ability to love only one of her puppies, but it made her think about her own mother's inability to shower her three children with equal attention. Sam had first place in their mother's heart; he was her baby boy, whether Lizzy understood it or not...whether she liked it or not.

Lizzy did not learn her caring and nurturing ways from her mother—that was apparent. She loved to read, and she was drawn to characters, like Fern in *Charlotte's Web*. Fern believed in Wilbur, the runt of the litter, and fought for his life when he was to be slaughtered. Lizzy wanted to save Girl's pups like that.

Lizzy dismissed her questions because children were not supposed to understand adult decisions. Besides, her job was being a child and not being concerned with adult issues.

CHAPTER VI

GOING HOME

The Davenports watched the morning news in silence as flames consumed a small cotton mill village, flames that were so vivid they seemed to extend from the television into the Davenport's den, glaring into Elizabeth's eyes, pleading for assistance.

Elizabeth listened attentively for updates on the tragedy and looked to her husband for hope. She wanted him to end the feelings that were overtaking her mind.

"Harrison, there's nothing you can do to stop this tragedy that's unfolding before our eyes. Nothing at all you can do," Elizabeth sobbed.

The only comfort she had was Harrison's strong shoulder and his tender, empathic smile. Dismayed, Elizabeth crossed her arms across her chest. She was desperate to keep the doors safely locked that held her secrets safe from everyone, including Harrison.

Bogged down with shame, humility, and a need for comfort, she pushed her body away from Harrison and curled into a fetal position. She needed her own space if she had to invade someone else's life.

Lizzy was calling her name. Elizabeth gazed around the den to make sure she was not in the all too familiar twin bed of her childhood home.

The room spun as the blue smoke seemed to encompass the entire den. The doors were now open, and the flames from the fire were reaching to expose the charred secrets of her childhood.

Harrison reached over, swept his wife into his strong arms, and took her to their bedroom. Elizabeth's body resembled a small fragile child ready to be tucked into bed. She was consumed with fear, anxiety and confusion.

After all these years, Harrison remained Elizabeth's calming hero in the midst of any storm. Gently tucking her limp body in their plush bed, he softly kissed her cheek.

Elizabeth required open space, dim lighting, and soft blankets for personal calming. Harrison quickly closed three shutters leaving the fourth shutter partially open. A low beam of light to brighten the room, as the sun rose would be comforting to his distressed wife.

"Elizabeth, are you comfortable?" There was no reply as Harrison stroked his wife's long black hair. If only he could see inside her heart, he could possibly understand her turmoil.

Harrison was accustomed to rising to the occasion in a crisis. He had always been the strong, wise solider who fought adversity lurking over his devoted wife's mind.

As Harrison recalled their morning conversation, he remembered that Elizabeth's carefully planned day included patients under the prominent doctor's care. He called his wife's office and instructed the secretary to cancel his wife's appointments until further notice.

Harrison rested his face in his large palms. He whispered a prayer, interceding for his wife's emotional health. Harrison knew his next steps on the battlefield were going to be risky. Elizabeth was unable to assist him, but he needed his wife to fight with him. He needed her assistance to plan the trip to her hometown, Shadow Village.

Harrison went to the bedroom to check on his wife who was still lying in the fetal position, clutching her blanket. "Elizabeth, we need to check on your relatives in Shadow Village. Please don't succumb to the unbearable monsters of your childhood. Elizabeth, can you hear me?".

Elizabeth did not respond. Harrison walked away. He hoped she would soon be alert and ready to discuss their travel plans.

Much to Harrison's dismay, Elizabeth was still in the fetal position when he peeped into their bedroom. It was apparent Elizabeth had resigned herself to confusion as Harrison looked at the clock on the den wall. It was near ten o'clock. He would have to plan for their trip without his wife's assistance so he packed enough clothing for a week for them both.

The trip to Shadow Village had the potential of bankrupting Elizabeth from her sanity. Harrison prayed it would not destroy years of profitable therapy. For some time it seemed Elizabeth was finding some peace with her past. He could not allow the emotional warzone claim his wife's mind.

"I've already packed for us Elizabeth; can you help me out and get up so we can get on the road? It will take us at least four hours to make the trip. I would like to get there before sunset." Harrison looked at his wife, resembling a lifeless ragdoll lying on the bed.

With no response from Elizabeth after several attempts, Harrison decided to wait patiently in the den for the love of his life to rise from her rest.

Several hours passed and Harrison heard the sounds of doors opening, drawers closing, and other clattering sounds coming from their bedroom.

Harrison walked toward the bedroom to greet his wife. Elizabeth is frantically searching for her watch.

"My goodness, what time is it Harrison?" Elizabeth asked as she stood in the doorway.

"It's getting close to one o'clock most likely. I fell asleep in my recliner waiting for you," Harrison explained as he looked at his wife who was fully clothed standing in the threshold of their bedroom door.

"Harrison, I'm ready to travel to Shadow Village." Elizabeth stood with a look of desperation upon her face.

"I've already packed Elizabeth. I'll take our things to the car while you finish preparing. I've taken care of everything. You get yourself together and we'll leave. It will be near dark before we arrive. My plans are to stop and reserve a hotel room prior to entering the village. That will assure us of having somewhere to stay while we investigate the situation," Harrison said realizing in the midst of all the turmoil Elizabeth seemed at peace.

As she unsteadily made her way through the hallway and into the garage, she quietly spoke to Harrison, "It's been so long since I've traveled to Shadow Village, Harrison. Seems like a thousand miles away."

"Are you feeling anxious Elizabeth?" Harrison asked as he touched Elizabeth's arm, helping her into the car. He began driving down the highway at a steady pace, trying to make conversation to ease his wife's anxiety and to keep himself calm and alert.

"Harrison, it feels like every nerve in my body is aching. I'm feeling rather helpless at this point," replied Elizabeth with tears welling up in her eyes.

"I'll be fine, Harrison," Elizabeth replied as she wiped her tears with a monogrammed handkerchief she had removed from her designer handbag. Harrison knew his wife very well; the signs of a panic attack were on the horizon. Harrison coached Elizabeth to finish her coffee in hopes of it rejuvenating her spirit.

"You're most likely afraid of the unknown Elizabeth," Harrison assured her as he continued to drive at a steady pace.

Harrison smoothed Elizabeth's hair from her forehead. She slowly lowered herself under her soft blanket. Looking up at the stars, she prayed for a calming mist to fall upon her.

Her mind was panicking, but there was no turning back.

Realizing Elizabeth's turmoil, Harrison reached and pulled the blanket over her shoulders. "Elizabeth, allow your body, mind, spirit to rest as we travel to our destination."

"Another thirty minutes and we should be arriving near Shadow Village. Are you awake?" Harrison asked as they turned on the long road that led to his wife's hometown.

"I've been awake for some time Harrison. I've been resting and thinking," Elizabeth faintly said which alerted her husband the stress was becoming unbearable.

As they continued to travel, Elizabeth asked, "Do you think my father and brothers made it out of that old house and are alive?"

Harrison had a look of compassion but refrained from answering Elizabeth's question. The look in Harrison's eyes made Elizabeth more anxious as she wrapped her blanket securely around her body.

There was complete silence in the car.

It was pitch dark with a smoky overcast as they turned into the parking lot of the hospital. The smoke was so thick it made it hard to see beyond two feet.

"Elizabeth, I think we should avoid trying to find out anything until the morning. There's nothing we can do at this point. You're exhausted so why don't we find a hotel and get some rest?

We can rise early and go about our plans," Harrison had everything under control.

"That's fine Harrison." Elizabeth was glad her husband was in control. She was in a state of turmoil. Elizabeth was tired.

Sensing Elizabeth's hesitation, Harrison informed her that they had just passed a hotel, and he was turning around to check on booking a room for a few days.

Elizabeth's mind was drenched with tormenting memories from her childhood. She looked into her husband's eyes with welting fear, "Harrison, there are years of horror tucked deep inside my mind. Feels as if the ghosts of Shadow Village are choking me and I'm not prepared to tackle the tormenting spirits."

Harrison patted his distressed wife's hand encouraging her to remain brave.

"Elizabeth, I understand it will be hard for you to deal with the negativity of your childhood. You've got to be strong for your family. Maybe this is your opportunity to start healing, let go of your fears and face the demons that have fought to control your mind for decades." Flashbacks of the village dulled her vision.

"You're correct Harrison, but this is going to be really hard for me."

"I know Elizabeth but, we can do this together. We're both strong individuals and our lives have been fruitful since our time in Shadow Village."

"True Harrison, but we're both aware I've been stuck in the past for decades. Oppressed? Depressed?" Elizabeth replied as tears streamed down her thin soft cheeks.

"Elizabeth, please smile. 'Cause when you smile the whole world smiles with you. You're amazing Elizabeth. Just simply amazing to me. You deserve to be free of anything that has held you hostage." There was dead silence in the car.

"I am going inside to book a room, or we may not have a place to stay. You sit still and I'll be right back, Elizabeth."

Harrison returned with a key and looks at his wife stating, "Sorry, it is an outside entrance; I know how you dislike this type of hotel, but it was all they had vacant."

Wiping the tears from her face, Elizabeth slowly asked, "I wonder what type of childhood I would have experienced if my mama hadn't died?"

"We can talk more once we get unpacked. Come on Elizabeth, I'll get you settled in the room and come back for our luggage."

Harrison was all ears for his wife once they settled in for the night. He sat next to her on the bed reaching for her hand, "Elizabeth, take me down the road you traveled as a child. I'm your husband. I want to know what it was like in Shadow Village with you. I want to know everything."

"Harrison, have you lost your mind? It is too late to walk to Shadow Village and besides I'm very tired." Elizabeth rebutted with a suspicious look.

He chuckled softly at his wife, and put his arms around her. "Elizabeth, I'm trying to make the conversation easier for you. I didn't mean to literally walk down your old road. I meant I'm ready for you to let me into your world. You know; tell me about your past, where you lived, the hurt, the pain. Let me visit your childhood with you; take me there Elizabeth."

"Harrison, coming back here was hard enough on me; do you really need me to talk about it with you right now, too? You should understand how much it pains me to think, let alone speak, about my past. Besides, I am feeling overwhelmed and exhausted." Elizabeth sat upright in the bed, attempting to divert Harrison's attention by readjusting the bed pillows again and flipping through the latest issue of Architectural Digest she had brought on the trip.

"Elizabeth, why don't you start with that Halloween night? That seems to be bothering you the most lately. It may do you some good to recall the details," Harrison pleaded with deep concern for his wife's wellbeing. Elizabeth turned her head away from Harrison and slowly placed her magazine on her lap.

She looked at her husband whose eyes were pleading to be welcomed into her world. Elizabeth was unsure of her ability to communicate, her mind was too weary.

"Harrison, it is getting late, and besides, it'll take too long to explain and there are too many memories harbored inside my mind to invite into this small hotel room," Elizabeth replied. "I'll get claustrophobic if I have to give pertinent details and may have an onset of panic attacks. So, can't we please get some rest and avoid all the drama tonight?"

"I really would like to know Elizabeth," Harrison pleaded. "It isn't drama. It is your life story, who you were and that makes you who you are today, a strong vibrant woman."

Realizing Harrison was not going to let up, Elizabeth felt compelled to soothe her husband's inquisitive mind. She dared not venture into the depths. It was too late and her mind was too tired for such stress.

"I'll do my best Harrison. But, there are still many unanswered questions which have haunted me since that dreadful Halloween night. If I'm awake all night…it will be your fault." Elizabeth tried to force a gentle smile but could not.

Suddenly, memories trampled her mind, flooding all her senses with unbearable pain. She broke down in a crying spell and placed her head against Harrison's shoulder.

With one last struggle, Elizabeth lifted her head and began to speak. She struggled to capture the images that she buried. Opening her eyes she waited for a moment and then traveled back in time as her mind was racing and anxiety flooded her thoughts.

"I can remember how my mother was bursting with energy as we prepared for the night's festive events. She was looking forward to joining us and our friends around the village to collect candy. We had even started to make candy treat bags out of brown paper sacks and homemade costumes together the night before.

"Mama reminded Albert Joe and I if the rain held off it would be a perfect night for roaming the cotton mill village and gather candy treats from neighbors. The aroma of penny candy Mama had placed on the counter floated throughout the house. She was prepared in case a knock came on our door from an early candy seeker. I remember everything, Harrison: the smell of the crayons as my fingers pressed down on the tip of the colorful wax cylinder still lingers in my nostrils; Sam's laughter running through the house as if he were Superman with his red blanket tied around neck floundering in the air like a gentle breeze; the chocolate he had around the edges of his tiny mouth from the tootsie roll candy I had given him earlier that afternoon." Elizabeth stopped and opened her eyes as tears streamed down her face like a dam had broken.

Harrison caught her as she leaned over and wept. Tremors wracked her body as she testified to him of her early years on the cotton mill village. He knew the memories were swamping her mind as she tried to snuff the silent screams.

"Mama's smile acknowledged it would be a memory-making night for the kids in the village. Our house not only exploded with the aroma of candy, but it had laughter; it was alive. Until death knocked on the door," Elizabeth explained, remembering the details she had locked away for decades.

She continued as Harrison listened with compassion, "The mere thought of collecting candy loot was enticing to all the children. The streets of the small cotton mill village were always crowded with inquisitive minds as each child waited at the door in suspense. Albert Joe coined the term 'Candy Loot Bags' one Halloween year in hopes of winning the coloring contests. He claimed Officer Joe thought one of the Jones children would surely win."

"That year was a special milestone for me as I helped supervise the festive event. The younger children would surely be safe in their homemade costumes. I was so excited and worked so hard on the treat bags; I had planned to give a candy bag to all the children that did not have one. "

Harrison tucked Elizabeth's skinny frame with her blanket. The warmth was a comfort as she spilled her heart with words that longed to escape.

"We all waited patiently for darkness to engulf the sky and signal it was time to celebrate each year on Halloween night but that year was an exception. The signal came and Halloween had yet to be celebrated for me."

Leaning her head back to rest, Elizabeth continued to unravel the web of deceit of that horrific Halloween night. She struggled to allow the memories to enter her mind. After a couple of minutes, the stage was set and the curtain opened.

"It was a misty evening and my mother was preparing dinner while we kids continued to decorate our paper candy loot bags. Mama seemed at peace. Not happy but a gentle demeanor."

Harrison knew not even the mental picture of Elizabeth's mother could make her words light and airy as she described the details spilling from her heart and mind.

"It was approaching 5:00 PM; time for my father's shift to end at the cotton mill. My mama was cooking supper and had called my name several times. She needed my assistance to get the clothes off the line. By now the mist had become a light rain. I did not respond to her call. The clothes were in jeopardy of being drenched.

After the third call, I heard Mama remind Albert Joe and me to wash up for supper. I knew the next sound would be the slamming of the back screen door. She would no doubt get the clothes off the line, and I may or may not suffer the consequences of a rebellious spirit," Elizabeth looked into Harrison's eyes, making sure he was still engaged in her confession.

"I sat on my bed and continued coloring the brown paper bags. Mr. Godwin, who owned the local supermarket, donated them to the school each year. Ms. Allen, my teacher, always gave me several, as she knew I enjoyed coloring and wanted to make sure every child had a bag. The excitement of Halloween kept my mind occupied for some time. I had planned to offer to take the clothes and fold them once Mama came in from outside, hoping maybe that would ease my punishment. I kept listening for my mama to reenter the house but never heard the door open. I went to the porch, looked toward the clothesline, and saw the wicker clothesbasket placed on the wet ground under the clothesline. It was empty, and my mama was nowhere to be seen."

Elizabeth continued with her eyes closed. "I called my mama several times. She didn't answer. All I heard was my own voice echoing. It was getting darker and the drizzle of the rain began to saturate the clothes. I left them hanging in the stillness of the night."

"I ran to the front of the house as Daddy was approaching the edge of the yard. He had his black, dented lunchbox in his hand and looked tired from a long day's work at the cotton mill. I explained that I couldn't find Mama, expecting Daddy to run to look for her, but he stood frozen. He dropped his lunch box and the sound startled me."

Sobbing uncontrollably, Elizabeth struggled to continue with her story. "I explained the events that led to the basket on the wet ground: the clothes untouched, and Mama nowhere to be found. He listened in silence."

"Was he upset with you, Elizabeth?"

"No, he didn't seem upset. Disbelief was in his eyes. He coughed several times to clear his throat." Elizabeth placed her hands over her face as she relived the scene, her body shaking with fear. "Dad fell to his knees, pleading for God to protect his wife from the hands of the devil."

"What type of sin was he speaking about, Elizabeth?"

"I have no idea what he was referring to at that time," Elizabeth held her head down as she twisted her hands together.

"Do you know now? Do you have any idea of the sins your dad was speaking about that night?"

There was silence in the hotel room.

Elizabeth gained control of herself as her husband gently stroked her face, encouraging her to continue with her story.

"Elizabeth, what did your dad do? Did he try to find your mama?"

"Yes. Dad slowly scuffled toward the back of the house calling for Mama. She didn't answer his call. He went next door to talk with our neighbors. They had not seen or talked to Mama in several days. I looked at him with sadness. He saw the tears welling in my eyes and walked away. At that moment, I placed the blame on my own shoulders. I had intentionally been disobedient. God was punishing me. The blame produced fear. The fear grew into extreme anxiety," Elizabeth said as she put her hands over her face, sobbing.

"Now Elizabeth, you can't still feel you are the blame after all these years," Harrison wondered how his wife could possibly feel such guilt but knew she was suffering, dismayed.

"To some degree I am the blame, Harrison," She replied. "My dad scratched his head and mumbled words I didn't understand. Later he asked if Mama seemed upset. I relayed she wasn't upset; seemed excited and happy."

My dad replied, "To the best of my knowledge Lizzy, Mama and I were doing just fine except for everyday disagreements."

"Elizabeth, what exactly happened on Halloween? I mean, once your dad knew for sure that your mama was missing. Can you give me more details of that night?" Harrison asked with concern as he pushed her long silky hair away from face.

"If you'll recall, I told you how I didn't answer my mom's call to get the clothes in off the line. That will always be a fact I remember until the day I die."

"I know, Elizabeth, continue on."

"After Mama didn't come home, many people in the village felt she was too involved with the Halloween celebration, and God had punished our family by taking her from us."

"What? Why would anyone feel that way, Elizabeth?" Harrison had a look of disbelief. "God doesn't punish people by taking their loved ones from them."

"Harrison, you have to remember that many people felt Halloween was the devil's night and bad things came to those who participated in the celebration. That was the culture of the cotton mill village. I know it sounds insane, but the village residents had been drilled with this type of information." Elizabeth paused, wiping her eyes.

"My dad didn't feel that way, and his mind was racing with thoughts of the possibility that maybe someone had seen my mama alone in the darkness, standing at the clothes line and perhaps taken her in the woods or something awful. Dad was concerned because he knew how excited Mama had been about celebrating and he didn't think Mama would disappoint us kids by disappearing on Halloween night."

"As the night progressed and with no luck of finding my mama, my dad reluctantly called the police department for their help."

Elizabeth told how a sudden downpour of rain had fallen by the time the police arrived at their home and how the tension grew as the officers continued without showing any concern as one said, "Mr. Jones are you sure your wife is missing or just maybe taking a break from the family?"

Elizabeth twisted a corner of the sheet around her fingers as the intensity of her gaze drew Harrison into her childhood. As if lost in the darkness of that night, she nodded and breathed a deep sigh of relief, "Harrison, the policeman's words sent my dad into a rage."

Elizabeth knew the response was due to numerous calls the officers had made to separate her parents as anger sparked between them. Flushing with slight embarrassment, Buck would always send the officers on their way with an apology. Elizabeth wiped her eyes and calmed her breathing. She had to stay alert.

"Okay. Keep going, Elizabeth." Harrison's deep brown eyes stayed focused upon his wife's face.

She shook her head in disbelief. "It was true my parents fought, but they loved each other."

"My dad was irate. He proclaimed that his wife was a good mother and a decent woman, no matter what the porch gossipers had spread around the village."

Elizabeth sighed and continued, "Daddy hoped the police officers would have pity on him, but the only pity shown was the smile one of the officers directed at the frail young child standing beside him: me."

Elizabeth shrugged as she looked at Harrison. "Dad got so mad when he saw the look in the policemen's eyes and the smirk on his face. I remember the policeman telling Daddy how they needed to leave because they had more important work, like patrolling the village for mischief, not chasing around the woods for Mama. Daddy stood in front of them with tears trickling down his puffy cheeks, aware he was at their mercy. His anger was replaced with fear and despair—much like the rest of us, Harrison. We all knew that Mama could be mysterious, but for her to disappear like that was still out of character."

"My dad mumbled some nonsense, and Officer Joe asked him to repeat his statement. He did, with anger: "Me and Katie Mae didn't have any issues…we settled them some ten years after the culprits left Shadow Village. Done told you that one time Officer Joe.""

"Officer Joe patted my dad on the back and said he understood and to give him some time to investigate my mama's disappearance."

"I had no clue as a child what my dad meant by his statement to Officer Joe, and I'm still not certain." Elizabeth was shaking her head as if the events were in real time.

Elizabeth looked at Harrison, who was completely spellbound. "Harrison, do you want to hear the rest of what happened that night?"

"Sure Elizabeth," Harrison placed his arm around his wife's shoulders.

"The next morning Officer Joe came to our house to speak with my dad. They went walking toward the woods together. Officer Joe looked up and saw the clothes were still on the clothes line and the wicker basked was in the same place on the wet ground."

"Did the officer say anything, Elizabeth? Could you hear the conversation between him and your dad?"

"No, not really, but Albert Joe remembered Office Joe saying it was as if our mama never made it to her destination."

"Albert Joe was standing on the back doorsteps trying to listen and I was in the house, taking care of Sam. Once they walked toward our family garden I put Sam in his crib and went outside with Albert Joe."

"Did they find anything in the garden area?" Harrison asked.

"Yes, they did. Officer Joe found my mama's shoes, her apron, and a piece of paper lying under the clothesline, drenched from the rain."

"What was on the piece of paper Elizabeth?" Harrison asked.

"It was a picture of my brothers and me that had apparently fallen out of Mama's apron pocket. The picture was soggy from the wet ground."

"My dad reached for the picture and Officer Joe told him it was evidence and he placed the picture in a plastic bag with Mama's shoes and apron."

"About that time the other two officers drove up and saw the evidence in the plastic bag. One of them chuckled, stating my mama couldn't have gone too far without her shoes."

"My dad drew back his fist, shaking it at the officer as his face turned flaming red. He was disgusted at his accusations. Officer Joe instructed them to go back to the police station. My dad settled down with Officer Joe's assistance." Elizabeth gently wiped tears that were slowly dripping from her eyes.

"Officer Joe was very nice to our family. As he left he assured my dad he would hold on to the report and if there was no sight of Mama in a few days he would be back to speak with him about further procedures."

"Once Officer Joe left with Mama's personal belongings in the plastic bag my dad fell to his knees on the wet ground and begged God to bring his wife safely home."

"From then on Halloween was no longer of importance to me. I picked up my paper candy loot bags and shoved them under my bed."

Tears streamed down Elizabeth's face, and Harrison gently wiped each one away. "Elizabeth, all will be well. Keep your faith. Just maybe this is a start for your healing; talking about that dreadful night is the beginning of a new life for you, for us."

"I've tried for years to forget what took place in my home on Halloween, Harrison, but the visions that have been so distorted for decades are now clear. It is all coming back to me, and there is no way to escape the emotions."

"Did Officer Joe return to your house and speak with your dad?"

"Yes, it was few days later and he came out with his notepad; did a complete report and told my dad to explain to his children that the police were looking for their mother. He was trying to smooth things over for us children, but Albert Joe and I knew the truth. I tried to hide things from Sam as long as possible, but Daddy was so distraught that even Sam knew things weren't right. I ended up having to take care of everyone and everything—Daddy, Sam, the house, the cooking, the cleaning. I didn't get to be a little girl anymore, Harrison. The one thing that I just can't figure out is why, how could Mama abandon her little angel, Sammy Boy—her porcelain doll? She loved that little boy more than anyone or anything."

"Elizabeth, you're getting tired. Maybe we need to call it a night and get some rest."

Elizabeth reassured him she was fine and continued: "Well, as the days turned into weeks, it was apparent trouble was brewing. Rumors in the mill village were flying out of control. Neighbors thought Mama had perhaps run off for a better life with fewer responsibilities and didn't want to be found."

A concerned Harrison asked, "Did your dad ever find out any concrete information as time went on? Was there ever a sign of your mom's body?"

"Harrison, my mama was declared dead when investigators found human bones deep in the woods about six months after her disappearance. My dad didn't believe the evidence found was truly my mother's bones. Regardless Katie Mae was pronounced dead, and Reverend Davis conducted a graveside funeral. Everybody felt it would help bring closure for the family. That was such a gloomy day in my life. It seemed so final, and I knew my life would never be the same."

"I'm so sorry Elizabeth. I only wish I had known more about your childhood. Perhaps I could have helped you."

"Maybe we should try to get some rest, Harrison." Elizabeth pulled the sheet up to her chin. "Maybe we can get up early and finish our talk over breakfast."

"Well, maybe we can, Elizabeth, but the morning will be busy and taxing," Harrison said, kissed her forehead and told her to rest well.

With her soft throw beside her Elizabeth closed her eyes. The hotel room was cozy, and Elizabeth felt safe with Harrison beside her.

The next morning, before the sun rose, Elizabeth was sitting at the table in their hotel room, waiting for Harrison to stir. She had so much to share. "Good morning sleepy head. About time your eyes opened," Elizabeth said as Harrison sat up in bed.

"What time is it Elizabeth?" Harrison asked.

"Around five I think," she replied.

"How long have you been awake?"

"I got up around four. I couldn't sleep. Have a lot on my mind that I wanted to discuss before heading out this morning."

"Well, come over here, and let's finish our talk," Harrison patted the bed, urging his wife to sit closer.

"OK, I'm coming. Let me get you some coffee first."

Elizabeth sat down beside her husband and picked up where she left off the night before. "After the funeral, I remember Reverend Davis was very concerned about the details of my mama's disappearance. He asked my dad if Jack Bradford, the cotton mill supervisor and his wife had moved from the cotton mill village; he said he saw a 'For Sale' sign in front of their house," she said, pausing momentarily to take a sip of her coffee.

Elizabeth took a deep breath and continued. "My dad told the Reverend that, as far as he knew, the Bradford's had moved. They hadn't been seen in the village since that dreadful night he confronted them. Dad reminded Reverend Davis that the Bradford family was a topic that had to remain confidential…said he and Mama had made a vow never to discuss Jack Bradford and his wife as long as they lived. Reverend Davis told my dad it was for the good of the village to keep that situation with the Bradford's confidential. Odd, shortly after, the Reverend died of a heart attack."

"I'm so sorry for all the things you had to endure as a child. Elizabeth, how did you ever make it out? How did you survive after your mama died?" Harrison waited for his wife to answer as he embraced her.

"Well, Harrison…I didn't have a choice in the matter. I had to grow up fast when I no longer had a mother, and my father grew even more distant than he was before. He was always working or partying with friends before Mama disappeared, but then…well, then he had completely 'checked out,' as they say. Someone had to take care of the boys. Besides, Katie Mae was not discussed after she was laid to rest. Life was never the same for any of us. It was as if she had never been a part of our lives. My dad refused to speak of Mama, and he made each of us swear to do the same. It was hardest on Sam, of course, since he was so little—he just didn't understand. Daddy became even more depressed and drank even heavier after his shifts ended at the cotton mill each day. He was intoxicated from Friday evening until Monday morning. So, you see; I had to provide constant care for my brothers. I gradually assumed my mama's responsibilities for cooking, cleaning, and other domestic chores. I often visited nearby relatives for short periods during the summer. I was reluctant to linger but going to other people's homes was a nice break. I enjoyed seeing how 'normal' people…families…really lived."

"Elizabeth, that was rather brave of you, to take on such a huge responsibility. But, way too much for your father to ask, let alone to expect, of a girl so young," Harrison had concern etched on his brow.

"Harrison, Dad didn't ever properly ask. He just assumed I would take care of the boys, and I did the best I could. I knew my father was sick. He was basically bedridden sometimes with bouts of depression and alcoholism. He had become a prisoner to the bottle. His skin was jaundiced, showing signs of cirrhosis of the liver. It became inevitable that I would become the sole caregiver to my father and brothers," Elizabeth related with tears shining in her eyes.

She took a moment to gaze out the window, looking at the mist engulfing Shadow Village before continuing her story.

"As the years passed, my responsibilities bogged me down, and I grew distant from my father and my brothers. I wanted a different life, but I felt guilty for wanting to leave my family, or what was left of it, behind.

After I completed high school, I earned an amount of money working two years as a babysitter. I also did odd jobs to help save money. I knew there had to be a better life beyond the tracks of the old cotton mill village and I was determined to find peace of mind and happiness as soon as possible."

"Elizabeth, how did you escape? What did you do? You were so young with no one to take care of you…is this when we met?" Harrison wondered aloud. He even looked surprised that the words were spoken outside the confines of his mind.

Elizabeth's eyes begin to shine with something other than tears for a change. "No, Harrison, we weren't ready to meet just yet. It was the beginning of the rest of my life at this point. With my mind made up, I packed my belongings in a few boxes and took a cab across the cold railroad tracks. I had planned my escape for months and saved every penny I earned so that I could rent a motel room near the local Furniture Gallery where I planned to seek employment. I knew it would take years for me to get where I wanted to be in life…and I knew that Maple Leaf Avenue wasn't the end result I had in mind. But it was a start, and I was willing to work hard. That was my plan, Harrison."

"Elizabeth, I know it took a lot of self assurance to leave the only place you had ever lived. And I also know how determined you were and still are, my love," Harrison said with encouragement for his wife to continue; he was all ears.

"Yes, it did, Harrison. As the cab passed 2020 Maple Leaf Avenue, I saw a 'Room for Rent' sign in a yard, and I quickly jotted the address on a piece of paper. At the motel, I unpacked the bare necessities, sat in a somewhat comfortable chair, and tuned in to one of my favorite classical songs. Life was surely looking much brighter for me as I slept my first night across the tracks as a free woman. Life was good; at last, life was good."

"Elizabeth, you said you had planned for months, but I know you had to be afraid of the unknown," Harrison said.

"Sure, I was afraid but I had to be brave. I had almost no one to turn to at that point in my life. It was somewhat exciting. I rose early to prepare for my adventure across the tracks. First I knew it was necessary to review my finances to make sure I could pay the deposit for the room on Maple Leaf Avenue," Elizabeth revealed.

"I walked confidently to the home where I had seen the rent sign and just stood there marveling at the exterior of the home. It was so beautiful Harrison. I couldn't believe I was actually standing on the front porch of such a lovely home. I rang the doorbell, and a beautiful, smiling woman in her forties was standing there. I swear she looked like an angel in her finest costume. I felt as if I were in heaven for sure, Harrison." Elizabeth had a sparkle in her eyes. Even as a young woman, she had an eye for the finer things in life.

"I introduced myself and inquired about renting the room. The poised woman introduced herself as Victoria Holiday and invited me in. Harrison, it was as if I had died and gone to heaven for sure." Elizabeth beamed as she recalled her first encounter with Victoria.

"Ms. Holiday ushered me into the hallway of the house, motioning for me to follow her. She told me about how the rooms had been recently redecorated and were fully furnished with the finest the Furniture Gallery offered. Ms. Holiday also offered to store any unwanted furnishings from the room in her attic. I was completely speechless, overwhelmed by the size of the room, the décor, and the enormous adjoining bathroom with a shower. I had never had my own bathroom before. There was a beautiful vanity and two huge closets. This was a dream come true for me, and it would be more than sufficient until I could afford my own home."

"I signed a six month lease immediately and thanked Ms. Holiday for her generosity. Harrison, Victoria was such an incredible hostess. She invited me to sit in the main parlor for brunch that consisted of sweet rolls and warm rosemary tea. Ms. Holiday was very open about her expectations and assured me the lease would be honored. We became instant friends; we had similar interests in fine fabrics, decorating, and reading. The following day I moved into my spacious bedroom with all the extras; it was a comfortable living arrangement for this young lady," Elizabeth said, finishing her story.

Harrison beamed at his wife. "Elizabeth, this is interesting. I wish I had known more about your introduction to decorating. It would have helped explain all the designer furniture and fabrics in our home over the years," Harrison teasingly said.

"Harrison, I thank you for listening to me. I should have told you much earlier, but many more memories remain confused. I pray one day I can sort through my memories; store the good ones and discard the bad so our lives can move forward."

"All will be well, Elizabeth, you'll see. Just think. You were brave enough to make it across the tracks, and you found a loving home with Victoria. It's time to face what lies ahead of us."

Harrison got off the bed and headed for the shower. "I see you've already had your shower. I'll be right out. We can grab a quick breakfast and head toward your home place. Maybe the police can update us. Stay put, Elizabeth. It'll only take me a few minutes."

CHAPTER VII

FACING REALITY

Harrison and Elizabeth stopped at the nearest diner to grab some breakfast before getting the latest update on the village fire. A flirtatious waitress led them to a booth. "Be back in a moment, handsome." She smirked, teasing Harrison with a faded, plastic menu. After they ordered, Harrison asked, "Elizabeth, do you want to finish telling me all about the good times of your life, such as…living on Maple Leaf Avenue?"

"Sure, Harrison, those were indeed the best days of my life, before I met you at the furniture gallery."

"Well, I'm ready to hear about that Holiday lady. You beam at the mention of her name. Talk to me while we wait for our food."

"Maple Leaf Avenue. It brought so much joy into my life. The beauty there was breath taking, Harrison, and I had such a wonderful landlady. At last my life felt meaningful."

"Victoria had a gift for making others feel valued. She loved to entertain, was known as the most prestigious woman in her neighborhood, and had superb hospitality skills. I will always be grateful to her; she gave me meaning in my life. I just wish I had kept in touch with her through the years," Elizabeth gushed.

"Elizabeth, when we instantly bond with someone and distance and time disrupt communications, the bond is never broken."

"I know, but she was different. She was tuned in to my feelings, my needs, and my fears. I fell in love with her the first time I met her. As soon as I had unpacked my belongings, there was a knock on the door; it startled me. I opened the door, and there stood Victoria. She quickly apologized…as if she were intruding."

Elizabeth smiled in remembrance and continued, "I told her all was well; I was just startled by the knock on my door. She told me I would get accustomed to living on Maple Leaf Avenue and would soon feel safe in my new home."

"Why was she at your door as soon as you unpacked? Sounds a little overbearing," Harrison asked.

"Would you care for more coffee?" the waitress asked, darting a wink at Harrison.

"Thank you," Harrison said to the tall woman standing in front of their table with a fresh pot of coffee, ready to fill their mugs. "And yes, we could use more coffee and lots of cream."

"Anything else you need?"

Harrison looked at Elizabeth to see if she needed anything. "That'll be all. Thanks again," he said to the waitress, hoping she would move on. Harrison quickly turned his attention back to his wife, wanting to hear the rest of her story.

"To answer your question, Harrison, Ms. Holiday was there to invite me to supper, which she reported would be served in the main dining room at five o'clock. I accepted her offer with eagerness. I longed to be in the presence of fine company…well, at that point, any company. I was starting to get lonely, and I could only imagine the delicious meal she had prepared."

She continued, "Dinner was served promptly, and the two of us sat for hours talking about our lives. I told her it was important to me to live across the railroad tracks of Shadow Village and that I wanted more for my life than being a mill hand worker," Elizabeth explained as she looked over Harrison's shoulder and saw the waitress bringing their coffee with a strut that was not appealing to her.

"Here you go. Sorry for the delay. Y'all from this neck of the woods?"

"Not a problem," Harrison assured her. "No, we aren't."

"Harrison, I told Victoria how I felt and how hard I had worked to get away from my old life. She assured me that she understood my ambition and had always hated to look of the railroad tracks. They reminded her of jail cell bars," Elizabeth said, whispering the last words, so as not to offend anyone nearby who might be listening.

"How did Ms. Holiday afford to live on Maple Leaf Avenue, Elizabeth? Did she ever tell you about her childhood, her ambitions?" Harrison asked as he raised his hand signaling they were ready for their bill.

"Here you go, sir. Thank you for stopping by. Hope you come back to eat with us soon," the waitress said as she gave Harrison the bill and another quick wink of the eye, turning and strutting away with her long legs.

"Harrison, Victoria was quick to let me know she appreciated her parents providing her with a good childhood and leaving all they owned to her. Victoria's inheritance had provided her with a good life including a home located on Maple Leaf Avenue."

"What happened to her parents?" Harrison asked.

"Car accident," Elizabeth reported with disbelief in her eyes. "I asked if she had ever married, but she wasn't keen on talking about her past. So I didn't press, even though I was eager to find out more about her.

Smiling, Harrison said, "Well, well. Who does that sound like Elizabeth? Looks like you and Victoria had a lot in common."

"Ms. Holiday did tell me one day that sometimes it is better to remain single than to marry someone your parents refuse to give their blessing to. She expressed her love of children and a desire to have her own family but said that had not been possible for her. So, she had taken pleasure in decorating, gardening, and renting to young women who become a part of her extended family. Once when Victoria and I were in a deep discussion, she reminded me that she never wanted to meddle in my business or hurt my feelings. I didn't really understand but told her I didn't think she could offend me."

Elizabeth continued, "Later Victoria said, 'Elizabeth, I would love to claim you as my adopted daughter, and I hope you find my offer acceptable to be amongst my extended family.' Victoria was so generous and had such proper manners. I was in heaven being in her company. She told me to reflect upon her offer because not all offers are what they seem, and once you accept…sometimes it is impossible to evade without consequences." Elizabeth paused for a moment.

"Now, that really threw me for a loop Harrison. I had no idea what she was talking about, but I assured her I felt at ease in her lovely home, and the thought of having her as someone she could call family was well received. From that day on she called me her adopted daughter. I was actually pinching myself as I gladly accepted Victoria's offer. We spent numerous hours talking and revisiting the good, bad, and ugly of our lives. Ms. Holiday was complimentary of my ambition and what I had achieved at such a young age," Elizabeth relayed to her husband. "She even told me I was like the daughter she never had…or maybe she said the daughter she once had? I can't quite remember her exact words, but nevertheless, she made me feel like a real member of her family."

"How old did you say she was when you met her? Sounds like she may have been lonely living in that big house by herself."

"If I remember correctly, she was approaching middle age, and I know for a fact she felt lonely because she told me many times I was a Godsend. She felt it was inappropriate to mention her personal life to me or to share her deepest secrets, but I assured her I would never judge her for anything in her past."

"You haven't answered my question Elizabeth. What was Victoria speaking of when she made that statement to you about the daughter she lost?" Harrison impatiently asked as he sipped the last drop of coffee in his cup catching a glimpse of the sassy waitress.

"Harrison, I'm really tired of talking and besides, I think the waitress is ready for us to move on so she can clean the table. Let's go," Elizabeth whispered as she stood, placing a tip on the table. "We can continue this conversation later. We really need to assess the damage in Shadow Village," Elizabeth added as she walked toward the door.

"Sure Elizabeth, we are facing a busy day, and we really do need to get going." Harrison opened the door for Elizabeth and went around. Getting in, he could not help thinking that Elizabeth was rushing him to avoid his questions about Victoria, but he would give her the benefit of doubt. "Are you sure you're ready for this Elizabeth?" Harrison asked gently, as he pushed the ignition button on their Lincoln.

"Sure as I can be, Harrison. Sure as I'll ever be," Elizabeth replied.

Elizabeth looked out the window as they headed toward Shadow Village. She hoped Harrison would understand. She had revealed far too much information about the days prior to meeting him. Besides, she held some things about her past in complete confidence, and the information Victoria shared with her that day was confidential.

Soon they would be on the street she grew up on, and Elizabeth was sure her mind would be overloaded with memories of her childhood. She said a silent prayer that her family had made it out of the fire. She also asked God to forgive her for stalling; she had intentionally put the trip off several hours while in their bedroom. She had been in panic mode and could barely breathe. She had to gain her own composure before checking on her family members, family members she had not seen in over thirty years. She could only pray they were still alive.

The area near the railroad tracks was secure, and they were told to come back in three hours for updates. Elizabeth was disappointed but understood that the authorities would need time to sort through the damage. The place was a total disaster, and if people were allowed into the area, they might disturb the evidence needed to determine the cause. In some ways she was relieved; she had at least three hours before she had to face reality.

"So, what do you want to do, Elizabeth? Do you want to head to the hospital to see if any of your family members have been admitted?" Harrison asked.

"No. I don't want to do that Harrison. I want to go back to the scene in three hours as the policemen instructed," Elizabeth said with disappointment and panic echoing in her voice.

Harrison heard the panic loud and clear, "Okay, I'll drive us back to the hotel. Maybe you can get a nap before we return."

Back in their hotel room, Elizabeth took Harrison up on his suggestion for a nap, and asked him to wake her up in an hour so she could prepare to go back over to Shadow Village.

"Sure. You should take a short nap Elizabeth," Harrison said as he pulled his black pen from his white starched shirt. "I'll complete my crossword puzzle while you rest."

Elizabeth closed her eyes and slowly returned to the day she and Victoria had had a sincere talk. The scene seemed to appear in real time in her dreams. Drifting into a light sleep, Elizabeth invited the past into her present. She wanted to relive the day Victoria had taken a tremendous emotional risk in hopes of finding a common bond with her new tenant. Victoria's eyes were puffy as tears rolled down her cheeks.

The fear of rejection had always overruled her need to discuss her personal life struggles dating back to her unleashed days at one of the most prestigious colleges in North Carolina.

As she and Elizabeth talked, Victoria opened the doors of her past to tell her life story.

For the first time in her adult life, she would take a step into unknown territory and break her silence. Now seemed the perfect time to spill her heart as Elizabeth sat in front of her with her legs crossed, sipping tea, and eager to hear what the woman that was held in such high esteem would reveal.

Victoria had tears welling in her eyes as she began, "Elizabeth, my mind is my personal prison. It has kept me captive for way too long. I wish to be free!" She quickly turned away so she could hide the hurt. A photograph sitting on a corner shelf caught her eye and for a moment, Victoria thought that Elizabeth had placed a portrait of herself in the parlor. She walked over and picked it up to examine it more closely through the tears in her eyes.

Wiping her eyes with a monogrammed cloth handkerchief, Victoria immediately recognized the person in the picture.

"For a minute my eyes were playing tricks on me," Victoria said, placing the picture frame back on the shelf, her face white as a ghost.

"What are you referring to, Victoria?" Elizabeth asked, with a questioning look on her bright, young face.

"Oh it's nothing, my dear. Sometimes my eye sight isn't as clear as it should be," Victoria said with a weak smile.

Victoria sat down in front of Elizabeth to continue their conversation, thinking how much the picture resembled the young lady sitting across from her.

"You okay Victoria? You look like you just saw a ghost."

"I'm fine. I was just remembering the day that the picture I was just holding was taken. It was my eighteenth birthday; it was such a wonderful time. I was noticing the resemblance of my photo to your beautiful face and that is priceless to me. I believe that we definitely share a kindred spirit and that soothes my mind as I continue with my story." Elizabeth sat staring at her new landlord, now friend, wondering what she was talking about. Since

Victoria had quickly placed the picture frame in its respected place on the shelf, Elizabeth was not privy to view the picture. Nonetheless, Elizabeth was all ears for Victoria and eagerly sat wondering what could have gone wrong with a person that had such a fairytale childhood.

"Elizabeth what I'm about to disclose has to be kept confidential," Victoria said firmly. Her tone made Elizabeth feel uneasy as she sipped her tea from the finest china in town.

Victoria continued to give a pre-speech to Elizabeth praying she would not risk losing this fine young lady due to her own selfish need to relinquish years of personal guilt in hope of receiving acceptance for mistakes committed two decades ago.

Victoria felt uneasy as she glanced at Elizabeth's face that seemed very confused about the words at the tip of her landlord's tongue. Victoria immediately put a halt to her tell all—life confessions.

She did not need to spook Elizabeth. Besides, it was unfair to expect such a young and tender girl to understand how the spiteful decisions her wealthy parents had made some twenty years ago had inflicted a lifetime of heartache.

"Now that's enough about me my dear. Tell me what is next on your agenda Elizabeth, what are your plans this week as you experience life on Maple Leaf Avenue?"

"Well, I need a job, sort of like yesterday. So, I'm going to apply at the Furniture Gallery tomorrow morning. I pray they'll have an opening." Elizabeth was crossing her fingers in mid air for good luck.

"That's a wonderful place to work Elizabeth. I'm sure they will welcome your beautiful face at their place of business. I'll be anxious to hear about your experience." Victoria was mentally making notes of her connections at the Furniture Gallery as she captured the fine furnishing in her lovely home, all purchased at the upscale business. It was time for a little payback for the years of patronizing the locally owned business, hiring her new tenant would give them a clean slate in her book. A simple call would take care of the situation, come morning. That was, if Anthony Bailey was there.

Elizabeth applied for a job as a sales décor representative at the Furniture Gallery. She presented herself in such a professional manner that the storeowner immediately offered her the job. She accepted with gratitude. It was within walking distance of Maple Leaf Avenue and surely, it would provide her enough wages to pay her rent and buy minimum groceries. Besides, if things continued as they currently were, Elizabeth would not need to purchase groceries at all. Victoria had personally cooked all her meals since she moved in.

It was past time for Elizabeth to pursue happiness beyond the mill village, and she was ecstatic to venture out on her own to taste independence. Anyway, she had been on her own as long as she could remember.

Elizabeth considered providing care for her siblings and assuming the responsibility of daily chores in their home as a sign of independence and had added these qualities to her personal resume. She also reminded herself with all this on her plate, she somehow had mustered up the ability to complete her senior year at Shadow Village High School with honors. Life was surely heading in a brighter direction for Elizabeth, and she could not be happier.

Victoria sat quietly in her favorite designer chair, which was purchased at the Furniture Gallery. She rubbed the fine fabric with her fingers and said a silent thank you to Mr. Anthony Bailey, the manager of the Gallery. He had given his word to hire Elizabeth if she indeed met his approval.

During a phone conversation, Mr. Bailey had informed Victoria that Elizabeth far exceeded his expectations, and he had indeed hired her on the spot.

"I told you, Mr. Bailey. I told you Elizabeth was a jewel."

"I never doubted you, Victoria. I've always held you high on a pedestal," Anthony Bailey said with a hint of resentment in his voice.

"Didn't say you doubted me Anthony? Will you ever forgive me?"

He hung up.

As she placed her jewelry box on the small table beside her bed, stroking the tiny ballerina's long hair with pride, Elizabeth looked up to the heavens and smiled to acknowledge her appreciation. She had a great sense of pride that she had escaped the mill village without being an employee of Mr. Roscoe Johnson.

Elizabeth's heart was full of joy. She thanked God for providing the perfect home and a delightful landlord. She also was grateful for her new employment at the Furniture Gallery. Mr. Bailey was charming.

It was time to get some rest. She was having lunch with Ms. Holiday at the Country Club. The mere thought of entering the long narrow drive that led to Shadow Village Country Club brought Elizabeth enormous happiness. She had never been near a County Club. She was so excited about her Saturday's agenda with her new landlord and found it hard to focus on the classical music softly playing in the background.

After breakfast, Ms. Holiday gave Elizabeth a typed agenda of the events that would take place with the exact time noted. Elizabeth was impressed. Here was another person with a need for precise order in her life.

Elizabeth memorized each time slot so she would be familiar with the order of the day's events. Ms. Holiday announced she was going to meditate and read her scriptures, water the flowers, and prepare for their afternoon together.

Elizabeth was so excited. She had to get back to her room, tidy up, and prepare for a day with the most wonderful woman she had ever met. It was hard to measure up to the awesome character of Ms. Allen, her third grade teacher. Elizabeth was sure Victoria surpassed. Elizabeth heard the doorbell ring several times and decided to go and check who was at the front door. Much to her amazement it was Victoria, standing there smiling with a bouquet of flowers in her hand.

She proudly announced to Elizabeth the flowers were a welcoming gift and gave her congratulations on her new job. Elizabeth felt tears welling in her eyes as she reached out to take the flowers from Victoria's hand. "Thank you so much for the beautiful flowers and how were you aware I had a new job?"

"Oh, I have my ways of knowing things…now I'll be right back with a vase for your flowers," Victoria announced as she turned and walked away, humming a classical tune Elizabeth found soothing and very familiar, the same tune from her music box.

In a few minutes, Ms. Holiday knocked on Elizabeth's bedroom door and was greeted with a huge smile, followed with a slight hug from her new tenant. Victoria walked over to the bedside table and placed the flower vase down. She was spell bound at the sight of the music box and nearly dropped the vase.

Victoria placed the flowers on the table. She reached out, took the music box in her hands and twisted the knob in order to see the beautiful ballerina twirl. She abruptly turned around and asked Elizabeth, "Where did you find the music box my dear, was it in the closet? I've looked for it several times through the years, thought I had packed it clear out of sight, up on a top shelf or in the attic. Glad you found it for me, been MIA for at least twenty years or more."

Elizabeth looked puzzled and said, "Oh no, I brought it with me. I've had it since I was born, according to my dad. I'm not sure who bought it for me, most likely one of the supervisor's wife at the cotton mill being that my parents would have never had the money to buy it for me themselves."

Victoria immediately placed the music box on the table and walked over to Elizabeth. She embraced the young tenant and whispered in her ear, "It is beautiful my dear. Fond memories; my mother gave me one just like it on my tenth birthday. Cherish it with all your heart my dear, it is priceless."

Their day at the Country Club was splendid. Elizabeth was in heaven as she touched each piece of furniture, each drape of fabric that embellished the windows, and each beautiful silver tray displayed throughout the rooms, loaded with fresh fruits, fragrant breads, and homemade candies.

They talked for hours, sipping warm rosemary tea and snacking on the delectable cuisine. Ms. Holiday assured her new friend nothing she could share would cause a negative effect upon their relationship, and she hoped they could build a lifelong trust for each other. Elizabeth agreed that she indeed wanted that, too.

Elizabeth took a sip of tea and as she lifted her chin, she noticed Victoria had tears flowing down her ruby red cheeks. "Ms. Holiday, what's wrong…are you okay? Did I say something to upset you?" Elizabeth asked with compassion.

"No my dear," Victoria said, "you didn't say anything to upset me, and I'm just fine. I was just thinking how my daughter would be near your age if she were still with me."

Elizabeth looked nonplussed and was unsure what to say to Ms. Holiday. How could she console a grieving mother who had lost her baby?

"I'm very sorry that your baby died, Ms. Holiday. That must be hard to live with, I'm so sorry for your pain," Elizabeth said softly as she sipped her tea.

Ms. Holiday appreciated Elizabeth's compassion, and she felt she needed to explain the tragic loss of her child.

"Elizabeth, I'll be brief with this explanation, and you feel free to ask questions. I need someone to listen and accept my wrongdoing. I suppose the music box brought back a mountain of memories for me," Victoria explained with shame covering her face.

Elizabeth was not sure what Ms. Holiday was going to tell her. Could it be possible she had unwillingly caused the death of her baby? Elizabeth felt her anxiety level rising as Ms. Holiday spoke softly with a mixture of tears streaming downward onto her lap.

"Elizabeth, I was about to spill my heart before but I stopped myself. You see, my dear, back when I was a senior in one of the finest interior decorating colleges in North Carolina, I was somewhat unsure of my future. I became involved with a young apprentice working on his internship at the same interior market. We fell madly in love and planned our future together. Both he and I had grown up in this area, and dated several years in high school. We had broken up prior to leaving for college. Being far from home, our relationship rekindled quickly. We truly were in love."

"Before graduation I found out I was expecting a baby. I was expelled from college, sent home to the most elite parents in Shadow Village who would not dare have a daughter under their roof that made such a mistake. They were disappointed in me. They assumed my actions could only be those of a rebellious young girl, not a young woman who was simply in love with a young man who she knew loved her equally. They sent me to a boarding school up state until it was time for me to give birth. I was only permitted to take the essentials with me, no personal keepsakes were allowed except the music box. I placed it in my luggage and would listen to it at night. The tune was so calming during such a lonely time in my life."

Victoria was trying to read her new friend's facial expressions, making sure it was appropriate to continue with her untold secrets Ms. Holiday softly said, "I never understood why my parents came to pick me up a few weeks prior to giving birth. The anguish on their faces showed severe disappointment that could never be repaired."

"My mother explained I would be returning to Shadow Village and would give birth at the local hospital where I would be denied the right to keep my baby. The unwanted infant, as my parents had coined my baby's name, would be placed in a home that had parents who were well equipped to provide appropriate care upon the child being born.

"Oh Elizabeth, I cried and begged them to change their minds, but they refused to budge on their decision. I fought for my baby and they threw threats even harder toward me," she paused momentarily to wipe the tears from her eyes and then continued with a trembling voice.

"My parents said they would banish me from their lives and also deny me my inheritance, further warning me that my life would be one of poverty, much the same as the trash across the tracks if I disobeyed them. Elizabeth, I was young and had no money of my own, and financially there was no way I could possibly support myself or my baby.

"I was so afraid, and I didn't want my newborn baby to suffer because of my parents and their lack of support, or another bad decision on my part. I broke down and signed the appropriate paperwork in order for my baby girl to have a decent life. I have long since forgiven my parents for the undue stress they placed upon my life, but I have never forgiven myself for signing those papers. I should have fought much harder for my baby girl." Victoria paused.

"Oh, Victoria, you are being much too hard on yourself. You didn't know what was happening to you, being so young and at the mercy of your parents," Elizabeth consoled with compassion. "I can understand your position and why you went through with the adoption plan."

Victoria nodded and continued, "The next few days are still a blur to me. I remember packing an overnight case, placing my music box securely at the bottom and then going to bed. I knew something was not right with my body; now I understand I was feeling the onset of delivery pains. I screamed for help, and my mother immediately made a call to someone informing them it was time for the baby to be born."

"Who did she call?"

"I have no idea. It was so secretive, and I can't recall many details that occurred following that conversation. I did ask many questions but was not told much. According to my mother, I was unconscious for three days. I do recall the emptiness that overtook my body when I woke up and felt my flat stomach. At that moment, I knew my baby was gone. I pleaded with my parents to give my baby to me, but they ignored my cries, sedating me for several days. I will always feel emptiness in my life because of the unanswered questions. 'Where was my baby? Was she with a good family?

Would I ever see her again?' It was cruel of my parents to withhold such vital information from me."

Victoria wiped tears from her cheeks. "The only solace I have is the phone conversation several weeks later when I overheard my mother and an unidentified person. My mother asked repeatedly had the infant girl been placed in a loving home and was the music box given to the adoptive parents. That was some twenty years ago, and I'm still held in bondage from the torment they inflicted upon my young life. I asked my mother several times, but I was always denied knowledge of my baby."

Elizabeth stood up, giving the grieving Mother a compassionate hug, acknowledging she understood her pain. Victoria sobbed uncontrollably. "I should have taken my baby and run from them but I don't remember giving birth. I only remember waking up and feeling my empty stomach; my baby was taken from my womb without my knowledge. I don't even know the date of birth. Elizabeth, my parents never forgave me for my indiscretions, and I have never verbally forgiven them for stealing my baby, although I vowed to always keep her close to my heart."

"There were months of bad blood between my parents and me. We didn't speak of the incident. It was forbidden. About a year from the date of my baby's birth my parents were both killed in an accident on the interstate. I received a call from their attorney informing me my parents never arrived for their scheduled appointment to make changes to their will. About two hours later, the highway patrol officer knocked on the door offering condolence of my parents' death. I felt God was punishing me for my sins. I lost the love of my parents and more importantly I lost the opportunity to hold my baby, to love and provide a home for her."

Elizabeth was wiping her own tears, explaining she understood death because her own mother had died at an early age and guilt lived in her veins as well. It was well agreed upon between the two new friends that their lives were bonded with unconditional love and acceptance.

Monday was the first day of the week, and an excited Elizabeth jumped out of bed prepared for her job at the Furniture Gallery. It was a new day of a new week and a new path to a brighter future. She was so proud to be an employee at such a fine place of business.

Elizabeth was finally experiencing happiness. She had taken a step toward a brighter life as a resident on Maple Leaf Avenue with the love and care of Ms. Holiday. Elizabeth had no idea how her life would change after only a short time at her new job.

Victoria was filled with joy as she felt a new hope within her spirit. Her new tenant was surely uplifting. She was also thankful that Anthony Bailey had given Elizabeth the position at the Furniture Gallery; at least he had kept his word.

The bond between Anthony Bailey and Victoria went back to the days when they were college students. They would forever hold a bond. He was the father of her baby girl. The baby girl neither of them ever held. Besides, they had both gone their separate ways after their college days, he marrying and having a family of his own and Victoria living a life of regret for signing adoption papers without his consent. Victoria often wondered if she had told Anthony Bailey she was pregnant with his child would things have turned out differently. She had lived with regret over twenty years.

Through the years, they had remained cordial; in their small town that was expected. Victoria felt no need to burden Anthony Bailey or rehash old news to a happily married man. So she assumed.

CHAPTER VIII

DEMONS IN THE NIGHT

"Elizabeth. Elizabeth. Wake up. You were screaming." Harrison stated. "We need to get on our way. You've been asleep nearly two hours."

Elizabeth sat up on the bed and scrambled to her feet. Her vision was blurred from the tears she had shed during her nap. Noticing her puffy eyes, Harrison knew Elizabeth was experiencing a great deal of inner turmoil and his thoughts were racing, trying to decide the best way to ease her pain.

"Where are we, Harrison?" Elizabeth asked with a panicky voice.

"We are in a hotel, in Shadow Village. You and I decided, together, to come back here to check on your family, your childhood home. Remember?" Harrison asked with great concern.

Harrison called the desk clerk. A man's voice wanted to know how he could be of assistance. "Can you please send two bottles of chilled water to room 122 and a bucket of fresh ice? Thank you."

"Yes sir, be right up," the clerk replied.

Within a few minutes, a loud knock surprised Elizabeth. "He' ya' go. I'm Snappy Happy. He's ya' water an' ice," said the tall thin boy with his hand out for a tip.

Harrison was concerned. "Now what were you dreaming about Elizabeth? You were tossing, turning, and unresponsive. I didn't think you would ever wake up. Drink some water."

"Just a bad dream Harrison. I'll tell you later. I really need to freshen up so we can be on our way. Hopefully we can find out what the status of things once we arrive." Harrison followed Elizabeth in the bathroom and stood beside her as she dipped a soft washcloth under the warm water flowing from the faucet.

When Elizabeth looked in the mirror, her swollen eyes explained why

Harrison was so concerned. She placed her hands over her face and prayed for her sanity...for survival.

"I will explain my dream later, Harrison," Elizabeth whispered from beneath the soft white washcloth that covered her entire face. "I'm trying to get some steam to help with the puffiness. Goodness, I can't go anywhere looking like this."

After washing her face, Elizabeth put eye drops into her bulging eyes and noticed the soft skin sagging underneath. A sense of sadness came over her. She longed to feel the warmth of Victoria's arms as she recalled their conversation that had taken place some thirty years ago.

Soon the Davenports were on their way to Shadow Village, a much-dreaded drive for Elizabeth. Harrison reached over to his wife and gently stroked her hair. "Elizabeth, I'll stop at the Quick Mart just ahead and buy you a Diet Coke with crushed ice, of course. You can also take your medication. You need to calm your nerves. No telling what we'll find, we should pray for the best and be prepared for the worst."

Elizabeth accepted her husband's offer to purchase her a soda, and added, "I forgot to bring my water, and I can't take my medication with the soda."

"One bottle of cold water and one diet soda with crushed ice coming up, Elizabeth. I'll be back in a minute."

"Thanks, Harrison," she replied with genuine gratitude.

Shortly Harrison returned and opened the car door. One look at his wife's face and Harrison knew that it was only a matter of time before Elizabeth slipped into a state of anxiety so deep he might never pull her out.

The opened door allowed the smell of smoke to flow into the car. Elizabeth covered her face with her lightweight jacket. The sound of the fire trucks and emergency vehicles added to Elizabeth's stressful state of mind.

Harrison knew he had to help settle his wife's nerves. He gave her a sip of cold water to swallow her medication. Harrison prayed his attentive care would calm the turmoil in his wife's mind.

Elizabeth's heart was pounding. Waves of anxiety washed over her body, and the smell of death coming from the village would not allow her to escape its tormenting grasp.

"I'm sick, Harrison. I feel so helpless. Please help me. My head is spinning out of control, and I can't concentrate."

"You'll be OK, Elizabeth...as soon as your medication settles in your system. I knew this trip would be hard on you."

Elizabeth was having a panic attack, as she feared the unknown that was ahead of them.

"Take a sip of your soda...should settle your stomach. Once you gain control again, you'll feel much better."

"Harrison, I'm afraid." Tears flowed down her cheeks as she took deep breathes to calm herself. Her body was shaking with fear.

Elizabeth glanced out the window as they approached the tracks leading to the mill village. Inquisitive bystanders crowded the streets, shuffling for a favorable view of the damage caused by the blazing fire.

A police officer bellowed on a bullhorn that no one was allowed in the area due to the extent of the damage. They had to park their car, walk across the tracks, and stand behind the rope barrier that provided safety from the smoldering fire. No one was allowed to enter Elizabeth's street, the last street behind the cotton mill. She wept.

The area reeked of burnt wood and smoldering ashes. The people along the taped off area speculated about the damages. Rumors ran amuck, causing unnecessary chaos among those whose loved ones lived on the last street behind the cotton mill.

"OK people. Listen up. I'm about to give an update," the fire chief said as silence fell upon the crowd. "It seems like all the houses on the street have major fire damage. We are still trying to assess the damages, and ask that you be considerate and patient with our team of professionals as they work diligently."

Elizabeth knew her old home was not able to withstand the fire and most likely nothing more than flakes of ashes surrounded the property.

Elizabeth's heart was beating fast, and it felt as if her entire body was in slow motion as she strained her eyes, looking all around to view the damage. The homes within Elizabeth's view were nothing but black dust. The boards had burned to charcoal wood flakes and concrete porches covered with smut and debris. Elizabeth's eyes gazed around the cotton mill streets trying to find answers. Her knees became weak, and she leaned over the security tape.

The place she called home, as a child, had burned to the ground, leaving flakes of charcoal dust. There was a faint remembrance of the house that once occupied the property. She could barely see the top of the aged chimney that landed near the weather rusted wire fence. She had to know if her playhouse was still standing. Just thinking about how such a massive fire could destroy an entire community made Elizabeth weary.

A fireman shook his head. "It looks like the two story white house was the raw diamond that made it out. It should be all good with a fresh coat of paint. It is such a southern colonial beauty with its white, two-story columns which was owned by Mr. Jack Bradford, the cotton mill supervisor."

A man standing next to Elizabeth in the crowd commented, "Apparently Mr. Bradford built himself a jewel with walls of steel and a guardian angel to oversee it."

The crowd was told the majority of the residents living in the homes at the time of the fire were successfully rescued and taken to the local hospital for treatment. Only two residents did not make it out of their house. Elizabeth's heart skipped a beat; she just knew her father did not make it out. He was dead.

Someone at the back of the crowd demanded answers from the authorities. "We heard it was the Old Lady Gunter and her maniac grandson that didn't make it out. We deserve to know the whereabouts of our neighbors and family."

The authorities explained the deaths were under investigation and no other information would be provided until further notice.

Elizabeth knew it had to be Old Lady Gunter and Lester. She turned to Harrison and said, "She has to be in her late 90's, Harrison, and her grandson has to be approaching his late 60's... poor people...they were both suffering from mental disorders. They were most likely sound asleep and overcome by the smoke."

Family members waited impatiently, but the authorities had no more information. They simply said, "A more in depth report will be given to all family members as the investigation is completed. This can take days or possibly weeks. Injured residents are safe in Shadow Village Hospital. We cannot release the names of the residents who did not survive the fire. That information will be released once we contact family members."

A bystander yelled, "They ain't got no darn relatives. They were crazy fools and most likely started the darn fire. Death serves them justice. Better off, they was two morons."

Silence followed the bystander's statement. No one was certain of his accusations.

Another bystander reminded everyone that visiting hours were over and said it would make more sense to arrive early the next morning.

The crowd was asked to leave and give the authorities time to complete their investigation.

People quickly faded into the evening dusk. Only the authorities were left with the smell of smoldering ashes mixed with the flesh of the two residents who did not survive.

When firemen tried to rescue the Günter's, they found the entrance blocked by blazing flames and furniture. Why the entrance was blocked seemed to be of great concern. Did Lester Gunter place the furniture at the entrance to keep outsiders from breaking in during the night, or was it possible someone else had blocked the entrance? Did foul play cause the death of Old Lady Gunter and her grandson, Lester Gunter, known as the community maniac? As the authorities have stated, the investigation might take a while, and Elizabeth had to settle her mind, but she was not ready to travel to the hospital.

Elizabeth and Harrison drove to their hotel in complete silence.

Harrison broke the silence when they got to their hotel room, "Why don't you finish unpacking Elizabeth?"

"I will, Harrison. I just need some time to think about all this. I'm feeling less anxious knowing my dad is alive and in the hands of competent professionals at the hospital."

Harrison smiled, "I thought this news would surely help you have a good night's rest, Elizabeth. You'll get to see your father in the morning."

"Harrison, I don't want to reunite with my father after all these years in a hospital room. That just doesn't seem right, does it?" Elizabeth wondered aloud to her husband. Harrison did not quite know how to respond.

They settled in for the night with Elizabeth's favorite classical music playing. Harrison hoped the music would help his wife fall asleep. He could only pray Elizabeth would have a restful night.

"Elizabeth, I hope you rest well. Remember: prayer calms the mind when the body is in turmoil."

"I know Harrison. I know."

The next morning Elizabeth and Harrison stopped at the hospital information desk to ask for Mr. Buck. The visitor's card indicated that he was in the intensive care unit on the third floor.

"I'm Dr. Elizabeth Davenport, Buck's daughter. I have my credentials if you want to verify my identity," Elizabeth said to the nurse sitting at the desk who was reviewing patient charts.

"Thank you, Ms. Davenport. I'm Nurse Bentley and I'll be glad to assist you any way I can. Yes, you can visit with your father, but you must remember he needs to rest, so your visit must be short, my dear."

Holding Harrison's arm for comfort, Elizabeth entered the room. She had no idea what she would find. She only knew it was unknown territory, and it made her feel nauseated and weak.

The room was dark. On a hospital bed in the far corner, a frail, old man with an oxygen mask was struggling to breathe. The medical equipment attached to him seemed to be his only lifeline.

"Harrison, I'm not sure this man is my father. I can't see his face clearly, the oxygen mask is covering his face," Elizabeth had uncertainty in her voice.

The man was sleeping soundly but twitched when the door opened. Nurse Bentley asked Elizabeth and Harrison to step outside for an update on the man's condition.

Standing outside Buck's room, the nurse informed Elizabeth that her father was fighting for his life. "Ms. Davenport, your father is indeed a miracle. Mr. Jones sustained several deep cuts and third-degree burns covering about one-third of his body while trying to escape the fire. We are fighting to keep infection from entering the wounds, which is critical to his survival. His condition is critical, and it will be days before the doctor can give the family a proper prognosis. It didn't help that your father was intoxicated," the nurse continued in a lower tone. "His lungs were damaged as a result of the smoke. Sweetie, his poor health contributes to the seriousness of his condition."

Elizabeth listened carefully as Nurse Bentley continued, "Your father has cirrhosis of the liver. That is making it much harder for his body to recuperate. Stay positive."

Images of her father guzzling moonshine from his mason jar flooded Elizabeth's mind

"The doctor will speak with you soon. I suggest you call your family members. The next twenty-four hours are critical. You might want to call your clergyman or the hospital can provide one for you."

"Harrison, this is too much information for me to handle. I'm overwhelmed," whispered Elizabeth.

Harrison led his wife to a nearby chair. "Here, have a seat and calm down. Give me the contact information, and I'll call your brothers and any other family members you want to let know about your father. I'll also request the service of the hospital clergyman for the family."

Elizabeth opened her mouth to speak but could not utter a word. She said, "I don't know how to contact my brothers or any other relatives. I can only hope they are still living and will find us here."

Harrison nodded and left the room. He found Nurse Bentley standing in the hall and requested the services of the clergyman, further informing the nurse that his wife would contact other family members as soon as possible.

"Thank you, Mr. Davenport. We are here to assist the family during this difficult time. Should I bring your wife a cot for tonight?" she asked with concern.

"A cot would be greatly appreciated for Elizabeth, and I would like a reclining chair," Harrison assured the nurse.

Nurse Bentley smiled at Harrison, ensuring that she would take care of his requests.

About 8:30 p.m., the hospital clergyman entered Buck's hospital room and moved close to the bedside. "Mr. and Ms. Davenport I'm Father Allen would you like to join hands with me in prayer?"

"Yes," Elizabeth said, closing her eyes.

They repeated the Lord's Prayer. Tears flowed down Elizabeth's cheeks. She opened her eyes and kissed her father's forehead. "I'm so sorry I left you, Daddy. Please forgive me for leaving you."

Buck's body twitched and he turned toward his daughter. Elizabeth gazed into his eyes, but she almost did not recognize his frail, aged face. Through partially opened eyes, Buck looked back at his daughter. He had sadness in his eyes. Elizabeth wept.

Elizabeth reached for her father's hand. Slowly his fingers moved. Elizabeth was not sure what to do. She was not sure if her father was trying to grasp her hand with his fingers or if it was just an involuntary movement.

Elizabeth certainly did not think her father would remember a face he had not seen in three decades. Guilt almost stifled her breathing as she watched him struggle to speak.

Nurse Bentley tried to reassure Buck. She patted his shoulder while stating, "Mr. Jones, you are in the hospital. You have multiple burns from a house fire. Please remain still. It's crucial that you get plenty of rest."

Buck continued to struggle. His eyes begged for understanding. The nurse moved closer: "What are you trying to say, Mr. Jones? What do you need?"

"Liz," he whispered. "Liz."

Nurse Bentley lifted the mask from his face to hear what Buck was saying. "Mr. Jones, it's normal to feel pain. May I offer you some something to help you rest?"

Shaking his head from side to side, Buck whispered, "Lizzy...Lizzy...Lizzy."

Elizabeth moved closer to her father's bedside, tears streamed down her face as she bent down and touched his forehead with her hand. "Daddy, I'm here. I'm going to stay with you while you rest."

Buck became more agitated. The compassionate nurse suggested that everyone leave the room, so she could administer a sedative to help him rest. Elizabeth took her father's hand and softly kissed it. She noticed the tears streaming down his face. Elizabeth slowly backed away from her father's bed and took her husband's hand as they both moved toward the door.

"Ms. Davenport, your father spoke. He's becoming more alert, and that's good, my dear. Don't be too alarmed if you don't understand his words."

Elizabeth was delighted that her father seemed to recognize her. Elizabeth also felt Buck did know what he was saying.

"Elizabeth, perhaps you can get an appointment with your father's doctor," Harrison asked. "I know you're anxious to speak to him. Why don't you speak to the head nurse?"

"I will do just that, Harrison. I will return momentarily, thanks for staying with my dad."

"Excuse me, Nurse Bentley. May I please speak with the head nurse on duty? Elizabeth asked.

"Yes, my dear, just a minute. I'll get her for you."

"Hello, may I help you," asked a tall slender nurse with excellent poise and professionalism. Her hair was dark black and very sleek. Elizabeth could not help but notice her skin had a light brown tint that glowed under the florescent lights; she looked so familiar to Elizabeth. She desperately tried to remember if she had been introduced to the head nurse and perhaps had forgotten in the midst of the turmoil.

"Hello, sorry to bother you but I have several concerns. My name is Elizabeth Davenport, and my father is Buck. He was hurt in the village fire."

"Yes, I'm aware of the village fire. Very sorry to hear your father was among those hurt. I can assure you we'll take excellent care of your father." The nurse extended a pleasant smile. "How can I assist you, Ms. Davenport?"

"First, could you arrange for my husband and me to speak with Dad's primary doctor?" Elizabeth inquired. "Second, I would like to have a list of all the medications my father is currently being administered so I can keep a personal log."

"I'll do my best, dear. It may take some time for the doctor to make his appearance; they are busy trying to cover this horrific accident in the village," the nurse replied kindly. "Your dad's doctor checks in with the staff and is a phone call away. On your second concern; I'll print you a copy of the medications ordered for your dad and have Nurse Bentley take this to you shortly."

"Thanks. We'll be in Dad's room. Please let us know as soon as you talk to his doctor." A grateful Elizabeth turned to go back to her father's room. "Excuse me. I'm sorry; I didn't get your name."

"Not a problem. I'll give you my card." The head nurse extended her personal business card adding, "Keep this card, and call me anytime. I'm so glad to see you, Elizabeth."

The nurse came around the desk and gently embraced Elizabeth and whispered in her ear, "Good to see you, Lizzy. I'm Emma Jean Smith Ward, and I made it out. Thank you for believing in me."

Elizabeth stood speechless as Emma Jean Smith Ward turned and walked toward an office with a nameplate on the door that had the words "Emma Jean Smith Ward, RN. Underneath her name: ICU Head Nurse.

Before her shift ended, Emma Jean Smith Ward stopped by Buck's hospital room to check on his condition and to speak with Elizabeth. She tapped on the door and slowly entered the room.

"I wanted to stop by and check on you and your father. How are you holding up, Elizabeth?" Emma Jean asked with concern etched on her face.

"Thank you, Emma Jean, for your concern. I'm doing much better now that I've seen Daddy and he is more alert. I'm so glad we met again. It has been a long time since we talked...decades to be exact." Elizabeth reported with a slight degree of apology.

"Maybe we can have lunch once your dad is better? We have so much to catch up on." Emma Jean replied to her childhood friend.

"That would be wonderful, Emma Jean. I would love to sit down and catch up."

"Well, if you'll step out, I'll check your father's vitals. His doctor should be stopping by soon," Emma Jean said as Elizabeth and Harrison were leaving.

Shortly after, Emma Jean opened the door stating, "You can come in. Everything is about the same. Your father seems to be a fighter."

"Emma Jean, Dad is a fighter and earlier this evening he called my name. Does that mean he remembers me? Do you think he knows who I am?" Elizabeth asked, tears brimming her tired eyes.

"Perhaps or he could be recalling the names of people he has known throughout his life. The doctor will be able to tell you more when he comes in," Emma Jean said with a gentle pat on Elizabeth's shoulder.

"It's crucial that a family member remain with your father for the next twenty-four hours and possibly longer."

Elizabeth nodded and turned to Harrison, "Can you bring me my overnight bag, dear? I plan to sleep here tonight."

"Sure. Do you need me to bring anything else? How about your blanket, would you like for me to bring it for you?" Harrison bent down to kiss his wife's forehead.

"Yes, thank you. Hurry back, Harrison, and be careful," Elizabeth said with appreciation.

Elizabeth walked with Harrison into the hallway, closing the door behind her.

"Okay darling, I'll be back soon with your things, but why not walk with me to the hospital cafeteria? You can get yourself something to drink, Elizabeth," Harrison said as he walked toward the elevator.

"Think I'll do just that. Wait a minute. I want to make sure my father is okay, and I'll need some money." Elizabeth said as she briskly open the door of her dad's hospital room, grabbing her purse.

When they got downstairs, Harrison went to the car, and Elizabeth walked to the cafeteria. Once in the cafeteria Elizabeth hesitantly ordered a cup of fresh coffee, knowing the house blend would have to do because gourmet coffee was not on the menu.

"Is that all you'll have, missy?" The clerk asked, with a seductive wink.

"That's all I need, thank you," Elizabeth sharply replied as she noticed his street-smart attitude. She knew his kind, living amongst dominant and overbearing bullies in the cotton mill village had taught her how to handle a smart mouth clerk that was merely nothing more than a first class jerk.

"Well, that'll be two quarters or five dimes, whichever you prefer." said the tall slender clerk that stood behind the counter. "So, what's your pleasure, missy? Could you speed it up, gotta help other customers."

By now the clerk was shouting with his crackling smoker's voice as the pupils in his eyes enlarged with pleasure upon his face, feeling he was surely getting to the sophisticated woman standing a few feet from him. Knowing he had the security of the protective shelter of the counter as his safety zone was a warm comfort that enable the clerk to be a first class bully.

"Here's fifty pennies, Mr. John Ross Johnson. I see you have yourself a nice red t-shirt with your name on it. Oh, here's a penny for your tip," Elizabeth retorted with a pleasant smile upon her face.

Elizabeth turned to exit the cafeteria with an extra twist in her walk. She was proud that Emma Jean Smith had made a good life for herself. Unfortunately, the same could not be said for John Ross Johnson, their childhood school bully.

Some things never change, Elizabeth thought as she closed the cafeteria door.

The elevator door opened, and Emma Jean Ward stepped out.
"See you got a cup of coffee, Elizabeth. Did you get a chance to greet the cafeteria clerk? If so, you most likely realized he hasn't changed at all…that John Ross Johnson."

"Oh, I saw him, and he had no idea who I was. He tried to be smart with me, so I gave him a handful of change for my coffee." Elizabeth smiled at her actions, her attempt to put the man behind the counter in his rightful place.

"That serves him right. That man will never change. He still tries to harass me every day… after all these years. Though I can say his tactics have changed lately. He uses slight sexual overtones instead of the physical taunting when we were in elementary school. Guess he hasn't forgotten that goose egg I gave him on the playground, that's why he refrains from trying to be physical with me."

"You should get to see Nurse Tori; she'll be on the morning shift most likely. You'll enjoy talking with her I'm sure; catching up on old times. You'll recognize her, nice but still same odd gal. Well, it has been a long night. See you tomorrow."

As Elizabeth returned to the hospital room, Nurse Bentley opened the door and updated, "Your father is resting. His body is responding well to the medication. I'll be back in about ten minutes, but call if you need me before then."

Elizabeth pulled her chair closer to the bed. She wondered if her dad would pull through. Being careful not to wake him, she laid her head on the side of the bed. Suddenly she felt a hand stroking her hair. "Harrison, I thought you left," she whispered.

As she moved her head, she locked eyes with her father. Buck was awake. He whispered, "Liz."

"Dad, did you say my name?" Elizabeth asked, looking into her father's eyes. Without a word, Buck closed his eyes. He was sound asleep. Elizabeth was speechless but relieved. Her dad knew she was there. She continued to watch over him as he slept. Leaning toward his ear, she whispered, "I love you Dad. I hope you rest well tonight."

Elizabeth suddenly remembered Emma Jean telling her about Tori being the morning nurse. She was puzzled as how that would play out, since Tori had been such a strange individual in her younger days. She also remembered how Tori could be very sociable. Elizabeth smiled, wondering if Tori still tried to cast spells on people, hopefully, not her patients.

She laughed as she heard the door open. She knew by the footsteps who was approaching her side. Such a predicable man. Her man.

Harrison returned with Elizabeth's overnight bag and blanket. Before kissing her goodnight, he noticed that she seemed more relaxed. He assured her that he would return in the morning. He took her hand, slightly squeezing it, he reminds her to concentrate on getting some rest. He closes the door behind him and walks toward the elevator.

Elizabeth prepared for a night watching over her Dad. She took a deep breath and leaned back in the chair. Suddenly, she heard a faint moan. "Dad, you need something?" She asked as she nervously walked toward his bedside. She prayed he would make it through the night. Seeing he was resting, Elizabeth sat down and pulled her blanket close to her body. She closed her eyes and started to think about her childhood. She was trying to find something humorous to settle her nerves. She thought of Old Lady Gunter and Lester, her grandson. Elizabeth let out a soft laugh. Those two had pulled all their resources together, trying to spook the neighborhood children. It had worked. As a child, she had been afraid of both of the odd neighbors. To this day, she declined eating figs of any kind. She laughed, praying her Dad would rest well.

Buck was somewhat resting; one eye closed and the other eye on his daughter. A tear fell from his open eye as he quietly fell into a deep sleep. He was at peace, and so was his daughter. The sun was peeping through the gap in the curtains. Elizabeth heard a knock on the door as Harrison entered the hospital room expecting his wife to greet him. However, Elizabeth's sleepy eyes were fixated on the nurse who was dispensing medication. "Tori, is that you?" Elizabeth asked.

"Yes Elizabeth. I heard you were back in town. Sorry for the circumstances, and I hope things work out well for you and your family. I'll be taking care of your father. Let me know if I can be of assistance," Nurse Tori replied with coldness in her voice.

"How is your dad doing this morning Elizabeth? Are there any improvements?" Harrison asked as he handed his wife some fresh coffee.

Before Elizabeth could utter a word to Harrison, Nurse Tori answered with authority, "I'm so sorry, but Mr. Jones' condition hasn't improved since he was admitted. His heart rate is very high, and we can't seem to control his blood pressure. We were hoping to see improvement by early morning."

"Thank you for the update. I'm sure you've spoken with my father's doctor concerning his yellowish skin tone?" Elizabeth asked. "It seems to be getting worse."

"Elizabeth, your father has cirrhosis of the liver. He lost a lot of blood before he was admitted. This makes it much more complicated, and hard on his system," Nurse Tori explained. "Continue to keep a positive outlook. Only time will tell if his condition will improve or worsen. The doctor will be here soon to speak with you," Nurse Tori abruptly turned to exit the room.

With tears in her eyes, Elizabeth turned her head away from her husband, "I was praying for good news, Harrison. I just knew my dad's condition would take a turn for the better."

"We'll just hope and pray your dad is feeling better soon, Elizabeth." He came to his wife's side stroking her hair.

Nurse Tori walked toward the door and quickly patted Elizabeth's shoulder. "I'll ask Father Allen to stop by and pray with you."

As her father's nurse left the room, Elizabeth stiffened her back and brushed the hair from her face. "Nurse Tori is an old childhood friend Harrison. She's just as weird now as she was as a child. I sure don't have time to deal with her mood swings," Elizabeth said as she took the local phone book from the old wooden table beside the bed and began searching for the names of her brothers.

"I think I located Albert Joe. But I don't see a listing for Samuel Jones," Elizabeth said with concern written all over her face. How was she ever going to find her brother? He could be anywhere by now.

"Elizabeth, I'm going to get a soda while you call Albert Joe. I'll be right back, you need anything?" He asked as he stood to stretch his legs and walk to the cafeteria.

"I'm fine but thanks for the offer." Elizabeth dialed the number listed for Albert Joe Jones. As the phone rang, Elizabeth wondered why Albert Joe had not been to the hospital to check on their Dad. She had so many questions for him if only she could locate her elder brother. Suddenly an automated voice picked up responding, "There's no one home. Please leave a message."

"Darn it. That's just what I expected." She left a detailed message, pleading with Albert Joe to come quickly. As she hung the phone up, she heard her dad mumbling.

"Dad, Dad! Can you hear me? Are you in pain? Can I get you something?"

Buck reached for the hand that was slowly stroking his arm. Elizabeth cradled her father's hand between hers, giving it a gentle squeeze as if she were projecting healing into his body. At first, she could not make out the words he kept repeating.

Finally, she understood: "Liz, my baby."

Elizabeth was not certain if her father recognized her or if the medication was causing him to remember things from the past.

"Dad, you're in the hospital. I'm here," Elizabeth said holding his hand tightly.

Buck struggled for the strength to communicate. He pulled on the mask with his other hand.

"Dad, you must rest. Save your strength for healing," Elizabeth tried to adjust the mask that was now half off Buck's face.

He continued to whisper, "Liz, my baby."

"Dad, you have to stop pulling the mask off your face or the nurse will have to restrain you," Elizabeth pleaded.

Elizabeth cried tears of regret as her dad locked his eyes on her face. As he continued to try to talk, she summoned the nurse who immediately sedated Buck.

Moments later Harrison returned. "Elizabeth, I've called your name several times. What's wrong? You look as if you just saw a ghost," He said as he handed his wife a pack of Lance crackers.

Elizabeth opened her crackers and laid them on the table. Her mind was not on eating. She had to tell her husband the good news.

Turning to meet her husband's eyes Elizabeth said, "My dad was so agitated. He kept calling my name and tugged at his mask until it fell off."

"He looks restful now, Elizabeth," he replied quietly. "Try not to worry so much, won't help a thing, and make you more anxious."

"Yes, he has settled down now, but not until he was given a sedative. I hope he'll rest for a while," Elizabeth paused. "Do you think if I had remained connected to my family, I would have had less anxiety through the years? I was always worried about the unknown."

He replied, "Elizabeth, I can't answer that since I never knew your family. Only you know the answer to your question. Search your heart, and you'll find the key to all your questions."

"I think if I hadn't removed myself from all the depression, drama, and poverty, I would have ended up in an asylum," Elizabeth replied with desperation.

"Well, there's your answer. So, stop doubting yourself and move on. Stay in the present, Elizabeth. Your father needs you now and you have to be emotionally stable," He answered with compassion for his distraught wife.

Looking back to her father, Elizabeth said, "I will do my best. It was a hard decision. I was so young when I left, but I can't look back. Even though I left, I have never been able to escape the stifling nightmares. They nearly won their fight for my sanity."

"Elizabeth, I know it has been hard through the years, but only good things await us. Keep the faith, and get some rest tonight," Harrison consoled as he prepared to go back to the hotel.

Elizabeth watched over her father as he slept soundly through the night. She was thankful for the opportunity to be alone with him. She could feel the warmth of his love for her as she lay on the cot within few steps of his hospital bed.

The next morning Buck's doctor knocked on the door and asked to speak with the family.

"I'm Mr. Jones's daughter, Dr. Elizabeth Davenport. Thank you for coming by to speak with me."

"Your father lost a lot of blood from the deep puncture wound to his abdomen," Dr. Price reported. "It was most likely from glass as he tried to escape the fire."

"Do you feel my father will make a full recovery?" Elizabeth asked quietly.

"Well, it's too soon to say. I can tell you that the hospital is short of your father's blood type. We need to find a donor as quickly as possible to increase your father's chances of recovery," the doctor said with urgency.

Elizabeth said, "I'd be happy to donate blood for my dad. That's the least I can do."

"I'll have the lab tech come and draw your blood. We should know shortly if it is a match," Dr. Price said as he turned to leave. "I'll return once I know something. Make yourself comfortable, my dear."

"Think I'll do just that, Dr. Price. Thanks for taking care of my dad," Elizabeth replied gratefully.

The lab tech came and drew two vials of blood. For safety and accuracy, two different labs analyzed the vials.

Within the hour, Dr. Price asked to speak with Elizabeth in a small office near the nurse's station. "Elizabeth, we noticed something peculiar in the blood work. Your blood is not a match for your father. Furthermore, the analysts concluded that there is no possible likelihood that you are blood kin to Mr. Jones." Dr. Price noted Elizabeth's reaction. "I'll leave so you can have some privacy."

Stunned, Elizabeth remained silent for a moment as she sat in the tiny space surrounding her. "Thank you Dr. Price. I'll notify you once my brothers arrive." Dr. Price left the office. She was startled by a knock on the door.

A familiar voice called, "Elizabeth, are you in there?"

Ears still ringing from Dr. Price's news, Elizabeth said, "Yes, but you can come in if you like."

The door opened, and there stood Emma Jean Ward. "Elizabeth, may I sit beside you?" she asked softly.

"Yes, that would be fine," she replied softly with her head bent down.

"Did Dr. Price speak to you, Elizabeth? How are you doing?" Emma Jean asked, while patting her friend's shoulder.

"Yes. It's still unbelievable. I can't understand what is going on or what to do." Elizabeth had tears beginning to stream down her face.

"Well, you can't do anything but move on and focus on your dad's health. Finding a perfect match is the most important issue. I'm sorry you're hurting, Elizabeth, but things will be better. You'll have time later to deal with anything that you don't understand. Time has a way of healing all wounds," Emma Jean assured her as she hugged her childhood friend.

"Thanks, Emma Jean. I appreciate your concern, and please keep this confidential. I need to internalize this news, and then I can talk about it," Elizabeth mumbled through her tears.

"By all means, everything is confidential. If you need to talk to someone, I'm here for you." Emma Jean stood and left the room.

Elizabeth sat quietly trying to gather her thoughts as a wave of claustrophobia swept over her in the tiny room. She abruptly left; fresh air was what she needed to clear her mind.

"Elizabeth, I was going to look for you," Harrison announced as he came out of Buck's room. "Where were you? I've been waiting in your dad's room for some time now."

"I was in Dr. Price's office. He wanted privacy to explain the lab results with me," Elizabeth explained to her anxious husband as they walked back together towards Mr. Jones's room.

"You sound distressed, Elizabeth. What's going on?" He asked with concern.

"Well, Dad needs a blood transfusion, and Dr. Price felt I might be a good match." Elizabeth placed her hands over her face. "Dr. Price told me he ran the blood analysis twice to make sure the results were conclusive."

"What are you trying to tell me, Elizabeth?" He asked.

"I'm not a match. I can't give blood to my dad," Elizabeth mumbled softly.

"Well, that happens all the time, Elizabeth. You take things too hard sometimes. I'm sure one of your brothers will be able to donate their blood to your dad," He tried to console his grieving wife.

"No. You don't understand. There is no way possible Buck can be my father." she exclaimed with exasperation in her voice.

"What?" He exclaimed.

"Buck is not my biological father, and I have no idea what is going on or what to do. Now I have no idea who I am! I thought it was bad enough growing up a poor girl on the wrong side of the tracks. But at least then, I thought I knew who my family was. Now I'm an orphan, an unclaimed, unwanted infant."

Elizabeth was becoming hysterical. He knew he had to refocus her somehow.

"Elizabeth, this is not the time to think about lab results. You are Elizabeth Jones Davenport, a strong ambitious woman. Don't flounder in this news, Elizabeth. Continue with your plan of finding a donor for your father," he commanded her softly.

CHAPTER IX

OLD FRIENDS

Elizabeth leaned over to check on her father, softly rubbing his hands. There was a knock on the door. "Come in," She said, standing to greet the visitor.

Nurse Tori entered the room. "I'm here to check on Mr. Jones and take his vitals. How's he doing?"

"He is still resting and seems nonresponsive but much calmer since the last sedative," Elizabeth reported. "Will you give him something to help him rest through the night?"

"Sure will. But, let me check his vitals first, then maybe we can talk," Tori said with a smile. "Seems we have a lot to catch up on Elizabeth, don't you think?"

"That will be nice, Tori, to reminisce about the old days and catch up on your current life too." Elizabeth thought maybe there was hope to rekindle an old friendship but doubt clouded her thoughts.

"Give me about twenty minutes to complete my rounds, and I'll be right back Elizabeth," Nurse Tori said with a warm smile upon her face as she walked toward the hospital door.

"Sure. I'll be right here," Elizabeth assured Nurse Tori as she closed the door behind her.

Elizabeth sat in silence, trying to collect her thoughts. Suddenly, a knock on the door alerted her.

"Elizabeth, you ready for a break? Would you like to go to the cafeteria with me?" Nurse Tori said, poking her head into the hospital room twenty minutes later as promised.

"Yes. I need to get up and walk. A break would be nice. Do you want anything?"

"No, I'm fine; you two have a nice chat, and take your time Elizabeth.

I'll watch after your dad," he promised as the two women walked out of the room.

"This will be a treat on me. What would you like?" Tori asked looking at the menu posted on a chalkboard which rested on the counter top.

"Thanks, Tori. I'll have a small coffee with a lot of cream and a small tossed salad."

"Why don't you go ahead and get us a table," Tori instructed Elizabeth as she prepared to order their food.

Elizabeth found a corner table. Turning, she saw John Ross wiping the tables across from her. Hoping he wouldn't notice her sitting there, she turned her head toward the window.

"Well, well. You're back, you couldn't stand being apart from me," John Ross whispered leaning on the table where Elizabeth sat. "You just had to come back down and see me again. Didn't get a good enough look last visit, did you, Lizzy?"

"John Ross, that's Dr. Elizabeth Davenport to you. I understand you're a slow learner, so I'll wear my name tag next time," Elizabeth punched back, giving the ill willed man a stern gaze.

"John Ross, are you harassing Dr. Davenport?" Emma Jean questioned, appearing from around the corner.

"No. Nurse Emma Jean, I mean, Head Nurse Emma Jean. I'm not harassing anyone," John Ross bellowed. "To be honest, she is harassing me, keeps coming to the cafeteria to see me."

"John Ross, do I need to give you a goose egg...again?" Emma Jean asked as she sat down beside Elizabeth. "You get back behind the counter where you should be, John Ross. You're nothing but a nuisance to the human race."

"Which race you speaking of, Nurse Zebra?" John Ross asked, not nearly as quietly as he should have as he walked away with his middle finger pointing downward, beside his left pants leg.

"Just ignore stupidity," Elizabeth said to Emma Jean who did not seem shocked at John Ross's comment.

"You would think after all these years the man would mature, but I suppose some things never change," Emma Jean remarked sadly to Elizabeth.

"Hi, Emma Jean, I was hoping we would all get to eat together." Tori said as she sat their food on the table.

"I saw you talking to Elizabeth, so I went ahead and got an extra salad and soda for you...figured once you put John Ross in his place it wouldn't be wise to order food from him," Tori chuckled.

"Thanks, Tori. I'll pay you back later," Emma Jean replied. "I have about an hour then I must get back to the floor. So, we can chat awhile and reminisce about old times."

The three childhood friends sat and talked about their school days and how the village had doubled in size and the many good changes throughout the years. Elizabeth caught them up on her life, career path and marriage to Harrison. She waited with anticipation to hear her old friends take her down the path of their adulthood.

Elizabeth secretly wondered why the two of them had remained in Shadow Village.

The three old friends continued to talk. It was Elizabeth's turn to ask questions and she could not wait to hear about Emma Jean's life.

"Tell me all about your life, Emma Jean," Elizabeth wanted pertinent details.

"Elizabeth, I've had a great life… a lot of ups and downs, but for the most it has been good. After high school, I completed my nursing degree at the local community college and then went on to the University and completed my Masters. I have been working at the hospital nearly twenty years."

"How is your family doing?" Elizabeth inquired.

"Well, Troy and Roy both died about fifteen years ago in a head-on collision, out on the interstate. They were intoxicated. My parents never recovered from their deaths. Dad passed away with a rare lung disease five years ago, and my mama has been in Shadow Village Guardian Care for last year with early stages of dementia."

"I'm so sorry to hear about your losses, Emma Jean. Are you married?"

"No, and yes," Emma Jean laughed. "I was married for about seventeen years, but we have been divorced for three years now. We have one son, Terrance. He is fourteen going on twenty-five. A good kid, but like most teens, he thinks he knows everything."

"Well, it's about time we get back to work, Emma Jean," Tori abruptly said, with authority protruding from her voice.

"We still have about fifteen minutes, Tori. Hold on," Emma Jean reminded.

"Tori, what about you; are you married? Have any children? Where do you live?

"I'm not married, never been and don't intend to ever marry. I do have a partner," Tori said with a look of disgust. "I don't have kids, never wanted them. My red convertible will not accommodate car seats," Tori said with a solemn smile as she stood and walked toward the trashcan at the back of the cafeteria where John Ross was standing. The two of them chatted; their heads slightly close to keep their conversation private.

"Did I say something wrong, Emma Jean?" Elizabeth asked. "Tori seemed uneasy with my questions, even though they were the same ones I asked you."

"Don't worry Elizabeth, Tori is moody. I take her with a grain of salt.

Some days she'll speak, act like we're the best of friends, and other days she'll walk by me as if we are strangers. As for the marriage issue, let's just say Tori and I have worked together over 15 years, and I've never seen her partner," Emma Jean added. "I have no idea who the mystery person could be. Rumor has it she is, you know…a little on the strange side, has some personal turmoil with her choice to go in a different direction than most people in Shadow Village. Tori's choices aren't well received by most."

"Oh, I see," Elizabeth said. "Sometimes those types of relationships are difficult to negotiate with family members, friends, and the community, even within one's own mind. That could explain the moodiness. It is my opinion that everyone should accept, value, and respect the choices of others," Elizabeth preached. "Just listen to me. I'm sounding like the psychologist of Shadow Village. I surely hope Tori doesn't think I'm being judgmental, had no idea and frankly her personal affairs are surely none of my business." Elizabeth rounded her shoulders as Tori returned.

"Well ladies, I'm about ready to get back to work." Tori briskly gathered her things as John Ross slowly walked past the table. He threw a darting, intimidating gaze at Elizabeth. Elizabeth stared him directly in the eyes.

"See you later, Tori," John Ross shouted as he looked back at the women. Locking eyes with Elizabeth, he placed his right hand on the towel around his neck and then eased four of his fingers out of sight. His middle finger protruded as John Ross gazed with a smirk on his face.

"Tori, I did want to ask you one last thing, if you don't mind."

"Sure. What's on your mind now, Elizabeth?" Tori sharply replied as she gazed out the window, uninterested in the twenty questions game.

"I was wondering if you had kept in contact with Albert Joe through the years," Elizabeth asked quietly as she tried to make eye contact with Tori.

"I've purchased a few pigeons from him from time to time. I've always thought a lot of Albert Joe and his love of birds, as you might remember. It was a bond we shared as kids," Tori replied with her lips pursed. "Well, I must be on my way…you two can chat if you like."

Elizabeth noticed that Tori seemed very uncomfortable speaking of Albert Joe, and her cheeks were blushed. Something did not seem right, and Elizabeth wanted to quiz Tori with detailed questions, but it was not the time or place. There seemed to be a hush among the three women at the mention of Albert Joe's name.

Elizabeth broke the silence. "Well, I asked about Albert Joe because I'm having a little difficulty locating him. I know you love pigeons, Tori, and I was not sure if you had kept in contact with my brother. I'm sure Albert Joe will return my call soon, and he'll update me on his life."

"Elizabeth, you and Albert Joe were close growing up, and I'm sure he has missed you," Tori said as she stood to leave, brushing her hair out of her face with a quick stroke.

"Thanks Tori, your words are comforting," Elizabeth said. "Tori, your lapel pin is very beautiful. Where did you purchase such a unique pin?"

"My partner...I mean a friend gave it to me years ago. Have no idea where he purchased it. Yes, it is very unique, one of a kind I was told." Tori blushed as she reminded Emma Jean they should get back to work. "Hope to see more of you while you're in town, Elizabeth."

"Well, guess it's time for the two of us to report back to the floor. Tori has reminded me twice." Emma Jean said with a puzzled look. "We'll see you later, Elizabeth. Let us know if you need anything."

As Emma Jean and Tori walked away, Elizabeth shuffled her feet faster, "Just a minute. We can walk up together. That is, if you don't mind?"

Elizabeth placed her trash in the can near the cafeteria's entrance.

"Don't think I'll be in good company once you two leave. I'm sure John Ross will be glad we're out of his hair. Besides, I need to get back and check on my dad."

"Emma Jean, we have a good five minutes until we need to clock in," Tori said, walking ahead of her friends with body language that spoke loud and clear as her arms moved swiftly against her jacket in a power walking mode.

"What's wrong with Tori?" Elizabeth asked Emma Jean.

"Tell you later, Elizabeth...long story. Remember, I told you Tori can be very moody sometimes. Guess this is one of those times." Emma Jean reported as the two of them walked toward the elevator. Tori stood anxiously waiting and repeatedly tapping the "up" button with eagerness to board.

Tori and Emma Jean returned to the nurse's station each going to their assigned post; Elizabeth went to her Dad's room.

"Harrison, how is Dad doing?" Elizabeth asked placing her purse in the coat closet.

"About the same; Buck hasn't made any attempt to wake up. Nurse Bentley just took his vitals. She told me the doctor wouldn't be back until early morning," he reported. "Think I'll go on to the hotel and turn in for the night. I'll be back in the morning."

Elizabeth and Harrison embraced, and said goodnight. Once he left, she sat in the recliner and covered herself with the soft blanket Harrison had packed for her. She could not help but feel uneasy, as if trouble was in the air, but she was not sure why. Suddenly, Elizabeth felt spooked; the hospital room became extremely cold. The hairs on the back of her neck began to stand up. She did not like the feeling of someone or something watching her. She cocked her head toward the hospital door. She heard a cracking noise as the door slowly began to close covering the shadow standing in the threshold. A cold chill ran through Elizabeth's body as she recognized the silhouette of Nurse Tori. Elizabeth refused to feel intimidated by new or old spirits. She was determined to be at ease. She slowly dozed off into a light sleep, clutching her blanket and book.

Dr. Price arrived in the early morning and checked her Dad's vitals. "Elizabeth, I'll have the nurses keep a closer watch on your dad today. He isn't doing as well as I would like."

Dr. Price nodded his head and left the hospital room. The door closed behind him.

A minute later Elizabeth was startled from deep reverie by a light knock on the door. "Come in," Elizabeth responded. She wondered why Dr. Price had returned so quickly, but to her surprise, Harrison stood in the doorway.

"Good morning. I thought maybe Dr. Price had forgotten a piece of his medical gear. He just stepped out of the room. You had to pass him in the hall."

"I don't recall passing anyone," He replied. "What was his report this morning?"

"Dr. Price didn't say much, just checked Dad's vitals and shook his head. Said he was still waiting on a couple of lab reports. I'm sure it's the liver panel he wants to review," Elizabeth said. "From the look of Dad's skin, the report will not be too promising. I think Dad's health has declined. His breathing has been more sporadic during the night," a teary-eyed Elizabeth said.

"You have to stay focused, Elizabeth. I know it is difficult for you. Perhaps it will help matters when your brothers arrive. Were you successful in reaching either of them?" he asked.

"No, but I left a message for Albert Joe, so maybe he'll return my call," Elizabeth replied with little confidence, but at that same moment, her cell phone did, in fact, ring.

"Here's your cell, Elizabeth. Perhaps its Albert Joe calling," He said hopefully.

"Dr. Elizabeth Jones Davenport speaking, how can I assist you?" Elizabeth spoke into the receiver with professional curtness.

"I'm returning a call from my sister, Lizzy. I must a dialed the wrong number. Sorry, ma'am," bellowed a rough, but kind, voice on the other end of the line.

"Albert, Albert Joe this is me, your sister, Lizzy." Elizabeth said quickly.

"Darn, Sis—you a doctor?" he asked incredulously.

"Yes Albert Joe. Listen—Dad is in the hospital. He has to have a blood transfusion or he'll die. You have to get here as quick as possible." Elizabeth paced the floor, looking out the window in search of her brother. "Where are you? Can you come to Shadow Village Hospital?" Elizabeth had so many questions and needed answers to settle her mind.

"Calm down, Elizabeth, your voice is breaking up. Bad reception, I suppose," Albert Joe paused. "I'm on my way home. Been in Mexico on business. I had a layover in Dallas but should be boarding soon," Albert Joe explained. "I'll try to be at the hospital tonight," he added.

"Good, Albert Joe. That makes me feel much better," Elizabeth sighed. "Did you have knowledge there was a fire in the mill village? Our whole street was destroyed."

"I've been in touch with the fire chief, Sis. He's keeping me updated," Albert Joe replied. "I'll have my cell phone on my hip. Call me if anything changes with Dad, and soon as I land, I'll give you a ring."

"Albert Joe, please get to the hospital soon. Dad and I need you." Elizabeth said with tears beginning to stream down her face.

After a long pause, Albert Joe spoke, "I know, Lizzy. I'm on my way."

Elizabeth heard a clicking sound and then silence on the other end of the line. "Albert Joe, are you there?"

Elizabeth turned to Harrison, "Hmmm...apparently bad connection, lost him, wanted to ask if he had Sam's number."

"I'm sure Albert Joe will contact Sam. Most importantly, Albert Joe is on his way home. Does that lift your spirits, Elizabeth?" he asked, but Elizabeth just stared out the window in deep thought.

Throughout the long day at the hospital, Harrison stayed by his wife's side, assisting as needed. Elizabeth remained close to her sleeping Dad who showed no improvement. Around midnight, Albert Joe called to say he had just arrived in town and would be at the hospital at sunrise. Elizabeth was boiling with anger.

Harrison, in attempts to calm his wife, said, "Elizabeth, there's nothing Albert Joe can do this late...best he get some rest from his trip to Mexico. It makes sense to me that he rest before coming to the hospital."

"You're correct. I'm still disappointed with Albert Joe's nonchalant attitude. He didn't even ask if there were any changes in Dad's condition," she replied in a nearly screeching voice.

"You have to remember: Albert Joe has remained in Shadow Village and is well known in the community. It's highly possible that he has been updated regularly on your Dad's condition. Take it easy and try to relax," he calmly said.

"Take advantage of the cot, Elizabeth. It actually looks comfortable. I'm sleeping in the recliner tonight. I'm not leaving you alone. No arguing with me, young lady."

Harrison turned the light out but kept his eyes glued on Buck as he mumbled and tossed in his bed. Did he have something he needed to say to his daughter? If so, he wanted to know so he could break the news to his wife who was not doing so well herself.

Elizabeth slowly succumbed to the voices calling her name, voices she knew all too well. Elizabeth felt her body falling like a snowflake on a cold, dark night. She had fought the dreams while at the hospital, struggling to avoid the sleep disturbances. Furthermore, Elizabeth had fought the dark illusions her husband called tormenting nightmares for most of her life.

That night she did not have the strength to fight anyone or anything. It was apparent the darkness wanted the undivided attention of her heart, mind, and soul.

Elizabeth's mind searched feverishly for a small ray of light to avoid another episode of the frightful movie that would play out in her mind. It was time for the late night show to roll, and Elizabeth only desired rest for her weary body and protective healing for her dad.

The bottled-up questions needed answers, and she had to be willing to answer their call or the movie clips would spin out of control. Submitting to the demands of the voice invading her mind, Elizabeth waited patiently. She knew that Harrison would rescue her if the nightmares got out of hand. She felt safe with him in the same room.

It was time for Elizabeth to confront the demons that had tormented her for decades. She wanted to be free of their calls. Her body seemed to float above the cotton mill in the midst of Shadow Village, overlooking Mr. Jack Bradford's two-story house that out shined all the other houses in the village.

She heard many voices, voices of men, women, the voice of her mother and father, a baby crying, a woman screaming. The visions were too vivid, and Elizabeth wanted out. She wanted to wake up from the nightmare as she felt her body shaking uncontrollably with fear. There was no turning back. The film rolling seemed to mock the pain in Elizabeth's mind.

Silently floating above a dark gloomy room in the basement of Mr. Jack Bradford's house, she saw medical equipment, patient beds, cabinets and huge sinks with long sprayers lining the wall. Her eyes were spellbound.

The room was cold, dark and uninviting. A long slender table was protruding from a metal door near the back of the room. There was a body on the table, but it was covered with a white sheet. Elizabeth could not see the face of the body that lay helplessly, perhaps dead.

Elizabeth glanced around the room at the stacks of fluffy blankets. The top shelf held blue blankets, the second, pink, and the third, black. A stack of wood crates with attached lids sat beside the cabinet.

Elizabeth had never seen the blankets so clearly in previous dreams. She felt the morbid spirit of death overtaking her body. She cried out for rescue to no avail. Harrison was in a deep sleep.

The crates were grouped in twos, and three areas separated the crates throughout the cold room. Signs above the three areas answered her question about the colored blankets. A pink sign was nailed above one area noting "girl", blue noted "boy", and the third sign was nothing but a piece of wood painted solid black. The crates under the black sign were nailed shut with the edge of a black blanket exposed through the opened slats. Did this symbolize death? Elizabeth was spellbound as her eyes carried her around the room numerous times.

The other two areas that housed the crates were open and beautiful pink and blue blankets overflowed the open lids. Elizabeth's mind wanted to reveal the contents of the crates that were nailed closed.

The morbid feeling of death was even stronger with such thoughts. She was sure the silence in this area was that of death.

Elizabeth glanced once again toward the areas where she saw the pink and blue blankets in the crates. A peaceful feeling flowed through her body. The lids were open as if to invite her to view the contents.

Focusing on the two crates underneath the pink sign, she saw movement within the crates. In the center of each crate was a beautiful tiny newborn, swaddled in a pink fluffy blanket, emitting cries that were so faint they sounded like a newborn kitten.

Likewise, the crates underneath the blue sign each housed an infant swaddled in a blue blanket. The infants were tiny but beautiful. Slowly wiggling in the crates, the infants seemed content with the softness of the fluffy blankets.

Elizabeth twisted and turned on the cot, trying to wake up from the dreadful twilight zone. It was the same nightmare that had haunted her for decades, even as a young child. Only this time, she could see details within the room and hear the voices of the people. A shadow of a man appeared. Who was this person? Never before had she experience such vivid details.

The man slowly turned and faced the light under the pink sign. He was gazing at the crates with uncertainty in his eyes. Elizabeth was shocked to see the face of Buck. If only she could identify the other people in the room, maybe she could put her mind to rest with the puzzle solved at last.

She began to focus upon the shadow of the second man in the room, and she was not only shocked but fear consumed her body. The man was wearing a white uniform jacket, the same jacket worn by the male supervisors at the cotton mill in Shadow Village. Through the mist in the room, she struggled to see the name sewn on the left side of the jacket. If only she could get a glimpse, she would surely recognize the name and piece her nightmare into some type of normality.

At last, the man sporting the white jacket turned to face the table with his hands raised in the mid air. He was screaming profanity at the top of his lungs. Elizabeth had a clear view of the name, "Jack Bradford." She had no idea why Mr. Bradford was screaming at her father. Why was her father in such a cold, dreadful room with Jack Bradford? As Jack Bradford continued to scream, Buck stared at him fearlessly.

"Some men find it easier to kill, Buck, than to face reality. You are a foolish, poverty-stricken, no good excuse of a man. That woman that you call your wife has always had a roving eye, Buck. Why can't you just admit it? Don't worry, Bucky boy, no one will ever know what took place here tonight." Buck stood tall without blinking an eye as the accuser continued ranting threats.

"I sure will not utter a word and risk my reputation on such trash as you and that piece of meat on the table. You old fool, take your woman home and grab the crate with the pink blanket, that is, the crate which has 'J' printed on top of the lid. The contents in that crate belong to you, Buck. You take that crate and run for your life, you fool. Can you even read, Buck? The 'J' is for Jones. No wonder your woman lusted after other men, you're an illiterate fool."

Buck turned around several times as he tried to find the pink crate and figure out how to assist the semiconscious woman on the table. Tears flowed freely down his ghostly colored face. He prayed for strength to save his wife and infant from the powers of evil that blinded his sight, causing him to stumble in a sober stupor.

"Bucky boy, you arrived just in time…minutes later and the problem would have been solved for good. I just lost thousands of dollars on this deal because of your ignorant self," Jack Bradford screamed, as Buck quickly plunged toward the crates. "Remember, Buck…you utter a word, and I'll come for you and the rest of your family. Get out of here before I change my mind. Wealthy folks across the tracks had bids on that baby girl of yours. You ruined that for me."

"You're an evil demon, Jack Bradford. I pray God will have mercy on your sick soul and not send you to hell to burn!" Buck yelled as he rushed to the two crates with pink blankets. He picked up the first crate he saw, not noticing the initials scribbled on the lids.

Jack Bradford continued to scream with his fists in the air. "Remember, once you get out of my basement your lips are sealed or you'll be minus that baby girl I spared. You utter a word, Bucky boy, and I'll be standing on your front porch banging on that dilapidated screen door. I'll take your entire family hostage and kill you, burn you in my incinerator. Best to keep your mouth shut."

Bradford scrambled toward him shouting, "I told you to get out of my basement. Run, Buck. Run like hell. Run like the devil is after you and your sorry, no good wife, and take that baby girl with you. Keep the crate as a souvenir."

Elizabeth heard the sound of feet scrambling up the steel steps; faint whimpers came from the baby wrapped in the pink blanket.

An object suddenly flew out the top of the crate, Buck stumbled on the steps as he recovered and replaced the small music box securely at the foot of the crate.

Elizabeth saw Buck glance at the initial "H" on the top of the crate lid. He panted for breath as he ran through the darkness, holding the crate with one hand and pressing on the back of the lifeless woman draped across his shoulder with the other. Buck stumbled several times, nearly falling to the hard ground.

Buck heard the banging of the music box inside the crate. Thoughts of how such an item had found its way into an infant's bedding crossed his mind for only a second. He had more important things to worry about than a music box. He had to make it safely home and prepare for battle in case evil knocked on his door.

Buck felt a sense of relief as he saw the shed at the back of his lot. A few more strides and he could embrace safety. He had to keep running for his wife and his baby to claim safety. He noticed fewer cries from the tiny infant in the crate, but by then his wife was moaning.

Elizabeth begged to exit her nightmare as the woman slowly turned her face. There was no doubt; it was the distressed face of Katie Mae Jones. Many questions invaded Elizabeth's mind as the nightmare continued.

Elizabeth's body was drenched with sweat as she pleaded again to leave the nightmare. Without a rescuer, the drama would continue. She was doubtful she could remember the late night thriller. Elizabeth wanted to recall every moment of the link to her lost childhood.

Elizabeth flipped on her stomach, buried her face in her pillow and hoped to be released from the tormenting performance before her eyes. She had seen enough for one night. Griping the sides of the cot, Elizabeth remained face down until she caught a glimpse of light peeking through the window of Buck's hospital room.

She had survived the nightmarish vision, but how could she ever explain the reality snippets to her husband, to anyone?

CHAPTER X

REUNITED

A loud knock at the door startled Elizabeth. "Just a minute," she said in a low tone but loud enough for the person at the door to hear. She jumped up and brushed her hair from her face.

"Excuse me; is this Mr. Buck's room?" A tall handsome man wearing a cowboy hat stood in the doorway, and he tipped his hat. His voice sounded vaguely familiar to Elizabeth, but she could not place it or his face.

"Yes. I'm his daughter, Dr. Elizabeth Jones Davenport. Albert Joe, is that you?" she asked through sleepy eyes and a foggy brain. She needed coffee, fast.

"Sure is, Sis! Buck's oldest son," he teased as he walked over to assess his father lying on the hospital bed. He then walked in the direction of his sister to take a closer look at her.

"You are a grown up version of Lizzy. Good to see you at last. Sorry about the delay, you'll have to forgive me. The trip to Mexico was stressful, and I knew I wouldn't be of any assistance to you in such condition," Albert Joe explained while embracing his sister.

Elizabeth felt odd to be so close to the brother she had not seen in over thirty years. She was not comfortable; something seemed awkward to Elizabeth as she pulled away from her brother's arms.

"I understand," Elizabeth softly replied, hinting her doubt in her elder brother's confession.

Albert Joe sat down beside his sister and looked at the recliner. "Is someone else here with you, Lizzy?"

"Yes, my husband slept in the recliner last night to keep me company and to help with Dad if needed," Elizabeth said. "He's an early riser...most likely in the cafeteria getting some coffee."

"Oh my, hope he didn't strike up a conversation with John Ross

Johnson," Albert Joe replied while he rolled his eyes upward in a negative manner.

"Well, tell me all about Elizabeth Jones Davenport," Albert Joe said with a big grin. "What do you do for a living? Am I an uncle?"

"I'm been married for over thirty years to Harrison Davenport. He's a wonderful man who is approaching retirement. We've never had children. Recently, we built our dream home in Brevard, North Carolina," Elizabeth continued, "I've had a wonderful life with Harrison. He is the love of my life. I'm sure you'll enjoy talking with him, Albert Joe."

"Well, looks as if we have a lot to catch up on, but for now update me on Dad's condition and prognosis," Albert Joe requested with concern as he leaned back in the chair, crossing his legs in a more relaxed manner, placing his hat on the bedside table.

"Albert Joe, Dad's condition is not stable. His doctor is coming by to speak with us. I do know it is crucial that he receive a blood transfusion. Seems I'm not a good match for Dad. Will you volunteer, Albert Joe?" Elizabeth pleaded.

"Sure, why wouldn't I? I'll go and let the nurse know…maybe they can go ahead and draw the blood," Albert Joe said as he stood and placed his hat upon his head, yawning to show his lack of sleep.

As Albert Joe turned to leave the room, Elizabeth noticed a small pigeon lapel on the collar of his black shirt. Once at the door she turned around noting Albert Joe's tall stature. She felt proud to have such a seemly well-rounded man as her brother.

The door closed and in a few minutes Elizabeth heard her name.

"Elizabeth, where are you, dear?" Harrison asked as he entered the room with two cups of coffee.

"I'm in the bathroom…freshening up a little," she replied.

"You didn't sleep too well last night, did you?" Harrison reported to his bleary-eyed wife. "I heard you tossing and turning. When you seemed to settle down, I didn't see the need to wake you. Did you have another nightmare?"

"Albert Joe is here, Harrison. He just went to the nurse's station to let them know he is willing to be a blood donor. Hopefully, he's a good match," Elizabeth reported to her husband. "He is tall and handsome and looks so good in his cowboy hat. I'm so proud of him. He seems to be a wonderful man."

"Did you say Albert Joe is wearing a cowboy hat?" Harrison inquired with a puzzled look on his face.

"Yes. Why?" Elizabeth asked.

"I just saw a tall man matching that description in the small office near the nurse's station with your friend, Nurse Tori. They seem to really know each other very well," Harrison said as he placed the coffee cups on the table.

"Why is there sarcasm in your voice, Harrison?" "For starters, they were embracing each other. They seemed rather intense," he reported with confusion on his face.

"Oh. Maybe Tori was updating Albert Joe on Dad's condition and perhaps consoling him, you know, out of respect."

"No. You misunderstood me, dear. Elizabeth, the door was partially opened. I'm sure they didn't know someone could see them. They were kissing, and it was not out of concern. It was passionate."

"That's not possible, Harrison. I asked Tori if she had kept up with Albert Joe, and she informed me she'd only purchased a couple pigeons throughout the years. Said she didn't know where he was, didn't keep up with his life," Elizabeth informed Harrison.

"Don't shoot the messenger, Elizabeth...just telling you what I saw. Now, there may be several men walking around Shadow Village Hospital that meet that description, but I don't think there is another man with a cowboy hat on the same hospital floor we are in," Harrison replied.

"What color was his shirt?" she asked.

"Black...long sleeves with a colorful pigeon on the back," he replied to his wife, beginning to tire of this game.

"I'm puzzled..." she said, her voice trailing. "I was under the impression Tori is the same sex as her partner."

Before Elizabeth could say more, the door opened, and Albert Joe entered the room.

"Nurse Tori went ahead and got the lab tech to draw my blood...put a rush on the results...should know something within the hour," Albert Joe stopped and extended his hand. "You must be the Harrison Davenport I've heard all about."

"Good to meet you, Albert Joe," Harrison shook his brother-in-law's hand and sat down beside Elizabeth.

"Well, guess all we can do is stay for the lab results," Albert Joe said with a grand smile.

"Albert Joe, I didn't know you and Tori had remained good friends," Elizabeth pried.

"We're not. We sorta lost contact years ago when we all went our separate ways," Albert Joe replied, looking at the floor as his entire face resembled a hot pepper ripened in the sun. "Why are you asking, Sis? You still have that lawyer voice you had as a young girl," Albert Joe chuckled as he turned his face toward the window.

There was a long silence. Then the phone in the hospital room rang.

"Hello, may I help you?" Elizabeth asked. "Well, that's good news. Thanks for the information, Tori. I'll let Albert Joe know."

"You're a perfect match, Albert Joe." Elizabeth reported. "Tori are escorting you to the lab. She'll be here in few minutes…said it would take about two hours for the procedure."

"Well, soon as it is completed, I'll be sure to have them escort me back to this room," Albert Joe promised.

"Albert Joe, Nurse Tori has offered to stay with you during the entire process, which should be comforting to know. Maybe you two can catch up on lost years since you went separate ways after high school," Elizabeth said with a hint of sarcasm that went unnoticed by her brother.

Nurse Tori came and escorted Albert Joe to the lab. They returned about three hours later…smiling and chatty.

"Albert Joe has been given strict instructions to rest in the recliner, or better yet, on the cot, for the rest of the day," Tori announced as she gave Albert Joe a wink of the eye.

Nurse Tori closed the door to Buck's room as she left.

There was silence in the room.

Buck remained unresponsive as his son's blood dripped slowly into his fragile veins.

As the day progressed, Elizabeth and Harrison returned to the hospital after spending some time away from Albert Joe. Rather than pursue their suspicions about what might be going on between Albert Joe and Nurse Tori, they decided to concentrate on the main reason they were together: Buck's health. "Besides, there will be plenty of time to quiz Albert Joe," Elizabeth reported with a hint of concern.

Albert Joe and Elizabeth sat together with fond memories as they continued to reminiscence about their childhood. They tried to avoid negativity as they watched over their father. It would have been easy for Elizabeth to bring up her battle with nightmares and her childhood plagued with too much responsibility, but that would not have accomplished anything. Making peace was more important.

"Albert Joe, where is Sam? Has he been contacted?" Elizabeth braced herself for her elder brother to speak.

Albert Joe's laugh startled Elizabeth.

"Albert Joe, keep it down—Dad is resting." Elizabeth chastised her brother lovingly.

"Sorry, Sis I forgot…I should have told you earlier about our younger brother. Sam's home is in Mexico, and he has a small house located on my land, not too far from here. You see, he and I own the business, Jones' Pigeon Farm. Samuel is, indeed, a fine man…an excellent partner with the family business not to mention he is making a fortune selling cars," Albert Joe reported.

Albert Joe explained that Sam's passion had always been cars and trucks.

"He buys a few here and there and parks them on my land. You wouldn't believe the sales he gets. Everything Sam touches turns to gold,"

Albert Joe said. "Yep, Sam is a progressive and successful business man. You'd be proud of him, Sis."

"I'm very proud of you both, Albert Joe. I'll be glad to see Sam," Elizabeth said with a gleam of hope in her voice. "Albert Joe, are you okay? Do you feel lightheaded? You should continue to rest as the nurse instructed. I'll have Harrison go and get us something to eat from the cafeteria."

"I'm fine, Sis. Just hope Dr. Price will come on and give us a good report on Dad. Hope this blood transfusion will surely be the answer to our prayers." Albert Joe wiped his face with a handkerchief with the letter "J" monogrammed in the center.

Elizabeth noticed a small-embossed pigeon in the corner. She was impressed with her brother's ability to search for the finest handkerchief.

Elizabeth was proud that her two brothers had actually made it out of the mill village. They were both owners of successful and thriving businesses, fine citizens of their hometown. She looked forward to reuniting with her youngest brother.

"Elizabeth, I called Sam after I spoke to you, and he's in route to the hospital from a car show…not sure what state he was in…didn't even bother to ask him," Albert Joe said as he rubbed his hands against his pants leg. "He should be here soon, and I know he'll be glad to meet you, Elizabeth Jones Davenport."

Suddenly Elizabeth heard a faint sound. It was Buck calling for his daughter. "Liz, where are you?"

Elizabeth walked over and patted her father's hand. "Dad, I'm right here beside you, and so is Albert Joe. Sam is on his way."

Her father stared straight ahead. Elizabeth wiped a tear that slowly fell from the corner of one eye.

Harrison knocked on the door and walked in with three cups of coffee and food for everyone.

"Thanks, Harrison," Elizabeth whispered.

Albert Joe stood to assist Harrison with distributing the food. Elizabeth caught him as he stumbled like a drunken ballerina.

"Albert Joe. Sit down before you break your leg. We'd have to get you a bed beside Dad," Elizabeth said with a hint of rebellion.

About that time, Nurse Tori came in to attend to Buck. She winked at Albert Joe and notified everyone that Dr. Price was seeing patients.

Nurse Tori left as Dr. Price entered the room. He pulled the curtain around Buck's bed. "Your Dad's condition is still critical," he reported to the family. "The good news is that the blood transfusion has been successful thus far, thanks to Albert Joe. Your dad will remain in ICU for some time because of the cirrhosis of his liver. A more concrete prognosis depends upon several things. First, we have to watch to make sure he truly is tolerating the blood transfusion. Secondly, we have to watch his liver panels. Your dad's liver is slowly shutting down; his skin has already turned a pale yellow. That's not a good sign," Dr. Price explained carefully. "The lacerations he sustained are another concern because of possible infections. We'll watch this and be as proactive as possible. I highly recommend that a family member stay with Mr. Jones, and other family members should be on alert and stay close by to the hospital just in case Mr. Jones takes a turn for the worse," Dr. Price said shaking everyone's hand as he walked out the door.

Elizabeth followed Dr. Price into the hall and asked to speak to him privately in his office. She asked him to explain why her blood was not a match for her father.

"Elizabeth, you of all people should know lab tests can be inconclusive," he said with a look of compassion on his face and doubt bleeding through his words.

"Yes, I know that is true, Dr. Price but I also know that the test was completed twice and the results were the same each time," Elizabeth persisted.

Dr. Price walked over to Elizabeth and sat down beside her. "I don't know how to say this, but the DNA is conclusive. The possibility of Buck being your father is very unlikely, my dear, as I've tried to explain."

"So it is true—he isn't my real father—he isn't my birth father?" Elizabeth sobbed as she cupped her hands together, twisting them into a tight ball. Shame overwhelmed her body.

"Elizabeth, I'm so sorry to be the one to give such devastating news to you. This is not your fault. There could be any number of explanations, be positive in your thoughts." Dr. Price patted Elizabeth on the shoulder. "You know, Elizabeth, of course you wouldn't remember, but it was a common occurrence for young, unwed mothers to place their babies for adoption when you and your brothers were coming along, it is possible that this could have been the case with you, perhaps?"

"What you trying to say?" Elizabeth asked as tears fell from her cheeks.

"Well, maybe your biological mother was an unwed young woman, wanted you to have a home with a complete family—a mother and a father, so she placed you up for adoption? It is a thought," Dr. Price said in hopes to ease Elizabeth's mind. "That would surely deem your parents as rescuers, Elizabeth. That says a lot about their character…to take an unwanted baby in their home."

"With all due respect Dr. Price, my parents didn't adopt me. They didn't have the financial funds for a private adoption or the cognitive ability to complete such a tedious task with the required paperwork," Elizabeth replied with a sharp tone that spoke volumes about her troubled mind.

There were many possibilities rambling in Elizabeth's head, yet no answers were known, except the fact her DNA proved Buck was not her biological father. Elizabeth extended her hand thanking Dr. Price for his expertise and care for her father. Walking toward his office door, Dr. Price nodded with understanding.

Elizabeth returned to her father's room with many unanswered questions weighing heavily on her heart as her mind wandered back to the nightmare she encountered the previous night in the room. That hospital cot had given her something to reflect upon as she searched for answers. That was more than the answers Dr. Price was able to give.

Buck was asleep when Elizabeth returned. She sat between Harrison and Albert Joe. They looked puzzled and Elizabeth wondered why all the curiosity in their eyes. Suddenly she heard someone in the bathroom and as the door slowly opened she saw a familiar face standing in the doorway.

"Sam. Is that you?" Elizabeth shouted covering her mouth to silence her squeal.

"Sam, I am." Her brother rhymed with a chuckle in his voice, standing tall and lean, dressed like he just walked out of an important business meeting.

It was the face of her baby brother Samuel Jones. He had arrived at the hospital.

Buck slept peacefully. Harrison suggested that the siblings go and eat supper while he stayed with their father. Elizabeth walked between her brothers to the hospital cafeteria in silence and sat at a table. She prayed John Ross Johnson was off his shift. They needed privacy.

She learned that her brothers had worked hard to complete their education and each made a good living. She was proud her brothers were well groomed, exhibiting excellent manners, and abreast on current events. Elizabeth was extraordinarily proud of the two successful entrepreneurs.

The conversation was primarily about the care of their father. Elizabeth wanted to know how he was surviving financially, what he did during the day, and if he was still heavily drinking. Albert Joe answered most of the questions.

"Well, Sis." Albert Joe said as he lowered his head and stationed his folded hands on his lap. "Dad remains at the home place because it is his home. It was in good shape...before the fire. We remodeled the house some years ago, giving Dad one large room for a kitchen and den and a small bedroom that had a half bath. Enough room for him to live comfortably," Albert Joe explained. "Feed bags and farming machinery parts were stored in the rest of the house. Basically, the house and lot were used as extra storage space for Jones' Pigeon Farm."

"I understand the set up, and I know Dad enjoyed spending time at the old home place," Elizabeth abruptly said with a smile upon her face to show her approval. "But, was Dad productive...did he work?"

"Well, we gave Dad odd jobs to keep him busy…let him earn his keep," Sam added with a slight smile. "He cleaned the barns, fed and cared for the animals in the pasture, and kept stock of the feed bags and parts."

"Sounds like you both kept Dad really busy." Elizabeth had a satisfied grin.

"Dad's a good man, a hard worker. As you know, he has lived a hard life. Now he's paying for his choices," Sam said with misty eyes and pity.

"Heck, once in awhile he would even pick up the phone and remind us to reorder items when the stock was getting low," Albert Joe said in hopes to lighten the serious mood within the room.

"We did everything we could to make it easy for Dad," Albert Joe assured Elizabeth. "We hired a local gal who stopped by twice a week to check in on him, do light cleaning, and keep him company."

"Dad said she was taking our money…all she did was sit on the sofa watching soap operas all day, eating his food. He often called her a lollygagger." Sam threw his hands in the air. "Just couldn't do anything to please the man."

Samuel looked at his sister, "You know, Lizzy, he never got over your leaving, and he has always loved you. I'm glad you've been successful and hope we can stay in touch. It's been hard on Dad not having Mom around to care for him…and then not having you, either…well, that was equally hard on him in the end."

"Guess it hurts to talk about Mama. I suppose the alcohol removes the pain…that is…for a short time," Albert Joe said as he tilted his head toward the ceiling.

Elizabeth asked Albert Joe, "What will happen to Dad now? Where shall he live once he's released from the hospital? I mean…since his house burned, he has nowhere to go."

"Dad can live with me until the insurance is settled, and he decides what he wants to do. I've got the space and will have health care provided as needed, but he may want to rebuild on his lot, that is if the town will allow reconstruction. The man loves the cotton mill village. It's in his blood and he has declared he will never be a resident of the Assistive Living Home across the tracks," Albert Joe said. "I'll need to check on the zoning ordinance, but I'll have plenty of time for that as Dad heals."

"We passed the living center on the way to the hospital. The landscape is beautiful," Elizabeth said with hope of a new home for their Dad. Her eyes lit up at the possibility of him living in such a beautiful place, similar to Maple Leaf Avenue.

Albert Joe patted his sister's shoulder. "Take it easy, Sis. Don't rush the old man. He is set in his ways and stubborn beyond your wildest imagination. Trust us. Dad will not agree to living anywhere but behind the cotton mill."

Sam added, "Dad might be like old man Bradford and outlive his family. Yep. Rumor has it that Jack Bradford outlived his wife and dog. Many still declare he is an active businessman, but, we're not sure what business he is practicing since he retired from the cotton mill over thirty years ago and hasn't been seen since. His house looks like it is lived in most of the time."

Albert Joe chimed in: "Rumors still float around the mill village that the mill yard crew continues to take care of the Bradford's lawn. Most likely to make the old cotton mill shine, lure in potential workers. It could be nothing but gossip floating around the village."

Samuel nodded to show his approval of his brother's comments adding, "Albert Joe, I was over that way the other week …not too sure the grass has been cut lately. Someone is falling down on the job. Well, guess it's a good thing old man Bradford remains hidden because he has never been a liked man in the community."

"Goodness Samuel, didn't you know Jack Bradford was actually a sought after man?"

"No Albert Joe. Never knew that. Are you kidding me?" Samuel smirked.

"Well, little brother…the women must have liked him because they sure did chase after Bradford, old and young ones. Rumor always was Bradford had a way with the women because he was a wealthy man," Albert Joe declared.

"That old man Bradford might be making moonshine in his basement. Heck, for all we know Dad is getting his weekly delivery from Bradford," Sam added with a laugh.

"Don't think that's correct, Sam. Dad always hated old man Bradford—still calls him a lethal crate farmer. He wouldn't take free water from that man, much less buy moonshine."

"Well, that sounds like our dad. He gets a disliking for someone and never trusts them again. Dad probably holds Bradford's poor farming skills against him. He always called old man Bradford a sorry, no good, lousy crate farmer," Sam said with a harsh tone.

As Elizabeth listened to the conversation, an uneasy feeling slowly crept up her neck choking her.

"Well, everyone knows Old man Bradford owns the only house standing on the street behind the dilapidated cotton mill. The same street called home by numerous other families. Heck, it is the only house in the mill village that has a basement," Albert Joe reported.

Elizabeth heard Albert Joe's slip of the tongue. "Albert Joe, I wasn't aware Mr. Bradford's house had a basement."

"Well, about time we head back to Dad's hospital room," Albert Joe said, ignoring Elizabeth's questioning invitation for more information.

"Well, I'm ready. I think I need some fresh air," Elizabeth said as she stood and smoothed her long black hair, making sure every strand was in place.

Back in her dad's room, Elizabeth recalled her dream as her brothers and husband chatted. She could not help but wonder if her dream was somehow real. She has so many unanswered questions, so many things she needed to find out before leaving Shadow Village. It may be necessary to prolong her traveling back to North Carolina for few days, but that would require her to purchase some lounge clothing, which would be much more comfortable.

Elizabeth was feeling very tired. She needed her soft blanket, anxiety medication, and total quietness. "Harrison, I really would like to go to the hotel and rest. We can return early morning," Elizabeth said. Just maybe, somehow she could sort through the conflicting thoughts within her mind in the quietness of their hotel room.

The ride to the hotel was short and pleasant. She made mental notes of her upcoming day. Returning to the hospital would require Elizabeth to plan a detailed agenda including questions to ask Dr. Price.

For the time being, all was well. Her brothers were watching over their father. Suddenly Elizabeth had a cold chill hit her body causing her to feel uncertain about many things that had taken place during the day. Too much had occurred in one single day, and her mind was racing too fast to comprehend the details, events, and possible outcome.

At last, the lights were out, and the Davenports were in bed. Elizabeth prayed for a peaceful night as she felt herself drifting off to sleep. Harrison's arm rested on her shoulder as he slept soundly.

"No. No. Please don't torment me with dreams. I need answers but, I'm way too tired," Elizabeth mumbled in her sleep.

She reluctantly succumbed to the calls of the twilight, wondering when the final chapter would evolve and bring the closure she so desperately needed. If she could only remember, understand her past, her childhood, maybe she could put the anxiety and panic attacks to rest and move forward with her life. Elizabeth longed for brighter days with her attentive husband, days free from the dreams and the nightmares.

Suddenly, Elizabeth became fascinated. She heard the voice of her father talking to her mother. "Look, that's the biggest billboard sign I've ever seen, Katie Mae." The colorful billboard proclaimed, "Men's night out," displaying a group of men sitting at a card table toasting with their bottle of South Carolina's best-brewed beer.

"Buck, you miss those days, don't you?" Katie Mae asked her husband.

"I can't say that I do, Katie Mae. Anyway, I made a vow to be a better husband and father," Buck said. "Gotta do my part to prove to you I'm a changed man, Katie Mae."

"Buck, don't be too hard on you. I don't mind you playing a game of cards with your buddies now and then…long as you don't wander home sloppy drunk," Katie Mae explained with a serious glance at her husband who was driving with his right hand, his left arm rested in a bent position on the edge of the open window.

"Katie Mae, I hope you see I'm really trying to be a changed man for our family. Can't hold my beer or whiskey…best I stay clear of it all…makes me a weak man when I drink," Buck said in hopes to explain his attempt to stay sober.

Katie Mae nodded. "Buck, I am proud of you for attending AA meetings. I think it'll help you to stay sober and give our family a better life together."

"I'm doing my best, Katie Mae. Don't give up on me…brighter days round the corner for us, honey, you'll see," Buck replied. "Just think. We'll attend the annual Christmas event at the cotton mill soon, just a spell off. I'm saving my money; Katie Mae…going to get you a pretty store bought dress for the Christmas party. I can't wait to show you off, and Mr. Jack Bradford can't wait to see you, thinks you are a pretty sight to behold."

Katie Mae did not respond as she sat quietly in the car, looking out the window. "Katie, dear, did you hear me? The Bradford's think you're lovely. They both told me so the other day."

Katie Mae was well aware that Mr. Jack Bradford thought she was lovely. His gestures were anything but welcome by Katie Mae. She thought it odd that his wife was in no way hindered by her husband's mingling with the women of the village. Katie Mae thought Mr. Jack Bradford and his wife were rather odd; it gave her an uneasy feeling when she was in their presence.

Elizabeth twisted and turned in the bed. Harrison shook his wife lightly, and she settled down. Her dream continued.

Katie Mae was sitting in the swing on her front porch. Mr. Jack Bradford approached the porch and stood in front of the swing as his eyes glowed with what Katie Mae considered nothing but lust. He continued to stare at her longingly.

"How you doin', Katie Mae? You lookin' mighty pretty perched in that swing."

Katie Mae blushed, naturally, but did not say anything.

"Let me get down to business, Katie Mae. My wife has few friends she can trust. She is taken with your politeness and beauty. The Missus wanted me to stop by and invite you for tea."

Katie Mae still could not speak. She could not understand why Mr. Bradford was inviting her to tea.

Jack Bradford continued, "Would you be interested in meeting my wife, having some good ole southern sweet tea with the two of us? If you will so kindly accept our invitation, we would be delighted to share our home with you tomorrow around 11:00 am. We'll call it brunch, some sweet bread with our tea."

"Well, Mr. Bradford...I wouldn't know what to do at your wife's brunch, but I'll be glad to give it a try. I sure do appreciate the invitation. It is mighty kind of you," Katie Mae said.

"It's all settled then. See you tomorrow for brunch. Good day, Mrs. Jones." Jack Bradford said in a sheepish tone as he gave a slight wink of the eye.

As Mr. Bradford left the Jones' porch, Katie Mae thought, no one in the mill village got invited to the Bradford's gorgeous home for anything. Katie Mae felt a sense of pride, although it was mired in confusion that Mrs. Bradford wanted to befriend a mill hand worker's wife.

Katie Mae opened her door and embraced the aroma of sweet honeysuckles. She brushed white flakes off her freshly starched pink dress, pressing any wrinkles hiding within the floral print of her frock. She was already experiencing the excitement and pleasure of the friendship she anticipated with Mrs. Bradford.

Proudly, she walked a few doors down the street to be the Bradford's guest at brunch. "Going to be a nice adventure I will remember forever," Katie Mae told herself as she placed her hand on the exquisite door made of imported wood.

She knocked on the front door, but no one answered. She knocked a second time with no luck. Then, she walked to the back door to find Mr. Bradford standing in the doorway. Jack Bradford was neatly attired in a starched white shirt, black pants, and black leather shoes.

"Hello, my fair lady." Jack Bradford whispered as he stepped back to allow Katie Mae to enter.

As she passed Mr. Bradford, she inhaled the expensive cologne he had apparently splashed one too many times on his body. It took her breath, and she commenced to cough. She required a glass of cold water to settle the sting of the perfume that lingered the air.

"Come, have a seat, you glamorous woman." Jack Bradford said as he eyed every move Katie Mae made.

"Here, I'll take that glass if you're finished. Maybe you would like more cold water, my dear?"

Feeling uncomfortable Katie Mae asked, "Can I assist your wife with the sweat bread and tea? I surely don't mind, Mr. Bradford."

"That is generous of you, Katie Mae, but everything is prepared for you. You're our guest, and I must say...a mighty fine pick Mrs. Bradford has made. Yep. You are a beauty, Katie Mae," Mr. Bradford said as he bent and kissed Katie Mae on the cheek.

"Welcome to our home," he added closing the back door and securing the latch.

Katie Mae was anxious to meet the reclusive wife of Mr. Jack Bradford. The reason why Mrs. Bradford wanted to befriend a poverty-stricken woman such as herself, the wife of a lowly paid mill hand worker, remained on Katie Mae's mind.

Thinking it more important to enjoy the visit and cherish the moment, Katie Mae glanced around the room, taking in every detail...from the beautifully crafted wood table and the two bone china place settings to the beautifully designed oriental rugs on the pine wood floors. The Bradford home was beautiful.

Katie Mae was relieved when Mr. Bradford summoned his wife to join them for sweet bread and tea. He poured her some hot tea and placed a piece of sweet bread on the fine china plate. Katie Mae picked up a white cotton napkin with the monogram "B" for Bradford on the corner. She placed the napkin on her lap.

Katie Mae was in heaven and never wanted to return to the old mill home she shared with Buck.

"Scoot closer to the table, my dear. I'll find a good tune on the radio."

Katie Mae obliged and waited impatiently to savor the taste of the fruity smelling bread. She was unsure of the proper etiquette. Should she wait for the host or was it acceptable to take a sip of tea and a pinch of sweet bread?

To be on the safe side, Katie Mae decided to chat with Mr. Bradford as they waited for his wife.

"Mrs. Jones, you like the song playing on the radio? It's Beethoven."

"Yes sir. Can't say I've heard it before, but it is a very soothing tune. Easy on the ears, Mr. Bradford," Katie Mae nervously said, looking around for some sign of Mrs. Bradford.

"I'm having hunger pains...how about you, my dear?" Mr. Bradford chuckled in a deep tone that reminded Katie Mae of a heavy smoker's voice. "Here, a bite of this sweet bread," He placed a crumb of the bread on Katie Mae's lips.

She did not open her mouth quickly enough, and the crumb fell on her dress.

"My apologies, allow me to clean up the mess," Jack Bradford picked the crumb from Katie Mae's dress.

Katie Mae blushed and dismissed the negative thoughts that were trying to enter her mind as Mr. Bradford continued to sweep his hand upon her freshly starched dress, pressing his hand against her abdomen.

"Think I got it all off that nice frock you're sporting. Now, you just sit back and relax Katie Mae. My lovely wife should be joining us soon."

Mr. Jack Bradford continued to talk with Katie Mae and serve her tea, even offering her a cup of freshly-brewed coffee.

How could she feel uneasy with such a fine man that exhibited proper etiquette?

As they waited for Mrs. Bradford to join them, the classical music on the radio tune grew louder, and Katie Mae became more at ease, enjoying herself in the presence of such fine host.

Katie Mae wondered again if eating before the host appears is an acceptable practice of the wealthy. Whatever the reason for Mrs. Bradford tardiness, Katie Mae is sure she will enjoy meeting her new friend. She was beginning to feel full and slightly nauseated. Besides, it was now noon, and Katie Mae wanted ample time with the Mr. and Mrs. Bradford to share life stories, get to know them better, but she had to be conscious of the time. It would soon be time for Albert Joe to be home from school, and she must be there to greet her young son.

Mrs. Bradford entered and extended her hand to Katie Mae. "My apologies Katie Mae I lost track of time; didn't mean to keep a new friend waiting. I see you and Jack have already broken bread together. I'm so delighted to have you in our home."

Standing, Katie Mae announced to Mrs. Bradford, "It's an honor to join you today, ma'am. Thank you for the invitation. I will cherish this time together for many years to come."

"I hope so my dear friend and it is truly my pleasure to have you in our home," Mrs. Bradford said as a soft faint laugh escaped her lips.

Katie Mae relaxed and dismissed any negative thoughts about the distinguished cotton mill supervisor. After all, she was sharing brunch with the two most talked about, prestigious residents of Shadow Village. What could go wrong in such fine company?

CHAPTER XI

BRADFORD EXCHANGE

"Come, Katie Mae. Come join us in a stroll to the music," Mr. Bradford said, beckoning to Katie Mae as he waved his arms in the air, motioning their guest to come closer.

It was apparent Mr. Bradford was not going to take no for an answer to his invitation. Besides, he was the rightful deed holder of the two story white house lavished with expensive furnishings. He was also the host who had invited her to such a splendid brunch. The show was in the making, and Katie Mae did not want to be cast in the designated role the Bradford's were forcing upon her. Katie Mae had never desired to be the main character in such a movie.

Mr. Bradford had one hand on Katie Mae's shoulder and the other resting on her waist, as he beckoned her to allow him to lead her in a dancing stroll. By then Mr. Bradford had placed his head on her shoulder as he slowly swung her body to the music.

"Excuse me, Mr. Bradford, but what the heck are you doing? I'm afraid I'm going to be sick all over the both of us if you don't stop all this twirlin' right this minute," Katie Mae pleaded as her face grew ghostly white with each unwanted spin. "Please, Mr. Bradford...I've told you I'm not feeling well."

Katie Mae was in the arms of a man that had a look of pure lust glaring from his disturbed eyes, and he had no intention of letting his prey free from his clutch. All of a sudden, Mr. Bradford came to a sudden stop when Katie Mae grasped her mouth with both of her hands.

Jack Bradford assisted his nauseated guest to a nearby chair as Mrs. Bradford turned the volume down on the radio. "Now, now Katie Mae did you eat too much sweet bread my dear?" Mrs. Bradford asked as she winked at her conspiring husband; acknowledging they were on to the truth, surely, Katie Mae just had to be with child.

"I'm just a little uneasy on my stomach. Not sure why," Katie Mae replied leaning back in the chair with her hands over her face.

"Jack, get the poor damsel a cold cloth and hurry! She's about to faint!" Mrs. Bradford shouted to her husband who was still trying to sway solo to the classical tune which he had blasting.

"I have a cold cloth coming right up. Hang on, my lovely ladies—I shall return," Jack Bradford shouted as he swirled around several times with a ghostly partner only he could see.

"I'm so sorry Katie Mae. Jack reverts to the first years of our marriage when he hears this music. I do apologize for his awkward, unnerving behavior," Mrs. Bradford explained with a hint of embarrassment etched on her brow and slipping through the tone of her voice.

"Jack, would you stop that foolishness, and please hurry? Give me the cold cloth," his wife hissed just as Katie Mae fainted, luckily into the nearby chair without injuring herself in the process. "Now look what you've done, Jack Bradford. You're such an ass. Why couldn't you just bring the cold cloth when I asked?"

"Hush your trap woman and get her awake. We have business to take care of," Jack Bradford instructed as he threw the cold cloth at his wife.

"Katie Mae. Wake up sweetie," Mrs. Bradford was lightly wiping Katie Mae's face with the cold cloth as she sheepishly bent toward her cheek, placing her lips on Katie Mae's soft skin. "Katie Mae, your skin is like silk, soft and beautiful."

Katie Mae slowly sat up and looked around to find Mrs. Bradford sitting beside her and Jack Bradford dancing with his make believe partner; the music much lower than before. "My goodness, Mrs. Bradford, I'm so sorry. I must have gotten too hot. I do apologize for fainting," Katie Mae blushed with embarrassment.

"No need to apologize," Mrs. Bradford said, while demanding her husband and his phantom partner settle to the sofa. "Jack Bradford, you need to stop acting like a man in your twenties right this instant—it is high time to settle down, you spunky old man."

"But darling, I love to be spunky and I enjoy dancing—even with my invisible partner. It allows me to have the perfect beauty at my side." Jack Bradford escorted an exaggerated wink and a loud chuckle that infuriated his wife.

"Jack Bradford, I'll not have that kind of stuff going on in front of our company. You settle yourself," Mrs. Bradford said as her husband shook himself into reality, quickly lowering the radio volume.

"Now Jack, you run along and go to the basement; finish up your crates, you're too full of life. Goodness, get some of that energy out of your body before night falls," Mrs. Bradford insisted.

Jack Bradford slammed the door that led to the basement as he blew his wife a mid air kiss. "That man, he'll always be young at heart," added Mrs. Bradford, rolling her eyes, as she ushered Katie Mae to sit on the sofa while she got some cold raspberry tea. Katie Mae is overcome by the generosity of the Bradford's as she marveled at the formal furnishings in the room, with the cold cloth on her forehead.

As Mrs. Bradford entered the room, Katie Mae notices the tea being served in crystal stemware on a silver tray embellished with gold trim, not the mason jars and plastic TV trays she used at her own house. Noticing Katie Mae's gawking stare, Mrs. Bradford explained, "Only the finest will do for you, Katie Mae. Drink up my dear, settle your nervous stomach."

Katie Mae slowly drank her tea, attempting to join in the casual conversation with Mrs. Bradford. She revealed that she was skeptical to accept the invitation of a stranger but felt it had been a wonderful experience getting to know her new friends.

"Did I say something wrong, Mrs. Bradford?" Katie Mae asked. "You have a puzzled look on your face. I hope you do forgive me for having a sensitive stomach, the light fainting and all."

"No, my dear not at all, you're a delightful guest and we hope to see more of you, Katie Mae, just a joy to be around," Ms. Bradford said while gently patting Katie Mae's hand and lightly embracing the embarrassed guest.

"My dear, you are the friendliest woman I've ever known, and my Jack thinks you're just a beauty to his eyes," Mrs. Bradford added, as Katie Mae pulled away from her embrace that had grown too tight…or was it just too uncomfortable?

"Sounds like Mr. Bradford settled down, found his tools. That Jack Bradford is obsessed with his saw and hammer. I'm sure he is making more crates. For the life of me, I can't understand his thinking but, he declares crates are a necessity for all families. He stores about anything he can gather in his homemade crates." Mrs. Bradford said with her ear against the basement door.

"Just look at that picture…he's such a charmer that handsome man of mine," Mrs. Bradford continued, pointing to their wedding portrait hanging on the wall. "Just look at us. We are still as much in love as the day that picture was taken, if not more. My Jack…he is such a heartthrob. He is one hunk of a man."

Katie Mae can hear hammering and the sound of a saw coming from the basement. She was curious as to what Mr. Bradford was building and remembered the mention of some type of crates earlier on. She dismissed any questions that were rambling in her head. Besides, she felt much better and it was approaching time to make a departure from the Bradford's and head home to greet Albert Joe as he got off the school bus.

"Katie Mae, I understand you and Buck have one son, is that right?"

"Yes, ma'am, Mrs. Bradford my boy, Albert Joe, will be home any minute. I'd like to get home to meet him from school," Katie Mae said with an uneasy feeling as she noticed Mr. Jack Bradford had rejoined the two of them, standing slightly nearer to Katie Mae than his own wife.

"Let's all sit on the sofa and talk a spell, Katie Mae." Mrs. Bradford suggested with a suspenseful look on her face, motioning for her husband to take a seat.

Katie Mae was beginning to feel claustrophobic with the two of them so close to her body. She began to squirm, "You know, as I said, I...I need to get home to Albert Joe. It's about time for me to leave. I sure do appreciate your generosity. The sweet bread was delicious and the tea was real nice. It tasted good."

Katie Mae started to make a bend of the waist and stand up when an unwelcomed touch forced her body to the sofa. Mr. Bradford's hand was on Katie Mae's shoulder, announcing their visit was not quite over. Silence was in the air for the first time since Katie Mae had entered the door of the Bradford home.

Jack Bradford had the look of desire in his eyes as Katie Mae stared into his pupils. He took her hand and said, "Katie Mae, you are the most desirable woman of all the mill hand workers' wives. Your eyes draw me to a place I have longed to be with a woman. You are the epitome of beauty wrapped with a desirable body. Every curve is fine-tuned to a man's whistle. Yes, Katie Mae, my wife and I desperately need you, my fair lady." All this was said with Mrs. Bradford looking on...approvingly?

Katie Mae sat between her new friends in a spellbound state of mind. Was she dreaming or were the two people sitting on the sofa completely drunk and out of their minds?

"Mr. Jack Bradford, I would like to think you've had too much gin in your tea. You're speaking nonsense," Katie Mae said as she yanked her hand from his clutch.

"I'm leaving, I'm leaving right now. Please remove your hand from my knee Mr. Bradford!" Katie Mae insisted as she stood to leave the house that was not as inviting as she had thought.

"Not so fast, Katie Mae. We're not finished with you," Mrs. Bradford screamed with the look of evil in her eyes.

Mrs. Bradford stood at the same time as Katie Mae, blocking her path to the door. "Katie Mae, I'm so sorry if I upset you. Sweetie, why don't you have a seat, just for another moment, please?" She commanded, more so than asked.

"We have a proposal for you. Once we've talked, you are free to leave" Mr. Jack Bradford said. "Just hear us out; this is for the sake of your family."

"All right, sir, I'm listening," Katie Mae said, sitting up straighter, more defensively, for she knew she was not going to like what was coming next.

"Now, now, Katie darling," Mrs. Bradford whispered. "No need to get all uptight, my dear. We are just concerned for the welfare of the residents of Shadow Village, and we offer our assistance to most of the young mothers. Sweetie, Jack and I are upstanding Christians in the mill village, and we want what is best for everyone in our community, you and Buck included. You must understand that a ripening seed is in your body, growing inside your stomach, Katie Mae," Mrs. Bradford said tenderly.

"What are you talking about Mrs. Bradford?" Katie Mae questioned.

"Just hear me out, sweetie. We're here to assist you. Jack and I are your answer to a life of luxury beyond the cold poverty-stricken railroad tracks of this cotton mill village. We want to provide you the tools to escape. You must abhor that which is selfish and evil, Katie Mae. You must sow the seed and give the plant to others who don't have rich, fertile soil."

"Escape what?" Katie Mae asked. She had no idea what Mr. and Mrs. Bradford wanted from her. "What are you talking about? Buck and I are good people. We aren't evil. We have grown our own crops and shared with everyone. We have raised our son well. We are, by no means, selfish," Katie Mae shouted. "I have to get myself home. My son will be there soon."

"Good enough reason for you to shut up and listen to me," Jack Bradford thundered at her, making both women in the room turn their heads sharply in his direction.

Katie Mae couldn't believe the turn of events. What happened to the pleasant brunch she was invited to attend? Mr. and Mrs. Bradford were not being very hospitable or reasonable.

"Well, you see, I need to just go ahead and explain something to you. You are not to discuss this information among the mill village residents, but it is rumored that you are planning to add to your family," Mrs. Bradford said quietly, deliberately.

Mrs. Bradford's tone sent a cold shiver up Katie Mae's spine as she spoke her next words: "Mrs. Bradford, what are you trying to tell me? Why would any pregnancy of mine be any of your business? Besides, Buck and I are not planning to add to our family anytime soon."

Mr. Bradford stared at Katie Mae with coldness and replied, "You see, my dear, I have a gift that enables me to look into the eyes of a woman and tell if she is with child. You are, indeed, with child. Your eyes, Katie Mae, have pregnancy written all over them. That's why I told my wife we needed to invite you to our home to discuss the new policy for the mill hands of Shadow Village."

"What the heck are you talking about Mr. Bradford? I am not with child, and if I were, as I've already said, it sure ain't any of your business. I thought you and your wife were honest, decent Christian people," Katie

Mae said accusingly,

"We are here to help, not harm you. Calm down, my child," Mrs. Bradford said while patting Katie Mae on the shoulder. "Just listen to my Jack; he is a very wise man."

As if there had been no interruption, Mr. Bradford continued. "You see, the owner of the cotton mill is only allowing one child to be born into a family every eight years. Your Albert Joe is only six, my dear. That means your insurance coverage will be null and void if you decide to keep the child you are carrying."

"What are you talking about? Are you both insane?" Katie Mae screamed.

"Listen and I'll explain. You see, Mr. Roscoe is only trying to keep his costs down, which will also help your family, too. He can't be expected to fork out large sums of money to cover insurance for all you ladies who continue to give birth to four and five babies. He has made a stand," Mr. Jack Bradford announced to his captive guest. "Families that have more than one child every eight years forfeit their insurance coverage. The rule is printed in the mill insurance policy book Buck was given three months ago. I suggest you speak with Buck and make a decision. You can pull your family out of debt with my offer or sink further in debt without proper insurance coverage." Mr. Bradford sat down and poured himself a tall glass of gin with a little sweet tea splashed on top.

"I'm not with child. Can't you two get that through your rotten brains?" Katie Mae implored. "Please, I beg you to let me leave!"

"Now, Katie Mae—you listen here, young lady. You can't continue to disrespect me and Mr. Bradford." Mrs. Bradford said as the papers she had in her hands tumbled to the floor. "I'll not have you disrespecting my husband. He's a fine Christian man." By now her voice was rising with every word.

Jack Bradford scrambled to pick up the fallen papers.

"Jack, put the darn papers on the coffee table and settle down. I'm in charge now. If you can't help me, get your gin and go elsewhere," Mrs. Bradford commanded with authority.

"Jack and I have a basement that is set up as a hospital to take care of our beloved friends in the village. I'm a registered nurse, and Jack has always had the gift of healing with his hands. We are called to save the unborn children of the village from a life of poverty. You see, we can deliver your baby in our care, and we'll have a family waiting to adopt the child. You'll be providing your child with the means of crossing to the other side of the tracks into a life of luxury and some barren women with a child to love. Everyone wins—you won't have to worry about a thing, including medical care, bills, or expenses."

"I have a good mind to go home and tell Buck y'all are nothing more than lunatics running a black market right here amongst the residents of the village. Y'all ain't nothing but baby snatchers. If I was with child, you would never get your hands on my baby," Katie Mae spat the words out of her mouth as she jumped up; preparing to leave the Bradford's home for what she hoped was the last time ever.

"Sweetie," Mrs. Bradford says, "We didn't mean to offend you. As I said, Jack and I are upstanding Christians. We belong to the First Missionary Church across the tracks. We would never harm anyone and surely not our friends in Shadow Village."

"You are both crazy lunatics, and I need to leave, now!" Katie Mae shouted.

"Think of it this way. You're about six weeks with child, so you have several months to let us know your answer. We're prepared to set you and Buck on the road to financial security if you'll abide by the rules of the owner of the cotton mill," Mrs. Bradford informed her guest who was ready to exit the front door.

Mr. Bradford, who had crept back in to the room after freshening up his "tea" again added, "I don't know what the big misunderstanding is all about, Katie Mae. It's the best situation a poor girl like you could ask for, don't you think?"

"Katie Mae, please take our offer," Mrs. Bradford pleaded, ignoring her husband. "Think of it as a way out a life of poverty, my fair lady, a way to cross the cold, glaring tracks that have held so many of the residents hostage in poverty."

"Now, here is the clincher, Katie May," said Mr. Bradford. "After the birth of your baby, your family will be moved one street across the tracks where Mr. Roscoe Johnson has built some mighty nice homes, selling them as fast as he can build. I'm talking about some real nice homes. It is all yours for the taking of my offer. Your family will be living across the tracks in luxury, my dear. Albert Joe will never want for anything — not a thing — Mr. Johnson will set up a college fund just for him."

Katie Mae's head began spinning like the thread on her sewing machine's bobbin.

"Go home. Discuss our offer with Buck, and come back with an answer, Katie Mae. I sure hope we can work out an arrangement that will meet the needs of all the parties involved because Mr. Roscoe Johnson is serious about the new insurance policy coverage," said Jack Bradford. "If you don't accept, I'm not sure how you and Buck will fare. It's all in the policy book provided to your husband."

"It just isn't logical for poor folks to have large families," Mrs. Bradford assured the lovely Katie Mae. "Likewise, it isn't fair that wealthy women are barren and can't experience holding and loving a newborn infant."

Katie Mae's mind continued to spin out of control. "I'm not with child.

How many times do I have to say this to you both? Can't you hear?"

"Katie Mae, we know you're upset, but you're a smart, charming woman, and we know you will make the right choice — the only choice. Won't you, dearie?" Mr. Bradford said, ushering her to the door and patting her back. He quickly moved her hair to the side and planted a kiss upon her neck.

Rushing to get away from the Bradford home, Katie Mae bowed her head and said a prayer: "My God, please have mercy on the Bradford's soul for they are bound for the pits of hell. God…please, please…protect me from these devils."

Elizabeth screamed in sheer terror and Harrison shook his wife firmly to awaken her.

"I'm okay, Harrison," Elizabeth assured him, sleepily. The terrible nature of Jack Bradford's proposal to her mother was too much for Elizabeth to comprehend, yet she wanted more information.

Elizabeth snuggled down into her soft blanket and slid into the mind and the world of Katie Mae as she continued to drift. She knew she was safe as long as Harrison was beside her, no matter where her mind was taking her.

Katie Mae's thoughts were elsewhere as she took care of Albert Joe when he got home, fixed dinner, and waited for Buck to get in from the mill.

She was still thinking about the turn of events when she got in bed. How could she ever explain the Bradford's offer to her husband? Buck had a terrible temper.

To make matters worse, the offer was actually from the mill owner, Mr. Roscoe Johnson, and he could be brutal if the mill hand workers didn't follow his orders.

Katie Mae could only think about the harm Jack Bradford and his equally demonic wife might cast upon her family if she were indeed pregnant and refused Mr. Roscoe Johnson's offer. What would be the aversion to her refusal? She couldn't fathom the thought of giving up her own flesh and blood to a stranger for money and social status.

The next morning Katie Mae got out of bed and ran to the bathroom. She was nauseated. With her head hanging over the commode, Katie Mae yelled for her husband. Buck came to her aide and saw his wife looking as pale as a ghost.

Buck spoke softly as he helped his wife back to the bed. "Katie Mae, what's wrong? You got some type of virus…Oh, Katie, darling. Could you be, you know…with child?"

She turned her face toward the wall so she didn't have to see Buck's face. Katie Mae was ashamed; she was withholding information from her husband. Her body shook with fear as Buck cradled her in his arms.

"Katie Mae, settle down, darling. What's all this fuss about? Goodness sake, told you more than once I want a house full of babies. We will have a good life together with our babies running around here, chasing each other, Katie Mae."

"Buck, why haven't you explained the new mill policy to me? What about your insurance benefits?"

"Katie Mae, that's not for you to worry about. It's a man's place to take care of his family," Buck said soothingly. "Besides, that ole Roscoe Johnson has no right to play God. He can't control how many children I have—he can't control any of us just because we work for him. That ain't right, Katie Mae. This is a free country—I work hard, pay my taxes, and take care of my family. I should be able to have as many kids as I want, as I can take care of. You hear me?" Buck's tone had changed dramatically.

Katie Mae could see the anger in Buck's eyes. She just couldn't tell him what happened at the Bradford's house. Buck would take his shot gun and make threats to Mr. Jack Bradford — what if he made good on those threats?

With her head bowed in prayer she said, "It is better to withhold some things than to cause more pain to those that you dearly love. God, please forgive my sins. Amen."

Across town, the Bradford's continued with their insidious plans.

"Come, my dear. Let's sit down and discuss Katie Mae," Jack Bradford's wife teased him with the rum she was getting ready to pour in his sweet tea. "Been thinking, Mrs. Bradford, how special it will be to have a December baby. Do you have your list of special requests available? Blessed is the Lord—December babies are in high demand these days. The seedless will pay the asking price, and we must prepare," Jack Bradford shouted as he took the glass of sweet tea, doused with an abundance of rum.

"By all means, Jack darling, I do have your list ready. I just love the month of December. We all know the holidays play on everyone's emotions," she replied

"That means more money in our pockets, my lovely wife." Jack Bradford replied, his eyes glowing.

"Let's see, looks like Mr. and Mrs. Belk across town are prepared to pay high dollar for a Christmas baby. I'll tag their name as the first to contact. I know they're loaded and don't mind handing over for their bundle of Christmas joy," Mrs. Bradford stated with her eyes glowing at the sight of fresh money for their bank account.

"You are a good judge of character, my love. Do you think Katie Mae will accept the offer and go through with the contract?" Jack Bradford asked his wife.

Mrs. Bradford was absorbed in the black book marked "Confidential" which contained a list of couples yearning for an infant. A red star was placed beside the names of those wanting a "Christmas" baby, and a double red star beside those that had the cash to hand over for their Christmas bundle of joy.

"Darling, did you hear me? Put that book down," Jack Bradford commanded.

"Mr. Johnson will have my job if Katie Mae doesn't come through for us. You'll need to influence that lovely girl…make her understand the pros of accepting our offer; might want to add the cons. Lay it on thick—paint the picture of the realistic life of a permanent resident of Shadow Village, Mrs. Bradford."

She replied, "Jack, it may be harder to convince our newest prey with Mr. Roscoe Johnson's usual monetary rewards. She's no fool like the others. He might have to beef it up some. You work on increasing the money, and I'll work my magic on Katie Mae."

"Remember we're indebted to Mr. Roscoe Johnson, my lovely wife. Now, you go and get all prettied up and get to know Katie Mae, be her friend, and make her dependent on you. Our plans will surely go in the right direction, and we'll be very wealthy once the Belk's make their payment in full," Bradford instructed his wife.

"I'll go the extra mile, Jack. I'll also find out if any other women are planning to bear a child and remind them of the new policy Mr. Johnson shared with their husbands. Don't think the information is being passed to the homemakers," Mrs. Bradford added. "This is going to be the best Christmas ever, Jack. We'll be filthy rich!"

"Well, I like your plan, but I want you to spend your time convincing Katie Mae to see things our way," Jack Bradford said. "I want her around for some time…she's a beauty and I can only imagine how her face will glow as that baby grows inside her womb."

"Jack, you're too wrapped up with the thought of delivering Katie Mae's baby. What's up with you?" Mrs. Bradford demanded.

"I told you, woman. I'm highly attracted to Katie Mae. I want her around. Now, you better do what I darn well say, or you'll pay dearly."

"Don't you dare threaten me, Jack Bradford," she declared.

"Not a threat, Mrs. Bradford. It is a promise. So, shut your mouth and get me what I want. Work on Katie Mae. Make her need me — like I need her," Jack Bradford said as he gulped his rum tea, smacking his lips with the thought of winning Katie Mae's trust.

"Yes, Jack. I'll do as you wish. I can see that you're engaged at the thought of having Katie Mae in our home."

"You got that right. I desire to be close to her and we need her baby to cushion our bank account." Jack Bradford yelled as his hair fell into his eyes and his head went limp from too much rum in his tea.

Mrs. Bradford removed the glass from her drunken husband's hand as she prepared for a good night's rest muttering, "Jack Bradford, the sight of your face repulses me. You're a slave to your lust, and your bottle."

CHAPTER XII

HIGHEST BIDDER

As December approached, Katie Mae had to find the strength to embrace the holiday for her son, Albert Joe. The offers made by Mr. and Mrs. Bradford tortured her. She didn't know how to fight the three money hungry beasts who sold newborn infants to the highest bidder.

The Jones' Christmas tree was small with few decorations—but it was theirs. It was quaint and happy, like their lives before the offer from the Bradford's. Katie Mae was dreading the annual Christmas event at the cotton mill where her husband worked. Buck looked forward to having his lovely wife on his arm, and escorting her to the event was always a proud moment in his life.

With swollen feet overflowing her Sunday-best shoes and a stomach protruding like a watermelon that had ripened in the summer heat, Katie Mae pleaded with her husband to be excused from the festive celebration at the cotton mill. However, Buck insisted they go.

The threat of Buck being fired by his employer had kept her from discussing the offer Mr. and Mrs. Jack Bradford made her in May. She couldn't entertain the possibility of exchanging her newborn baby for money. In a few weeks, Buck's job would be in question, as soon as Mr. Roscoe Johnson realized that she had opted out of his proposal.

When Katie Mae's feet touched the cold linoleum floor each morning, her mind raced back to that warm May brunch at the Bradford's home, the day her faith in mankind was lost forever. How could she entertain the idea of accepting money in exchange for her own flesh and blood?

The infant growing inside her belly would forever be a symbol of the love she and Buck shared. She couldn't exchange the life they made together for one of luxury promised by the Bradford's.

Katie Mae reluctantly accompanied Buck to the festive Christmas event at the old mill. Santa Claus charmed the kids with his gigantic sack of stockings filled with fruit, nuts, candy, and toys, no doubt, a special treat from Mr. Roscoe Johnson, the mill owner, and Mr. Jack Bradford, his right hand man.

The sight of both men disgusted Katie Mae. They were deceitful men in positions of power who tried to control the residents of Shadow Village. She had to give the devil his due; they had left no rock unturned in planning an event for the families of the cotton mill village. It was a gloriously festive party.

Since the repulsive offer was conveyed to her in May, she had kept it confidential as instructed by the Bradford's in fear of retaliation upon her family. As she walked around the mill with Buck attached to her arm, she kept her eyes on the culprits. Her heart was full of fear as her baby kicked with force at the sight of evil.

As usual, the Bradford's and Mr. Roscoe Johnson were the stars of the night, beaming as each family entered, shaking hands of the guests and planting a gentle kiss on the cheek of the women, winking at them with gratitude.

"Well, well, what we have here, my lovely lady? Looks like you will have an addition to the family rather soon," Jack Bradford thundered, as he patted her protruding stomach, blowing the unborn child a kiss.

Katie Mae stared him dead in the eyes, unable to speak. She flinched so hard her whole body seemed to jump.

"Excuse me, darling; I just love the sight of a pregnant woman with spunk in her eyes," Bradford said with a wink as he reached and pulled Katie Mae in his arms. Katie Mae jerked from the clutch of evil. Buck looked on with shock of his wife's behavior.

"Ah, Katie Mae is a little under the weather these days, sorta touchy. Guess it is those raging pregnant hormones I heard about on the talk shows the other night" Buck replied, with loud chuckles, as Katie Mae's face turned five shades of red.

"Excuse me," Katie Mae mumbled, as she pushed past the two men towards the ladies' room.

Katie Mae was well aware of Jack Bradford following her. She stopped near the corner of the room that was stacked with colorful gifts for all the children, who are bustling around with candy canes hanging out their mouths.

Jack Bradford placed his hand on her shoulder and whispered in her ear, "So, you're about eight months with child my lovely Katie Mae? My predictions are always within a few weeks of accuracy. I think we need to have us a good talk. How about you come by our house tomorrow at 11:00 for brunch, not an option my fair lady, remember Buck has a lot to think about, such as his loss of a good job and benefits," Mr. Bradford said, reaching out to kiss Katie Mae on the cheek. He quickly slid to her ruby red lips and kissed her deeply as she pushed him away from her, stomping his foot with her heel.

"Bad decision you just made my dear one. I'll show you some grace; since you're upset—what was it your husband called it? Raging hormones? Best you show up at my house as planned tomorrow," Mr. Bradford threatened; as he reached down to rub the pain that was swelling in his foot.

Katie Mae darted to the powder room, shaking with fear. The decision was hers. Follow Bradford's commands or remain a recluse in her home the rest of her days.

Elizabeth, sweating and shaking in her nightmare, silently prayed for the truth to unfold, putting a closure to her years of being plagued with anxiety. Elizabeth watched with eyes of steel, wanting to absorb each segment. At last, Elizabeth was relieved to hear her mother's words as Katie Mae pleaded with her father to leave the Christmas party. Katie Mae declared it was due to being exhausted with swelling feet that needed rest. Buck agreed, and they walked toward the huge door that led into the darkness.

The Bradfords were within eye view and followed close behind their bait. Katie Mae and Buck walked closer to the door. Katie Mae saw Mr. Bradford's eyes watching her protruding stomach as he disappeared into the crowded room. Then, out of the darkness, the Bradford's reappeared. Turning to Buck, Bradford slyly asks, "May I kiss the cheek of your lovely wife and wish her a Merry Christmas?"

"Sure, no harm showing little affection to a woman with child," Buck said with a slight smile. Katie Mae stared directly in the pupils of Mr. Bradford's sly eyes as she carefully bent down to pick her purse up that conveniently fell on Mr. Bradford's sore foot.

Gaining his composure, Mr. Bradford waved at the couple leaving. "See you soon, Katie Mae." Katie Mae looped her arm in her husband's and walked in front of Jack Bradford. She spitefully stomped his good foot as she eased past him. Into the night, refusing to look back at the eyes of the devil staring at her, Katie Mae had feelings of pleasure and fear overwhelming her soul.

Elizabeth, in her vision, saw her parents walking hurriedly toward their home, a short stroll behind the cotton mill. Katie Mae inhaled the fresh cold air as it swept across her face in the darkness of the cool December night, refreshing her mind from the stifling effects of Jack Bradford's gin-doused breath.

The freedom of space from the crowded room also gave Katie Mae much needed solace. Jack Bradford's face to face encounter replayed in her mind as she walked in the darkness. Suddenly she felt herself becoming sick. Holding her hands under her protruding stomach, Katie Mae doubled over in pain and screamed.

Buck assisted his pregnant wife to their home, washed her face, and helped her to bed. He kissed her gently on the forehead and instructed her to get some rest. "It must have been too warm in the mill for you, Katie Mae. You look exhausted, darling," Buck said as he turned out the light and left the room.

The next morning, Buck's feet hit the floor much earlier than usual. "Mr. Bradford got a truck load of wood crates being delivered to the cotton mill, and he needs me to put them on the tow motor and carry them to the shed behind his house. I've got to be there bright and early."

Katie Mae waited for the sound of the screen door to slam. Reluctantly she dragged herself out of the bed and prepared breakfast for Albert Joe, rushing him off to his bus stop. She watched her son run for the bus and slowly walked back to her bed. Feeling like a zombie, she crawled to the center of the mattress.

Covering her head with the thin shabby sheets, Katie Mae wanted to end her pain, but that was not a choice she would dare entertain. Sleep would be useful. She lay on the bed waiting to be in a zone where she was at peace at least for a few minutes.

The sound of barking dogs startled her. She sat up in bed and glanced at the clock noting it was nearly 10:00 am. She said repeatedly, "I have decisions that must be made, but I only want to sleep my life away. My God help me; send an angel to rescue me."

Knowing she must make a decision that would forever affect her life, Katie Mae placed her feet on the floor, trying to find the warmth of her bedroom slippers. Standing at the edge of the bed, she reached for the tiny white Bible on the nightstand. Katie clutched the bible against her heart and felt a powerful force run through her body...strength she had never experienced and hopefully would provide the courage to face the Bradford's.

"My God, please protect me and my unborn child from the Bradfords. I need your arms around my shoulders today," Katie Mae continued to pray as she slowly searched for something to wear. She held the tiny white bible tightly in her hand before lifting her bra and placing it as close to her heart as possible.

Elizabeth's eyes streamed with tears as the sounds of the movie began to fade into the darkness of the room. She mumbled in her sleep as she tossed and turned. She pleaded with God to put an end to her nightmare soon because she couldn't take much more of the drama filled show.

Elizabeth watched, wide-eyed, listening to each word and each movement made in the tiny bathroom where her mother sobbed profusely. Elizabeth's mind was like a sponge floating in a tub of soapy water, she refused to fade by sinking to the bottom. She found herself in the tiny bathroom, stuck in the corner where her mother was seeking refuge from the voice of Jack Bradford.

The truth was forcefully protruding through her mother's stomach with each kick of the tiny life that was in distress. Elizabeth was ready for the truth to escape as she waited patiently in her sleep.

Katie Mae knew she had to confront the Bradford's at the appointed time given by his raspy voice at the Christmas party. She slowly pulled her maternity top over her head, making sure the tiny white Bible was intact, secure against her skin.

She caught a glimpse of her swollen eyes in the mirror. Only God could rescue her from the offers she would be faced with today at the Bradford's home. Katie Mae had great faith in God and knew He would rescue her if she was placed in a position that threatened her life. God was her comfort; indeed He would protect the unborn child she carried in her womb from any harm.

As she pulled the elastic pants over her protruding stomach, Katie Mae could not help but wonder why Mr. Bradford wanted to see her.

Arriving at the Bradford's home, Katie Mae noticed that the screen door was partially open. She knocked, and immediately a touch on her hand sent chills up her spine. It was Jack Bradford.

Startled, Katie Mae pulled her hand away and entered the door. "Katie Mae, you're as beautiful as ever." Jack Bradford slithered in a raspy evil voice as he eyed Katie Mae with seductive eyes. "We've been waiting for you all morning, my lovely lady. That helpful husband of yours brought his last load of wood crates to my shed about thirty minutes ago. He's such a hard worker at the mill, and we sure hope to keep him employed and also increase his salary soon."

"What do you want with me, Mr. Bradford? I don't have anything more to say to you," Katie Mae said as she walked toward the kitchen table, the same table she had had brunch with the Bradford's. There was no entrancing aroma of fresh sweet bread, just an evil presence that sprayed an aroma of filth throughout the kitchen.

"Have a seat, my lovely lady. Let's talk awhile about your situation…must be very taxing on the mind, but I think we can make things much better for you, Katie Mae," Jack Bradford said charmingly as she limped toward her, making sure to protect his sore foot from harm's way.

Once seated, Katie Mae felt her infant kicking as if it were trying to escape the darkness of her stomach in fear of the evil that made the mother shake. "Mr. Bradford, I don't want any trouble, please, leave me be. Buck and I will make it somehow; we don't need your offer. Katie Mae placed her hands around her protruding stomach in hopes of calming the fear within her body.

Jack Bradford stood directly in front of Katie Mae, his eyes exploding with intimidation. "Katie Mae, you're our favorite woman in the mill village.

My wife and I chose you as our partner in business. We want to assist you monetarily and express our gratitude," Jack Bradford said impatiently as he slowly paced back and forth on the hardwood floors, being careful to nurse his hurt foot. "I don't think you understand that you owe us that unborn infant. We made a deal months ago. The unborn infant does not belong to you!" Jack Bradford screamed, as he raised his hand toward Katie Mae's face. She abruptly, instinctively, bent sideways to avoid his rage. "Please. Mr. Bradford, I'm begging you to stop your nonsense, and let me go home. Please, don't hurt me."

"You see, the pleading is over. The contract has already been signed, sealed, and delivered to Mr. Roscoe Johnson. It will not be voided by anyone. Death will oblige if you refuse to deliver our infant," Jack Bradford screamed in her ear as he slammed his hands on the table, causing her to slouch over in the chair.

"Drink this hot tea and relax, silence your whimpering. You must realize who is in charge of you and your future. Don't you remember the deal we made?" Mrs. Bradford appeared, bearing a cup of steaming liquid. She handed it to Katie Mae and joined her at the table.

Katie Mae drank the hot tea as tears continued to roll down her cheeks. "Here, here, my love. Stop those tears. We just want what has been promised to Mr. Roscoe Johnson. You must follow his policy, or you will conveniently become a missing person like the others gals who reneged," Bradford warned with a harsh laugh.

Mrs. Bradford chimed in to persuade Katie Mae, "Look at your life beyond the tracks as a fair exchange for the infant."

Katie Mae shifted her weight in the chair to find the slightest comfort from the hellish treatment. "Please stop. Allow me to leave Ms. Bradford. I'm getting very sick, I must leave." Katie Mae pleaded to no avail.

"You hear us out, Katie Mae. The infant has been sold to the highest bidder, wealthy parents who will offer it a carefree life." Mrs. Bradford said.

"Mr. Roscoe Johnson will not allow the mill wives to bankrupt his cotton mill due to the insurance premiums spiraling out of control. Too many babies are being born in the village. Mr. Johnson had to do something to save his empire," Jack Bradford said.

"This last form must be signed now. Don't force us to take your baby. We are prepared, but that is not the best medical procedure. You see, Jack isn't up to date with C-Section procedure, and you'll surely meet your death," said Mrs. Bradford.

"Katie Mae, once you sign the contract all will be fine. You'll deliver here in the basement, a safe and sterile environment my Jack has prepared."

Smiling, Mrs. Bradford pushes the wet strands of hair from Katie Mae's face.

Katie Mae found it difficult to speak without trembling and opened her mouth to answer Mrs. Bradford but nothing came out except muttering sounds. She stood up and prayed for the strength to address their questions and defend her decision.

"Mrs. Bradford...I appreciate your concern for my family's financial security, but I can't accept your offer. I could never live with myself if I exchanged my baby for money. That would be severely heart wrenching. Besides, I don't remember signing any contract."

Mr. Bradford looked Katie Mae dead in her eyes. "Katie Mae, let me explain something to you. The offer is one that you should reconsider, my dear. Mr. Roscoe Johnson is aware your baby is due soon. He is anxious to compensate your family well above any offer he has ever extended."

"Katie Mae, there is a couple who are in desperate need for a bundle of joy have paid top dollars for your unborn infant. Heck, Buck would never have to cross the tracks to work a day the rest of his life with Mr. Roscoe Johnson's offer," Jack Bradford informed the grieving mother-to-be.

"You need to listen to Jack, Katie Mae. He is trying to save your family," Mrs. Bradford commented. "Have you taken your husband's health into consideration? How are you going to feel when Buck is dead, knowing you could have saved his life? Besides there is no backing out, Jack already signed the contract. Excuse me. I meant you've signed the contract."

"What did you say, Mrs. Bradford? What about Buck's health? What you talking about? Is my Buck sick?" Katie Mae had a look of confusion on her face. Tears welled in her eyes as she fainted and fell at Jack Bradford's feet.

"She's dead, Jack. What will we do now? Katie Mae is dead. You killed her, Jack Bradford," Mrs. Bradford screamed as she pulled Katie Mae's limp body off her husband's shoes.

"My foot, my foot is hurting. Get her off my sore foot. Just look at my shoes. She vomited on my new shoes. That no good woman," Jack Bradford bellowed as he assisted his wife by shoving Katie Mae's body off his shoes. Jack Bradford was in a raging fit as he limped back and forth.

"Shut up, you foolish woman. Katie Mae isn't dead. She fainted," Bradford hissed as he tugged at Katie Mae's arm. "Get up, Katie Mae. Get up now!" He screamed.

Katie Mae's breathing was sporadic as Mrs. Bradford propped her body against the kitchen wall. "Jack, get her some cold water and a wet cloth. Hurry, Jack."

"Yeah, yeah I'm coming. Give me a darn minute to think...plan what to do next!" Jack Bradford screamed as he threw a wet cloth at his wife and brought tap water in a paper cup.

When Katie Mae's eyes opened she wailed out a scream for help.

"Shut up, you fool," Jack Bradford shouted as he pressed his hand against Katie Mae's mouth.

Katie Mae opened her eyes and screamed at her attackers. "Jack

Bradford, I'll have you arrested…you and your wife. You'll both rot in prison. You're both liars. My Buck isn't sick. You're both foul liars."

"Well, Katie Mae…maybe your husband is the liar," Jack Bradford replied as he sat in a chair, leaning against the wall.

"I surely didn't want to be the one to divulge Buck's illness, but apparently he has kept this from you in hopes it would spare your mental health, you being pregnant and all. Buck is very sick, Katie Mae. He has a serious lung disease, and the doctors say he'll likely be on disability soon, not able to work at all. Buck is going to need extensive medical care the rest of his life."

"Now, Mr. Roscoe Johnson is prepared to pay his health insurance as indicated in the contract with the documented plans to relocate your family into a home across the tracks and set up a trust fund for Albert Joe's college. Katie Mae, I have a check made out in your name for $25,000 from Mr. Roscoe Johnson and another check from the prospective parents for $10,000. Katie Mae, this is the largest sum of money Mr. Johnson's ever given to anyone. It's more than a fair offer, so let's go ahead and seal the deal and stop this foolishness. It will cover any medical expenses for you and your family. I know this is a lot of information, but weigh your option. You simply don't have any other options, do you? Now, what is your answer?"

After thinking for a few moments about the last few weeks and how Buck had seemed to be sick with a cough, breathing problems, Katie Mae replied, "Mr. Bradford, I had no idea Buck was so sick. My God, what should I do? How can I allow my husband to die when Mr. Roscoe Johnson is willing to supply lifetime insurance coverage that will provide my husband the proper medical care? How could I dare risk Buck's health when I hold the key to him living a longer life? I can't risk losing my husband, my son's father."

"Well, Katie Mae, now, you're listening to reason. You see, we've been trying to help you all this time and you refused to listen, darling," Jack Bradford said while kissing Katie Mae on the forehead.

Perplexed, Katie Mae replied to his offer, "Yes, Mr. Bradford…I'll sign the contract, but please, please, let me carry the baby full term, until December 14th. While Buck is at work, I'll deliver the child here at your home."

"You've made the right decision, Katie Mae. We knew you would come to your senses. And remember: no one, not even Buck, needs to know about our agreement," Bradford reminded her.

"Yes sir. I understand, and I'll return within a few days," Katie Mae whispered as she stood to receive the contract from Mr. Bradford. Tears rolled down her cheeks, but she felt there was no other choice if she wanted to save her husband and her life as she knew it.

Katie Mae went home with a heavy heart. When she opened the door, Buck was lying on the sofa, resting. She walked over and felt his forehead, burning with a fever. He was too weak to sit up. Katie Mae felt she made the right decision and scheduled a visit to speak with the Bradford's the following day.

The next day, Katie Mae spoke with Mr. Bradford about Buck's failing health; she needed two grand to have him admitted to a decent clinic. Mr. Bradford agreed to grant Katie Mae the advance and noted the revision on the original contract. He handed her another one of Dr. Wayne Lee's cards, suggesting Katie Mae call as soon as possible so Buck could be seen by the well respected professional.

As Katie Mae signed the contract, Mr. Bradford explains that once she delivered the infant, she would be paid in full. He and Katie Mae shook hands to seal the deal, and Mr. Bradford gave Katie Mae a check. She left the house feeling as if she had made a step in the right direction to save her husband's life, but she still felt sick in the pit of her stomach.

Back at home, Buck looked at his wife to assure her he is fine. "Just a bad infection, but the medication is working now. I'm feeling much better, darling."

Albert Joe, full of energy, arrived from school, asking for a snack. He settled down and sat with Buck to watch a movie while Katie Mae prepared supper.

After supper, Katie Mae went about her normal routine, clearing and washing the dishes, and assisting Albert Joe with his homework. Once Albert Joe's bath water was prepared, she reminded him to wash behind his ears and scrub his feet. She quietly went to the kitchen and prepared fresh ginger ale for Buck as he rested on the sofa.

"Thank you, Katie Mae," Buck wrapped his body in a thick quilt. "Why you look so worried, Katie Mae? Look like you just saw a ghost."

"Well, I'm very concerned about your lungs. You have been so sick, darling. I want you to see a doctor in a nearby city, one of the finest specialists in lung diseases," Katie Mae replied.

Buck gave Katie Mae an odd look. "Katie, I ain't got no lung disease. My doctor said he thought I had pneumonia. I need to return tomorrow for an x-ray," Buck paused. "For all I know, I might got some cotton fibers caught up in my lungs. Don't worry so much because I'm feeling much better."

This was good news to Katie Mae; she thought Mr. Bradford had told her the truth. With tears in her eyes, she recalled Mr. Bradford saying that her husband was suffering from a potentially fatal lung disease, a disease that would take years of medical care to heal, if he didn't die first. No doubt, her husband was indeed a sick man and was trying to hide the truth from her, thinking he couldn't dare cause her to suffer by worrying about his health.

Katie Mae was a step ahead of Buck. Thanks to Mr. Bradford's offer and his generous advance of $2,000 to her account, she had sufficient money to take care of Buck's immediate medical care. Soon, with the birth of their child, she would gain access to enough money to provide long term care for Buck. She was at peace with accepting the Bradford's offer; it would save her husband's life.

Katie Mae was sure that, with time, Buck would come to understand why she accepted the offer Mr. Roscoe Johnson master minded. Besides, Katie Mae knew Buck would have done the same thing to save her or Albert Joe's life. She prayed that God would ease her mind for handing her baby over to total strangers.

She kept reminding herself that it would be very wealthy parents who could offer the infant a life that she and Buck could never afford. Katie Mae could only pray. Pray, hope, and believe.

After expressing her concerns, Buck decided to appease his wife by giving her permission to make an appointment with the specialist. Katie Mae made a note to call the doctor the following day. She was pleased that Buck was being proactive with his health, and at last he was going to receive the best medical treatment available from a lung specialist.

CHAPTER XIII

THE LIES BENEATH

As Buck prepared for his trip to the lung specialist, Katie Mae prepared for a baby sitter to help with Albert Joe so she could travel with Buck to the clinic. When they arrived, Buck was ushered off for routine lab work and x-rays.

Buck needed the best medical care, and it seemed Dr. Wayne Lee was indeed the best money could buy, and money was no issue thanks to Mr. Bradford and Mr. Johnson.

After Buck's examination, Dr. Lee suggested that Buck and Katie Mae go to the cafeteria for some lunch and return in an hour for a conference.

Buck and Katie Mae enjoyed their meal together. They rarely had time to be alone, but it was soon time to speak with Dr. Lee. They arrived just in time, the nurse was calling Buck's name. In the doctor's office, Dr. Lee gave them some promising news.

"Well, let me first say that your blood work was a little disturbing, seems your white blood cells are low but that is something we will watch. I'm somewhat concerned about the severity of your lung infection. I'm waiting for one last test result from the lab. I've also called a colleague of mine so he and I can collaborate for possible future treatment."

"Dr. Lee, does my husband have a lung disease or an infection?" Katie Mae asked.

Dr. Lee replied, "Mrs. Jones, we won't know until the tests have been analyzed. I'll have the receptionist make an appointment for your husband one week from today. Until then, I've written him a prescription for a stronger antibiotic. He should feel much better soon."

On their way home, Buck asked about the payment arrangements for his medical care. Katie Mae quickly assured him she had taken care of the payment and asked him not to worry.

In the early morning hours, Katie Mae felt the baby kicking so hard it woke her from a deep sleep. Katie Mae walked to get something to settle her stomach, and hopefully the stirring infant, so that she could get some more rest. As she stood, she felt excruciating pain stabbing through her stomach.

The next morning, Katie Mae quickly took care of her duties to her son and her husband, and then attempted to settle her nerves by reading her Bible. She felt a sharp kick from the baby and realized she was in labor. She had to get to the Bradford's home for medical assistance. She checked on Buck after calling the baby sitter to come immediately after school to help with Albert Joe. Then she would hurry to the Bradford's home.

Katie explained she needed the sitter to take care of Albert Joe while she traveled out of town for couple days to speak with her husband's doctors. She explained, due to Buck's illness, it was important she meet with his doctors to discuss possible treatment prior to their next visit.

The sitter vowed to keep her whereabouts confidential and to take care of Albert Joe. "I'll need you to give my husband a note, so please read it to him when he wakes up," Katie Mae instructed.

"Yes ma'am. I'll read the letter to Mr. Jones as soon as he is alert," the baby sitter assured Katie Mae she would and asked her to travel carefully.

Katie Mae wrote the note quickly, and read it again to herself: "My dearest Buck, Please don't worry. I've gone to speak privately with your doctors to discuss your upcoming appointment. Dr. Lee wanted to review your treatment plan, and I needed to consult the business office clerk so we can set a manageable monthly payment. I didn't want you to worry about this entire process, Buck, so I am taking care of everything. I will meet with Dr. Lee mid morning but can't meet with the business clerk until around 4:30 pm. I'll get a hotel room so I can rest. I'll be home tomorrow by noon. The sitter will take care of Albert Joe and prepare your meals. It is important that I meet with Dr. Lee, and I apologize for not waking you.

Katie Mae knew it would not be long before her baby would be born. It was imperative she keep her end of the bargain so Buck could receive the best care for his lung disease.

It was time to make the exchange.

Katie Mae placed her tiny white Bible in her pocket as she threw her overnight case in the front seat and drove toward the Bradford's home.

Flashing before Elizabeth's eyes were distorted segments of her mother's secret life and the untold scenes that had cheated Katie Mae of a rightful mind. Elizabeth was eager to behold the final stages of her mother's pregnancy…her last days on earth.

Elizabeth prayed for deliverance, for the healing of her mind, and for the noose around her neck to be broken. She wanted an end to the tormenting nightmares that had devastated her life far too many years. She felt the touch of Harrison's hand, clutched tightly around her own. She was safe in his care, and it was time for closure.

Katie Mae drove down the street toward Jack Bradford's home. Her fingers felt like ice as she gripped the steering wheel as if it were trying to escape. A blur of pain shot through Katie Mae's stomach.

Mr. and Mrs. Bradford meet Katie Mae at the door. She pleaded for their assistance, screaming at the top of her lungs, "Help me, it's time."

"I've been waiting for you," Bradford mumbled greedily.

"I think I'm in labor, please help me. My baby is coming" Katie Mae pleaded as she fainted at the threshold.

Mr. Bradford picked her up and carried her to the basement as Mrs. Bradford fetched Katie Mae's overnight case from her car.

The delivery room was prepped and waiting for Katie Mae to enter. Katie Mae woke up and realized she was on a cold table, wrapped with mounting blankets that weighed her body down.

Mr. Bradford was standing over her, and she could hear him and his wife talking. Katie Mae whispered, "Am I in labor? Is it time for the baby to come?"

"Yes, it is time Katie Mae, and you're in good hands. Relax and before long this will be over, and you can return to your family. Your secret is safe with us," Mrs. Bradford whispered soothingly.

"Did you make the proper preparation with Buck, covering your absence?" Bradford asked.

"Yes sir. I told him I would be at Dr. Lee's office as you instructed, discussing his medical treatment plan," Katie Mae whispered through the sharp, stabbing pains.

Mrs. Bradford started the IV in Katie Mae's arm. Katie Mae fell into a light sleep and was startled at the sound of the faint cry of an infant. An evil spirit enveloped the freezing room. A soul-shivering shadow of a vile demon stared at Katie Mae through her tightly closed eyes.

"Is it over? Is my baby breathing?" Katie Mae asked as she tried to free her arms.

"Yes, my dear all went well. You need to rest and let us take care of business," Jack Bradford said, as he turned and walked out of the room with Katie Mae's infant in his arms.

The next morning the Bradford's came to check on Katie Mae, informing her that her baby rested well and had been placed in the appropriate crate for Mr. Roscoe Johnson to deliver to the new parents.

"A...a girl?" Katie Mae shouted between her cries, glancing to two crates nearby, each having a pink blanket. "I gave birth to a girl. Didn't I? Please tell me."

Katie Mae continued to cry as she screamed, "Let me hold my baby. Please, let me see her."

Mrs. Bradford explained that it was not a good idea for Katie to see or hold the infant; she reminded her that the contract she signed prohibited physical contact with the infant. Mrs. Bradford walked over, and closed the lid on each crate as Katie Mae watched in horror.

"The babies will suffocate; open the lids before they die!" Katie Mae screamed.

Mr. Bradford appeared and opened the lids half way to settle Katie Mae who was hysterical.

Katie Mae made a mental note of the initials on each crate. The letter "H" was written on the first crate, and the second crate had the initial "J." Each initial was scribbled in black ink.

Katie Mae continued to scream, "Why are there two crates? Did I have twin girls? Please, tell me."

Mr. Bradford explained softly to Katie, "No, sweetie you gave birth to one infant girl, but you don't need to worry about all this. All is well, and you need your rest."

We'll be back in a few hours to get you on your feet and start some liquids so you can return to your family. Meanwhile, we'll get all the paperwork completed so this infant can bond with its parents. You must remember we have other patients to assist, my lovely lady."

Katie Mae watched Mr. Bradford's lips moving but refused to listen to his nonsense. "Rest, Katie Mae. You are at the end of this journey; you and your family can move on with your lives across the tracks just as we discussed. Your new life is going to be worth the exchange."

Katie Mae nodded in agreement, but the emotional turmoil and screaming episodes continued. Katie Mae bellowed for her newborn baby. Becoming frustrated with Katie Mae's screaming, the Bradford's gave Katie Mae a sedative, turned the light off and closed the door.

After a short time, Katie Mae was startled by loud voices in the hallway. She lay quietly on the table so she could hear the Bradford's discussion. It was a mixture of hostility and medical jargon of their patients that had delivered at approximately the same hour.

"Seems she has settled down for now, but we'll need to be prepared for her screaming fits," Mr. Bradford said. "If that foolish woman continues, the authorities may be called. We sure don't need them looking around our property. I don't plan on pulling time because of this foolish lunatic," Jack Bradford shouted to his wife.

"I'll silence her Jack. Darn you, Jack Bradford, give me time to draw up some morphine. That'll shut her up so we can map out a plan to take care of this," Mrs. Bradford informed her impatient husband who had walked toward another delivery room.

"Jack, snuff that cigarette. You idiot, the babies don't need to smell like a bar. You're such a foolish man. Besides, when did you take up smoking?"

Mrs. Bradford asked. She thumped the cigarette out of the side of her husband's mouth. "I'm going to give Katie Mae a lot more morphine. Be right back." Mrs. Bradford opened the door to the delivery room. It reeked of Clorox.

"Katie Mae is sound asleep. I also gave another dose of morphine to our second patient. She's a fighter, too, and is becoming harder to manage," Mrs. Bradford informed her husband when she returned.

Mr. Bradford chuckled, "Katie Mae is so ignorant, and she bought the line about Buck's lung disease taking him to an early grave...hook, line and sinker."

Katie Mae was so drugged and exhausted that she could not muster the strength to scream for help. Uttering the Lord's Prayer, her eyes opened from the dark gloom that had taken over her body. She heard a woman's voice nearby begging for her baby girl. Katie Mae thought she was hallucinating, hearing her own voice echoing. "God, please don't let me die," Katie Mae pleaded for mercy. She continued to hear voices beyond her bedside. The very thought of others being in the same situation as she sent fear through her body. Could there possibly be others? She prayed she was hearing her own pleading and not of another woman.

"God, please deliver me from the hands of these people, and save my baby from evil-doers," Katie Mae turned her head toward the door and silently prayed for help. "Father, I've been made a fool by these two evil beings, they are trying to profit from my baby. My God, have mercy on my ignorance and forgive me."

Katie Mae could hear the voices getting closer. It was no doubt the voice of the Bradford's, making mockery of her Buck and their successful plot to deceive the couple. "Oh my God, my Buck was not on his death bed. It was a hoax. They forced me to sign their contract," she whimpered, "Oh, mighty God; I've sold my own flesh and blood. My Father, send your angels down to rescue me from this evil."

Katie Mae, half conscious, raised her head in search of an exit door. She screamed for help. Elizabeth continued to watch her mother struggle, to view the exit of this nightmare. How could this be? How could another human being cause another to hurt, steal their baby, and cause them lifelong harm? Elizabeth felt empathy for Katie Mae. For the first time she could feel her pain and understand her inner struggles.

Katie Mae continued to struggle as she witnessed the hands of the deceitful Bradford's gain control over someone. Katie Mae was sure there had to be others. How could this happen in a small cotton mill village? Katie Mae was trapped. Life would never be the same. She wanted to die. No, she wanted to live! Katie Mae wanted her baby in her arms. She prayed.

Suddenly, the child within Elizabeth cried.

"Where's Katie Mae?" Buck asked the baby sitter when he woke up.

"She left you this letter, Mr. Jones," the baby sitter replied, handing Buck the piece of paper, folded into a small square. Taking Albert Joe with her, she left the den to give Buck some privacy.

He read Katie Mae's letter and placed it on the sofa. Buck was aware Katie Mae seemed stressed and his medical care and mounting bills were causing excessive anxiety.

That night, Buck went to bed with an unsettled mind. He got up early the following morning to help see Albert Joe off to school. Picking up the letter, Buck read it several times. He realized the words seemed rehearsed, unlike Katie Mae's writing.

He called the baby sitter into the living room. She sat down as Buck questioned her again about Katie Mae's frame of mind and her whereabouts.

"Mr. Jones, Katie Mae had an overnight case. She said she was going to take care of business for you at the doctor office. That is all she told me 'cause she was in a hurry, sorta worried looking…bending over several times with sharp pains."

"Katie Mae is with child. My God, she is uneasy driving a few miles from home to shop for groceries. Surely she wouldn't drive an hour to a city." Buck stood and started pacing in front of the sofa.

"Mr. Jones, I'm so sorry. I should have stopped your wife, but she was determined to take care of business at your doctor's office."

"Not your fault. Besides, Katie Mae has been acting strange lately. She may be sick herself. Who knows?" Buck replied. "I can't put my finger on what's wrong, but something is not right. I'll give her a little longer to call me, but if I don't hear from her soon, I'll call Dr. Lee's office to see if she made it safely."

By late afternoon, Buck had not heard anything from Katie Mae. He was frantic about his wife's whereabouts. "My God, she could be lost, or stranded," he said to the baby sitter who was also getting worried.

"Mr. Jones, you think Ms. Jones was in labor and drove herself to the hospital? She was bending over in pain when she left. I saw her face, and she looked sick, Mr. Jones," The baby sitter reported with tears in her eyes, feeling responsible for allowing Katie Mae to leave in such condition.

Buck just had to find his wife. He prayed she had not gone into labor while traveling to another city to take care of his medical bills.
He would not be able to forgive himself if Katie Mae was in harm's way.

He called Dr. Lee's office and explained that his wife had an appointment to meet with his doctors. He asked if Katie Mae had arrived.

The receptionist reported that Katie Mae was not at the clinic, and that it was not possible for her to have an appointment because all the doctors were at a conference for three days. The receptionist added, "Mr. Jones, don't forget you have an appointment in a few days to see Dr. Lee."

Buck was disturbed and even more puzzled about the whereabouts of his pregnant wife. He decided to get dressed and search for her throughout the mill village. He would walk down each street and yell for his wife. Surely, he would find some clue to her whereabouts.

Buck asked the babysitter to take care of Albert Joe while he looked for Katie Mae. She nodded and agreed to stay at the house in case Katie Mae returned.

Buck gently closed the door and walked down the cold cement steps. He reached down to pick up Albert Joe's red bike from the ground and placed it against the Chaney ball tree. As he walked down the street, he looked everywhere for Katie Mae's car.

About half way to the corner of their street, Buck stopped short in his tracks. He heard a faint scream that sounded like a wounded animal. There must be a fox or 'possum in the woods across the tracks. As Buck continued to walk toward the end of his street, he heard the noise again, but that time, it was clearer to him—it was not a wounded animal. It was a woman's scream.

Buck turned his head toward the sound. It seemed to be coming from his left. Nervously, he stopped directly in front of the prestigious home of the cotton mill supervisor, Mr. Jack Bradford. The cries continued with more intensity as Buck walked toward the Bradford's back yard. As he followed the sounds, Buck saw the half-open garage door. He placed his hand underneath the door to pry it open, but it was stuck.

The screams were becoming louder. Buck decided to crawl under the garage door to rescue whoever was in trouble. As he slid his body under the garage door, Buck lifted his eyes to see a familiar car.

He slowly stood, walked closer to the car, and peered into the driver's side window, then the passenger's side window. It was Albert Joe's Matchbox cars on the backseat of the car.

Buck looked for Mr. Bradford's truck; it was not in the garage. He frantically lifted the lever and raised the garage door, running toward the Bradford's back door screaming, "Mr. Bradford, you home? You home, Mr. Bradford?"

No one answered Buck's cries for help. He pulled the screen door open and started banging on the wooden door with his bare fist. "Please. Mr. Bradford, open the door."

Buck ran to the front door and repeated his pleas to no avail. He raised his leg and slammed his foot into the door hoping it would open but nothing happened. The door was not budging. Buck did not have time to waste, so he threw his body against the front door to gain entrance to the Bradford home.

With a loud bang, the door opened on the third try, glass shattering from the top windowpanes that slammed against the wall. Buck quickly entered into the house screaming, "Mr. Bradford, anyone here? Please. Where is Katie Mae? I know she's here—I've seen her car, Mr. Bradford!" He screamed, but no one answered.

Buck ran toward the kitchen in a panic, yelling to the top of his lungs, "Mr. Bradford, where are you?" The sound of an engine starting caught Buck's attention as he stood in the spotless kitchen of the Bradford home.

He glanced out the kitchen window and saw the side of a van as it sped from the back of the Bradford's garage. A large box fell out of the back of the van. Small blankets were flying in mid air as the van sped off. For a moment, Buck thought he had seen the word "Candy" on the side of the van.

He knew his eyes were most likely playing tricks on him. Besides, a candy truck with a box of blankets did not make any sense. It surely did not have any reason to be at the home of Jack Bradford. Buck dismissed his thoughts and ran into each room screaming for someone, anyone to answer him.

The faint cries returned. Buck fell to the floor and looked under the kitchen table, unsure of what he would find.

He glanced toward a closed door where a beam of light was escaping through the crack under the doorway. He heard the cries again, and they seemed to be coming from inside the door. Without hesitation, he jumped up and yanked the door open.

He saw steps that lead to the basement of the Bradford home; a dim light was on. Buck yelled, "Anyone down there? Mr. Bradford, you working in the basement? Are you hurt? Mrs. Bradford? Are you down here?" There was no answer, except the cries.

He placed his right foot on the step that led to the basement. The area was so dimly lit that Buck could not see a thing. He held onto the banister and began running down the steps. He placed his hand around the cold knob of the door. It was locked. He pounded on the door, but no one answered. He was too tired and desperate to wait any longer, so he pushed with the last bit of energy he had left and it was just enough to throw the door off its hinges.

He entered a basement that was in total darkness. He flipped a switch on the wall, a dim light appeared providing enough light to see a long hallway that extended to the left, but a door blocked the entrance.

There did not seem to be anyone in the basement, only the faint cries that now sounded as if they were embedded inside the walls of the basement. He suddenly felt the urgency to flee and go to the nearest hospital, perhaps the Bradford's took Katie Mae there.

As he turned to make his way up the steps, Buck saw a dim light under the locked door at the end of the hall where he had just left.

He ran down the hall and pulled on the knob and much to his surprise the door opened. Buck screamed for Mr. Bradford as he looked around seeing several doors down the long, dimly lit hallway. A door about ten feet from where Buck was standing opened, and someone came out.

"What the heck are you doing here, you foolish man? Get out of my house or I'll call the police and have you arrested for breaking and entering!" Jack Bradford shouted at Buck who was standing like a zombie.

"Mr. Bradford, what in the name of our Lord are you doing wearing a doctor's jacket?" Buck yelled. He tried to push Mr. Bradford aside so he could see what was in the room Bradford had left.

Jack Bradford continued to scream as veins of anger swelled on his forehead. "Stop, Buck, you must leave. Leave now, Buck, or I'll have to kill you. Get out of my house, you foolish man! Don't you open that door, Buck. I'm warning you for the last time."

Buck yanked the doorknob from Mr. Bradford's hand, and opened the door. He heard a woman's faint voice. "Buck, Buck, help me." Buck distinctly recognized the voice. Katie Mae. "Where are you, darling? I'm here for you," Buck shouted as he continued to search for his wife, screaming her name at the top of his lungs.

He stumbled over a large square object. As he flipped the light switch on, he saw it was a cardboard box. Baby blankets toppled out of the box and fell on the cement floor.

The sight of the black blankets took his breath, and Buck's body shook in fear of the unknown.

The morning after Buck rescued his wife and newborn baby girl from the Bradford's basement his mind was swirling with questions for his wife.

As he sat at the kitchen table with a cup of coffee, Buck eyed the shotgun he had propped in the corner, always within arm's reach. Besides, if the Bradford's took one-step on his property, he was darn well prepared to defend his family.

He got up and glanced out the window, making sure no intruders were near. Buck was shocked to see Katie Mae's car parked in their driveway. As the sun beamed through the thin curtains hanging over the windows of the Jones' living room, Katie Mae sat up and scanned the room for Buck. "Buck, where are you?" Katie Mae asked softly.

Buck entered the room and walked toward the end of the sofa. He retrieved the little bundle of joy from the crate and held the baby tightly in his arms. He walked to his wife and placed their newborn baby girl in her arms. Katie Mae held her baby against her body as fear surfaced in her eyes.

"Buck, we must talk but afterward never mention this to anyone," Katie Mae cradled the tiny baby in her fluffy pink blanket as the infant searched for Katie Mae's breast.

"She's hungry Buck. Do we have any fresh milk in the refrigerator?"

"I have a bottle of fresh goat's milk warming on the heater, no worries

Katie Mae."

Buck was still confused about what happened in the Bradford's basement.

There was only one thing he knew for sure; he had rescued his wife and newborn from harm's way. Now, they both were home in the safety of his care. Buck vowed to take care of the Bradford's...call the authorities, but Katie Mae continued to plead to put the events behind them and move forward with their lives.

"I'll do as you wish, Katie Mae, but, tell me what happened. I have to know the details. I give you my word to never bring this up again if you explain what happened." With tears in his eyes, Buck put his arms around his wife and baby girl.

Katie Mae assured Buck that she would provide the details if only he would be patient. "Buck, in early May I was invited to visit the Bradford home for tea. I went with good intentions, and Mr. Bradford tried to convince me I was with child and needed to think about the new policy Mr. Roscoe Johnson had given his mill workers," she paused for a deep breath and continued.

"The Bradfords told me they had excellent intuition and could foresee pregnancy in the eyes of a woman. I assured the Bradford's I was not with child, and Jack Bradford laughed in my face. When I went to the doctor, I found out I was indeed expecting." She stopped to catch her breath again and kiss her baby girl on the forehead as the infant sucked on the end of a clean cloth that Katie Mae had dipped in the warm milk.

"Buck, I was too ashamed to tell you how they coerced me. Besides, I felt it was better to leave matters alone...so you would not go into a rage and lose your job at the cotton mill. After that first encounter, I avoided the Bradford's ...until the Christmas Party at the cotton mill. The coercion started again, but it was much more intense," she continued as tears dripped on her gown.

Reluctantly, Katie Mae said, "I need to tell you more Buck, but you gotta promise to listen to me and not let your temper get the best of you."

"Katie Mae, I give you my word. I'll keep my temper under control," Buck declared to his grieving wife. He wondered what could be worse than the news she had already shared.

Katie Mae explained the events that took place at the Christmas Party. She bowed her head in shame as she said, "Mr. Bradford instructed me to be at his house by 11:00 the day after the Christmas Party to discuss the offer they presented to me earlier."

"My goodness why did you go to that house all by yourself? Why didn't you come to me?" Buck asked looking at his wife in disbelief.

"I went out of fear, Buck. Fear he would kill us," Katie Mae said with firmness in her voice. "I wanted closure. I wanted to make it clear to the

Bradford's that I intended to keep our baby," Katie Mae said, patting the tiny infant on the back.

"Buck, they informed me you were deathly ill with a lung disease, and I had no choice but to take their offer in order to save your life."

With tears streaming down her cheeks, Katie Mae continued her story. "Buck, I couldn't discuss this with you because I was afraid for your health, afraid that you might die. I signed my name to a contract to sell our newborn baby, so I could save your life. It was a scheme. A lie, and I fell for it Buck. I sold our baby," Katie Mae sobbed uncontrollably.

Buck trembled with fear; he had no idea what his wife's next sentence would be.

"Buck, you gotta swear you will not explode with anger," Katie Mae said with doubt in her voice that her husband could keep his word.

"I gave you my word, Katie Mae. Tell me everything."

"The Bradford's told me the money would enable you to get the best care possible, and they even gave me the name of the lung specialist that would help you live a long life. Dr. Wayne Lee, your lung doctor, was also part of their scheme. I heard them discussing all this in the hall after our baby girl was born. They were laughing at us and called us simple-minded fools. Buck, I fell for everything they told me, and I'm so ashamed of myself," Katie Mae confessed through her sobs.

Katie Mae held her head up. "Buck, there is more. The Bradford's advanced me $2,000.00 for Dr. Lee, to help with your medical bills. I paid the entire amount on your account when I took you to your first visit."

"Why did you do that Katie Mae? Why did you pay them all that money?"

"Buck, I didn't want you to die, and the Bradford's convinced me I had no other choice. They told me you needed the best medical care, and we surely could not afford such without assistance. The contract even had a provision for Albert Joe's college fund, and a new home for our family. We would be on our feet, Buck. You would be able to stay home and live a good life," Katie Mae explained.

"It's all in the contract, Buck, the legal contract that I signed," Katie Mae shouted, while pointing to her pocket book where she had placed the papers. "Oh, my God, they could sue us and take our baby, Buck. I signed a contract and took their advance," Katie Mae continued, wiping tears from her cheeks.

Buck looked at her and walked towards the purse.

"Get it out, Buck. You can read all their promises, the things they were willing to do for us in exchange for our baby. Buck, I would have never done such a thing if I didn't think you were going to die, Katie Mae gasped, crying uncontrollably as Buck went over and opened her pocketbook and pulled out the contract.

Buck read the contract and rubbed his head in frustration. He looked at his wife and said, "Katie Mae, the Bradford's sure had it all figured out. I can see why you fell for their deceit. Heck, I would have done the same if I had been in your shoes, Katie Mae. I don't hate you for what you did; you were taken advantage of by Mr. Roscoe Johnson and the Bradford's. They must pay for their sins. They will surely be cursed for all eternity for putting you through that! You could have died, Katie Mae, you and our baby girl could have died."

"No Buck. You can't cause any trouble. They will do harm to our family; you heard Mr. Bradford's threats. Besides, I signed a legal document to give our baby to them. I was a fool Buck…just a foolish woman. If they seek legal action against us, the judge may feel I was being selfish. He might think I was hoping to have the opportunity to live a different lifestyle across the railroad tracks. Buck, the courts may favor the Bradford's, and we'll lose our baby girl." Katie Mae was pleading with Buck not to cause any problems.

"My God, Katie Mae. Listen to yourself. You're speaking nonsense," Buck shouted, startling the baby in Katie Mae's arms. "They will be put in jail for running a darn black market. They are selling babies, and they will go to prison. What they're doing is against the law, illegal, Katie Mae. They will not come after us. They should be afraid of us reporting them to the authorities."

"Buck, I think you're right about the black market scheme. They put our baby in a wood crate, you know, just like the crates you took to Bradford's shed. The Bradford's basement is full of those crates.
I heard them talking about the other babies they've sold to the wealthy people," Katie Mae sobbed.

"Katie Mae, I'm aware of the wood crates in the Bradford's shed and basement, and I will testify against them in a court of law. I'll put them in prison." He stroked Katie Mae's hair, assuring her that the Bradford's are evil and must go to prison for committing a crime.

Buck stood and said, "Katie Mae, stop crying, hush my love. I can assure you I will not leave your side until this is settled."

Buck's mind was whirling as he tried to sort the information his wife had just disclosed. Thoughts rambled through his mind, the Bradford's invitation to his wife early in her pregnancy, and the contract offer Katie Mae had signed without his knowledge, and the birth of their tiny baby girl.

Buck muttered to himself, "What if Katie Mae is correct? If I report the deceitful schemers for running a black market, they may come after my family."

CHAPTER XIV

TRUTH IN THE LIES

"Buck, I don't think the baby got enough milk. She still seems hungry," Katie Mae said as she instructed her husband to search for one of Albert Joe's old milk bottles in the cabinet.

"I will look Katie Mae, be patient," Buck searched in the cabinet and found a milk bottle. He washed it and poured some warm milk for his daughter. Handing the glass bottle to Katie Mae, he wiped a tear that fell from her eye. "Hush, Katie Mae, calm your nerves. Our baby girl needs you."

"I will be fine Buck. I'll feed our baby. All will be fine," Katie Mae assured her stressed husband. "Please Buck, don't be upset with me. I need you."

Buck walked into the bedroom and closed the door behind him. He fell to the floor and prayed to God to forgive him for not understanding that Katie Mae was suffering during her pregnancy.

"Buck, where are you?" Katie May asked as she placed their newborn daughter on the end of the sofa. She covered her with Albert Joe's blanket. "I'm feeling really anxious, Buck."

Buck came into the living room and sat down in the recliner. "I'm right here, Katie Mae. Take it easy," He said with a smile.

Katie Mae placed the baby in her husband's arms and whispered, "Buck, I have to dress, and we have to go to Dr. Hunter's office so he can check me and the baby. We have to explain that the baby came during the early morning, and you assisted with the birth of our child. We must get a legal birth certificate. The time of birth will be after midnight; let's say around 2:00 in morning. Buck, we have to stick to our plan."

Buck nodded his head, and they prepared to travel to Dr. Hunter with Albert Joe in the back seat of the car. Buck knew that Katie Mae was right;

the newborn must have a legal birth certificate.

Albert Joe sat quietly until a loud cough followed by several sneezes came from the small boy. "My goodness, Albert Joe, you must be coming down with a cold." Katie Mae added, "I'll get the vapor machine out tonight and put it in your room for that cough. You'll need a cloth and some vapor rub for your chest, too."

Albert Joe replied, "No, Mama, please don't put that stinky stuff on my chest. The kids will bully me at school and call me names."

Buck assured Albert Joe that the rub would surely help prevent the onset of a cold. Besides, he reminded his son that he had to think about protecting his baby sister.

Albert Joe could already smell the vapors from the rub and shook his head in disbelief. He did not like having a cloth placed on his chest to unclog his stuffy nose. The worst part being the stench stayed on his skin for days.

At Dr. Hunter's office, the nurse said, "Buck, didn't know you had the skills to deliver a baby…gotta get you on our payroll as a mid-wife. That would sure help Dr. Hunter in the wee hours of the night. You could assist in the delivery of the village babies."

"What do you have here, Buck?" Dr. Hunter asked with a chuckle. "Nurse Bettie said you delivered the baby with your bare hands. Is that true?"

With a slight grin, Buck nodded and said that Katie Mae gave birth around 2:00 am. "Dr. Hunter, we appreciate your checking Katie Mae and our baby girl."

"Sure, Buck. I'm elated to do so. It'll take a few minutes, and I'll be on your way home." Dr. Hunter shook Buck's hand and escorted him to the waiting room where Albert Joe was doing a crossword puzzle in an outdated "Highlights" magazine.

Dr. Hunter completed the exams and had Nurse Bettie bring Buck to the small office. "All is well with Mama and the baby. The birth certificate will be mailed to your home within a few weeks, Buck. You take care of them and call me if you have any questions." Dr. Hunter reported to Buck. "Wait just a minute. What name shall I put on the birth certificate for this beautiful baby girl?"

"Elizabeth Jones. We'll call her Lizzy, after my grandmother." Buck replied as he beamed with pride.

Turning the corner to enter their street, Buck saw a sign in the Bradford's yard: 'For Sale by Owner'. "What the heck's going on here? Guess the Bradford's fled town, and best they did," Buck said with hatred exploding.

"Maybe they moved out of state, and our problem has been solved," Katie Mae replied. She prayed that the Bradford's were gone, but in her heart, she knew they would come looking for their money.

A wave of panic was overtaking Katie Mae's body as Buck parked the car. Katie kissed her baby girl on the cheek and prayed for God to protect her family from the people who had tried to steal her flesh and blood. Buck helped his wife get out of the car and led her to the sofa to get some rest. He would take care of the children and their home until Katie Mae could resume with her daily schedule.

Buck returned to work to learn that Mr. Roscoe Johnson had sold his share of the cotton mill to someone in upstate New York, and the Bradford's had been transferred to a cotton mill in a nearby town. Buck was relieved, but he still wanted to get his hands around Jack Bradford's neck. Buck knew God would not be pleased with evil for evil. Silently he prayed for peace within the village, a protection from higher powers to settle the dust of the enemies.

The following months were tough for both Buck and Katie Mae as they waited in fear of revenge from the Bradford's. There were days when Katie Mae felt there was life within the Bradford's house. She kept her doors locked and always had a careful eye roaming for the safety of her family.

Buck assured his wife that Jack Bradford had taken a job out of town. He explained to Katie Mae that rumor had it that the cotton mill union had purchased the house, as a favor to Mr. Bradford, and the union did not intend to rent the dwelling. The elaborate house made the mill shine and the village more reputable.

Months turned into years with no sight of the Bradford's. Buck and Katie Mae went about their lives raising their two children in as much normalcy as possible. Katie Mae's guilt led to deep bouts of depression throughout the formative years of her children. Lizzy became "the little Mama" for the family.

Through the years, Katie Mae grew distant from Buck and withdrew from her friends in the village. Katie's heart ached for the outpouring of truth, but it could never be revealed. She wanted wrongs corrected; she wanted justice for the Bradford's and for Mr. Roscoe Johnson.

Katie Mae knew that, by keeping silent, the authorities might never bring the Bradford's or Mr. Roscoe Johnson to justice. She wondered if she and Buck had made the right choice by agreeing never to mention the events surrounding the birth of their daughter.

Over the years things did not return to normal. Buck turned to the bottle to ease the pain he saw in Katie's eyes. He was not able to save his wife from the hands of the deceitful intruders, and it had caused her to lose her mind. Katie Mae never returned to a normal life. She was always paranoid that the Bradford's were coming for the check they had given her in exchange for her baby.

Katie Mae was overcome with guilt and the shame of taking a monetary offer in exchange for her flesh and blood. Every time she looked at little Lizzy's eyes, she felt the shame. She could not face her daughter without drowning in guilt. Katie Mae felt if the truth leaked, no one would ever forgive her for agreeing to sell her baby, even if it was under the pretense of saving her husband's life. Katie knew the residents of the mill village had always felt Mr. Jack Bradford was an upstanding mill worker, a community guard. They would never believe that he was selling babies from his basement.

As the days came and went, the front porch gossipers focused on Katie Mae's hourglass body as they questioned her loyalty to her husband. It was no secret Buck had turned to the bottle and was an absent husband and father.

The porch gossipers noted that baby Samuel's birth brought Katie Mae out of her depression. They speculated that the newborn was a love child from Katie Mae's dark sins.

Ignoring the porch gossipers, Katie Mae spoiled Samuel with her undivided attention and unconditional love. He was her world, her porcelain baby boy who brought her much needed hope for a brighter day. It was she and Samuel against the winds of the world. They were inseparable.

Katie Mae called the women nothing more than gossiping hens that had nothing better to do than plaster her name against the mill walls and trample her reputation.

She was hostage to the unspeakable events that brought many days of seclusion from the outside world. She sought peace within her troubled soul in order to protect her unspeakable secrets. Secrets she and Buck forever put to rest, secrets that came from the deceitful minds of three evil people: Mr. Roscoe Johnson, Jack Bradford and Harriett Bradford.

Life with her porcelain doll could not heal the troubled soul of Katie Mae for long. As her newborn developed and grew into a child, he was no longer a distraction from her unspeakable secrets. Katie Mae carried darkness in her heart and had days of bed rest to ease her depressed soul. Katie Mae's days of solace remained mixed with sadness and guilt from the birth of her only daughter, Lizzy. The child's face would always remind Katie Mae of her unspeakable sins and the darkness of evil.

Katie Mae's depression was not a secret. Buck knew the face of their daughter was a constant reminder of how Katie Mae willingly exchanged her flesh for money and benefits offered by the Bradford's. Buck tried to show Lizzy his love and protect her from the wrath of Katie Mae's wounded heart. Even Albert Joe, their eldest, could see how distressed his mother was and how she treated Lizzy differently than she did her sons.

Even though she had been held hostage by the characters in her nightmares, Elizabeth hoped for healing in the last episode that flashed before her eyes.

It did not play out in the manner Elizabeth had hoped. The truth was difficult to comprehend after being taken hostage by Jack Bradford on Halloween night; Katie Mae fell to her knees. She could no longer live under his tyranny. The sight of the pink blanket covering the tiny infant broke the silence within her soul, bringing back memories of her own child. Katie Mae opened the door of the incinerator to throw the broken pieces of wood into the fire. She heard a voice echoing from the flames, "God have mercy upon your soul, Katie Mae.," she slammed the door shut.

Katie Mae clutched her heart as she fell to the basement floor, ready to meet her maker. Pains rip through her chest. Katie Mae died, alone in the basement, at last at rest. Her debt was paid and she was no longer in bondage.

After the Bradford's disposed of Katie Mae's body, Jack Bradford lamented that he had just lost his best black market worker. He and his wife, with the help of Mr. Roscoe Johnson, continued with business as usual.

Bradford and his helpmates continued to take the babies of innocent women in exchange for money. They were in the moneymaking business, selling newborns to the wealthy for lifetime profits.

As a reminder of Jack Bradford's distorted love for his first devoted bait, a picture hung on the wall of his office of deceit. The picture of Harriett Bradford, his wife, hung in the middle. To the right of Harriett Bradford hung a picture of Katie Mae, a picture marked with a red spray-painted cross, apparently signifying the broken contract. On the left side of Harriett's picture hung a picture was another woman, but Elizabeth couldn't make out the name on the frame. The picture of her mother was heart breaking. It seemed to signify failure in Jack Bradford's eyes.

Elizabeth was unable to make out the names of each baby picture hanging beneath its mother, but she felt the important piece to the puzzle was solved.

Elizabeth was startled to feel a cold rag on her face.

"Elizabeth. Elizabeth, wake up. We must get ready to head to the hospital," Harrison pleaded.

Even though Elizabeth felt somewhat cheated because she did not see the final episode, she felt a peace that she had never experienced.

She and Harrison would have a busy day at the hospital, and she desperately wanted to check on her father and speak with his doctor. Nodding towards Victoria's house, she said, "Harrison, I have such fond memories of Maple Leaf Avenue. This is where I first felt peace in my life. Victoria gave me long awaited peace to move forward and a firm foundation to stand on in times of trouble." Harrison nodded his approval.

"Harrison, I had a dream last night, and so much of my childhood, my life, was exposed. I feel a sense of relief, and I hope and pray the nightmares are at rest."

Harrison replied, "I know darling, you tossed and turned all night, and I thought you would never wake up. Hope you got plenty of rest, sweetie…this could be a long day. We might have to wait a while to speak with your father's doctor."

Elizabeth and her husband walked hand in hand through the entrance doors. When the elevator door opened on Buck's floor, John Ross and Tori stood looking like two ghosts nearly causing a bystander to stumble as they pushed through the crowd.

Looking suspicious, John Ross and Tori went their separate ways.

"Goodness, Harrison. Why were those two in such a hurry?"

"Not sure, Elizabeth, but John Ross dropped something on the floor," Harrison replied as he picked up a piece of plastic tubing.

"What's that in your hand, Harrison?" Elizabeth asked, almost whispering with fear.

"I have no idea. It fell from John Ross's back pocket," Harrison stammered in confusion.

Over the loud speaker, a voice called, "Code red, Room 214. Code red, code red. Room 214."

Elizabeth's heart stopped in her chest—was that her father's room? She and Harrison bolted down the hall toward her father's hospital room. Harrison opened the door to Buck's room. His bed was surrounded by medical staff performing CPR.

"The time of death, 8:44 AM.," the doctor said professionally, without emotion. He looked at Elizabeth and her brothers. "We tried to save him. I'm so sorry for your loss."

Elizabeth and her brothers joined hands and said a prayer. Tears flowed from their eyes. At last, Buck found peace in the arms of his savior. He looked content as the nurse covers him with the white sheet.

The doctor explained that Buck's fragile health could not withstand the trauma from the house fire, the deep lacerations, and the increasingly worsening cirrhosis. His lungs were too weak, and it was only a matter of time for his death to occur.

Harrison walked toward Buck's bedside. He bowed his head to show his respect as the three adult children of Buck joined hands. With his eyes fixated on the tile floor in Buck hospital room Harrison noticed something that resembled a straw on the floor. Reaching down to pick the object up Harrison saw that it was the same plastic tubing that had carried oxygen to Buck's body through his mask. It was jagged in several places as if a rat had chewed through the tubing.

Harrison tilted his head upward stating to the family, "There is something wrong with Buck's oxygen…" quickly being interrupted by

Samuel Jones; Harrison didn't have the opportunity to complete his sentence.

Samuel looked at his siblings as he moved their clinched hands toward heaven and he abruptly said, "Dad, you're at last in the arms of your maker; rest in peace."

At the funeral, each of Buck's children placed a red rose on his chest and said a prayer. They exchanged personal contact information and reaffirmed their desire to keep in touch. They embraced one last time and reaffirmed their love for each other.

Albert Joe turned to Samuel, "Well, brother...you need a lift to the airport?" Samuel responded to Albert Joe with a slight nod of his head.

"Then, get to my truck, Sam. I'll take you to the airport, and then I must get home and filter through the unopened mail. I'll also need to check on the whereabouts of my pigeons."

The two brothers walked side by side as Elizabeth and Harrison followed behind, holding hands. Elizabeth reminded Harrison they must go by the hotel before heading to the Brevard.

"Harrison, I have one last request before leaving Shadow Village."

"What's that my dear?" Harrison asked.

"Could we go by my home place for one last look before we leave?"

"Sure, Elizabeth, maybe that will bring final closure and healing," he replied obligingly. They made a right turn into Shadow Village traveling toward the street where she had lived. Once over the railroad tracks, Elizabeth saw the yellow crime scene tape had been taken down and laid on the rocky tar streets she walked as a child.

Elizabeth's eyes took note of each lot where a house once stood. "Look, that's odd. Mr. Bradford's house looks as if it has been power washed recently—clean as ever."

"Firemen probably washed it down as a favor to the cotton mill village," Harrison replied.

"Harrison, pull in the driveway and let's park here," Elizabeth requested.

Harrison was puzzled but pulled into the Bradford's driveway.

"What's wrong, Harrison? You look upset," Elizabeth noted.

"Nothing, Elizabeth I just had a cold chill come over me as we got out of the car. Looks like no one have lived here in years, the front yard has been kept manicured, but the back has been taken over by weeds," Harrison said. "Look, there's a light on in the house and a path that leads to the back door. It looks to me like someone is staying here, Elizabeth. It may be a homeless person who has taken up residence.

My goodness, I wonder if a homeless person started the fire."

"I don't think anyone is living here, Harrison. Rumor has it the light has been burning for years, and the mill hands keep the front yard manicured. As for as who started the fire—we may never know the answer to that question," Elizabeth said reluctantly as they walked toward her home place.

Gaining her composure she said, "Harrison, see that chaney ball tree? It is still standing. Samuel loved to climb that tree and throw those nasty, smelly Chaney balls at me. The ditch bank is nearly gone. Guess over the years it eroded. I have such fond memories of my dad and me flying kites there. I miss the good days with my dad," Elizabeth quietly said as she turned toward the pack house that was half standing.

"My playhouse—it's nothing but black ashes. I had so much fun playing inside that old pack house. It was my safe haven from reality," Elizabeth covered her face with her hands.

"Elizabeth, maybe this wasn't a good idea. Let's get back in the car," Harrison gazed a worried and concerned look at his wife.

"I'm fine, Harrison. I just needed to see the house one last time. My home place did have some good memories, and I wanted to take a mental picture with me to Brevard," Elizabeth replied as she held Harrison's hand.

Walking back to the car, Harrison paused for a moment. "I heard something at the back of the house, Elizabeth. Did you hear anything?"

"No, but I am not in any shape to listen for strange sounds." Elizabeth replied.

Staying on the clear path that led to the back door, Harrison walked toward Jack Bradford's house.

"It's probably an animal, Harrison let's just go I'm starting to get a bad feeling," Elizabeth said as her body began to quiver.

"That's odd, Elizabeth, the garage doors have no grass underneath them, looks as if someone has been using them all these years. There's a path leading to back of the garage as well as the backdoor," Harrison reported.

"Guess they keep the lawn equipment in the garage, easy access when the mill crew cut the grass," Elizabeth replied with a look of uncertainty. "Let's go Harrison. I don't feel well."

"Just a minute Elizabeth, let's make sure no one is trapped in the house."

As they got closer to the back door, they noticed it was open. They were amazed to see everything in perfect order as if the house had been a happy dwelling place for decades.

A rock wedged between the doors, apparently leading to a wine cellar, caught the eye of the Davenports.

"I should have known Jack Bradford's house had the best of everything, even a wine cellar," Elizabeth said incredulously.

Harrison opened the door, "I think it is a basement, not a wine cellar."

"My God have mercy upon their souls," Elizabeth murmured.

Elizabeth, moving closer to her husband, whispered, "Are you sure it's a basement, Harrison? Are you sure?" The door was wide open. Fear gripped her heart, shaking her with horror as she remembered her nightmares.

"Harrison, we need to leave now. I'm afraid of this place. I want to go to the car," Elizabeth insists.

Harrison was concerned and insisted they go to the basement to make sure no one needed assistance. He reminded Elizabeth that, with the recent fire, a homeless person might have been hurt and made his way to the basement looking for shelter. "You just never know Elizabeth. We would always wonder if we could have helped if there was someone trapped in the basement. They may be unconscious, Elizabeth," he insisted.

"No Harrison. Please, don't do this," Elizabeth pleaded to no avail. Harrison was determined to rescue the helpless.

Slowly they walked down the steps. Elizabeth was afraid for her life while Harrison was in suspense of the unknown. As they turned the corner, Harrison flipped the light switch on, and suddenly Elizabeth's body began to tremble with the mental pictures that lurked in the basement of Jack Bradford's home.

"Elizabeth, it's okay—I'm here. Hold to my arm, and I'll help you up the stairs so we can leave," Harrison reassured his wife who was white as a ghost. She was speechless.

Elizabeth stood still. "No, I must face the evil in this room Harrison. You see, this is the torment I've fought for years. This is the room where my mother gave birth to me. I remember the dreams so vividly. Oh, Harrison, I can see it all, the eyes of a man and woman as they took me from my mother upon delivery, wrapping me in a pink blanket and placing me in the wood crate."

"What are you talking about, Elizabeth?" Harrison was in disbelief.

"Harrison, I understand my entrance into this world, my birth, my mother's torment. I've seen this basement in my nightmares, for decades. I'm sure of it," she whispers.

Elizabeth begins to explain to her husband. "This house was used to sell babies to the highest bidder. I remember Harrison; the dreams and visions are coming back to me. My mother was given an offer by the Bradford's and coerced into their scheme."

Elizabeth walked closer to what she thought was a safe and slowly opened the door. The smell of smoldering ashes rushed into her nostrils. She slammed the door and screams. "Harrison, this is where my mother met her death. I can hear her screaming. I've heard the screams in my nightmares. I can see my mother on the floor; she died of a broken heart." Elizabeth backed away from the incinerator door as fear gripped her body.

She sobbed as she held tightly to Harrison's arm. At last, it was over.

"Harrison, the stairs—they are metal, and that is the sound I've heard all these years, a man running with a small wood crate and a woman over his shoulder. That was my father with my mother slung over his shoulder, and

I was in the crate, Harrison."

"Elizabeth, stop it. You're confused," Harrison gently guided Elizabeth up the stairs as she trembled violently.

Taking one-step toward the metal stairs, Harrison saw the shadow of a light flickering down the hall. "Wait here, Elizabeth. Sit on this step and wait for me. I need to turn the light off in the back room. We need to leave this place and call the police."

Harrison walked toward the dim light. He saw a large name printed on a plaque. He pushed the half-opened door that bore Jack Bradford's name and realized that someone was in the room.

A man sat at the desk with his head bowed and resting on his arms.

Harrison whispered, "Excuse me sir, and is everything ok?" The man looked familiar as he slowly tilted his head until he was eyeball to eyeball with Harrison.

"Oh, my God what are you doing here, Harrison? You should not be in this house. It's the devil's dwelling."

Harrison immediately recognized Samuel, "Why are you in Mr. Bradford's office, Samuel? What is going on here in this basement?"

"Never mind why I'm here, Harrison; you should leave immediately. Get my sister out of here and never mention this to her. Harrison, you must vow to always protect Elizabeth from the truth, and she must be protected from this evil house."

"Why, Samuel? Why? I don't understand what is going on."

"Because, you see Harrison, I'm the product of Katie Mae. The depression took her mind after the Bradfords stole her innocence and coerced her into selling her flesh and blood, her baby daughter. Katie Mae could never forgive herself and always knew Jack Bradford would one day trap her—as he did that Halloween night when I was just a young lad.

"My mother was taken by the Bradfords. I saw Jack Bradford talking with my mama at the clothes line; he stabbed her with a needle. Her body became limp as a rag doll, and she fell to the muddy ground. Jack Bradford drugged her.

"I knew Jack Bradford would come for me once I was of age, and he could use me for his evil work. When Elizabeth left the cotton mill village, I was alone and afraid. Sure enough, Jack Bradford approached me one night when I was walking home after school—I had stayed late for some extra help. Jack Bradford offered to let me see my mama if I would work for him and keep my mouth shut. At first, I thought he was lying. I had no idea my mother was still alive after all those years," Samuel revealed, and continued,

"I agreed, and Jack Bradford took me to the basement where my mama was working folding blankets. She was lifeless, just going through the motions. I could not leave her there with them. I made them an offer; I would work for them rest of my life if they would only let Mama go free."

"What are you saying Samuel? I don't understand." Harrison pleaded.

"Well, Harrison, I took the offer and I joined them in the black market. My mama refused to leave the basement. Besides, she was so mentally disturbed there was no way she could survive after being locked in the basement all those years," he continued. Samuel paused for a moment, looking at the floor. He then looked back at Harrison, shame and confusion written on his face.

"There were times Mama acted as if she knew me; she'd call me her Sammy Boy. The next hour she was in a corner rocking her baby doll, Lizzy. Total messed up mind she had at the expense of Jack Bradford."

"My God have mercy upon you all," Harrison whispered as fear overtook his body.

"So you see Harrison, I'm a millionaire at the expense of my mother's life. Katie Mae died at the hands of the Bradford's, and I know one day they will pay. Besides, if I dared to turn them in, they would kill me too. I am the supervisor for the home base, ordering medical equipment and supplies for their black market. My job is simple. I order, assist as needed and keep my mouth shut—to stay alive." He began to shake with fear. "Go Harrison. Elizabeth cannot ever know what I do. Just go. Get out of here."

Harrison could not believe the words that came from Samuel's mouth, and he needed fresh air to survive the stench of the basement.

"Harrison, if you'll look at the pictures on the wall, you'll see Jack Bradford's prize processions, the women who gave birth in the basement, babies that made the man a millionaire. His own wife was his first victim. You'll also see the infants' picture beside each woman. Jack Bradford kept track of their names once the adoption was completed. Jack Bradford is one sadistic man."

Harrison looked at the wall—gasping at the family tree displayed for Jack Bradford to reminisce.

Harriett Bradford – Baby Boy "B" (Adopted Name-Harrison Davenport)

Katie Mae Jones – Baby Girl "J" (Failed Adoption – Lizzy Jones)

Victoria Holiday – Baby Girl "H" (Adopted Name - Tori Belk)

Harrison turned his head and viewed numerous other pictures that lined another wall in Jack Bradford's office. "My God, how could this be? How could anyone be this cruel?"

"God have mercy upon their evil souls," Harrison prayed as he tried to wake himself from a horrible nightmare.

With horror whelming in his body, Harrison turned to look at the pictures once more. His eyes could not believe Jack Bradford was so inhumane he actually took a picture of each baby in their crate. Gazing at Katie Mae's picture, he saw the baby in the crate was small, almost like a premature birth.

Moving his eyes downward, he was stunned at the crate that held baby girl "H." He saw the object placed beside the tiny, plump baby. It was a music box. It was Elizabeth's music box. How could that be? Why was Elizabeth's music box in the baby girl Holiday's crate?

Harrison had a cold chill as his eyes focused on the huge picture of Harriet Bradford, the wife of Jack Bradford. The baby boy "B" looked so tiny in the crate lined with a blue blanket. His eyes scrolled across the picture once more landing on the words "Harrison."

Harrison screamed aloud, begging God for mercy. His name identified as Baby Boy "B"—it could not be true. It had to be a huge mistake or a prank. Harrison's knees buckled as he slowly moved away from the wall of victims. He stumbled, shaking in fear.

"My God have mercy on the innocent people. They have taken many women into their pretended care. They were master minds of a black marketing scheme, and the basement was their delivery room for the baby mill."

Harrison turned to Samuel Jones who was still at the desk sobbing.

"You're right, Harrison. This basement is nothing more than a baby selling black market, a baby mill. I'm just as guilty, I know, but I was pulled in—I just wanted to see my mama again, Harrison. That was all," Sam wailed.

"You should go to jail just as the Bradford's and anyone else involved. All involved need to be charged and put in prison for the pain and suffering you've inflicted upon innocent, desperate women." Harrison shouted. "Why Samuel, why would you do this? Why would you be a part of Bradford's hellish scheme?" Harrison asked with tears streaming out of his eyes.

"Why wouldn't I, Harrison?" Samuel Jones shouted. "You were shipped off to a couple across the tracks, given a much better life than I ever had. Why are you so angry? At least you had an opportunity to have a good life. Don't you see? I did this in hopes of seeing my mother, taking care of her the last years of her life."

"Sam may God have mercy on you. May God forgive you for your sins," Harrison shouted as he sobbed.

"They made an offer to me when I was down and out, just like the women they preyed upon. I was a victim. Yes, I am a millionaire Harrison, but it has cost me my self-respect, my dignity, and entangled me in a life of deceit," Samuel shouted as he wiped mucus from his nose, cursing between each wipe.

"Katie Mae, I did it for her, for my mother. I did not have a clue that she was so mentally disturbed she would not recognize me. Jack Bradford knew. So you see, he coerced and lied to me as he did to my mother and all the others in his web of foul deceit," Samuel justified.

"But, why did Jack Bradford kidnap Katie Mae?" Harrison asked.

"I had no say in the matter. My guess is that Jack Bradford grabbed my mother to repay her debt. You see she skipped out on her contract when Lizzy was born. Katie Mae backed out on their deal, was rescued by my dad, and took her newborn home. In the eyes of Jack Bradford, my parents were indebted to him. Jack Bradford was not about to allow the debt to go unpaid. He wanted the infant girl or next best thing—Katie Mae. He enslaved her."

Samuel continued, "Guess you could say I'm carrying on his legacy. And you, Harrison, you're nothing but the first born son of Harriet Bradford, who was also Jack Bradford's bait. Both you and my sister were born in the basement owned by the Bradford's, both of you are end results of their black market baby mill."

"You see the name 'Holiday?' That infant's crate marked with the letter 'H' has been displayed behind Buck's shed since the day he brought the baby home with my mother. You understand me, Harrison?" Samuel shouted.

"Samuel, are you saying Buck got the wrong crate the night he rescued Katie Mae from this basement? Are you telling me Elizabeth Jones is not the daughter of Katie Mae and Buck?"

Samuel chuckled, "Buck grabbed the crate with the initial 'H' that night when he rescued my mother. He kept the crate to protect the innocent; it was a memento to Buck. No one was allowed to touch his crate. Now, as far as where my biological sister is located, I have a good idea. The Belks, rich couple across the tracks adopted an infant girl about the same time Lizzy was born. Named her Tori. She was good friends with Lizzy, went to school with her."

Samuel nodded his head. "Yep, all this is very confusing. The infants got switched at birth."

Samuel continued, "I would guess the crates were side by side, and my father grabbed the first crate as he scrambled out old man Bradford's basement. He was in fear of being killed. He kept that secret to his grave; so he thought. But, Bradford exposed the well-kept secret years ago in hopes of controlling my mind."

Samuel further explained displaying excruciating hostility, "...only difference between you and my sister, you were sold to the highest bidder across the tracks because your mother, Harriett Bradford, took her husband's offer. She took the money and invested in the stock market, made her a wealthy woman. She sold her first born son, you!" Samuel chuckled.

"Katie Mae, my mother, couldn't go through with the deal and was rescued by my dad. Lizzy lived a life in the mill village in poverty while you had a life of luxury with the Davenports. We had to endure poverty on this pathetic cotton mill while you had the best of everything, Harrison. You got your picture on the wall as the son of Harriet Bradford, but you are nothing more than their bait. So, be proud of that fact, you foolish man. Your mother went through with the offer and placed you in a home filled with love and sane parents. If you had stayed with the Bradford's, you would be sitting in this chair, not me."

"I will follow in the footsteps of the Bradfords. No one will stop me. Jack Bradford spared Katie Mae's life for only a season because he owned her with that contract she signed. He planned all along to kidnap her one day; he would not allow anyone to outwit him. Katie Mae was always a special woman to the Bradford's. She lived a horrible life because she loved her baby and refused to allow Jack Bradford to take her flesh and blood," Samuel paused.

"I own this empire established by Mr. Jack Bradford. It has made me a wealthy man, and by darn if you or my sister will demolish my kingdom. So, if you betray me, I'll have to take revenge upon your life. You hear me, Harrison? Think about the mixed up crates. How would Elizabeth feel if she knew her biological mother was Victoria, not the woman who raised her from birth?" He stopped his ranting for a moment.

Samuel finally gave Harrison a chance to speak.

"Samuel, Jack Bradford will kill us all; he will not spare a living soul. There is no way he will go to jail for his evil. He'll get rid of all of us sooner or later. Please. Please. I beg you to set yourself free from this black market baby mill. Go to the police with me, Samuel. Together we can have Jack Bradford and his demon wife locked away forever."

Harrison heard a noise down the hall. Could that be Jack Bradford? "He'll kill Elizabeth!" Harrison gasped as he ran toward his wife.

Samuel looked at him and yelled, "I know who it is, and you're a bigger fool than I thought. I can assure you it isn't Jack Bradford. He will not be bothering anyone. I solved that problem last night," Samuel replied with a smirk on his face. Harrison came to an abrupt stop.

"I don't understand, Samuel. Where are Jack and Harriet Bradford? What did you do to them? Please, tell me you didn't harm anyone."

"You're such a fool, Harrison. It was me or them. Jack Bradford took my mother's life decades ago. He made her a freaking lunatic. Buck turned to alcohol, had lived a miserable life. The Bradford's ruined my family, and I took care of them both. I had enough of their control. To be honest, I should have done it years ago. The same incinerator Bradford chunked the crates with runt infants swaddled in black towels. That's where he and his deceitful wife met their destiny."

With his eyes bulging, Samuel warns Harrison one last time. "If you want to live, you better take the last opportunity I will extend to you and my lovely sister. Run and never look back. Go now or you'll force me to take you and Lizzy.

"God, I can't harm Lizzy; she was a good sister, taking care of me when the Bradfords destroyed our mother. I truly love my sister. Run, Harrison. Get out of this basement; it's full of evil. I don't want to hurt anyone else."

Harrison turned and ran toward Elizabeth who had remained on the stair steps. Crying uncontrollably, she could no longer hide from the truth of her life. She stood firmly on a path of wavering sand in the midst of Shadow Village.

Elizabeth fell to the floor, overtaken with anxiety and exhaustion. Harrison leaned over to sweep his wife up with his strong arms. Elizabeth was clutching a tiny, yellowish-white Bible she found wedged under the stairs.

Throwing his wife over his shoulder, he darted up the metal steps, fleeing the basement filled with evil. At the car, Harrison put Elizabeth in the passenger seat and buckled her seatbelt. Just before starting the engine his eyes were drawn to Elizabeth's clutched fist. Her bible was securely surrounded by her long slender fingers. She would be protected…from the truth by the word. That was a signal from the Almighty above. Suddenly his train of thought was interrupted by the sound of gunshots from the Bradfords' basement. My God, has Samuel killed himself or was he firing at someone, perhaps the person in the hall?

Harrison realized the danger he and his wife might encounter. They had to leave Shadow Village immediately. Harrison prayed that whoever was in the hall had not seen him and Elizabeth. But, could others be aware of the black market operation? He had no idea who was a part of this hellish illegal scheme. Harrison needed answers but knew he most likely would always have to be on guard. At that moment he made a vow to never mention Jack Bradford's wall of victims to his wife. Never.

The son of the devil; Jack Bradford's son. Harrison Davenport could never admit the truth to anyone. Jack Bradford, his father, the man who sold his own flesh and blood to gain wealth. The Bradfords were heartless, wicked people. Such gruesome news would surely burden Elizabeth's mind to no avail. She could not live with…the truth. Both she and Harrison were products of the black market baby mill. However, Harrison was a direct descendent. He was the Bradfords' son. An innocent victim but the son of foul demons.

Harrison was in shock as he backed out of the driveway. He had to get his wife to safety, make a mad dash for freedom. A fast escape from the pits of hell; the Bradfords' home. His home.

Once on the street, he looked at the house, clamped his hands around the steering wheel, and tried to get as far from Jack Bradford's house as he could. Glancing back, he saw a red truck partially hidden behind the garage. There was a red convertible parked beside the truck, but Harrison had no time to investigate.

Harrison knew the answers to all his questions. He was now convinced there was, indeed, a curse upon the cotton mill village, a hot, raging curse that Roscoe Johnson, the Bradfords and their cronies fed through evil endeavors. He was speeding to cross the threshold of the cold tracks. Secreting vowing to himself he would never look back.

Harrison's memory was plagued with seeing both the red truck and convertible. Suddenly he recalled seeing both vehicles parked side by side at the hospital. A cold chill race up his neck as he visualized the baby blankets neatly folded in a basket that sat on the back seat of the red convertible: Nurse Tori; it had to be her car.

"I know who was in the hall and heard the gun shots...my God, Samuel. No! How could you do such an unthinkable thing to your only brother, Albert Joe and his friend, Tori?" he thought incredulously, wiping the sweat from his forehead as visions crept into his mind in slow motion. The crates.one marked with "J" and the other marked with "H"...the rich Belk couple. Tori. How could this all be happening? Tori...my God! Tori and Elizabeth were switched at birth. Tori...she was the daughter of Buck and Katie Mae Jones. Harrison could never reveal such devastating news to his fragile wife. He prayed Elizabeth would never put the pieces of the puzzle together.

Quickly, Harrison gathered his thoughts, comprehending that the secrets revealed had to be securely locked inside his heart to protect the only woman he had ever loved, to protect their marriage and his identity.

It was apparent decades of deceit had tormented and damaged many families; by the hands of malicious schemers. Greed had taken control and ruled in the dark basement located behind the old cotton mill. Now it had been revealed to Harrison Davenport. The pictures that hung in the basement were proof of the black market baby mill operated by Jack Bradford and his demonic wife. A scheme that was no doubt backed financially by the cotton mill owner Roscoe Johnson.

Harrison had to lock his discoveries tightly within his mind for eternity. He had to spare his wife's mind. He must rescue Elizabeth and allow her to heal from the monstrous childhood memories which had tormented her for years.

Being a truthful man Harrison was not fond of withholding the facts from anyone, especially his soul mate. However, he vowed to himself to be much stronger than Buck Jones who had not saved his wife from the hands of the Bradfords. He would rescue his wife from the tormenting truth. But he felt confused as his mind and conscience were at war. How would Elizabeth feel about her husband if she knew his true heritage? He couldn't...he wouldn't take a chance of her knowing. Never, he would not never utter the truth.

Harrison felt secure revealing some of the truth; knowing it may shine some light on Elizabeth's dark nightmares. Just maybe fate would favor him. He knew what he had to do. He would explain that Elizabeth's nightmares had led her to Victoria; her biological mother.

Harrison meticulously planned his speech; he would reunite mother and child. Victoria would be as delighted as Elizabeth with such glorious news. Besides, Elizabeth and Victoria had truly felt a strong connection from their first meeting. Harrison prayed his news would be the miracle Elizabeth and Victoria needed. Their healing.

Harrison waited for Elizabeth to open her beautiful eyes. The tiny bible still clutched in her fist. He could only imagine the sparkle that would remain for eternity as he made his speech: "Elizabeth, you'll never in your lifetime understand how your dreams tried to set you free all these years, my love. Your dreams were visions trying to lead you to the truth, to peace, and a sense of belonging."

Suddenly Elizabeth opened her eyes, holding tightly to her tiny bible. Harrison had to think fast, he looked at his dismayed wife as she fought for her mental wellbeing and emotional balance, and said, "Elizabeth, let's stop by and visit your mother, before our fast escape to our home.

Just maybe we can plan a family reunion. Better, we'll plan a winter vacation." Elizabeth smiled at her husband as he nervously made a turn onto Maple Leaf Avenue.

ABOUT THE AUTHOR

Dr. Bonnie Vause was born in Smithfield, North Carolina, a typical "mill town." She resides with her husband of thirty-eight years near Raleigh, NC. Her 1st novel, Fast Escape won the 2014 Dan Poynter's Silver Award in the category of fiction suspense. Bonnie earned an M. Ed. from East Carolina University, and Ed. D. from Walden University. Dr. Vause has been a teacher for over twenty years and finds great satisfaction in working with special needs students.

Additional information about the author and her books, including links, video, and excerpts, can be found on the author's web page: http://www.BonnieVause.com.

How to contact Bonnie:

Goodreads: https://www.goodreads.com/goodreadscombonnievause

Facebook: https://www.facebook.com/bonnie.vause

LinkedIn: http://www.linkedin.com/pub/dr-bonnie-w-vause/2b/238/2b0

Where to purchase books by Bonnie Vause, Ed. D.:

www.amazon.com and www.createspace.com

To Be Published, By Bonnie W. Vause, Ed. D.:

WINTER VACATION

THE ENTITLED STRANGER

CROSS KEYS INN

MISSING FROM MILL CREEK

YOUR REVIEW IS IMPORTANT!

In advance, we are very grateful for your review of *Fast Escape*. Please post a review, with your thoughts, ideas, and feelings at:

www.amazon.com, www.createspace.com, or www.bonnievause.com

Bonnie Interviews Dr. Elizabeth Davenport, protagonist in *Fast Escape.*

Author: Hello Dr. Davenport, and thank you for your time.

Dr. Davenport: Oh, please call me Elizabeth. You've known me long enough that we should be on a first name basis.

Author: Ok, Elizabeth. Since your time is short, let's get right into some of the questions. What has been your biggest fear? Who have you confided in? Were you able to overcome your fear?

Dr. Davenport: My biggest fear has always been 'Failure' incessantly fed by 'Self Doubt'. My husband, Harrison has always known and been supportive.

As to why I have fear of failure: Growing up as a poor child in Shadow Village projected a lifetime passage in poverty. It was expected the children would remain in the village and work in the cotton mill. It was our legacy, but I did not want that for my life. However, at times I had self-doubts that I could break the cycle to escape the destitution. I was strong-willed and determined in the eyes of most people yet there was always a nagging voice reminding me I was a Mill Village girlothing more. However, I was more, and my faith and determination carried me through the difficult times, the periods of self-doubt, to escape the poverty.

Author: Elizabeth, there were many secrets that you held in your heart. How did this affect your daily life? Were you able to help others with their lives by reflecting upon your own hidden secrets?

Dr. Davenport: Yes, secrets ruled and troubled my life for decades. The effects of hidden secrets were anxiety and depression. My marriage to Harrison is wonderful however; the anxiety and depression took a toll upon our relationship at times.

I definitely use my own life experiences to assist patients. I empathize with the inner struggles they fight. I feel their pain and understand their needs, wants, and desires. I attribute my personal life growing up in Shadow Village with unbearable secrets as the link to helping others out of their cultural and psychological bondage.

Author: You speak of assisting your patients break from their bondage. However, you also state you suffered for decades. Why couldn't you break free from your own turmoil?

Dr. Davenport: Good question. Despite my career as a renowned child psychologist, I fought the demons within my own spirit. I call it a 'transition period' in which I was fighting for the chains to be unlocked. However, my subconscious could not or would not surface until that night in the Bradford's basement. I had to be emotionally ready for the outcome. I kept my eyes open, refused to escape the torment until I knew…I knew the truth.

You see, a person must be prepared for the enlightening truth once it rises to the surface. How to handle the outcome of digging for years of knowledge and knowing what to do with gained truth. I am grateful that I found the courage to unlock the secrets from my childhood, process, and work through gained insight. It is torment at times and I still have to remind myself to move forward. One day at a time is the key for me and my supportive husband is my safety net.

Author: As a child you speak of your mother's homemade grits and the 'butter pot' that was spooned out in the middle. Why was that so important to you?

Dr. Davenport: As a child, I valued the little things. The tasty butter was the start of a new day and it brought me comfort. A part of me felt 'loved' by my mother; knowing she scooped deep into that butter dish to create a tempting butter well for her children.

However, on the same note: I knew the butter well was not intended for me.

Author: How did you know your mother didn't intend for you to be the recipient of the savory butter?

Dr. Davenport: I was a wise young girl with a gift of intuition. My mother was rather easy to read. Her facial expressions, lack of touch and nurturing was evident.

Author: What is your strongest memory that has stuck with you throughout your life causing a positive impact for you?

Dr. Davenport: Holding on to the small things in life that are not monetary, such as my music box. No amount of money could replace the warmth that music box provided to me. The music soothed my soul during the turmoil and the dancing ballerina brought hope. Hope that one day I could dance with freedom, twirl into another life. At times, I wanted to crawl into the box with her and hide from that hellish childhood. However, something in her eyes gave me hope. The music box was powerful in the fact it was mine and there was a connection that provided warmth during hard times and again, hope for my future. I still have the music box. No, I would never consider parting with it.

Author: Thank you Dr. Elizabeth Davenport for sharing your incredibly empowering insights. I hope some of my readers see and understand the message you carry.

###

Bonnie Interviews "Old Lady" Gunter, a supporting character, in *Fast Escape*.

Author: Hello Ms. Gunter. Thank you for taking time to answer some questions my readers have. Let's jump right in. What is your birth name?

Gunter: Now, some things best let rest. 'Old Lady Gunter' that's best how I answer folks in Shadow Village.

Author: Lester is your grandson?

Gunter: That be correct.

Author: There is no mention of Lester's mother. What was she like?

Gunter: Lester's mother died when Lester and his brother slid out the birth canal. Bad scene. I couldn't afford raise two heads. Gave the other youngin' to a man in town.

Author: Who would that be and how did you decide which child to keep?

Gunter: Didn't have no choice. Lester's head looked like a cone; he wouldn't bring no good to no one. Other one, well—he looked normal.

Author: There was no mention of Lester having a twin brother.

Gunter: I know. As I said, "Best not to stir trouble, let it be."

Author: Did you know Mabel Jean well? If so, what was your connection to her?

Gunter: Mabel Jean was distant kin. She was the Mill Village healer. Take off the biggest warts ever seen by human eye. People far and near came to see her spit on warts.

Author: Tell me about Lester, his character. What made him laugh and cry?

Gunter: Lester Ray was a sight! Big ole boy. Simple minded, loved jump around and dance like a butterfly. Had big feet and hands. Boy helped me pick figs. We had to make fig jam and brews. Lester love to laugh at the children when he frightened 'em.

Author: Now, I know you were a part of his pranks at times. Why?

Gunter: Well, you best be right. Lester liked for me to ride on the handle bars, gave the boy a thrill of life time. He frightened little Lizzy many times. I always helped Lester to keep him safe. Didn't want no-one to hurt him. He was really just a simple-minded overgrown boy. Couldn't speak much at all. Lester helped me, had some strong bones. Couldn't help he was born with a cone head.

Author: What was Lester afraid of?

Gunter: Fire. Lester was afraid of flames of fire. Thought it was sign of pits of hell.

Author: Many felt your home was haunted. Was it? Did you make magic potions? If so, why?

Gunter: We didn't have the money to keep a nice yard. Did best we could. Trees were overgrown and frightened the yungins of the Village. Yep, house is haunted with spirits. Some good. Some bad. I liked 'em bad spirits most.

Yep, me and Lester made magic potions, bottled 'em up and took to Mable Jean. That's how we got money. Spit and figs mix good, make some fine brews.

Author: Do you consider yourself to be a "witch" as many thought?

Gunter: Yep. I practiced witchcraft, wrote Mable Jean's mumble jumble sayings. How you think those warts fell off so fast? I was born into a family of witches. Our potions all had one main thing—figs.

I need to go now. Too many questions keepin' me 'way from things I gotta do.

Author: Thank you Ms. Gunter for answering and clearing up some of the issues my readers had. I'm sure they still have more later.